THE DIDYMUS CONTINGENCY

Tenth Anniversary Edition

AUTHOR'S PREFERRED TEXT

JEREMY ROBINSON

THE DIDYMUS CONTINGENCY

BREAKNECK MEDIA

For those who doubt.

An Introduction to the Tenth Anniversary Edition

The very first draft of *The Didymus Contingency*, titled just *Didymus* back then, was a screenplay. It was the year 2000, the world hadn't come to its Y2K end, and I was living in a crappy apartment in downtown Lowell, Massachusetts. I was sitting in the small living room, which I had painted (with the landlord's approval) in a rough brownstone texture, upon which I painted a border of petroglyphs—symbols, human figures and animals. I was pump-ing out screenplays, encouraged by the phone calls I was getting from Antonio Banderas's production company. During a brain-storming session, I asked myself, if I could go back in time and witness any single event, where would I go?

The answer to that question—the death and resurrection(?) of Jesus Christ—became my story. I wrote the screenplay, and on the first day of the New Year, I loaded up a truck and began a trip westward that began with a blizzard and ended with the 85 degree heat of Los Angeles. While in LA, *Didymus* (the screenplay) was optioned for film, but as these things usually go, the production company failed to raise the funds, the script entered development hell and the rights reverted back to me.

Now, around this time, I started reading—and really enjoying—novels for the first time in my life, thanks to James Rollins's *Subterranean*. So, while living in another crappy apartment with a view of downtown Los Angles to the south, and the San Gabriel Mountains to the north (on the two days of the year both weren't cloaked in smog), I considered writing a novel of my own. I wasn't a novelist, but I was a storyteller, so I studied my wife's copy of *The Elements of Style* and Stephen King's *On Writing*, and I launched into writing my first novel. It was based on the screenplay, but I expanded it to include more time-hopping and frightening elements.

When the novel was complete, I got in touch with my literary hero, James Rollins, who had written just three novels at the time, and I was elated when he replied not just with praise, but with my very first blurb: "Jeremy Robinson's novel, *The Didymus Contingency*, blends the cutting-edge science of Crichton with the religious mystery of the *Left Behind* series to create his own unique and bold thriller. It is a fast-paced page-turner like no other. Not to be missed!"

i

Mind blown. And my next step was publication, right? I'd written a novel that the believers and non-believers alike would enjoy...or hate. When talking to James about my options, we agreed that it was unlikely that mainstream publishers would get past the religious elements, and that religious publishers would freak out because I used the word 'Bitch.' So I shelved it and wrote two more novels, both based on screenplays: *Beneath* and *Raising the Past*.

Tired of living in LA's constant heat and smog, and missing out on big family events (weddings, births, etc.), my wife and I moved back to New Hampshire, where we lived in another crappy apartment overlooking a bar where brawls were common. And that's where we had our first child, and I thought, *we need to stop living in crappy apartments.* I decided I was done playing by big publishers' rules. I self-published *The Didymus Contingency* in 2005, five years after asking myself that fateful question. After a few slow months, the book became an online bestseller at the famous bookstore chain with the *B* and the *N* in the name, beating out Dan Brown (for a few days), and I sold a good number of books.

The success of *The Didymus Contingency* led me to create my own small press, Breakneck Media (that's a story on its own), attracted the attention of Scott Miller at Trident Media Group, who has been my literary agent since, and launched my career. It's been fifteen years since I wrote the screenplay and ten since I first self-published the book. A lot has changed since then, but this story that I worried no one would like has been read and enjoyed by a large number of people from various backgrounds with divergent beliefs. While I'd still love to see this as a movie, or even on store shelves, I'm proud of what this book has done, and if you haven't read it before, I hope you enjoy this freshly edited and newly published tenth anniversary edition. And if you do, I hope you'll take a moment to post a review online. Each and every one helps! Thanks for reading!

Jeremy Robinson
December, 2015

ARRANGEMENT

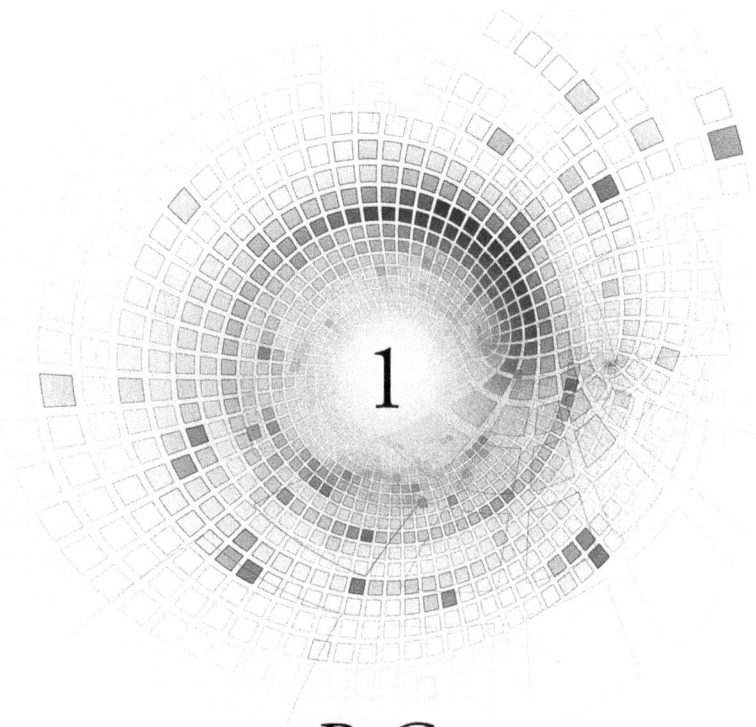

1

B.C.

1985
2:35 P.M.
Zambia, Africa

Tom Greenbaum was captivated. Herds of blue wildebeest and zebra scattered in all directions as Mpundu, the dirty, mild tempered pilot of the small Cessna rental, took Tom down for a closer look at the flora and fauna of the Zambian plains. It would have been easy for most people to lose track of time, staring at the creatures, whose lives and deaths played out on the brown-tinged grass below. But Tom wasn't most people. As a quantum physicist with an IQ of 167, the calculations needed to time a quick jaunt over the African plains were as easy as clipping fingernails.

Tom had planned this distraction well. His international flight from Israel to Zambia's capital, Lusaka, touched down at ten fifty three—ten minutes early. Megan expected his arrival at four o'clock, and the flight to her mission took two hours. Tom scheduled his flight with Mpundu for twelve, giving himself an extra two hours' time in the air. He was glad to be seeing his wife again, but experiencing this wild, untouched world from a bird's eye view was too much to pass up. Besides, she would never know.

Time flew past and they were soon cruising over a lush, green canopy of jungle trees, waterfalls and rivers. The peaceful surroundings and white hum of the Cessna's engine propelled Tom to sleep, much to the relief of Mpundu, who had grown tired of Tom's wonderment. Not until they were making their final approach did Mpundu break the silence.

"Mr. Greenbaum…Mr. Greenbaum, we're almost there."

Tom sat up and wiped the drool from his cheek. Embarrassed that he'd slept, he quickly ran a hand through his wavy black hair, making sure it was free of the bed-head that frequently plagued him.

"Mirror is there," the pilot said, pointing to a mirror taped above the windshield. Smiling, he added, "But no one out here will care what you look like."

Tom ignored the man as he looked at himself in the mirror. His brown eyes looked tired but he'd managed to shave, which helped highlight his strong, square jaw. *Just the way she likes it*, he thought. As he squinted against the lowering sun he asked, "What time is it?"

"Two forty-five. Tell me, why do you come to Zambia? You have seen the animals, but where you are going now has no animals."

"Visiting my wife," Tom explained, his voice softening with the thought of her face and smile. "She's been here two weeks, but she'll be staying another two after I leave."

Mpundu's face became visibly confused. "You say your wife? Here in Zambia for two weeks without her husband?"

Tom nodded. "It's the longest we've been apart."

"And you let her come here?"

"I would have stopped her if I could." Tom said. "Trust me. Since she found religion, it's been impossible for me to get through to her. I swear the whole lot of them has a death wish."

Mpundu's smile faded. "This is the worst place to come with a death wish."

Tom's forehead wrinkled with concern. "Why's that?"

"Because, Mr. Greenbaum, it usually comes true."

Tom's smile shrank away.

"We're almost there," Mpundu assured. "Try not to worry."

3:50 P.M.

Megan wasn't the type of woman to run from a fight, but this was slaughter. Tom was flying into a deathtrap. She had to warn him. Megan peeked around the corner of a grass-roofed hut, which served as the chapel. She knew the thatched wall of the hut was thick enough to hide her, but it would do little to slow a bullet. She saw her brave co-workers, lined up, arms behind their backs. The men holding them prisoner remained out of sight, but she could hear their voices: strange, demanding and broken.

"Spet on his face! You do id nah!" a man shouted.

She knew all of her new friends would never give in. She knew they would all die. Just like Charles. He had been the first to refuse; he'd been dead for ten minutes now.

Megan could see Jennifer's legs shaking. It was her turn now. She was eighteen, an eager intern from small-town Kansas. She'd been on the job for two days, yet her convictions ran the deepest. She managed to say, "Forgive them, Lord," before a bullet cut her down as well.

Jennifer's body slumped to the dirt. Megan covered her mouth, terrified she would scream and alert the butchers to her presence. But she couldn't let that happen. Not while Tom was coming. This wasn't his fight. This wasn't his place to die.

Eyes wet and unblinking, Megan turned and ducked into the woods as another gunshot echoed through the forest. Branches stretched out for her—scratching at her, clawing at her. They wanted to slow her down. They wanted to kill her, too. But her legs were strong from years of running, and the thickets that blocked her path exploded away from her, tearing open her flesh and exposing an open path. Megan turned right and ran, ignoring the streaks of blood slipping down her legs.

Movement in her periphery caught Megan's attention as she rounded a tree. She slowed and focused her vision. Four men were beating a fifth…but she didn't know him. She took in the assailants. They had rifles slung over their shoulders. Each man was dressed in half-military fatigues and half-tribal garb, the kind of people you'd expect to see in a National Geographic full-page spread. The angriest, most savage and most passionate man wore a New York Yankees baseball cap.

Megan wasn't sure how long she had been staring at the sight, but it was long enough for her to be noticed.

"A woman escapes!" one of the men yelled, blood dripping from his knuckles.

Megan's gaze was frozen on the man who lay on the ground, covered in blood and beaten to a pulp. He looked up into Megan's eyes using only his right eye—the left was swollen shut. Oddly, she noticed his clothing. Blue, button down shirt. Polished shoes… *Polished shoes in the Zambian jungle?* His un-swollen eye grew wide, and he yelled desperately to her, "Megan! Run!"

As Megan's eyes snapped away from the man, she saw that the four locals were almost upon her. She launched into the forest, praying her feet would carry her fast enough, praying for the poor man she left behind. How did he know her name? Was he a friend of Tom's?

Boom! Birds launched into the air behind her. She knew the stranger was dead. It made her run even faster.

The path was thin and winding, but Megan had run it every morning for the past two weeks. She knew every depression, every curve and every fallen tree. They would never catch her here. But the path would soon end and she would be running through an open field. She was fast, but she was no Superwoman. She couldn't out-run a bullet.

Mud splashed across her legs, mixing with blood, as she hurdled over a moss-covered, rotten tree. She could see the sky through the branches in front of her. The clearing, and Tom, lay just ahead.

3:57 P.M.

The Cessna pulled up and over a line of tall trees, emerging over a clearing, where a crude runway was chiseled into the earth. Once the plane had come to a stop, Tom and Mpundu began unpacking the luggage and the supplies Megan had asked him to bring. Grunting with exertion, Tom heaved a wooden crate onto the ground. After straightening back up, he removed a bandana from his back pocket, then dabbed away the stinging sweat that trickled into his eyes. Tom had expected help—workers from the mission, locals, whatever. At least Megan should have been there by now. It wasn't like her to be late.

"Tom!" It was Megan's voice, but from where?

Scanning the field of tall, suntanned grass, Tom found what he was looking for. His face lit up as he saw Megan running toward him. She was yelling, but Tom couldn't make out the words. He started forward. As Megan grew nearer, it wasn't her words Tom finally understood, but the tone of her voice.

She was afraid.

Before Tom could launch toward Megan, Mpundu's firm grasp on Tom's shoulder held him in place. "Do not enter the grass, Mr. Greenbaum. There are predators."

Tom looked back at Mpundu, whose eyes were locked on a flock of birds bursting from the jungle on the opposite side of the field.

"Lions?" Tom asked quickly.

"Worse."

Pulling away from Mpundu, Tom plowed into the field, determined to reach his wife. "Megan! MEGAN!"

"Mr. Greenbaum! Come back! We must leave now!"

Tom ignored Mpundu's call and continued forward. Mpundu ran back to the Cessna and started the engine.

Megan grew closer, and her words became distinguishable, "Get away! Go back to the plane!"

Tom ran faster.

Boom! A gunshot pierced the air. Tom instinctively ducked down. His chest burned with each panicked breath. What should he do? Who fired the gun, and at whom? When he picked his head up again, Megan was gone. Tom's eyes grew wide. "Megan?"

Ignoring the danger, he ran forward. "Megan! Where are you? Megan!"

Fifty feet away, Megan stood up and looked at him. "Run!" she yelled, as her feet carried her toward him.

Tom surged forward, shrinking the distance between them. As they grew closer, he could see Megan's normally smooth face twisting with fear and pain. His eyes darted to her blood red shoulder. She'd been shot.

Boom! A second shot pierced the air as Tom and Megan came within ten feet of each other. Her body arched back. Blood exploded from her chest, covering Tom's body and face. He stopped in his tracks, and the world around him moved in slow motion, as though the entire scene were happening underwater. The thick ruddy liquid felt warm on his face. Roaring blood rushed through the veins in his head, making it hard to hear. Dizziness swept through him with each pounding heartbeat. He felt himself falling, but his feet were firmly rooted to the ground.

Megan stumbled forward, her eyes locked with Tom's. He could see her: brimming with enthusiasm over a new job, snuggled up by the fireplace with a new book, glossy with sweat after a long run. And then she was gone. Her eyes hardened and her muscles fell limp. She fell forward and landed at Tom's feet, flattening a section of grass with her body.

He looked down. His wife was dead.

Breath raspy and full of anguish, he fell to his knees and rolled his wife over, as tears condensed on his lower eyelids. He pushed his hand against the flow of blood pumping from her body. It looked like a ruptured gallon of milk. "Megan? Megan, please…"

Had Tom been more aware, he might have noticed Mpundu streaking down the runway in the Cessna. He might have noticed the crunch of moving brush and the smell of gunpowder. Instead, he sat in the grass, cradling Megan and rocking back and forth like a caged animal.

It wasn't until Tom felt warm metal against the back of his neck and heard the click of weaponry that his attention was thrust back into reality. He could see four sets of bare feet standing around him. His head was too heavy to look up.

Standing above him were Megan's four pursuers, led by a man with a Yankees hat.

"Do you balieve ahs dis wuman deed?" asked the Yankees fan, as he pressed the barrel of his rifle into Tom's temple. "Ansah me, now."

Tom looked up toward the voice. The Yankees fan's face was silhouetted by the bright sun behind him. "W—what?" Tom asked.

The Yankees fan walked to the side. The sun cleared, and Tom could see the man's dark face, painted brightly with dry, red ink. What was most striking about his face were the expressions—twisting and contorting with confusion. The Yankees fan looked at Tom from all angles. Then he smiled and stood up straight.

"Do you balieve as dis wuman deed? Do you balieve en her God?" The man's voice seemed deeper, more demanding. "Ah you not a disciple?"

Tom's lip began to bleed as he bit down.

"Tell us! We want to know!" the man screamed.

"No, damnit! I don't believe what she did! I never will!"

The four men instantly lowered their rifles. The Yankees fan squinted his eyes skeptically, then relaxed and smiled a rotting grin. "Thun tuday ees your lucky day."

The other men laughed and patted each other on the back for a job well done. Satisfied, all four turned and walked away, disappearing back into the tall grass.

Tom was left on his knees with Megan in his arms. His muscles began to shake. His eyes twitched to a maddening rhythm and blood pumped adrenaline through his veins. He let his wife, whom he had clutched to his chest so fondly moments ago, fall to the ground. He stood to his feet and cut into the tall grass.

The four men walked away slowly. Tom caught them quickly. He pounded his fist into the head of the first man before they heard a sound. The man toppled over and dropped his rifle, which fired upon impact with the ground. The bullet split several shoots of grass and then shattered the ankle of another man who fell backwards into the grass.

The third man swung around and raised his rifle, but he was too slow. Tom was upon him. Tom's left hand held the rifle at bay while his right hand smashed the man's throat. The man fell to the ground gasping for air, leaving his rifle in Tom's shaking left hand.

He raised the rifle toward the Yankees fan, who had already taken aim at Tom. They paused. Breathing. Staring. Listening. A dragonfly flew between them, and both men fired.

Tom was clipped in the shoulder and screamed in pain. The Yankees fan stood unmoving with a hand held to his chest. Tom quickly regained his composure and raised his rifle a second time. But the man with the Yankees cap stood still, with a look of shock frozen on his face.

"So it's true," the man said with a smile, "You ah not a disciple."

The Yankees fan's hand slipped from his chest, revealing an open wound. He fell to his knees and slumped over dead.

Moans from the other three men writhing in the grass gained Tom's attention. He aimed the rifle. One man raised his hands over his head and begged in his native tongue. Tom looked away from the men, toward the area of crushed grass where Megan's body still lay. Then he took aim again and asked, "Do you believe as she did?"

"W—what?"

Tom pressed the rifle into the man's head. "Do you believe as she did?"

"No! No! We do not!"

"Then, maybe I'll see you in Hell."

The gunshots could be heard for miles away. Three. And then three more.

2

PRECIPICE

2005

7:00 A.M.

Arizona

D avid Goodman knew what day it was. Tom told him the story ten years ago, and David had since learned how to treat his partner on this day: just like every other day. As David threw away the soggy cereal he never got around to eating, he thought about Tom and wondered how a man who had no hope for the future, could bear the burden this day represented.

Tom had thrown himself into his work since Megan's death, but that was required of them both. David had never been married and probably never would

13

be. He was fond of saying, "Fifteen hour days locked in a secret facility, six days a week aren't exactly conducive to dating."

Whatever the case, they were each all the other had. The only variation in the pair's schedule was that David drove forty miles every Sunday morning to attend the nearest church. Tom did not. God was often a source of heated debate.

It was a topic David would attempt to avoid today. He quickly adjusted his paisley tie, slipped into his perfectly polished black shoes, attached his LightTech Industries ID card to his blazer and looked at himself in the mirror. He looked old. Older than he should. His blue eyes seemed to have faded nearly to gray. The crow's feet stretching out from his eyes, which deepened when he smiled, looked good on Hollywood actors, but not on him. They made him feel old. He turned sideways and sucked in his gut. The old skinny David was in there somewhere, buried beneath a few inches of chub.

With a sigh, he left his bedroom and grabbed a 20oz. bottle of Wild Cherry Pepsi from the fridge. With the recent addition of a breakfast soda, this had been his morning routine for the past fifteen years—as boring and stale a routine as the average person's. But it never bothered him. Particle accelerators, nuclear reactors, black hole generators, heavily armed guards and secret tunnels kept the rest of his day a tad more interesting.

As soon as he left the front door of his smooth, adobe home, the morning heat struck his head. David grumbled under his breath as his armpits instantly began to perspire. It took him ten years of Arizona heat before he had found a deodorant that could keep him dry. Last year they stopped selling it. He had never been fond of heat and even lobbied to have the whole operation moved to New Hampshire's White Mountains. The official LightTech response was a hearty laugh and pat on the shoulder.

It took David ten seconds to walk from his air conditioned home to his burgundy Land Rover, which was parked as close to the front door as possible without crushing his collection of cacti. In years past, he parked the vehicle in the attached garage, but it had become so full of old computers and spare parts that there was little room to walk.

14

He had considered cleaning out the garage on several occasions, but couldn't bring himself to do it. The computers in the garage were part of his past—LightTech's past—and if he and Tom succeeded, all of it would be part of history.

David hopped into the Land Rover, slammed the door shut and glanced at his reflection in the rearview mirror. His neatly bearded face looked as if he had just run a race through the Australian outback during the rainy season. He wiped the sweat from his pasty, white forehead and felt glad that those ten seconds represented his daily time spent in the sun. He started the engine with a surge of gas and cranked the air to full, so it blew his graying hair back and dried his skin.

It took him five minutes to navigate through the LightTech owned and operated neighborhood. The neighborhood was the only visible group of buildings for twenty square miles, and it housed two thousand employees, from physicists to janitors. Tom was waiting by the sidewalk as usual.

Tom was dressed casually, as he tended to, in blue jeans, a white T-shirt and an open, plaid, button-down shirt. Of course, LightTech had a dress code, but Tom had never cared about codes, rules or outside guidance. Besides, he knew they couldn't fire him. He was too important. His eyes had narrowed over the years, his face was more carved and his cheeks were rough with stubble. David was sure Tom was going for a Clint Eastwood look, minus the gray hair—Tom's was still solid black and wavy. Tom had also managed to stay fit, which vexed David, because he never saw the man exercise and they had similar diets.

Seconds after Tom entered the SUV, David cracked open his Wild Cherry Pepsi, signifying the start of their morning banter.

Tom looked at David with amused disgust. "You're going to rot your teeth out," he said.

"What do you know?" David retorted with his thick Hebrew accent, dodging any real response.

"I know that I'm going to keep my teeth longer than you," Tom added, with a gleaming grin.

"We've been friends since we both came to this country, what, fifteen years ago? Don't presume to come between me and my true love," David replied, as he took another swig.

David and Tom were both born and raised in Israel. Their homes there were two miles apart, yet they had never met until LightTech hired them both. They came to America and both quickly adopted it as their home country. David had been sent to a prestigious private school from which he had graduated top of his class, while Tom was home-schooled by his father, an ex-Rabbi, who no longer held the Jewish faith. David remembered their excitement in the early days, when freedom to do groundbreaking research in a privately owned facility was somewhat of a novelty.

Tom smiled and leaned back into the plush leather interior of the Land Rover, enjoying the conversation. "And what if I do, old man? Will you cane me?"

David fumed. "Cane you? I don't use a—Old man! I'm your senior by three years, and you presume to call me 'old man?'"

"I suppose I presume too much?" Tom asked.

David nodded as he sucked down some more cherry-flavored liquid sugar.

"About as much as you use that word," Tom added.

"What word?"

"Presume."

David shifted in his seat and said, "Don't presume to tell me how to... Huh, I guess you're right."

Tom smiled, "Aren't I usually?"

"Bah," David blurted, "The only thing your brain is good for is quantum mechanics and attacking Chri—"

David managed to stop his sentence short, but Tom's jagged facial expression revealed he already knew how it ended. The silence that ensued was nerve-wracking. How could David forget! Of all the days... It was Tom who finally spoke, "Better step on the gas; we have to meet the bitch in a half hour."

16

David was immeasurably relieved that his transgression had done no permanent damage, and he gladly resumed his role in the conversation. "Language!" David shouted.

"C'mon, David. You have to admit she's—"

"Just doing her job. I admit she's forceful at times. I'm just saying, watch your tongue," David said in his best patriarchal voice before taking another drag of soda. "You know, if you had all the responsibility she does, you might not be nice all the time either."

Tom looked at David, waiting for the punch line. "You're serious?"

David nodded, and Tom laughed, relaxing and turning in his seat.

"What?"

"Nothing."

The motor hummed and the crunching of soil beneath the tires rumbled for what felt like ten minutes, but was closer to ten seconds.

"You'd be grouchy too, if you worked for you," David stated.

Tom raised an eyebrow and cracked a smile. David saw him. "You know what I mean!"

Silence resumed as dust blew over the windshield, kicked up by a warm gust of wind.

"What *do* you mean?" Tom asked.

"You can be hard to deal with sometimes. That's all I'm saying." David guzzled some soda.

Tom smiled, "Yes, well, at least I won't be sucking my food through a straw soon."

David huffed and turned his full attention to the road.

Tom watched David drive, smiling at his friend's wrinkled brow, knowing that David would never give up his Pepsi habit, even if it did take his teeth. All of David's convictions ran that deep. It was one of the things Tom liked most about David, but would never tell him. It reminded him of someone he knew once.

17

☙

For miles in every direction, there was nothing but red dirt, craggy rock formations and deep blue sky. Dust sprayed up behind the Land Rover and covered the vehicle as it came to a stop in front of the only landmark for miles: a rundown wooden shack with a missing wall. The wooden structure looked as though a strong breeze could blow it over, but it had stood in this very spot for twenty years, never collecting dust, never losing a nail and never drawing any attention.

David steered the Land Rover into the shack and put it in park. Tom and David unbuckled their seatbelts, leaned forward toward the windshield and continued a conversation already in progress, paying no attention to the loud *clacks* and *whirs* emanating from all around them.

"All I'm saying is that I'm not sure," Tom explained.

"It will work. It's our design," David replied.

"That's what concerns me."

A small device, disguised to look like a knot of pine, lowered over the Land Rover's hood from the shack's ceiling. A shimmering green laser investigated the vehicle from top to bottom, front to back. The laser passed across the windshield and into the SUV. Tom and David looked forward, eyes wide open, allowing the laser to scan their facial features and retinas.

"You know what you need?" David asked rhetorically. "Faith. Just a little would do you some good. You always have to see it, touch it, smell it, before you believe anything."

"It's called science, David. It's what we scientists are paid to do."

"*You* got here through science. I got here by faith," David said with a wink and a smile.

18

"Well then, should we go see what your faith has to say about the malleability of space-time?"

"Gladly."

The laser disappeared, and the knot of pine retreated into the shack's ceiling. Seconds later, a cloud of dust exploded up around the Land Rover and the ground beneath it lurched downward. Light poured out from under the ground in a circle so perfect, it might have been drawn by a compass. The light grew brighter as the platform, which the Land Rover rested on, moved downward.

The vehicle descended into a bright, white, open cavern. The rounded walls were smooth, like the inside of an egg. The round platform was held aloft by a tall, white, hydraulic pole, which was disappearing into the floor. Four support cables strung from holes in the ceiling were attached to the platform's edges. Two hundred feet below, every make and model of vehicle, belonging to thousands of employees, filled the football-stadium sized parking lot.

As they reached the first floor level, simply designated *Parking Level One*, they exited the Rover and left it with Fred, the wiry, thin, valet parking attendant. He had the physique and style sensibilities of a young Bill Gates, which was a common look for not just the scientists in the facility, but also for the support staff. Aside from security, and Tom, most of the men working for LightTech, whether men of science or valets, perfectly fit the nerd stereotype.

"Any news from the future?" Fred asked.

"Not yet," Tom replied, "We might be paddling up the quantum stream in the wrong direction."

Fred snorted gleefully. Even the parking attendants at LightTech Industries were smart enough to understand quantum humor. "Good one, Dr. Greenbaum."

"Not to worry, Fred," David added, "Today is the day."

Fred brimmed with excitement. "Really?"

"Don't get your hopes up," Tom said, "Dr. Goodman here thinks we'll succeed because he has faith, and we all know faith is more important than science."

Fred laughed again and found an opportunity to brown-nose, "Two for two, Dr. Greenbaum. Faith more important than science? Please."

David responded with a scowl directed toward Tom. Fred wished them well as they entered the complex through a pair of glass doors that were etched with the LightTech logo—three beams of light converging to a point to form a cone. Through the doors, they entered into a bright white tunnel that appeared to continue infinitely. Both men strolled fifty feet and stopped, seemingly for no reason.

"Think she's here yet?" David asked.

"A snake can usually be found in its den."

"Especially when the snake has spent two billion dollars building the den," David said with a smile.

"She's going to kill us if we don't come through today," Tom said, as he shook his head. "Two billion dollars on a project we proposed... We should have been salesmen."

David forced a grin. "We may still get our chance."

The illusion of an infinite hall faded away as the image turned milky and then solidified to reveal a single door, which opened automatically. Tom and David entered, the door closing behind them with a clunk and the hallway reverting to its never-ending appearance.

Tom and David entered the control center, waving hello to fellow scientists bustling around the room and working at various computer consoles. The day had just begun and it was already a madhouse. The control center was a masterpiece of modern engineering and electronics, the science for which wouldn't be available to the outside world for another twenty years. The walls and ceiling were rounded like a black, half-shell amphitheater. Level after level of computers and workstations were staggered down the floor like an audience, all culminating in a sheet of four-foot thick glass separating the control center from Receiving Area Alpha. Light streamed from the grated floor like glowing square waffles, illuminating faces from below. David sometimes joked about how the lighting made the team look like they were about to start telling ghost stories.

Moving down the center aisle, David and Tom headed for the wall of glass where Sally McField stood over the shoulder of a very nervous scientist. David thought Sally was beautiful in a power-suit kind of way. She stood six inches taller than him and her taut calf muscles hinted that a fit body hid beneath her masculine suits. He was often tempted to compliment the woman on her bunned black hair that hung straight when freed from the bun, or how the shade of maroon lipstick accentuated her full lips and softened the stern look of her frequently furrowed brow line, but he held his tongue for fear she might have him executed. Only one man dared ruffle her feathers.

Tom scurried toward Sally from behind, a nervous David in tow.

"You watch," Tom whispered to David. "She has eyes in the back of her head."

"Shush!" David urged, not wanting to be berated first thing in the morning. "She'll hear you!"

Tom replied by pointing to his eyes with his index and middle fingers and then at the back of Sally's head, reiterating his statement in pseudo sign language. David widened his eyes back at Tom as a final warning.

"Dr. Greenbaum. Dr. Goodman. You're both late," Sally said, without looking back at them.

Tom, in his best sideways whisper, said, "I told you."

In a swift move, Sally spun one hundred and eighty degrees on her high heels, so she faced Tom and David, who quickly morphed their expressions into sweet smiles.

"Miss McField." David greeted her with a kind voice, as he raised his hand to shake hers.

"Sally," Tom said with a wry smile, "so good to see you again."

Sally ignored David's extended hand and got right down to business, "It won't be if I don't see some results by the end of the day. To put it mildly, doctors, impress my ass off or I pull the plug."

Tom's button was instantly pushed, but before he could unleash his fury, David interjected as diplomatically as he could muster, "Miss McField…today you

21

will witness something we cannot yet explain. It will, in seconds, change the course of human history, or more accurately, human *future*. I assure you—"

"Tom might enjoy your speeches, David, but they don't impress me," Sally said. "All I care about is results. We've had you two bottled down here for years. It's about time we saw something for it."

David's blood pressure rose to terminal levels, but he managed to contain his personal meltdown, "You will, Miss McField. Soon enough."

"I better," Sally said, as she used the same high-heeled pivot maneuver to spin and strut away.

David stared at Sally, throwing imaginary grenades at her head. In his blind anger, he let slip a simple word that instantly changed Tom's mood from rage to pure glee, "Witch."

Tom's eyes nearly launched from their sockets, "W—what did you say?"

David scrunched his face. "What?"

"You called her a bitch," Tom said with a grin.

"I absolutely did not!"

"I heard you."

David huffed. "I said, 'witch,' with a W."

Tom's smile faded, but not completely. "Ah, one of your religious curse replacements. Fudge, shoot, gosh darnit, Jiminy Cricket. It's all the same, you know. You still mean the curse, even if you don't say the actual word. Changing bitch to witch might alter the sound, but the emotion behind it is still the same."

David and Tom stared into each other's eyes. Tom knew his constant gaze and slight smirk would eventually wear David down.

"Bah! No one's perfect," David said, as he stormed away. "We have work to do."

Tom laughed and followed after his friend, thinking that maybe this wouldn't be such a bad day after all.

❧

A n hour passed before David was calm again. Tom knew Sally could get under David's skin like no one else, which made him wonder why David looked at her the way he did. He'd been watching David attempting to write out some calculations for the past half hour. But every time Sally walked by, it was as if she were a magnet and David's face was made of metal. His head would follow her across the room and then linger as she disappeared from view. Could he be interested in such an ice queen? Did David see something in her that Tom couldn't? Tom decided to discover the answers to these questions, but right now, there were more pressing matters demanding his attention.

A slew of scientists sat behind the myriad of consoles that filled the control center. The place smelled of warm computers. The excitement in the room was nearly uncontainable. Every member of the science team, led by Tom and David, had dreamed of this moment for years. Some had spent their entire careers at LightTech for the slim chance they would succeed.

David, Tom and Sally stood in front of the glass wall, peering into Receiving Area Alpha. The room was smooth from top to bottom; not one ninety-degree angle could be seen. The walls were brushed silver, like a giant frying pan. The massive sheet of glass separating the control center and the receiving area made the whole scene feel like an oversized children's aquarium. Tom's eyes eagerly searched for something—any anomaly that would suggest a breach in the time stream had occurred.

Sally looked at her watch, "By my time we should see something in forty-five seconds. Not that I really expect to see your entire future life's work suddenly appear."

"If we succeed within our lifetimes, we'll see something. Even if it's just a fluctuation," Tom added.

"Then I don't expect we'll see much, because if my future self is anything like my present self, she will have pulled the plug on this little—"

Tom interrupted, "Hey, that's not—"

"Quiet!" David yelled. "Both of you. All this talk, this bickering—it's all pointless. In ten seconds, our world will change forever, and all you two can do is nag each other. Please...for the love of Moses, just shut up."

"For the love of Moses?" Tom said with a raised eyebrow. "Really?"

Sally's reaction caught both David and Tom by surprise. A smile cracked onto her face, if only for a moment, before she smothered it and began waiting patiently as David had demanded.

Tom glanced away from the receiving area and saw David eyeing Sally, inspecting her soft lips for any sign of the smile's return. He imagined David was even more shocked by the emergence of Sally's smile, especially at a tense time like this. But it wasn't important now, and Tom certainly wouldn't let David miss a second of what they hoped would happen next.

"David," Tom whispered.

David jerked his eyes toward Tom, who motioned with his head for David to look at the receiving area.

"Right." David turned toward the wall of glass.

Tom shook his head. What was with him?

Silence consumed the room. Tom glanced at his watch. Five seconds overdue. Tom closed his eyes and lowered his head in disappointment. They were defeated.

David's fingers tapped against the thick glass, expelling his nervous energy. Sally crossed her arms and tapped her foot. Ten seconds late... This was not good.

A sound like the popping of popcorn began to fill the air.

Something was happening.

Scientists around the room began checking their equipment, recording the sound and preparing for more. The sound grew louder, crackling through the thick glass, and causing the control center to shake. A metal cabinet at the back of the

24

room popped open and its contents crashed to the floor. There was a flash of light inside the receiving area, and then everything went black.

After a moment of silence passed, the room erupted with cheering. Tom looked at David, and their eyes were wide. "Not quite what I expected, but a good turnout nonetheless," David said with a tinge of disappointment.

"I expected more of us, too," Tom replied.

They shook hands as Sally approached in the darkness. "Congratulations. Your funding will be doubled."

As Sally spoke, she failed to notice the light level in the room was rising. Blue light slowly lit up the room, glowing on Sally's face. David and Tom noticed right away. With wide eyes, they stared just beyond Sally, into the receiving area.

"But we better get a little more than a light show next time..." Sally noticed their fixed gazes.

She followed their eyes back to the receiving area, which was glowing with a dull blue light, luminescing from nowhere at all.

The control center fell silent again. Scientists frozen in mid-hug watched the receiving area with beaming eyes.

Tom lifted his head and rested his hands on the glass wall. His jaw slowly dropped open like a drawbridge. "It's happening," was all he could say.

A small, white shimmer appeared inside the receiving area. The light glowed steadily at first, but then began to fluctuate. It strobed slowly, and with each burst of light came a loud, bass *Whump.*

Whump... Whump... Whump.

Faster and faster. Light swirled and flashed like at a rave nightclub.

Whum. Whum. Whum. Whum. Crack!

Several brilliant, vertical streaks of blue and white light ripped into the air within the receiving area, creating thunderous booms. One after another, cracks of light tore into reality and then disappeared. In the wake of each spear of light, an object was left behind. A table covered in diagrams, charts and graphs; a cabinet full of supplies and tools that had yet to be invented; and several countertops covered in small devices. Several large chunks of electronic equipment also appeared. An ozone-like odor filled the room and grew stronger with each explosion of light and materials.

The raw power unleashed by the event was both fascinating and horrifying. Everyone in the room, except Tom and David, took a step back. Computers began to malfunction. Sparks exploded into the air. No one noticed. All eyes were transfixed on the tears in time-space opening up in the next room.

The show concluded with a loud *boom*, causing everyone in the control center to jump. As the final streak of light blinked out of existence, the control center was plunged into darkness. The receiving area still shimmered with light, like a luminous snowstorm, as thousands of blue, glowing particles fluttered down to the floor. No one moved. As the last particles extinguished, the emergency lights suddenly burst on. David yelped like a Chihuahua. The room full of normally composed professionals exploded with clapping and uproarious laughter.

Tom's hands squeaked down the glass wall. He looked at David. "We did it… We did it!" Tom yelled, as he picked David up off the ground and administered a crushing hug.

"What did I tell you!" David shouted. "What did I tell you!"

Tom bounced David in the air and danced around like a child on Christmas morning. Sally stood still, staring into the receiving area. "I don't… I can't…"

Tom put David back on his feet, strode up to Sally's face and yelled at the top of his lungs, "HA!"

After Tom had expressed his victory to Sally and moved on to shake the hands of several excited colleagues, David approached Sally with a smile. "Thank you for letting this happen. We owe you everything."

"I… You're welcome," Sally replied.

David extended his hand and Sally took it. Rather than shaking her hand, David let their hands linger together, while he looked kindly into her eyes.

And then she did it again.

Sally smiled.

3

TEETERING

2005

7:00 P.M.

Arizona

T om and David gleefully spent the next eleven hours sorting through the piles of documentation, equipment and tools that had been sent back in time from their future selves. The idea that this could work originated from David's brilliant mind, but was quickly supported by Tom when they first met. David grew skeptical of Tom's motivation after learning about Megan's untimely and violent death. But Tom had assured David endlessly that if success came within their lifetimes, he would not try to alter his tragic past. Tom knew that doing so would mean he and David would never meet. Having never met, any success they would experience in the realm of time travel would cease to exist, meaning Tom couldn't go back in time in the first place. This was only one of the many theoretical paradoxes of time travel, which they now faced in the futuristic items laid out around the room.

David rubbed his weary eyes and continued on, driving his thoughts into a particular schematic that diagramed how one might navigate through the time stream without creating a cosmic wake. David's mind wrapped itself within the blanket of the schematic's quantum calculations. His eyes twitched back and forth, as he sucked up the information like a computerized leech. Then, an epiphany, "Look! Look!" he yelled. "Of course. Why didn't I think of this sooner?"

Tom looked up from fiddling with a silver watch. "How do you know you thought of it at all?" Tom asked and went back to exploring the contours of the watch.

David crinkled his forehead. He began, "Well, I started working on—"

But Tom cut him off with a question of his own. "Why did we send back watches?" Ten watches were lined up on the table next to Tom, but before the issue could be further addressed, Tom asked another question. "Whose handwriting?"

David grew confused, "What?"

Tom answered, not looking up from the watch. "Whose handwriting is on the schematic?"

"What are you talking about? I don't know," David replied, with a tinge of impatience.

"Well, look," Tom said.

David begrudgingly held up the schematic and inspected the handwriting. As David continued his detective work, Tom puzzled over the watches. "There are ten of these watches. All the same."

David placed the schematic on a table and moved it nonchalantly aside. Tom never looked up. Thinking he got away with his sleight of hand, David relaxed and attempted to steer the conversation further in the direction it was already headed. "Here, let me have a look," David said as he reached for the watch in Tom's hand.

Tom pulled the watch out of David's range and asked, "Whose handwriting? Yours or mine?"

"Ugh, just give me the watch," David pleaded.

"Tell me."

An agonizing moment passed. Agonizing for David at least. It was sheer pleasure on Tom's part.

"Yours," David conceded.

Tom smiled smugly and handed the watch over. David snatched it away quickly, eager to move on to more productive topics.

The watch face was silver, lined with what David thought must be gold. Could these be gifts celebrating their success? *Not likely*, David surmised as he looked at the lines of small buttons, tracing each side of the watch with his index finger. In all, he found eight buttons. The diamond quartz display showed the time, which was wrong, but left plenty of room for several other sets of information—numbers, codes, percentages—to be viewed.

What are these watches for?

David found the chance to recover from the schematic fiasco. "It's digital," he said, "So you'll be able to read it."

Tom feigned a laugh as David continued. "I don't know what it's for, but the time is wrong."

"I'll fix it," Tom said, as he snatched the watch from David's hands.

"Hey," David blurted, as he attempted to recover the watch from Tom, who made a hasty retreat.

Tom stopped and pushed several buttons. "Okay, here we go," Tom said with confidence, as he sat in a smooth, metal chair.

As Tom worked the buttons, both men leaned in close to see what was happening to the watch face. The screen displayed several sets of numbers, the meaning of which Tom and David could not fully grasp. Losing patience, Tom pushed the buttons at an ever-increasing rate until one finger landed on a button that had yet to be depressed.

31

Nanoseconds later, a crackling noise filled the air around them. With no visible source for the audible emanations, both men looked around in confusion. The noise grew louder and then, both men recognized it. Their eyes met.

Between their faces, a small light began to pulsate. It started again…

Whum… Whum… Whum…

WhumWhumWhumWhum.

The pair's eyes widened and they dove apart in separate directions. David ducked behind a trash barrel, while Tom overturned a table, sending stacks of diagrams to the floor, as he crouched behind it.

"What's happening?" David shouted.

"How should I know?"

"Look!"

"You look!"

David peeked up over the barrel. The intense flashing light sent him back down. His mind scrambled for answers.

"We triggered another time event," David whispered to himself.

A thought struck him and he yelled over the increasing noise. "The watches… They're the time devices. We triggered the event with the watch."

David was sure Tom couldn't hear him over the noise and didn't bother repeating himself. His eyebrows raised as a new realization reeled into his mind. Not only had they created a time travel device in the future, they had created several—and they were portable.

WhumWhumWhumCrack!

Bright light flashed through the room as time and space exposed itself again.

Boom!

The chair ceased to exist and the light faded. Tom and David gradually peeked out from behind their hiding places. Only a handful of bright blue sparkles now floated to the floor where the single watch had fallen.

Tom was the first to move, crawling out from behind the table. David followed, holding the trash barrel in front of him for protection. The two converged on the watch, where the chair once stood. Amazement was stretched across their faces as they stood over an area of the universe that had been torn apart by a device they created. A device that now lay at their feet. Both men fell to the floor, crying with laughter.

☙

T he smell of heavily buttered corn and five different kinds of barbequed meats lingered in the air. Peggy's Porker Palace was the closest thing to a decent restaurant within one hundred square miles of the LightTech facility. That was Tom's opinion anyway. Tom and David had become regulars at the 'all you can eat' buffet. They were no longer distracted by the four hundred pound, gravy-loving, plaid-shirt wearing hicks who consumed entire tabletops worth of food in one sitting. Waitresses hustled back and forth from table to kitchen, carrying trays full of half gorged-on food, repeating the cycle infinitely. Tom and David sat in a booth to the side of the action, bellies full from their celebration dinner.

While David sipped on a soda and scribbled notes on a napkin, Tom finished off his eighth bottle of Heineken. One of the time-modified watches rested on the table between them. Tom blinked his heavy eyes and focused them on the watch. He wondered how it worked, but knew he was too mentally diminished to even consider figuring it out. That's why he let David take a whack—that, and David was better at math.

David chuckled lightly.

"Well?" Tom asked with a slurred voice. "Where'd it go?"

"Let's just say some paleontologist is going to be very confused when he digs up a Neanderthal sitting on our chair," David said, grinning ear to ear.

"My God, we might have changed the course of human history," Tom blurted sarcastically. "Imagine! Chairs invented earlier, leading to the idea of having a throne, upon which a king is crowned and a monarchy is born centuries earlier than we currently know. By my calculations, the time change shift hits us in three… two… one…"

Tom finished his countdown with an impressive belch that went unnoticed save for the rotund cowboy at the next table over who raised his chicken leg to Tom and nodded his head as if to say, 'Nice one.'

David shook his head. Tom was a silly drunk if you stayed on his good side. "While I don't think our chair will have any effect on the time stream, we do need to be more careful in the future," David said.

"So puh-artna," Tom said with a drunken smile. "Tell me how our little invention works."

"You're not going to remember a word of this in the morning," David said, thoroughly amused.

"C'mon buddy, humor me…" Tom replied as he blinked his eyes, trying to clear the cobwebs.

David picked up the watch and held it up in front of Tom's face. Tom focused on the watch as best he could. David worked the buttons with skill and spoke as he did so, "Look here. This sets the date—not today's date mind you, but the date to which you wish to travel. We even included settings for B.C. and A.D. Here is the time of day. And look at this. Anywhere in the world you want to go to. After picking the year and time, you can enter global coordinates, which are then automatically adjusted for continental shift. Just push this button and poof, you disappear…to another time…another place…another way of life, in the blink of an eye."

"Okay," Tom said. "So then the real question is…if the watch…which was on the chair…which belongs to the new king…created the time…warp? Wormhole? What are we calling it anyway? Forget it. Not important… Why didn't the watch disappear, too?"

"I thought about that. It's elementary, but I think the watch might have to be attached to whatever it's sending back in time," David explained.

"Huh. I still can't believe this works."

"Believe it," David said. "It's about time you believed in something."

David's comment sank in slowly and got twisted in the process by Tom's tanked brain. "What's that supposed to mean?"

David spoke quickly. "I didn't mean what you think. I—"

"You what?" Tom said, his voice growing angry. "Want me to believe in your God? Your Jonas…"

Tom squinted his eyes, attempting to free his mind of the alcohol's effects, and said, "Your *Jesus*? It was my lucky day. That's what he said, you know, my lucky day. My lucky day…"

Tom spoke through gritted teeth. "Megan dedicated her life to 'saving people.'" Tom's nostrils raised and his lips turned down. "Saving people… She called it that. She died for being a Christian. She died… She died because she believed in an ass of a God, who could care less about those who served him."

David looked around the room. They were beginning to get an audience.

"Here God! I want to serve you, so I can die, too!" Tom shouted toward the ceiling. He looked back at David. "I hold Jesus… Jesus is *responsible* for her death. She's dead. It's his fault. How could I ever believe in him? If he were who everyone says he is, why did he let Megan die?"

David spoke slowly and softly. "Sometimes bad things happen to good people, and we can't see why. But the greater good—"

"Greater good? David, my wife was gunned down in front of me and died at my feet. Right at my feet. And the blood… What good could possibly come of that?!" Tom fumed as his mind raced. "You weren't there, David. If…if you believed in Megan's God, you died. They killed you. Fffft, that was it. If you didn't…if you didn't, you lived. It was that simple…that easy. Be glad you weren't there. You'd be dead, too."

"She died for what she believed in, Tom," was all David could say.

"Why do you think…? What… Yeah, you know, you're right. She died for what she believed in: nothing. She died for nothing… Megan died for nothing."

Tom wound up and punched the tabletop with all his might, getting the attention of everyone in the restaurant. Tom's chest heaved with each passion-filled breath. He thought of Megan and how he wished he could save her—go back and save her—but he knew he couldn't. Time would be changed forever and the time travel device he invented would cease to exist, trapping Tom in an unbreakable cycle of self-defeat. But there was something he could do. Something that wouldn't change time, but would prove once and for all that Megan died for nothing and that David's naïve beliefs were ill founded. At least David could be saved from a life of worthless devotion to a dead god.

Tom shoved away from the table and pounded toward the door.

"Tom, wait," David urged, not sure what was happening. He fumbled with his wallet, attempting to pay for their meal before leaving. Tom had plenty of time to make his escape.

David careened out of the restaurant unsure of Tom's plans. Would he find Tom crying over the loss of his wife? Would he encounter a swift fist to his jaw? Would Tom pass out and wake up with a headache?

The Land Rover skidded to a dusty stop in front of David, nearly crushing his feet. Tom was behind the wheel. David approached the already rolled down window. "What are you doing?"

Tom looked at David, his eyes clear. "If you could go back in time…and witness any event…from beginning to end, where would you go?"

David was exasperated and didn't want to spend time on silly questions, "Tom, I don't know."

"Well, I do," Tom informed him.

"Tom…"

"I'm going to prove it to you, once and for all. I'm going to prove it to the world. My wife is dead and so is your God, dead and buried," Tom said. "Don't worry. I won't change anything. I won't get involved."

"You're drunk!" David shouted. "You can't drive!"

"You can't stop me, David."

"Give me the keys."

"Goodbye, David."

"Give me the keys, now."

"See you around."

"What are you going to do?"

Tom was finished with the conversation and slammed his foot on the gas. The SUV peeled off, leaving David to choke on a cloud of dust. David coughed as he chased after Tom, yelling, "Wait! What are you going to do?"

David stopped running in the middle of the road and caught his breath. He mentally sifted through all the possibilities Tom's drunken mind could be considering. He thought about what Tom had said. Where would he go? What event would he witness?

David opened his palm, looked at the heavy metallic watch and found the answer. They had unlocked the door to the past, and Tom was going to step through and face the man he blamed for his pain.

David's face contorted into sheer panic and he said aloud, "No... Oh, no, Tom..."

He smashed through the doors of Peggy's Porker Palace. "Help! Somebody help me! I need a ride!" David shouted. A room full of slovenly, bibbed truckers stared at David, annoyed by the disturbance to their feast. David met their eyes and knew he was going nowhere fast.

❧

A dark blue Chevy pickup with bull horns tied to the front stopped amid a cloud of dirt only ten feet from the inconspicuous shed in the middle of nowhere. David flung the door open and jumped out.

"Thanks," he said to Betty, the waitress who had used her smoke break to drive the frantic David to God-knows-where, for God-knows-what. Betty leaned out the window and spat. "Sure this is where you wanna be? Ain't nothin' out here."

David smiled and nodded his head, anxious for the woman to leave. "Yes, I'm positive. Thank you again for the ride."

"All right," Betty said, with one eyebrow perched high on her forehead. "It's your walk back."

David watched as Betty spun her tires, sending the truck into a quick one-eighty spin. She disappeared into the darkness, speeding through the night, country music blaring. As soon as she was out of sight, David ran into the shack like a child whose bladder was overflowing. The green laser dropped from the ceiling and scanned David's head.

Once he reached the parking level floor, Fred greeted him. "Salutations, Dr. Goodman. What are you two doing here this late?"

"When did Dr. Greenbaum arrive?" David asked.

"He came through not twenty minutes ago. Didn't quite seem himself though. Nearly ran me over."

"Maybe I'm not too late," David said to himself.

"Too late for what?" Fred asked.

Waaooh! An alarm sounded throughout the complex, so shockingly loud that David and Fred had to cover their ears. Red lights flashed on every wall. Just as quickly, the noise of the alarm disappeared, but the light remained.

David knew he was too late.

He entered the control center and was met by raw chaos. Scientists were running in every direction attempting to make sense of what had happened. Armed guards lined the walls and aisles, watching for anything out of the ordinary, which was everything as far as David could see. Sally was at the center of it all, giving orders to every soul in the room, like a general in the trenches.

Her eyes caught David's, and he saw an expression on her face he determined that second to never forget: relief. Sally rushed to him and said, "Someone used it!

Someone went back! I don't know how this could happen. Only you, Tom and I had... Where's Tom?"

David dodged the question. "Are the other watches still there?"

"One is missing," Sally replied.

Spencer, a timid scientist with thick glasses and a slight hunch, approached Sally with his head down and waited for her to acknowledge his presence. "What is it?" Sally barked.

"Uh, well, closer inspection of the data sheets from the time of incursion shows two additional time-space distortions," Spencer explained.

"Meaning?" Sally asked.

"Meaning two or three people—" David said.

"Or objects," Spencer added.

"—traveled through time in that room, at roughly the same time," David finished.

"How is that possible?" Sally asked. "All but two of the watches are accounted for and you still have yours, right?"

David removed the watch from his pocket and held it up for Sally. "Which means someone or something transported into the room and then back out after the first watch went missing."

"Is anything else from the room missing?" Sally asked Spencer.

"We already compiled an inventory. Absolutely nothing, other than the one watch and the unfortunate chair, is missing," Spencer said with unusual confidence.

"What about added?" David asked. "Was anything added? Maybe our future selves sent something else back?"

"We would have found that during the inventory," Spencer said. "Nothing inside the room has changed. But..."

David's impatience grew. "What?"

"Perhaps the monitoring equipment is flawed?" Spencer said, looking a little uncomfortable at suggesting such a thing. "This is, after all, the first time we've monitored space-time distortions. What if what we're seeing are, for lack of a better term, ripples?"

"Like aftershocks?" David asked.

Spencer smiled with relief. "Exactly. What if the second and third distortions we detected were simply aftershocks, or ripples, created by the first?"

"It's possible," David said. "That might make sense, but we should keep an eye out for the phenomenon in the future, just in case it repeats."

"Good," Sally said, the subject put to rest for the moment.

David patted Spencer on the shoulder and said, "Good work, Spence."

"Thanks, David. See you in the past," Spencer said, as he hustled away.

See you in the past?

"David, what are your thoughts?" Sally asked.

David's mind left his thoughts about Spencer's odd comment and focused on their predicament "My best guess," David said, "is that it's either a side effect from all the time distortions created in the last day, or our future selves were adding or subtracting from what they sent back. If it wasn't from an internal source, then there's nothing we can do about it anyway. I suggest we focus our efforts primarily on the problem at hand."

"Agreed, but I want another inventory done, just in case something was missed," Sally said, as they entered Receiving Room Alpha, which was swarming with guards.

David scurried to the eight remaining watches, resting on a table. He picked one up and glanced over it. "Good, they're identical. I still might be able to catch him," he said, without thinking.

"Catch who?" Sally demanded. "And how on God's green Earth can we find where 'he' went?"

David put the watch down and pulled out the one from his pocket. He strapped the watch to his wrist and looked up at Sally, "Because I know where and when he went. And since the watches are identical and most likely function similarly, I'm sure he could have—"

"David, for the last time...who?"

David paused. Should he tell her? Would she still trust him after knowing the truth? David's honesty won out. "Dr. Greenbaum... Tom went back."

Sally cocked her head sideways, apparently confused. "What? Why would he?" she asked.

"It's a long story," David said. "I don't have time to explain, and I'm going to need a few things."

David began mentally preparing for the ordeal, which he knew was his to face alone. It had been years since he held a conversation in his native Hebrew tongue, let alone his school-learned Greek and Aramaic. Thank God they had been required learning throughout his years at private Israeli schools. He feared Tom would be even worse off. He began making a mental list of items he would need: Authentic clothing could be created. Money: gold and silver in moderation would probably do. Some padded sandals...and a disguise for the watch.

David decided he would take a test trip into the past. He thought it would be best if he witnessed first-hand the event that drove his partner and best friend to risk changing the past to prove a point. He had to see it for himself. He had to understand. His mind was made up.

He was going to Zambia.

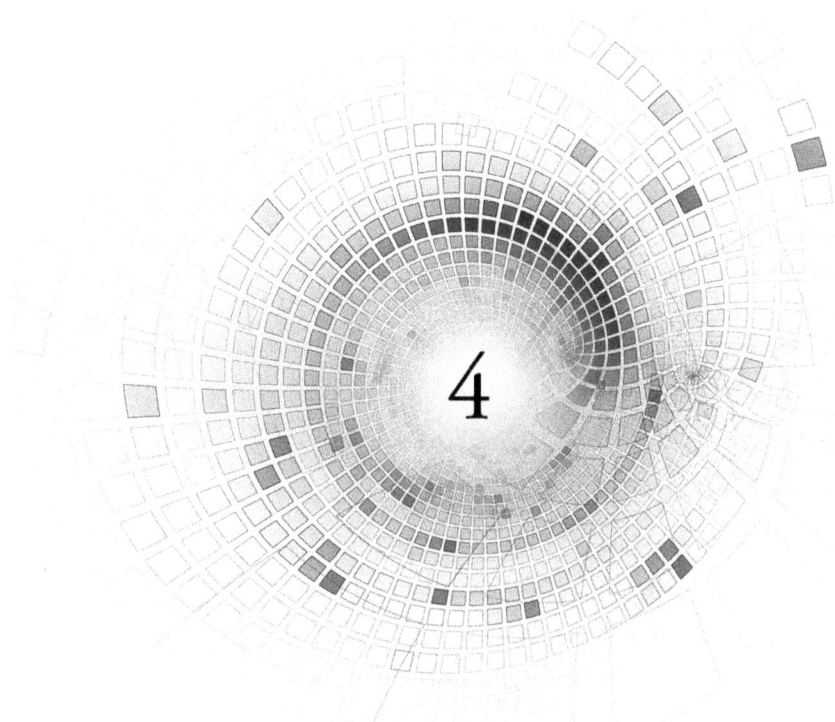

4

THE FALL

1985
2:02 P.M.
Zambia, Africa

An unfamiliar cracking noise filled the jungle, causing birds to jet away to the safety of the sky. Light flashed through the thick foliage like a frantic photo shoot. A shard of light split open, just above the ground, and spilled David out. He appeared, stumbled a few feet and leaned on a moss-covered tree for support. *Boom!* With a clap like thunder, the light vanished. Glowing blue sparkles twinkled to the wet ground around David, signifying the completion of the event.

David struggled to take another step, but fell to the ground and vomited into a patch of ferns. Perhaps this wasn't such a good idea? For all he knew, time travel was only safe for inanimate objects, even though the design of the devices as watches suggested otherwise. David pulled himself back to his feet and looked at his surroundings—lush jungle as far as the eye could see. This had to be Zambia, but were his coordinates correct? A thought occurred to David, and a smile came to his sickly face. It had worked! He had traveled through time and space. He—

Crack!

A gunshot pierced the air in the distance, and David remembered what he had come to see.

He carefully made his way through the dense wilderness toward the sounds of gunfire. He crept low to the ground, while attempting to avoid the many snakes, spiders, and larger predators that he couldn't see but thought must be lurking nearby. A metallic click froze David in his tracks.

"Tuhn arownd," came a deep voice. "Slohly."

David did as he was told and came face to face with four men he thought must be from a local tribe. Their dress was half-modern, half-tribal, and one of them wore a Yankees baseball cap… David's memory was triggered. He remembered the night Tom broke down and told him the entire story. Four men, in tribal clothes with rifles…and one of them, Tom called him 'the Yankees fan,' because he wore a Yankees hat. These were Megan's killers! These were the men Tom was going to kill mere minutes from now. David's mind raced with thoughts and theories about what his presence would do to this past and his future.

He thought about transporting himself back to the future, right before their eyes, saving his own life, but perhaps distracting or frightening these men enough so that the events of the past never occurred. David cringed at the thought that he might be changing the past just as he feared Tom would.

David winced as he felt cold steel press against his forehead. "Who ah you?" the Yankees fan demanded. "Ah you wit de missionaries?"

"No," David replied. He wondered if that was his ticket out of this. "I have nothing to do with the missionaries."

The Yankees fan leaned in close and inspected David's face. "Do we know you? I tink we do."

"No," David answered. "I'm a scientist."

David's answer seemed to cause the men some confusion. It was not an answer they had anticipated. The Yankees fan noticed David's LightTech badge still attached to his outer shirt. He lifted it up and looked at the picture, then back at David. He looked up and down David's body, taking in his ornate tie, his pressed shirt and polished shoes. They seemed to dissuade any suspicion that David was lying. The four men held a quick discussion in their native tongue, and then the Yankees fan said, "You ah fortunate, Mr. Scienteest. You do nah balieve as dey do, so you weel live... But we tink we will see you again. Yes, we will."

David felt a pang of guilt as he stifled the urge to stand by his fellow believers and tell these men that he did believe in the same God. But he felt—no, he *knew*—that the fate of space and time depended on him keeping his mouth shut.

The Yankees fan had more news to deliver. "Howevah," he said, trying to sound smart in the presence of a scientist, "you have trespahssed on tribal lahnd and must beh punished."

David didn't like the sound of that, and he dove fast into the jungle. He had to lose these guys before it was too late for them to murder Megan. David nearly froze with horror at the fact that here he was, in a position to stop Megan's murder, and all he could think about was helping her killers. What the hell was he doing?

The four men moved like stalking lions and sprinted after David. Thorns and branches tore at David's clothing and flesh. He tumbled through a heap of brush and crashed down onto a path. To his right he heard a gunshot, and to his left lay a field. David's memory was triggered again. Tom told him of the field, with the tall yellow grass. That was it! This is where it happened.

Quick to his feet, David managed to make it only ten more steps into the forest on the other side of the path before the four men caught him. There was no dialogue between them, no chance for David to redeem his actions. The four men simply began beating him. He felt the butt of a rifle bruise his ribs. One of their heels pounded his back. A fist to his jaw struck next. These men were punishing David for trespassing, but he knew another minute of this would mean his death sentence. There had to be a way out, something he could offer them. David's train of thought was brutally interrupted by a popping noise as his shoulder dislocated.

He screamed as his shoulder sent surges of electrical impulses to his mind, telling him his body couldn't take much more. He was sure his life would soon come to an end. His eyes began to twitch. He was feeling the impacts of fists to his head and boots to his body, but the pain delivered by each blow was now only a numb throb. His body's natural painkillers flooded his bloodstream. He was going into shock.

One of the men tried frantically to remove David's watch from his wrist, but was fumbling the job in his excitement. David thought he heard someone yell, "A woman escapes!" He looked up through his one good eye—the other was swollen shut. Standing not ten feet away was a woman on the path. She was staring at David with a confused expression. The four men must have been confused, too, because they didn't take action right away. This delay gave David the time he need- ed to put the pieces together.

David recognized Megan from pictures he had seen at Tom's house. She was as beautiful and strong as the photos showed and as Tom had told. But she wasn't moving. Why wasn't she moving? "Megan! Run!" Blood sprayed from David's mouth as he yelled.

Megan wrinkled her forehead. David thought she must have been trying to figure out how he knew her name. But his message seemed to sink in. She pounded dirt and ran toward the field. The four men leapt toward her in pursuit, and as they did, David thought he saw something unusual. He watched as the Yankees fan ran, and there, trailing behind him on the forest floor, were two shadows, as though there were two sources of light. But one of the shadows was different; it didn't follow the man's every move, and at times it seemed to have a will of its own. David was sure his failing vision and beaten mind were playing tricks on him. He had seen enough and would surely die if he remained any longer.

David looked at his watch through his clear eye. Thank God, they weren't able to get it off his wrist. David punched in a series of numbers and hit one final button. A bright light began to pulsate over his head. He prayed the loud noise his tear in time would create wouldn't distract Megan's murderers from carrying out their evil act.

The light expanded toward David's face. He watched it increase in speed through his good eye. He felt his head spinning, his ears thrumming with each pulse of light. He fell back into the grass and watched the passing clouds overhead as his eye closed shut. David lost consciousness and light enveloped his body.

In a flash, David was gone.

Boom!

Time resealed itself.

❦

Sally gasped when David reappeared seconds after he had disappeared. He was a bloody mess, sprawled out on the floor. Sally thought something must have gone wrong with David's time jump. She imagined David's insides being twisted and disfigured by the time travel process—the side effects of which, if any, had yet to be documented. Sally kneeled down next to him and said, "David! David, please be alive. Please, David…"

David's good eye cracked open and he saw Sally looking down at him. "Sally, thank God… It works… It works…" was the last thing David said before passing out again.

When he woke up, David found that all his wounds had been tended to. He could see out of both eyes again, and he looked around the room. It was a standard hospital room—nothing fancy. An old TV was bolted to the ceiling in the corner; the room stank of dry cleanliness and to his right was…Sally? She was sitting in a chair to the right of his bed, sound asleep.

David couldn't believe what he was seeing. How long had she been with him? How long had he been unconscious? He slid out of bed and picked up the clipboard containing his vital stats. He strode to the window and looked out. The skyline of Phoenix greeted him. A sign by the road read: Phoenix Baptist Hospital & Medical Center.

They must have flown me in, he thought.

David looked at his chart and read the damage report. Three bruised ribs, a dislocated shoulder—now repaired—and a few scrapes and bruises. Nothing life threatening, but he knew it would have been if it weren't for Megan. He remembered the sparkle in her eye, the long hair and smooth skin of the woman Tom loved. While David had never loved a woman so deeply, he had a better understanding of what Tom survived and how it could've shaped his life and beliefs.

"Ahem," Sally coughed. "You're, ah, exposing yourself."

David nearly jumped out of his white-and-blue, polka dot, hospital johnny as he spun around, realizing his backside was bare and exposed. His bruised face flushed red, and he said, "Sally, you're awake. I, uh… I…"

"Relax," Sally said. "It wasn't that bad of a thing to wake up to."

David froze. *Was that a compliment?* On his butt? Sally must have realized how it sounded, too, because she quickly corrected herself. "I mean, it could have been worse. How are you feeling?"

David was relieved the subject had changed. "I've been better, but I'm glad to be alive."

"What happened?" Sally asked.

He sat on the edge of the bed and cringed in pain, as his ribs flexed slightly. He stared straight ahead, as he relayed it to Sally. "I saw her," he said. "I saw Tom's wife."

David thought for a moment, staring out the window. "The only adverse effect of time travel is temporary, but extreme: nausea. After I arrived, already disoriented,

I was confronted by four men. The ones who put me in this sorry state," David said, as he waved his hand over his injuries.

"I would have died, had it not been for Megan. She was running toward the field, no doubt to warn Tom, when she saw me being beaten. She stopped... I recognized her. She was so beautiful, so afraid. I told her to run, and she did. The rest, as you know, is history," he said with a frown.

"I was lucky this time," he continued. "My presence could have changed the entire event. If they had let her go and killed me, if she hadn't stopped on the path, if that one man hadn't spotted her, we wouldn't be here having this conversation."

"But it works? They work? The watches?" Sally asked.

"Without a hitch." David managed a slight smirk.

"That's good news. That's great news. Think of all the things we can learn. All the things we can do. We're going to—"

"Sally," David's voice was stern. "Don't forget, Tom is still out there, and if we don't get him back, you and I and our entire world might cease to exist as it does right now."

"Worst case scenario, how much of our world could Tom alter by visiting ancient Israel two thousand years ago? That's where you think he is, right?" Sally asked very seriously.

"He's there. Trust me," David said. "Worst case scenario? Imagine a world without Jesus Christ."

Sally got a sickly look on her face, which then changed to amused. "You mean a world without Christianity? No more TV evangelists? No more Jehovah's witnesses banging on my door? Tell me how I can help."

David was not amused. "This isn't a joke. While you might not hold my particular beliefs about Jesus, you can't deny the influence his life had on the entire world for the past two thousand years."

Leaning back in her chair Sally began to wrap her mind around the endless possibilities.

"The Roman Empire, the Catholic Church, the Crusades, countless lives, deaths, marriages, births—all shaped by that single life," David said.

David took Sally's purse and opened it.

"Hey!" She began to protest, but David quickly found what he was looking for. He pulled out a dollar bill and thrust it in Sally's face.

"What does this say?" David asked.

Sally glanced over the bill. She knew what David was showing her and she read the words aloud, realizing the ultimate meaning of 'In God We Trust.'

"Exactly," David said. "'In God we trust.' The God this currency refers to is Jesus. This country, like many others, was founded on a belief system created by the man Tom now seeks to debunk."

Sally's eyes began to widen.

"If Tom proves to the world that Jesus was a fraud, he will destroy everything we know and everyone we hold dear. This isn't just Christianity that is being threatened; it's millions of human beings for the past two thousand years."

Sally looked at David, her face pale. "When can you leave?"

David stood to his feet, "Is everything ready?"

"Yes."

"Today."

"You can't. You're—"

"In no mood," David said with authority. "Tom has to be stopped and I'm the only one who can do it… Now, give me my pants and turn around."

Sally smirked, picked up David's pants and tossed them at him. "I'll be outside."

As David watched Sally leave, a feeling snuck into his consciousness. Amid the tumultuous scenarios playing out in his mind, something unfamiliar and equally as frightening dug in deep. Affection.

⁏

Looking at himself in the wall-sized mirror, David didn't recognize the man he saw. Not only did he look authentic, he looked downright ancient. It took only two days for LightTech to get all the necessary supplies. He didn't like waiting to leave, but his wounds needed time to heal and with time travel, David could leave in ten years and still get there on time.

He was dressed in a red-tinged, brown robe and sandals, and his watch had been cleverly disguised as a twine bracelet—not exactly standard issue for ancient Israel, but it shouldn't attract any attention. David knew that retrieving Tom could be as risky as Tom's own jaunt back in time, and he wasn't taking any chances.

Sally laughed at David when she entered the small orientation room, which had been designed for times like this, when people would be preparing to travel through time. "Not bad," she said, as she handed him a small pouch.

David opened the pouch and looked inside. It was full of ancient gold coins, gems and jewels. David's eyes lit up. "You don't think this is a bit overboard?"

"I want to be prepared for every contingency. Just because you have the money, doesn't mean you have to spend it," Sally explained.

"What contingency needs me to be filthy rich?" David asked.

"Do you know how to tend sheep, work the fields or grow olive trees?" Sally asked him.

"No, but I'm only going to be there for a few days at most, probably less. Once I find Tom, we'll both be back. I couldn't spend this much in a lifetime," David said, as his own comment began to sink in. "Oh."

"If you get stuck back there, if your watch breaks or malfunctions or…"

David tied the pouch to his twine belt. "I get the idea."

"Just find a hole in the wall little town and try not to interact with anyone…for the rest of your life."

David hadn't considered getting stuck in the past as an option. He cursed himself for not thinking of it after his last adventure through time. He had come close to losing the watch even then, and he had only been in the past for a few minutes. David would make sure he and the watch would never be separated.

"I'll come back," he said with confidence. He looked into Sally's eyes and smiled. "I promise."

Sally smiled back and said, "You better get to the prep station. The boys are getting antsy."

"Will you be coming to watch?" David asked, trying not to sound too hopeful.

"Wouldn't miss it for the world."

As David turned to leave, Sally suddenly said, "David, wait."

He froze in his tracks. What was this? David turned toward Sally as she walked over to him. Her face looked softer and her eyes were locked on the floor.

"I wanted to apologize," she said.

David nearly passed out but managed to stay standing.

"I know I've been a real ass over the years," Sally said slowly and deliberately, "but try to understand that it's not who I really am. My job is...complicated, and I have to sometimes say and do things I don't like, to make sure things get done. I just wanted you to know...in case something happens."

Through his smile David said, "I understand. Thank you for apologizing."

He thought he should leave before anything more was said—or done—that might cause him to change his mind about risking his life to retrieve Tom. "See you down there," David finished, and he started for the door.

"David, let's keep this between you and me. I can't have anyone else knowing I'm not a complete bitch."

He stopped at the door. "Your secret is safe with me." He closed the door behind him on the way out.

Sally stood alone, looking at the door, as a wave of sadness swept over her. She closed her eyes, but quickly composed herself when the door behind her opened. Three men entered and she turned to greet them with the cold gaze she had perfected over the years.

The man in the blue suit was George Dwight, CEO of LightTech and one of only three people with more clout than her. He was like a politician stuck forever on the campaign trail. His hair was slicked back and his nails were impeccably manicured. George had more power than Sally, but she knew she still intimidated him.

Jake Parrish, a tall and astute man with squinty eyes, was George's assistant. He was George's voice, his errand boy and a constant thorn in Sally's side. Every executive order from George came from Jake's lips. He took such joy in delivering those orders, too. Sally knew that Jake lusted for power. She could see it when he gave orders, smiling fiendishly. She watched him like a hawk, whenever he showed his face in her department. Today was no different. He had a look of 'I know more than you,' on his face. She could swear his eyes were smiling at her.

The other man was a stranger—tall, shaved head and clean. Sally imagined that there wasn't a loose flake of skin on the man's body. There wasn't a trace of stubble on his slick, cleft chin and even less intelligence behind his eyes. Sally didn't like him.

Smiling his pearly white, phony grin, George said, "You handled that well. I think that's a new low, even for you Sally, leading him on like that."

Sally swallowed hard. "Whatever it takes."

"Glad to hear that's still your policy," George said.

"Why?" Sally raised an eyebrow. "You have something planned?"

George gave a sideways glance to Jake, who promptly stepped forward. "Director McField, as you know, one of our lead scientists, Tom Greenbaum, has traveled back in time using LightTech owned equipment. Not only is this a crime against LightTech, but taking into account Dr. Greenbaum's intentions, it is a crime against all humanity. Given what is at stake, we believe it necessary to implement a few safety precautions, a few…failsafes."

"Meaning?" Sally asked, seemingly unfazed by this information.

"Meaning, Director McField," the stranger said, in a voice that screamed military, "if the situation cannot be contained, it must be eliminated."

"And you are?" Sally asked.

"Captain John Roberts."

George intervened. "Captain Roberts is the head of our Time Enforcement Division."

"Time what? Why wasn't I told of this?" Sally crossed her arms tightly across her chest.

"You're in charge of technology development. You didn't need to know. Captain Roberts has been training for years in case your division succeeded," George explained, as he chuckled. "And as soon as you succeeded, you lost control."

"What are you planning to do?" Sally asked, already knowing the answer.

"You heard Captain Roberts. If the situation cannot be contained, it will be eliminated. Roberts has been trained for every situation imaginable. He speaks fifteen languages, is a master of cultural blending and is trained in several kinds of hand-to-hand and special weapons combat."

"That's just what we need, a gung ho G.I. Joe killing people in the past," Sally said with a chuckle.

"Miss McField," Roberts said, "I assure you, I am the best equipped man alive to handle this situation. If Dr. Goodman fails, I will not."

"What event are you planning on going back to?" Sally asked.

"We've calculated the date on which Jesus was most likely crucified. If Dr. Greenbaum wants to disprove the story of Jesus, that is where he'd start," Jake explained.

"I'm leaving right after Dr. Goodman," Roberts added. "If he hasn't retrieved Dr. Greenbaum when I find them, I'll take care of the situation in the most expedient way possible."

"Sacrifice their futures to save our past," Sally said, understanding the plan.

"Exactly," George said with a smile.

"I expect you'll keep me informed?" Sally asked, as she headed for the door.

"Naturally," George replied. "Oh, and Sally, keep this to yourself."

"Naturally." Sally left the room wondering how she could have let this happen. Tom and David had been sentenced to death, and she was the only who could save their lives.

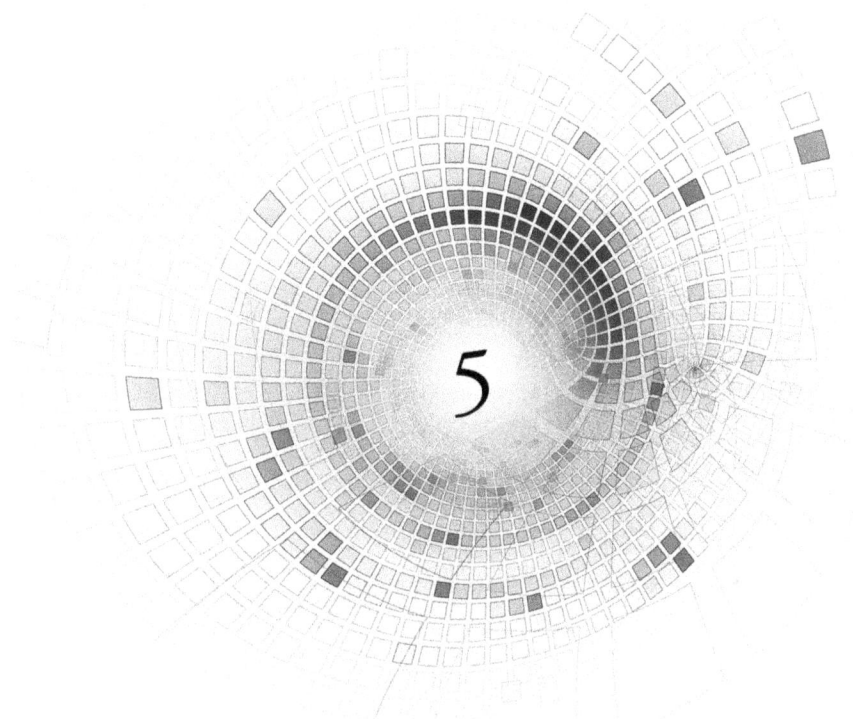

5

DESCENT

28 A.D.
3:33 P.M.
Bethany, Israel

Tom woke up feeling sore. His head was pounding and his dry eyes stung as though he had spent too much time in an over chlorinated pool. His throat burned as though he'd swallowed a vial of acid; he was parched for even the smallest drip of water. He climbed slowly to his knees and rubbed his eyes.

His direct surroundings were strange and confusing. He was inside a bush. That wasn't a good sign. As Tom braced himself against some branches, he remembered their success the day before. He remembered eating with David at Peggy's. And he remembered drinking...a lot. He thought he must have made a fool of himself, but after his fourth beer, the night was a blank slate. From the headache, dryness and odd surroundings he deduced that he must have gotten thoroughly drunk. How long had he been unconscious? Why hadn't David found him and dragged him home?

Stumbling from the bush, Tom leaned up against a tree. After taking a moment to relax his body and clear his mind, he realized what he was doing—leaning against a tree.

In the middle of the Arizona desert?

He absorbed his surroundings. He was encircled by trees, bushes and a dazzling array of colorful flowers—orange, yellow and red. He breathed deep as the smell hit him. The fragrant odor of the flowers was like none that had tickled his nose before. Tom had no idea such oases existed in Arizona. Wherever he was, it was beautiful, and he decided he would try to remember how to get back, just as soon as he found a way out.

He trudged through the thick forest for what felt like an hour, but it was closer to ten minutes. He stopped to rest for a moment and fell asleep. He wasn't sure how long he was out, but he knew he hadn't awoken on his own. A tingling sensation rippled across his head, causing his hair to stand a little taller. He was not alone, and judging from the amount of wilderness around him, his company probably wasn't human.

A crack of twigs in the near distance widened Tom's eyes and caused his chest to rise and fall a little more quickly. He was in no shape to outrun, outfight or outwit a grumpy animal. He pushed himself up and hugged a tree, pressing his body into the bark, in an effort to look as treelike as possible. He sensed that whatever was out there—whatever creature was stalking him—was growing closer.

Hands tense around the tree trunk, he leaned out for a peek. He saw nothing. He leaned in the other direction and let his head slowly emerge from behind the tree. His heart beat to a maddening rhythm. He could feel his pulse in his neck. Then he saw it.

A floppy eared goat foraged through the forest floor, ruffling through pine needles and leaves as it searched for fallen fruit. Tom sighed. The goat looked up at him and immediately went back to searching for a meal. Tom watched the creature, his confusion growing with each slowing breath.

A goat? In Arizona?

Eyes closed, he turned, leaning his back against the tree, trying to think. *Where am I and how did I get here?* His nose twitched. He smelled something odd, carried by the breeze, which had changed directions. He opened his eyes and his heart skipped a beat.

Ten feet away and low to the ground was what looked like an African lion. But it was built differently. Its head was thicker and its body was massive. Tom's limbs locked as his mind shut down. The lion crawled forward slowly, its muscles tense, ready to pounce.

Then it jumped.

The speed of the creature was amazing. Tom screamed as the lion burst into the air and sailed past his head. He heard the beast land and the whine of the goat before its neck was snapped. Tom's head spun around. The panting lion was lying on the ground holding the goat's neck firmly in its jaw.

Tom now knew he was no longer in Arizona. But he felt it wise to worry about where he was after the immediate physical threat of becoming a lion dessert no longer existed. He slowly crept away, keeping the tree between himself and the dining lion. As soon as he was sure the lion could not see, hear or smell him, he ran.

Trees and shrubs flew past in a blur. He knew this run would do him in, but dying of exhaustion or dehydration was far more appetizing than being eaten alive. He did his best to take in his surroundings as he ran. All around him were things that should not be. The trees were like none he had ever seen and some bore fruit: dates, figs and pistachios.

Tom grew more and more annoyed by his predicament as his run slowed to a jog. In all his years spent in Arizona, he had never once encountered a mosquito. But now a ravenous swarm of the pests were draining him, as if he was a living blood bank. Now walking, he used a branch from a pine tree to swish the pests away. A large bird of prey circled overhead, taunting him and making the situation feel that much more perilous.

His thighs burned and his shins stabbed with pain, but he pressed on. Between the drinks he had the night before and the scalding heat, he knew he wouldn't last much longer. He pushed through a low branch and stumbled into a clearing. *Not a clearing...a road.* A wave of relief surged through him as he reached his first sign of civilization. He looked in both directions. The road was empty. He reached into his pocket, pulled a quarter out, flipped it and caught tails. He headed left.

It was only ten minutes before he saw three objects moving toward him on the path ahead. He moved forward as quickly as he could, desperate for help and human contact. After all he had done in his life and believed he would still do, he thought it a shame if he died now, like this, in the middle of nowhere.

As he came within fifty feet of the strangers, he could see that one of them was an animal. *A horse*, he thought, but he soon realized it was a donkey. Tom then noticed how strangely these two people were dressed. One, a man, wore a red robe tied at the waist by a brown sash. The other, a woman, was wearing a mustard yellow robe complimented by a white head covering. Tom stopped in his tracks; exhaustion delivered its final blow and his legs began to shake. He saw the two strangers rush toward him as he fell to his knees.

He opened his eyes and looked up at the sky as he lay on his back. The woman and man were standing above him, speaking to each other in a language that Tom recognized but couldn't understand. They were clearly confused by what Tom was wearing, and they were debating what to do with him. Tom's mind began to function and put together the pieces of the puzzle. The land, the flora, these people, the donkey, the language and strange clothes... Tom rolled his head to the left and looked at his wrist. He was wearing a watch, but not his own. It was different.

It was...the watch...the time travel device.

Tom's heart nearly stopped as nervous tension tied a tight knot in the small of his back. The events of the previous night slammed back into his conscious mind like a runaway freight train. He had traveled back in time.

"My god..." Tom said aloud.

The two people standing above Tom stopped talking and stared at him, obviously trying to make sense of the words that just spilled from his mouth. He felt their eyes on him and knew he had to make an attempt to communicate.

"Water," Tom said in his native Hebrew tongue, hoping that two thousand years of modernization hadn't changed the dialect too much. That, and he hadn't held a conversation in Hebrew for fifteen years.

He was in luck. The woman quickly retrieved a wineskin full of water and poured it into Tom's parched mouth. When Tom finished drinking, the man spoke. "Tell me stranger, are you a Jew?"

Tom thought about the question before answering. He had been an American citizen and held to none of the Jewish beliefs for so long that he no longer considered himself to be truly Jewish. But under the circumstances, he thought it wise to not stand out any more. "Yes," Tom said in his best Hebrew, "I am a Jew."

The response Tom received was not expected. Both man and woman took a step back. "Then we will help you no longer."

Tom panicked. "Wait! Why?"

The man and woman looked at Tom through squinted eyes. He was a true enigma to them. "We are Samaritans; surely you do not want our help?"

"I will take help from anyone who offers it," Tom said.

The man and woman shared a look, and it was enough for them to come to an agreement. "We will take you to Bethany and find you lodging. Then you are on your own."

"Thank you," Tom said.

"But first...tell us, why are you dressed so strangely?" the man asked.

Tom looked down at himself. He was dressed in blue jeans, running sneakers and a short-sleeved, red and blue plaid, button-down shirt. He wracked his mind for some kind of answer.

"I was a slave," Tom said. "In...Asia...and I escaped. They dressed me like this."

The man and woman were shocked. "A slave?" the man asked and then continued, "I have heard of this *Asia*. You have traveled far to escape your slavery. Like Moses from Egypt, you are now free. Come, follow us, and we will see that you are taken care of. I know of a man in Bethany who can care for your needs."

The man pulled Tom to his feet and helped him up on to the donkey. Tom thought the donkey smelled foul but his exhaustion overpowered his sense of smell. He clung to the creature and fell asleep, as the two Samaritans led the donkey back the way they had come.

2005
2:50 P.M.
Arizona

D avid was as ready as he could be on such short notice. He looked the part, could speak the part, at least better than Tom could, and he knew the beliefs and culture of ancient Israel. Unlike Tom, David had never given up his Jewish heritage. True, he was a Christian, which practicing Jews considered blasphemous, but the Christian faith is based on a Jewish man, who lived in a Jewish culture. David knew more about biblical times than the average man, but he also knew that two thousand years of history books could never capture how things really were in the day-to-day life of ancient Israel, his homeland.

Prepared or not, David was going. He knew where and when Tom had gone. When David found an instruction booklet in the receiving area, he thought perhaps his future self had foreseen this predicament. He learned that each watch had built-in tracking devices. Any one watch could be used to track down another—any place on Earth and in any time. David had kept the instruction booklet a secret, even from Sally. The moral issues involved with time travel had already boiled over, and David didn't want anyone else knowing how to use the watches to their full potential. He read the instruction manual, committed it to memory and destroyed it.

Sally entered the receiving area where David was preparing to leave. She approached him quickly, wringing her hands together. "Listen, David," she said, "When you find Tom, grab him and come back as quickly as possible. Try not to do any sightseeing."

"That's the plan," David replied.

"I was wondering...where and when do you think Tom went?" Sally asked.

"The most logical choice for someone who wanted to disprove the story of Jesus would be his death and resurrection, just outside Jerusalem," David said, knowing that was the plan, but not wanting to reveal he knew more.

Sally looked slightly disappointed. "Just don't hang around too long, okay?"

David was confused. Was Sally trying to tell him something? "Got it," David said, "I'll be there and back with Tom before a minute of your time has passed."

Sally smiled at David's confidence and her shoulders dropped an inch. "You have everything you need?" she asked.

David looked himself over. "I'm just waiting for Tom's clothes."

A man carrying a pile of clothes, identical to David's entered the back of the control center just as David finished his sentence. When the door swung open, David saw three men. The first he recognized as George Dwight. He also recognized George's assistant, Jake. But David had no idea who the third man was, and he took a mental snapshot of the man. He was dressed in ancient clothing, tattered and authentic looking. He stood tall and straight and had a look in his eyes that longed for action. And then, as the man moved his arm, David saw a shard of light reflect off what looked like a handgun.

This is not good.

Sally saw them, too, and she attempted to stand in David's field of view, but it was too late.

"Who is that man?" David asked. "And what is he doing here?"

Sally was unsure how to answer.

"Tell me, or I'll ask him myself," David demanded.

Sally mulled over the question and answered, "His name is Captain John Roberts. He's the head of LightTech's Time Enforcement Division."

"Time what?"

"He's our...backup plan."

"Backup plan?"

"In case you don't make it back for some reason. He's going to the time just before Jesus's death, where we're most likely to find Tom. If you can't find Tom, he'll track him down."

David nodded like he agreed with this assessment, though he knew better.

"So what you're saying is if we *choose* not to come back, Roberts is the permanent solution."

"It's not my call," Sally said. "George is taking over. You're lucky he's letting you go at all. This was put in motion years ago, without my knowledge. Just stay away from him. If he finds you, come back without Tom."

"Why?"

"Just do it," Sally said. "Now go. The sooner you leave the longer you'll have to find Tom before Roberts follows."

David knew that wasn't true, with the mechanics of time travel, but he let the comment slide.

"I think Roberts might have a harder time tracking us down than he thinks," David said with a smile.

"What do you mean?" Sally asked.

"Just that time is on my side."

David watched as George, Jake and Roberts entered the back of the control room. "Time to go."

Sally glanced toward the control room.

"Better leave the room," Sally heard David say behind her.

She turned around and looked at the bright light flashing between them. "Be careful," she said and quickly left the room.

WhumWhumWhumWhumBoom!

David disappeared in a flash, leaving only glowing particles in his stead. It was a sight the LightTech staff would never grow used to.

Sally watched through the wall of glass as the little blue flakes settled to the floor. She wondered if she'd ever see David again.

"We'll give him one minute before I go back and finish the job," said Captain Roberts, standing behind Sally.

Sally pivoted toward the man. "Try to bring them back alive, Captain Roberts. We've invested a lot of money in these two men, and no one knows more about this technology than they do."

"I'll try," Roberts said, "but if your boys give me any trouble, I'm going to have only two choices..."

Roberts pulled a military knife from inside his ancient robe. "rare..."

Roberts then drew his silencer-laden handgun. "...or well done."

Sally glared at Roberts as he chuckled. Only a man trained like him could find this funny.

28 A.D.
1:22 P.M.
Bethany, Israel

The room Tom found himself in was unfamiliar. The walls were scarcely decorated and constructed from some kind of clay and straw bricks. Tom sat up; he still felt a bit of nausea, but his headache had subsided. He stood from the bed, which was cushioned by straw and covered by a thick handmade blanket. He stumbled as he took his first step. He was more dazed than he thought. But he wouldn't let that stop him. He had to get his bearings. He had to find out where he was and how he was going to find Jesus.

Tom remembered why he had come back, and while it was true he would have never done it had he been sober, he was here now. The least he could do was prove to David that it wasn't complete buffoonery on his part. His pride demanded it. He could picture David now, storming around in the future, fearing the end of the world was near. It brought a smile to his face.

After throwing on a tattered robe that hung on the wall, Tom managed to walk his way through the humble home and out the front door. A small, but bustling town greeted him. The streets were dirt and the buildings were all made from the same pale bricks, but what struck Tom was the architecture, and also the layout of the town. It was beautiful. He wandered out into the busy street looking around in awe, listening to the ancient dialects, smelling the pungent odor of cooking lamb and the sweet scent of flowers. The colors were brighter than he had ever imagined as a child. People were dressed in colorful robes, buildings were decorated with flowing sheets and the flowers...the flowers grew everywhere.

Dizziness spun over him and he raised his hand to his head. He surmised the effects of time travel had taken their toll on his body. Before he could take action to prevent falling down or passing out, he careened into a passersby. The man yelled at him in Aramaic, "Watch where you're going, swine." But he could not understand the language.

Tom rolled from the hit and slammed into an old woman, whose arms were full of food. Her bread and fruit fell to the ground. Tom bent over as best he could and started to help the woman pick up her goods, but she swatted at him like a pesky dog. "Back! Get back! You beggars won't be getting any of my food," the woman yelled.

The woman's language sounded strange to Tom, but the message was clear. He tried to explain in bad Hebrew, "I'm just trying to help you."

Wide, angry eyes stared at Tom from the woman's wrinkled face, and she yelled, "You speak like a man with half a mind!" She spoke in perfect Hebrew. "Away with you!"

The woman took one last swat at Tom, who moved away from her quickly and in doing so, he ran into a large man's elbow. Tom heard a crack in his nose as the cartilage twisted from the impact. As Tom fell to the ground, the large man simply looked down at Tom and walked away, seemingly unfazed and uncaring about the collision. Pebbles on the dirt road dug into Tom's palms when he caught himself on the ground.

He grimaced in pain. His first time travel experience was not going well. He pushed himself up onto his knees and looked at his hands. They were covered in muddy blood. He did his best to remove the rocks, which caused him great pain, and to wipe away the dirt from his wounds. He trembled at the idea of how many foreign bacteria were now invading his system.

Still on his knees in the middle of the road, Tom removed the last stone. He grunted in pain and clenched his hands together.

"That's not the best place to be praying," came a deep voice from behind Tom. The man spoke perfect Hebrew.

Tom looked up and saw the man standing over him. He was rugged, like a man gets from years of physical labor. His facial features gave the initial impression that this was the kind of man you wouldn't want to get into a barroom brawl with, but at the same time, he had kind eyes.

"I'm...I'm not praying," Tom said.

"Of course not," the rugged man said with a chuckle. He reached down for Tom's hands. "Here, get off the ground before you're trampled to death."

Tom took the man's hands and was pulled to his feet. The rugged man eyed Tom curiously. "Are you a slave or a prince?" the man asked.

"What do you mean?"

The man pointed at Tom's clothes and said, "You are dressed like a beggar or slave..."

The man took hold of Tom's wrist and held it so the time watch could be seen and said, "Yet you are adorned with an object that is no doubt from a faraway land and worth fifty sheep."

Tom smiled at the comment. The watch he wore was far more valuable than fifty sheep. It was probably the most valuable object in human history. *Well, one of the ten most valuable*, he thought. He tried to explain. "I'm...from far away, where it is not uncommon for people of average stature to wear such things."

The rugged man seemed to understand. "That explains why your Hebrew is so bad. Do you not speak Aramaic?"

"No," Tom replied.

The man didn't seem shocked. "If you plan to stay in Israel, you must learn."

Tom smiled, "I'll try."

"You look weary, my friend. Come, let me buy you a drink," the rugged man offered.

"That would be great," Tom said with a tinge of guilt, knowing he shouldn't even be talking to this man, but he thought one drink with a historical nobody shouldn't do much to alter the future. Besides, he was thirsty as hell.

The rugged man led Tom down the road. As Tom began to walk with the man, he brushed his hands off against his dirty robe. Brush...Brush...Brush. Dust clapped away into the air, revealing Tom's bare palms, which were no longer cut or bleeding. All that remained were dry bloodstains. His wounds were healed completely, as if they had never been. Perhaps from lack of pain, or confusion from his whirlwind tour of the past, Tom never noticed.

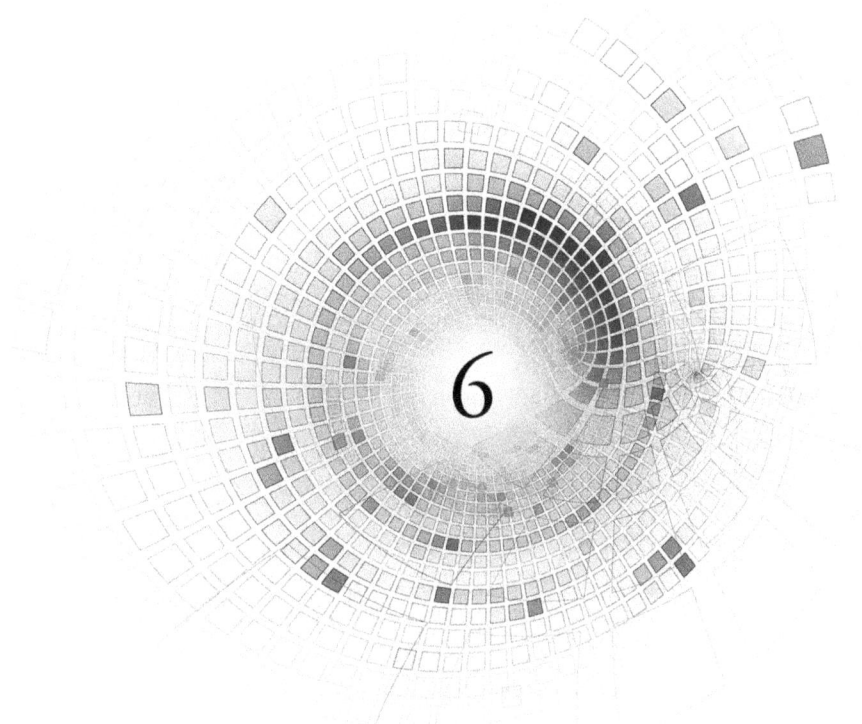

6

IMPACT

28 A.D.
4:46 P.M.
Bethany, Israel

A flock of sheep contentedly chewed on juicy grass, atop one of several rolling, green hills. As though it could sense something amiss, a single sheep at the center of the pack raised its head, like a lighthouse amid a sea of white. It searched the area with nervous eyes, scanning back and forth. The wary sheep took a step back and bumped into a second sheep, passing on a wave of nervous tension, like a shockwave emanating from the center of the flock to its very edges. The entire flock raised their heads, ears at the ready for the slightest noise or smell of a predator.

Boom!

A bright light exploded at the center of the flock, and the noise created was like thunder. Several sheep passed out and hit the ground with fluffy thuds. The rest burst into panic, hopping and kicking around the field, wailing like broken police sirens.

David squinted and attempted to focus his eyes, trying to make sure he was really seeing what he thought he was seeing. The confusing side effects of time travel combined with the flurry of obnoxious activity surrounding him was dizzying. David's head churned and his vision muddied. White clouds of sheep danced around him, while the glowing blue sparkles fluttered to the ground. It was like a sickening merry-go-round. The flock's maddening cacophony became noxious. The pungent smell of sheep dung and urine added to the cauldron of confusion. David planted his hands firmly on the ground, partly to get some kind of bearing, partly to brace himself as he wretched into the grass with force.

The entire flock stopped their wild flailing and stared at David, who was wiping off his mouth. He looked up into hundreds of dark eyes, probing him. Where was he? Had he miscalculated? Was this the right time?

A voice from the distance answered his questions. "What was that noise?" the voice asked in Aramaic.

"I don't know. Did you see the light?" came a reply.

The two men ran closer.

Feeling like Ulysses evading the Cyclops, David stayed close to the ground, under the sheep, half crawling and half dragging himself in the opposite direction from the approaching shepherds. He managed to slide his way to the bottom of the hill, then clambered into a patch of trees. He finally felt moderately safe and turned to watch the wary shepherds.

The two shepherds walked through the herd, looking for anything out of the ordinary. They had never seen the sheep so upset, even when the lions attacked.

But they were calm now, and no apparent danger could be found. As the shepherds prepared to leave, one of them stepped in something wet. The man looked down and grimaced. He was standing in vomit. Human vomit.

The man's eyes burst with realization and he yelled, "Someone's in the flock!"

The men split up and began hurrying the sheep in all directions, attempting to spur any intruders from hiding. Sheep poachers had robbed them once. They would not let it happen again.

David spied from a safe distance, but he believed the search would expand into the surrounding area soon enough. He knew with the amount of money he had, he could probably bribe the shepherds from taking any action against him. But then, what was to stop them from robbing him? Then these two shepherds would become rich and without doubt change a portion of history. David realized he should have never brought the money. If he failed and couldn't return to the future, better he be a beggar or dead.

He rubbed his eyes in an attempt to clear his head. Bracing himself against a tree, he stood up. The world was spinning less quickly now, and he stumbled deeper into the woods.

Five minutes later, he cleared the tree line and emerged onto a dirt road. He staggered up a hill, following the indicator on his watch. He knew Tom was close by, within a square mile from his current position, and probably in some kind of trouble. He imagined having to rescue Tom from a prison, or worse: having to dig up Tom's dead body.

David neared the top of the hill and noticed he was palpably wet. The temperature hadn't struck him until now. He thought it must be over ninety degrees, and the humidity was tangible. He had already spent more time in the sun than he would during a good year. He tried not to think of his skin roasting, but the itchy tickle on his arms served as a constant reminder.

After reaching the top of the hill, he saw a view that erased all concerns from his mind. Before him was an Israel he had never imagined. Fertile and green, it was nothing like modern Israel. At the bottom of the hill was a city, which he believed to be Bethany. A thought struck him then—he had stood on this hill once before, on the side of the road, as a teenager hitchhiking with his friends...two thousand years in the future.

How the world had changed.

David's view was green for miles. Trees and flower-speckled grass covered the hills. He saw why this was called the Promised Land, and he finally understood why this small chunk of land would be fought over for generations. Emotions swirled through him and seemed to worsen the effects of the time travel. Nausea took hold of him and squeezed, until he fell to his knees. He felt like crawling into bed and sleeping for days, but the stony road would have to do. As his mind slipped, he lay down in the center of the road and got comfortable.

As he began to slide from consciousness, he heard a noise—a crunching of soil on the road next to him. He looked up and saw a man, a woman and a donkey standing above him. The last thing he heard was the man say, "Not another one."

⋐⋑

When David woke up, he had insisted that the kind people who had brought him to town not help him any further. He quickly shooed them on their way and left to attend the important business of locating Tom.

David became engrossed by the new world around him. The smells of flowers and foreign foods cooking enticed his nose. And the sight and sounds of these ancient people, animals and buildings was almost enough to completely distract him from his mission. He caught sight of a pair of Roman soldiers patrolling the street and was reminded of Captain Roberts, the man with a gun in the future.

David knew that if he didn't find Tom soon, Tom might alter the future. At the very least, he and Tom might be on the receiving end of a bullet, eight hundred years before gunpowder was invented.

As the sun began to fall, David frantically searched the streets of Bethany. The watch was great for generalizing Tom's location, but David found it impossible to pin down his exact whereabouts. He grew desperate as the hours wore on, and he decided that simply asking people if they had seen Tom wouldn't make any changes to the future. It might even aid in the finding of Tom, thus preventing a larger disaster. David asked twenty people about Tom, describing his dress, his poor verbal skills and his physical characteristics. It was a half hour before he got a bite.

"The buffoon knocked me over and tried to steal my food!" the old woman shouted.

David couldn't believe his ears. Tom was only here for a few hours and had already left a lasting impression, at least on this woman. How much more damage had he already done?

"This man, what is he to you?" the woman asked, growing suspicious of David.

"He's my friend," David replied. "He's out of his mind, and I am trying to find him before he causes any permanent damage."

"I saw him enter a tavern with a man who had pity on the fool."

"Which way?"

The women stabbed her crooked finger toward the east.

"Thank you for your kindness," David said, as he moved past the woman in the direction she pointed.

"Kindness has nothing to do with it," the woman explained. "Personally, I hope the Romans have run him through already, but if they haven't at least maybe you can get him off the streets."

David picked up his pace.

How many taverns can there be in one town? David wondered. He had searched three already and had seen no sign of Tom. The sun was almost completely extinguished, and David had no light source to search at night. He loathed the thought, but he knew he had to find lodging for the night. He prayed he didn't take the room where an important traveler was supposed to stay or where one of his ancestors was supposed to be conceived. The possibilities for tragedy were incalculable.

David decided on a tavern that also rented rooms. He could make one last search for Tom and get a room at the same time. He changed his mind about the money, realizing that without it he would have been sleeping under the stars and most likely would have been pilfered in his sleep.

Drinking patrons filled the tavern and greeted David with their eyes as he entered. As he walked through the tavern, he scanned people's faces, taking care not to linger too long and offend. He approached a man he assumed was the tavern's owner and shouted a question that couldn't be made out because the noise from the next room was ear-splitting. Before David could repeat his question at a higher volume, he heard a familiar laugh mixed in with the shouts from the adjoining room.

He made a break for the side room. As he entered, David clumsily tripped over a jug and fell to the floor in a confused heap. The entire room fell as silent as death, and then, all at once, they burst into laughter. David found a thick hand thrust into his face, offering to pick him up. He took hold and was pulled quickly to his feet by a strong arm. David looked at the rugged man and said, "Thank you."

"You're all right?" the man asked.

David nodded.

"You're the second man I've pulled off the ground today. It's becoming something of a habit," the man said with a smile. "Why don't you join our table? Have a drink? I must warn you, our conversations are being held in Hebrew, as our other new friend cannot speak Aramaic, if you can believe that."

"I... Thank you, but no, I..." Other new friend? David whipped his eyes toward the table and saw Tom, sitting with a group of men, laughing at a joke! He was more than interacting. He was forming relationships!

Tom glanced at David and didn't recognize him in this setting, with David dressed as he was, but then he took another look, and the smile vanished from his face.

"David?"

"You two know each other?" the rugged man asked.

"Tom, we need to talk," David said in Hebrew, with as much authority as he could muster.

"How did you find me so quickly?" Tom asked.

"Not now," David said, while making a face with his eyes that screamed, 'not in front of the locals!'

The rugged man looked slightly confused by this exchange, but he was unwilling to let the disturbance ruin the night's fun. "This is a friend of yours?" he asked of Tom.

"Yes," Tom replied.

David grabbed Tom and pulled him away from the table and the rugged man, with a sudden burst of energy. David's English whispers were loud enough to hurt Tom's ear. "You're interacting with them! Do you have any idea what the consequences could be?"

"Nothing that will alter the future," Tom said. "These men would be here with or without me, and the conversation hasn't gone beyond dirty pigs, Samaritans and the Ten Commandments, of all things."

"I'm taking you back... Now," David demanded.

"How?" Tom asked. "You wouldn't dare do it in front of this many people. And we both know you can't physically drag me far enough out of town."

David's rage was close to meltdown proportions. "Tom, this is stupid! Even for you."

The rugged man interrupted with a smile, "Come friends, sit and drink."

Under normal circumstances David loathed being rude, but he knew the magnitude of what was at stake justified his next words. "Not now! Stay quiet and let us talk!"

"David, cool down," Tom implored. "An angry outburst is more likely to have negative effects on time than a few friendly drinks."

David took a breath and collected himself. "You mean like the little old lady you tried to rob?"

"You met her?" Tom asked, his forehead creased with concern.

"Yes, but that's beside the point. Any effect on time is a negative effect. We need to go back, and go back now."

"But I didn't try to rob her, I just—"

"I don't care what happened. We're leaving."

"No."

"What?"

"No."

"This isn't funny. You were drunk, and I can forgive it, but now you're being ridiculous."

"I am serious. I'm not leaving," Tom said. "I'm going to do what I came here to do—prove that Jesus is a fraud."

"Have you even stopped to consider the consequences? The next two thousand years of global, human history is shaped by the events of Jesus's life."

"I'm not a moron," Tom said. "I have no intention of sharing what I discover with anyone other than you. Don't you see? I care about you enough to risk my life to save yours from a meaningless existence spent believing in a lie."

"Like Megan?"

"David, if you had seen what happened to Megan, if you had been there… Seen the life in her eyes before she died, you'd—"

"I *did* see it."

Tom's breath caught in his lungs.

"Before I came here, I went to Zambia. I saw her. I saw the men who killed her. They almost killed me, too. I risked changing the future once already, just so I could understand what motivated you to come here and try something as insane as this."

Tom was shaken to the core. "You saw her? Alive?"

"Yes."

Tom grew somber and said, "Then you understand why I'm here."

David tossed the question around in his mind, remembering the vibrant woman he saw in Zambia and imagining her being gunned down feet from Tom's arms. "Yes," David said, not believing he had said the word.

Neither could Tom. "What did you say?"

"I understand."

A smile snuck onto Tom's face.

"Come, friends," the rugged man said again. "Join us for the night."

Tom and David stared at each other for a moment, having a silent argument with their eyes. David softened. "It's really quite amazing, being here... It would be a shame to go home without a firsthand cultural experience."

"You won't regret this," Tom said.

"We go home in the morning," David said sternly.

Tom smiled in response. The two headed back to the table full of strangers from another time and place. The rugged man handed them both drinks. "Welcome, friends."

Tom and David clunked their clay cups together and drank. David gagged and spit his drink out in a thick spray. "What is this?" he asked.

"Wine, of course," the rugged man chuckled.

"I'm sorry, I don't drink wine," David explained. "Could I have some water?"

The entire table of men burst out laughing. "My friend, the water here will do much worse to you, I'm afraid."

David raised his eyebrows with understanding and looked into his cup of wine.

"I have a feeling he's telling the truth," Tom said.

David took a sip and swallowed it down, while clenching his eyes and crinkling his nose.

"It's a miracle," Tom said to the rugged man. "I've been trying to get him to do that for years."

The rugged man laughed and said, "It's a shame he's only now becoming a man at his age!"

The entire table exploded with laughter again. Tom seemed to be enjoying all this thoroughly. These were his kind of men and this was his kind of place.

David smiled involuntarily, brought on by all the laughing around him. He took another drink and swallowed it down with a little less effort. Maybe this entire mishap would end without a tragic event and perhaps even with a fond memory? Hopefully Tom wouldn't get drunk again and transport himself to the Triassic Period.

Of course, David thought, *there Tom couldn't do any real damage*; *here the next two thousand years are at stake.*

CONCEPTION

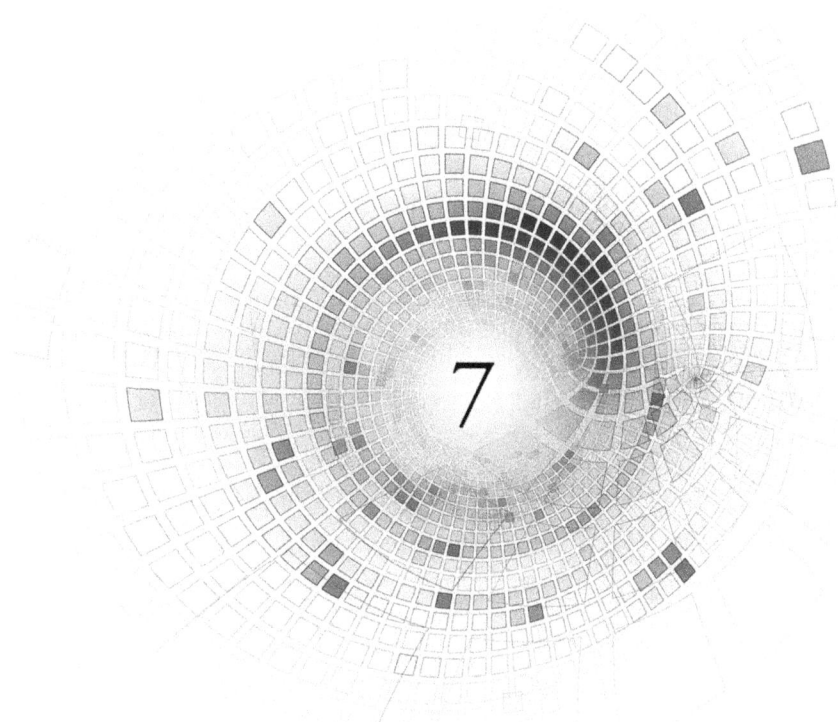

7

STANDING

28 A.D.
7:32 A.M.
Bethany, Israel

When Tom and David met that morning, their conversation was brief and to the point. Tom still wasn't leaving, and David still demanded that they leave right away, only this time Tom noticed the argument didn't last as long. After David cooled down, Tom convinced him that they should go for a walk with their new friend, the rugged man, and see their homeland the way it used to be. They would just be tagging along, doing nothing of consequence, Tom explained. After demanding that they remain distant observers—he didn't

81

even want to know their names—David conceded, and the two headed out with the rugged man and his friends.

Twenty minutes later, Tom wished he had never convinced David to go.

The new clothing David brought from the future was uncomfortable, itchy and too hot for the weather. More than that, it was identical to David's outfit. David explained they were going for authenticity, not fashion sense. He had never planned to stay this long, and if they looked funny wearing the same clothes, so be it. But Tom knew it was only a matter of time before their witty new friends poked fun at them, and time just ran out.

The rugged man approached Tom and David from behind and slapped his heavy hands on each of their shoulders. "Beautiful day for traveling, eh?" the man asked.

"Uh, yes, yes it is," David said, still wary of who he thought was an overly friendly man, in any time period.

"I was wondering..." the man continued.

Here it comes, Tom thought.

"It's nice, during these times, to see two men like you being true friends. As though you are brothers," the man said.

Tom wondered if their clothing had been overlooked.

"Brothers who wear the same clothes!" The man burst out with laughter.

The other men walking with them, some from the night before, others new, laughed heartily. The rugged man shook Tom and David playfully and said, "I'm sorry my friends, but it could not be helped. You brought it upon yourselves."

"No kidding," Tom said, under his breath.

After a moment of silence, the rugged man spoke again, though his voice had become sincere and quiet. "Tell me, why have you two traveled so far? What is it you have come to find?"

Before David had time to shoot a glance at him, Tom had answered the question. "Jesus," Tom said. "We came to find Jesus."

"Ignore him please. He doesn't want to find Jesus," David said forcefully.

"That's too bad," the rugged man said.

David couldn't resist. "Why?"

"Because we're on our way to see him now."

David's face fell flat.

The rugged man pointed to a tall hill in the distance and said, "That's the Mount of Olives. Jesus will be there soon."

David looked like he had just been slapped in the face. "The...the Mount of... Oh my..."

"What?" Tom asked, not understanding why this Mount of Olives held any significance with David.

"The Mount of Olives is where—" David broke off his sentence, realizing the rugged man was still listening. He grabbed Tom and pulled him out of earshot of the rugged man.

David whispered in English, "The Mount of Olives is where Jesus calls the twelve—"

"C'mon, David, it won't hurt just to get a look at the guy," Tom interrupted.

"I know what you're trying to do, stringing me along from one event to the next, until you've proved your all important point. We're not going any further, and that's final!"

"We won't talk to him. We'll catch a peek and leave. I promise. Besides, we've already covered the fact that you physically can't stop me. Unless you plan on resorting to violence, that is."

Before Tom could finish laughing at his own joke, David had wound up. He flung his fist square into Tom's jaw. *Whack!* Tom was barely fazed by the blow. He rubbed his chin lightly.

Tom chuckled. "Well, that was a noble try."

David was huffing and puffing, ready for a retaliation that never came.

"I didn't know they gave boxing lessons in the geriatric ward," Tom said.

A small smile crept onto David's face, half from the joke and half from relief that he didn't have to fight a battle he knew he'd lose. "I had to try."

Tom put his arm around David and the two walked back to the rugged man, who was clearly amused about what he had just witnessed. "You are the strangest friends I have yet to encounter," he said to both of them. Then he turned to Tom. "I told you that drink made him a man...though he still hits like a boy!"

David laughed out loud for the first time since coming back in time. This stranger, who had made them his friends, was a lot like Tom—even his sense of humor was like Tom's. David found that refreshing. "You said we're going to the Mount of Olives, to see Jesus?"

The rugged man nodded in agreement.

"Do you know him? Have you seen him?" David asked.

"Every day," the rugged man replied with a smile. "David and Didymus, come, follow me."

The rugged man turned and headed toward the tall hill in the distance.

Tom turned to David and asked, "Didymus? Is that supposed to be a nickname?"

David replied with a grin, "I think so."

"What does it mean?"

"The twin."

Tom smiled.

☙

As Tom, David and the rugged man drew closer to the Mount of Olives, David found his heart beating quicker and his feet treading more swiftly. While what they were doing violated his better judgment, he could not deny that the idea of seeing the man—who he believed to be the savior of the world—was irresistible. When they arrived at the base of the Mount, they found a large crowd had gathered, eagerly awaiting Jesus.

Making their way through the crowd seemed easier than David expected. He imagined that people of the ancient world would be far from polite, but these people quickly opened a path for Tom, David and the rugged man as they proceeded up the incline toward the front of the crowd.

When they had arrived at the highest point, above the crowd, David could no longer control his excitement. He climbed onto a boulder for an even higher vantage point and peered out over the crowd. He imagined that spotting Jesus, even among all of these people, would be a simple task. *The mere aura of the man must be tangible,* David thought. He was focused on his task. The breathtaking view of the green countryside no longer held his interest. The mixture of languages and cultures gathered before him had become inconsequential. He was determined to see Jesus, and then silently escape back to the future. That was his plan, anyway.

Tom, on the other hand, was content to wait patiently. "See anything?" he asked David, while leaning against an olive tree.

David quickly shook his head. "No."

Tom redirected his attention to the rugged man. "So when's Jesus supposed to show up?"

The rugged man smiled and said, "He's already here."

Tom grew incredulous as he looked out over the crowd. "Where?" Tom asked. "I don't see anyone who could possibly—"

"That's because you don't have eyes with which to see. You are blind," the rugged man interjected.

David caught the words from the rugged man, and they sank in slowly. Once they had, his reaction was violent. David craned his neck around toward the rugged man so quickly that he flung himself off the boulder. He hit the ground hard, but quickly picked himself up. His eyes were wide as he moved toward the rugged man.

Could it be?

The rugged man saw David coming and their eyes met. The rugged man smiled, and David felt a surge of energy as he realized the truth. David pushed a bewildered Tom aside and fell to his knees in front of the rugged man. "My Lord!" David said with a quivering voice.

David felt his limbs begin to shake and his vision became blurred with tears, as emotion took his mind hostage.

Tom didn't understand. "David, what are you doing?" he asked.

The rugged man replied to Tom. "He has eyes that can see and ears that can hear." Then he looked down and said, "Stand, David."

David did his best to stand, but his knees had become as stable as a bowl of Jell-O. He clutched his kneecaps and stiffened his arms so as not to fall over. David had never felt such emotion in all his life. He had been a believer in Christ for twenty-five years. He had gone to church, been born again, received the Holy Spirit—everything that Christians might relate to a supernatural experience with God. But everything paled with this experience. David was undone.

The rugged man placed a hand on David's head and said, "Peace be with you."

Instantly, a wave of serenity washed over him. He felt his strength return and his mind clear. The adverse effects of extreme joy disappeared, and he was left feeling lighter than air.

Tom finally understood. "Jesus?"

The rugged man removed his hand from David's head and nodded at Tom. He said, "Your eyes will be opened soon enough, my friend."

Jesus turned and walked toward the crowd of expectant followers. Tom looked into David's wet eyes. Each was as befuddled as the other. They turned their eyes back to Jesus, who had walked to the boulder David had climbed earlier. Jesus turned to them and said, "Now make yourselves useful and help me up."

The most important man in the history of the world was asking Tom and David for a boost, and all they could do was stare at him.

∾

Ten minutes passed before Tom or David spoke. They had broken every rule imaginable for time travel scenarios. They hadn't just observed an event. They hadn't simply carried on idle conversations with meaningless people in the past. They had become friends with Jesus Christ! They'd had drinks with him! Joked with him! David was beyond playing out doomsday theories with Tom; they were already in the midst of one. David sat on the grass next to Tom, while Jesus addressed the crowd on the hill below them.

"What's he doing?" Tom asked.

David looked at Jesus speaking to the crowd. He used to think going back in time would be romantic, like watching a movie, but this was real. They were witnessing actual events recorded in the Bible. His stomach twisted as he answered, "I tried to tell you before...he's calling the twelve."

"The twelve what?" Tom asked.

"The disciples," David explained. "Peter, John, Matthew. You know, *those* guys."

"Right... How much money did you bring? We're going to need—"

David burst out laughing. The idea of staying was ludicrous, and it pushed him beyond rage to unrelenting laughter. Then he realized Tom was serious, and the laughter was suddenly silenced. David knew that simply calling Tom a fool wouldn't do the trick. Perhaps he could prove his beliefs to Tom with the events they had already witnessed? David started, "Tom, you've seen him now. You saw how he stopped me from shaking with just a touch. You—"

"Still can't believe you think he's God," Tom said. "Granted, he's a nice guy. He's funny. He drinks. I like him."

Tom pointed a finger toward Jesus, still standing on the stone, waving his arms as he spoke. "But I'll never believe *he's* God."

David took a breath and said, "If we stay any longer, we risk changing the future worse than we may have already. Do I really have to explain this all to you again? You might plan on keeping the results of your quest for atheism between the two of us, but our mere presence here changes things. We might swat a bug that would have transmitted a disease to man. Our conversations might change the way someone thinks—like the old woman in Bethany. We've spent an entire day with Jesus already. Who knows how many historically important conversations we've already distracted him from."

"We'll distance ourselves from everyone. We'll stay in the shadows and observe. Just until he dies and doesn't come back to life three days later," Tom said.

David threw his hands up in the air and said, "It's two and a half *years* until that happens! We can't stay here for two and a half years. There's a very good chance that if we stay that long, Roberts might track us down."

"Roberts?" Tom asked.

David grunted. He'd forgotten about Roberts until now. "LightTech's backup plan. 'Time Enforcement Division.' Basically, he's a killer with a crew cut, a gun and a time traveling watch. We do *not* want him to find us."

"TED," Tom said.

"What?" David asked.

"Time Enforcement Division. They created time cops with the acronym: TED. Someone wasn't thinking."

David smiled.

"Sally approved this?" Tom asked.

"She had nothing to do with it. In fact, she made sure to warn me about him. Though she did say to leave you here if Roberts found us."

"How kind of her," Tom said with a grin.

"The point she was making," David said, "is that Roberts will shoot first and likely not care about asking questions."

"You didn't think of mentioning this before?" Tom asked, looking around for anyone with a crew cut.

"Well, he's going to the crucifixion, so—"

David stopped himself too late.

"So we don't even need to worry about him for a few years?" Tom asked.

With a sigh, David said, "No. Unless he figures out how to track us with the watch. But he didn't strike me as being that intelligent."

Tom thought for a moment while David caught his breath. "If we stay...and I'm right, then you'll have to give up your silly beliefs. But... If we stay and you're right...and Jesus rises from the dead...well, then I'd be a believer."

"Tom, you can't—what did you just say?"

"If you're right. If I see him alive, after I see him die, I'll believe."

David's mind raced.

"C'mon, we're smart guys. We can do this right. If we're not going to observe the past, what good was inventing time travel devices in the first place?"

David shifted. Tom was getting through.

"Look at it this way," Tom continued, "the risk of staying here, of witnessing these events unfold isn't set in stone. We control our exposure to this world. We control the impact our presence here has. But if we go back now, in your mind, my fate is sealed right? I'm going to Hell."

David shifted again, and Tom moved in for the kill.

"Are you willing to take the risk to save my soul, David? Are you?"

David was silent. He had dreamed of the day when Tom would share his faith and his beliefs. And no matter how truly he believed that if they stayed Tom would indeed see Jesus die and rise from the dead, he couldn't risk the lives and souls of countless people that might be affected by he and Tom playing time tourist.

"Tom, no matter how much I'd like to—"

"C'mon, what's the worst that could happen?"

"You two bicker like a farmer and his ass," Jesus said, as he caught them by surprise. "I'm not interrupting, am I?"

David attempted to play it cool. "No, no, of course not."

"Do you know what I was just doing over there? With the people?" Jesus asked.

David felt sick to his stomach as he lied to God, face to face. "Umm, no?"

"I called eleven to follow me, to learn my ways and the ways of my father, that they may continue to spread the good news when I am gone," Jesus said.

"Eleven?" David asked.

Tom forgot they weren't supposed to be in the know and said, "Looking for a twelfth, huh?"

Jesus raised an eyebrow, as though he were impressed with Tom's apparent intuition. "Indeed," he said.

Tom said, "I'm sure there are plenty of good men to choose—"

"I'm afraid you don't understand. I've already chosen the twelfth," Jesus said.

"Who's the lucky guy?" Tom asked.

David began to sweat with panic as he suspected what the next words out of Jesus's mouth would be.

"You, Didymus."

Tom stared at Jesus, waiting for the punchline. It never came.

"You're not serious?" David begged.

Jesus nodded. "I am."

"But I...I can't." Tom said. "You don't...I...David?"

The portion of David's brain that sent the signals to his mouth had shut down. David watched silently as Jesus put an arm around the baffled Tom and led him away. Suddenly a thought slammed into his cortex, and he snapped out of his daze.

"It can't be..." David said aloud to himself.

David ran to Tom and Jesus, and he said, "Tom, I'll be back. I have to check some-thing at home."

"What? You can't leave!" Tom was near panic.

"I'll be back!" David shouted as he ran down the hill.

Tom was beside himself with horror. He now completely understood all of David's fears and reservations. He had violated time in a way that might change every facet of the future he knew. He had gone from a respected quantum scientist to the destroyer of time—his own specialty! Tom was sure that even if they discovered that Jesus was in fact the savior of the world, he would still burn in Hell for what he'd done. Tom's thoughts were shattered when a strong voice interrupted.

"Come, Didymus, let me introduce you to the others," Jesus said, as he led Tom toward a group of men who looked just as wide-eyed as he did.

8

PERSPECTIVE

28 A.D.

11:48 A.M.

Bethany, Israel

David spent an hour walking through the wilderness in an effort to make sure he wasn't observed by any ancient Israelites. He thought about the ramifications of a man or woman seeing the light and sound show created by time travel and forming a new religion around the spectacle. Until his percolating theory could be proven in the future, he wasn't going to take any chances.

After scoping out the area, David tucked himself away in a thick patch of trees and sat down to formalize a plan. The equipment he needed was in LightTech's Receiving

Area Alpha. But it was a small window of opportunity between the time the equipment arrived and when Tom had stolen the watch. Almost every hour before and after these events would reveal David's actions to LightTech and possibly worsen their situation with the ruthless Captain Roberts.

While Roberts wasn't currently a threat in ancient Israel—he'd actually jumped to the time of Jesus's death, two and a half years later than Tom—David himself could still be dangerous in his own time. The presence of two Davids at LightTech could trigger a security response *before* Tom ever got a chance to leave. More than that, David's actions now could make things hard for the David at LightTech and potentially keep him from following Tom into the past. If his activities were discovered, LightTech would—

A thought struck David and he smiled. He knew exactly where and when to go, because he had already done it! The second time distortion that was detected when Tom stole the watch. David knew it was himself who had caused the second and third disturbances—the supposed ripples—because he was seconds away from creating them. He worked his watch with quick fingers, setting the date, time and exact location for the most technologically advanced theft in history.

David normally frequented the bathroom several times before events like this, when he was about to embark on something dangerous, but this time he was unusually calm. He knew the outcome. He knew he would succeed—because he already had. He would get in and out of LightTech with the equipment he needed, and no one would be the wiser. And then his future/past self would actually advise against researching the event. David was smiling ear to ear. Birds rocketed into the air as he pushed the final button and exploded back to the future.

2005

11:00 P.M.

Arizona

With a flash of light, David appeared, and then the receiving area went dark again. The lab had been shut down for the past few hours, and the morning shift would soon fill the premises, not to mention Tom's theft incident. David fell to the floor and struggled to keep from throwing up. Any evidence left behind would be quickly found and scrutinized.

The nausea passed and he got to his feet, searching through the room, which was lit only by a dim red light from the control room. He quickly found the equipment he needed: a machine he had learned was a Time Recorder. It looked like a fancy external hard drive, and much to David's delight, it appeared to be compatible with a PC serial port as well as a USB port. From what little David read of the notes from his future self, he knew that the Time Recorder worked by recording time. If time was altered completely or partially, the Time Recorder's storage unit, which was shielded from space-time itself, would remember the way things were. David planned to access the information recorded on the device and attempt to detect the minor, or major, distortions he and Tom might have already created without even noticing.

And now that he had found the time recorder, he had to abscond with it without being noticed.

David paused before typing in a new set of coordinates. He had planned up to this point, but not beyond it. He didn't know where he was going. He deduced that the most logical place to go was his own home...but when? If he went during the present, he would certainly be found out. Security had been tightened after a series of break-ins three years previous. David's mind made a logical hop, skip and jump to a related topic, and he began to see his past and present merging again.

But there was that time...ten years ago. He had gone on vacation for a month, to Israel, visiting family. When he had returned, he found that his house had been burglarized.

His food had been eaten, his fish, Franklin, which he had assumed he would find dead upon his return, had been fed and his computer had been used. He had reported the incident to the police, but since there were no signs of forced entry and nothing more than food missing, they didn't see the point in pursuing the matter. Besides, whoever it was had saved David's fish. He now suspected that he *was* that burglar.

He punched the date and time into his watch, but before he could hit the last button, someone crashed into the room. Clutching the Time Recorder, David ducked behind a table full of equipment. He peeked out and saw Tom stumbling around the room, murmuring to himself about David and Megan, and saying, "I'm not drunk... I'm not drunk! I can drive fine!"

A heated debate exploded in David's mind. He could end everything right here and now; he could stop Tom and end this nonsense. Or he could let Tom go and risk altering the past. But David couldn't stop him, not until he knew for sure if time was being changed. Not until he knew whether or not Tom was who David suspected him to be. David watched as Tom picked up one of the nine remaining watches and strapped it to his wrist. Tom punched in some coordinates and with a bright flash and boom, disappeared into the past, where he would befriend Jesus Christ.

"Dr. Goodman? Is that you?"

Eyes wide, David sat unmoving. He recognized Spencer's voice. He was caught! He whipped around and faced Spencer. He didn't remember Spencer saying anything about this encounter...but then, he had made that comment... What was it he had said? *See you in the past.* It occurred to David that this meeting had already taken place. He grinned again; it seemed he was leaving unintentional breadcrumbs for himself.

"Yes, it's me," he said, as he stood up.

"Do you know what happened? The computers detected a time fluctuation. Did someone go back?" Spencer was wide-awake and full of jittery energy.

"What are you doing here, Spencer? You don't have to come in for another four hours." David said, trying to move the subject to less dangerous topics.

"I...I never went home. Thought I could get some extra work in while no one was here. I went to go get some coffee and when I returned the computers were... I'm sorry. I should have told you I was staying." Spencer was growing nervous.

"Don't worry about it. Your ambition is admirable and will take you far, I'm sure," David said.

Then Spencer's eyebrows sank. He was looking at David's clothes. "Sir, why are you dressed like that?"

David walked to within a foot of Spencer, took him by the shoulders, looked him in the eyes and said, "Spencer, listen to me very carefully."

1995
3:45 P.M.
Arizona

The past snuck up on David and grabbed hold. Rather than testing his theory, which if proven, would ease his nerves and clear his mind of impending worldwide doom, he spent the afternoon rummaging through his own house. He explored the pine cupboards, which were now cherry wood. He wondered how he had ever lived with the sixties-style linoleum floor. The house smelled differently, but it was familiar, bringing back a wave of memories and emotions attached to the events of his life during this time. It was an amazing experience.

A two-liter bottle of Cherry Coke sat emptied on the counter. After rummaging through the fridge, he had found the soda and became perplexed by it. Cherry *Coke*? He remembered that during this time period, Cherry Coke was the only cherry flavored soda available. It wasn't his beloved Wild Cherry Pepsi, but it was sweet and he was happy to finish it. He then turned his attention to edible food and devoured a large slice of apple pie he had felt bad about leaving to spoil before departing for Israel. He fed Franklin the fish enough food to keep him alive for the next week and looked through some photos, which in his future album were faded, but here, in this time, they were fresh from the developers.

He flipped through images of himself and Tom, working hard on their dreams of time travel, posing next to the newly built semiconductor, faces smiling. They looked so young, so eager…so in-over-their-heads. If only they knew how deep they'd eventually get, would they have continued with their work?

David eventually made his way up the stairs and into his sparsely decorated office. The carpet was brown and the walls were covered with dark, wood paneling he and Tom would rip down a year later. The house had changed much over the years, but it still felt like home.

The room was impeccably clean and boring, he noted. Over the years, his penchant for neatness had taken leave for creative genius and not having time to clean. He pulled out the tower of his then top-of-the-line Pentium I, 200-megahertz PC and installed the Time Recorder. It fit perfectly using the free serial port cable at the rear of the computer. He just prayed the ancient Windows 3.1 operating system would be able to detect and use the futuristic device. As he reached for the power button, he realized he had no idea what would happen next.

He felt his hands grow clammy. The past days had been filled with so many dramatic discoveries, breakthroughs and close calls, he wasn't sure he would be prepared for the potential information this device would supply.

The computer whirred to life as he depressed the power button. He sighed with relief, but before all the air escaped from his chest, he sucked in a panicked breath. The computer screen flashed with vibrant colors, and he feared he had fried the computer. Then again, he remembered the computer working fine when he had gotten home from Israel.

The screen went black for a moment, and then a face appeared on the screen. David almost fell over backwards with shock as his own wizened and old eyes stared back at him.

"David, what I wouldn't give to see your face when you see what this device proves. It's changed the way we think about time and will provide you with the freedom to embark on a great adventure," the older David's voice echoed from the computer speakers.

David stared at his face on the screen, wrinkled and tan. *Tan?* Had he spent time in the sun? Before he could continue his line of thinking, the computerized recording continued its one-way dialogue.

"I know what you're thinking, David," the future David said. "You'll be spending a few more days in the sun than you're used to. Remember, I was once you, sitting in front of our old computer monitor, listening to myself talk to myself. Heh, I could make your life boring and tell you how things turn out, but that would ruin the fun now, wouldn't it?"

The image of the older David leaned in close and smiled wide. "I will tell you one thing, though..."

Younger David leaned closer to the computer as though he were about to hear a secret.

"Modern science will make amazing advances in dentistry in the future, so don't trouble yourself with Tom's teasing about your soda habit."

David leaned back with a smile on his face. He was funny.

"Enjoy," his future self said with a wink.

Then his face disappeared and was replaced by a black screen. Two sets of numbers appeared and began scrolling higher and higher, into the billions. Both numbers stopped at 598,098,982,001. Two jagged lines appeared, labeled True Time and Present Time. The lines stretched across the screen, stopped and then overlapped. They were identical. A number labeled Time Variance, in the bottom right of the screen, began to scroll backwards from 100. David watched eagerly, waiting to see his theory be proved by machinery created by his future self. The number stopped at 0.00000000000. He smiled as a message, appeared on the screen.

Time Variance Not Detected—Time Stream Intact

He leaned back in the chair, relieved, because he finally knew beyond a shadow of a doubt, time could not be changed. But then his stomach sank. He knew the truth. He knew the inevitable outcome of Tom's past and future. He knew when, where and how Tom would die, and telling him wouldn't do any good. It was set in stone, recorded in history.

Tom was going to die thousands of years in the past.

28 A.D.
4:00 P.M.
Bethany, Israel

Tom was beginning to wonder where David had gone. David left more than five hours ago and time wasn't an object. If he stayed away for a year, he still could have come back just seconds after he had left. Tom worried that something might have happened to David—maybe some kind of malfunction with the time travel devices, or maybe David needed his help.

Tom's thoughts were crushed by the loud laughter from the men around him. Jesus was to his right, and the other men around the table were just a few of the other eleven disciples Jesus had appointed earlier that day. Tom formulated a plan and was about to excuse himself, when David entered the tavern.

"Tom!" David said excitedly, as he moved to the table full of men, "Tom, can I talk to you for a minute?"

"Is this a friend of yours?" Matthew asked. He was a rotund yet muscular man sitting across from Tom.

"I don't go anywhere without him." Tom turned to David. "Isn't that right, David?"

"Ha ha! Welcome!" Matthew shouted to David, and then more loudly to the barkeep, he called, "A drink for our friend!"

Matthew expertly flung a coin to the barkeep, who caught and pocketed it. David was about to try to speak again, but Tom wouldn't give him the chance. "David, I'd like you to meet, Matthew."

"M—Matthew?" David would later realize how stunned he must have looked. Here he was, meeting one of the disciples and future authors of the Bible.

David's jaw was wide open.

Not that Matthew seemed to notice.

"Fine to meet you!" Matthew shouted, as he gave David a firm whack on the back that nearly knocked all the air from David's lungs.

Matthew leaned back as best he could and revealed a small mousy man sitting behind him. "Our shy friend here is Judas." Judas gave a little wave.

"Judas? Him?" David couldn't believe who he was meeting, and the look on his face said it all.

"You have a look of knowledge about you. Perhaps you have met Judas before?" Jesus asked David, with a suspicious look in his eyes.

"No... No, I haven't," David replied.

The man sitting next to Jesus extended his long, skinny arm to David. "I'm Peter."

David tried harder to repress his shock this time around, knowing it was bound to happen at least eight more times. "Hi, hello..." David said, as he shook Peter's hand. "Tom, we need to talk. It's important that you know this."

"You're among friends here, David. You have nothing to fear from us. Speak your mind," Jesus said.

"Yeah, what's so important?" Tom added.

David was in a corner and struggled for words. "I, uh, I just wanted to congratulate you on becoming one of the twelve apostles—uh, I mean disciples! Disciples I meant."

"Bartender, cancel his drink," Matthew shouted. "He's had too much to drink already!"

Tom smiled and said, "Well, thanks for stopping by... Hey, we're heading out to the Sea of Galilee tomorrow. You want to join us?"

David was on the spot and could see Tom was enjoying it. Everyone's eyes burrowed into David, urging him for an answer. David smiled. It was time to turn the tables on Tom. "Yes, of course."

Tom's facial expression went blank.

"Excellent," Matthew said.

David turned to Jesus and said, "Is it...would it be all right if I traveled with you? With the disciples?"

Jesus mulled over the question briefly and then replied, "You may travel with me and the twelve, but some of my teachings you do not need to hear. Do you understand?"

Butterflies filled David's stomach as he realized that this was Jesus, the man he believed to be God. Surely, Jesus knew who he was, where and when he was from. Was that comment, that question directed toward David as someone who knew what was going to happen in the years to follow, who already believed? "I understand," he replied.

"Good," Tom said. "The walking will do you good. You need to give those flaccid, old muscles of yours a workout."

The group burst out laughing. Even David, no longer held captive by fears of catastrophic time alterations, was able to find the humor. He chuckled with the group.

"Be nice," Jesus added. "He's in excellent shape...for someone his age!"

The group laughed again and David's laughter was among the loudest. Tom was laughing too, but his was a skillful ruse, deployed so that no one would notice the fear in his eyes. He had heard and seen enough to know that life here in ancient Israel was no picnic. He had begun to reconsider his plot to stay. Maybe it was too risky? Maybe they would change the future? Tom cursed himself for not talking to David when he had asked. He fully expected David to throw a fit, drag him outside and demand that they leave. What did David know, and why did he agree to stay?

Tom couldn't make sense of anything since Jesus had appointed him the twelfth disciple. The only thoughts Tom could hold on to kept repeating in his head: *How the hell did this happen? And why is David suddenly making things worse?*

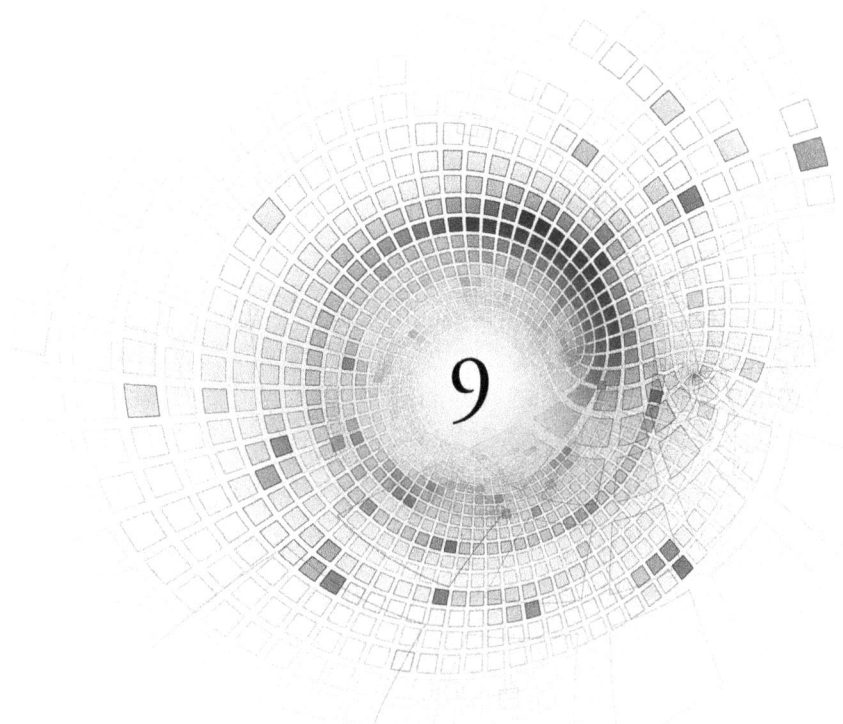

9

FIRST STEPS

Five months of life in ancient Israel proved to be the most challenging, rigorous and most spectacular of Tom's and David's lives. They had survived the summer, traveling through the countryside, villages and cities of ancient Israel. Tom was beginning to speak Aramaic, and David could pass for one of the locals. David's speech, dress and knowledge of ancient customs were impeccable. But what annoyed Tom more than anything else was David's sixth sense about what was going to happen next, what stories were going to be told and what they meant.

105

David traveled with Tom and the other eleven disciples, but as he had agreed with Jesus, he did not participate in all discussions and did not attend every event. At the same time, Tom had the pleasure of a front row seat, and like a cocky child at a magic show, he searched and scrutinized for the slightest sign of forgery, misdirection or illusion. Over the months, he had witnessed the healing of lepers and cripples, and had heard the teachings of Jesus. He had become swift friends with the bulky Matthew, the tall and slender Peter, the short and timid Judas and the ever-rugged Jesus. The six men, including David, were nearly inseparable.

Tom had come to respect Matthew's knowledge of mathematics. For a man in ancient Israel, Tom was convinced Matthew could grasp Quantum Science if given the chance...and he was funny as hell. Tom also found Peter's firm and honest grasp of reality to be refreshing. And Judas...quiet Judas. Tom admired the man's drive. Judas desired so powerfully to do something important with his life that Tom became convinced he would.

Then there was Jesus.

Tom shared a love/hate relationship with Jesus. When on worldly subjects, the two saw eye to eye, but when it came to matters of religion, Tom openly and blatantly questioned Jesus's teaching and miracles. Tom was dedicated in his quest to debunk Jesus, but he was continuously frustrated. He had never met a man who could talk circles around him, but Jesus could manage it with ease. The group of them didn't share the same beliefs, backgrounds and educations, but they had bonded the way travelers in a dangerous land tend to do, and they trusted each other with their lives.

And it was a dangerous land. Even now, the threat of being crushed by the overeager crowd before them became unmistakable. The fourteen of them were backed against the gently lapping waves of the Sea of Galilee by a pushing and shoving mob, like crazed fans at a World Cup soccer match. Matthew and Peter did their best to fend the people off, but their best efforts wouldn't last much longer, as those desperate to be healed of every affliction, from allergies to skin cancer, vied for position at the front of the crowd.

Even Jesus seemed uncomfortable with the situation. "I think it is time we departed," Jesus said.

A woman in the crowd caught wind of Jesus's comment and screamed, "You can't leave yet! I'm still sick!"

The crowd surged forward and Matthew spread his beefy arms like a wall. "Stay behind me!" he yelled to Jesus.

Tom couldn't believe what he was seeing. These people were crazy. Tom was sure Jesus 'healed' people by paying them to feign illness, and upon Jesus's cue, whether it be a hand gesture, touch or word, they would be miraculously healed. Now, every fool with a bruise for thirty square miles had shown up to receive a dose of false hope. Tom decided that someone had to come up with a plan, and being the person with the highest IQ, he volunteered himself. He scanned the area behind them and saw a small boat tied up in the water, only a few feet from shore. It looked seaworthy and large enough to accommodate the fourteen. "Let's take the boat," Tom said to Jesus.

"It's not ours," David objected.

Jesus patted David on the shoulder with a smile and said, "Then we'll return it."

The disciples acted without having to be told. They ran into the water and loaded themselves into the boat, while Matthew remained on the beach, continuing to hold the crowd at bay. Jesus calmly waded into the water and was pulled aboard by Peter. The crowd pushed forward; Matthew was losing ground.

David stood outside the boat and said, "This isn't how it's supposed to happen. It's not our boat. We can't just take it."

"David, I'm positive the owner of this vessel would rather us escape the mob than see us die before our time. Don't you agree?" Jesus replied, as he extended his hand to David.

David took Jesus's hand and was pulled aboard.

"We're all in!" Peter yelled to Matthew, who was still on shore.

People began to pull on Matthew's clothes, begging him not to let Jesus leave, pleading with him to change Jesus's mind. Matthew pushed the crowd back with a mighty heave and then splashed into the water, running as fast as he could through the waves. He rushed for the boat, which was already floating out to sea.

Matthew kicked and splashed, pushing through the water like an oversized St. Bernard.

Tom thought the sight was hysterical, but he dared not laugh, as Matthew, who clearly did not know how to swim, was dog paddling for his life.

Matthew made it to the boat and shimmied to the side. Tom, David and Peter took hold of him and pulled with all their strength. Matthew didn't budge. He weighed three hundred pounds and was currently water logged.

Jesus moved in and grabbed Matthew's garments. Together, Tom, David, Peter and Jesus pulled Matthew into the boat, while the rest of the disciples sat on the opposite side of the boat to keep it from capsizing.

Once inside the vessel, Matthew flopped to the floor, panting for air. "If I knew... I was going to be swimming...I would have brought...extra under garments!" Matthew shouted between breaths, followed by a hearty laugh and then an out-of-breath fat man's cough.

The tension of the boat's crew was relieved by Matthew's antics. A light chuckle escaped from the group and expanded into full-blown laughter. David, however, was not laughing. His thoughts lay elsewhere. Today's events did not transpire as he had imagined they would. Was taking this boat stealing or was Jesus right? Could they safely assume the boat's owner would have no hard feelings when the boat was returned? And David had witnessed Tom influencing Jesus! It was Tom's idea to take the boat. David decided to watch Tom's actions more closely and make sure he wasn't trying to find a flaw in Jesus by creating it himself. As for taking the boat, David decided that Jesus was right. But David couldn't shake the awful feeling in his stomach since the events on the beach. When Jesus approved the taking of the boat, all of David's beliefs were instantly called into question. David still couldn't believe the thought had crossed his mind. He tried to erase the question from his mind, but was unable. It repeated over and over, tormenting him and tempting him to doubt.

Did Jesus sin?

❦

After the excitement on the beach, the quiet of the sea was a welcome experience to all on the boat. Many were sleeping. Matthew was rowing, putting his large muscles to good use, while David and Tom enjoyed the view from the bow. For the first time since their trip through time began, Tom was in Heaven. He had spent summers as a child on his uncle's boat. The sweet air filled his lungs and brought back memories that wouldn't happen for two thousand years. A light breeze caressed his growing, black hair while his thoughts drifted.

Tom had seen what Jesus could do—he didn't buy it, but he had to admit Jesus was impressive. Jesus was the ultimate motivational speaker and could sway crowds with just a few words. Even Tom felt a tug at his heart now and then. The passion of the man was undeniable, and had Tom been a less educated man, without knowledge of the future, being swept into the teachings of Jesus would have been easy.

Tom searched the clouds overhead, white wisps of water vapor, like hair...like Megan's hair. Soft and lovely. He closed his eyes and could see her making breakfast. Cream of Wheat, of all things, was her favorite. She always cooked it too long, so it clumped into balls, which she would then douse with brown sugar and coat with two-percent milk. Tom couldn't stand Cream of Wheat, but he would sell his soul for a bowl of Megan's right now.

"What are you thinking about?" David asked.

"Nothing," Tom replied.

"Nothing nothing, or nothing you want to talk about?"

"Just looking at the clouds."

David had been watching Tom for a few minutes and saw his eyebrows lower and his forehead wrinkle. He knew Tom was thinking about Megan. It was the inescapable force that drove him forward.

"They look like they're getting darker. Might have a storm soon," David said, as he gazed out over the sea.

Tom took a breath and let it out slowly. This trip had put David and him at odds over so many issues, but David had always been there for him and always would be. Tom didn't see the use in keeping him in the dark. "I miss her," he said.

"You know..." David started, "And let me finish before you tell me I'm a fool..."

Tom crossed his arms, leaned back and raised his eyebrows as if to say, 'I'll try, but don't push it.'

"Megan was a Christian... She believed in eternal life after death. She believed in that man," David said, as he motioned to Jesus, who was sleeping on the other end of the boat.

"She believed he was God and that he died for the sins of humanity. Imagine, just for a moment, if she was right and you were wrong. It would be a shame if I saw her again...and you didn't. The risk of believing all this Jesus nonsense might be worth taking. We might not be able to change the past, but the future is still ours to create."

Tom sat staring at the sky and appeared to be thinking hard on David's comments. Then he said, "I think you're right... There is a storm coming."

David looked up at the sky and saw dark, heavy clouds moving toward them, smudging out the bright sun. His thoughts raced through what he knew of the Bible. He tightly clutched the side of the boat and said, "This is going to be interesting."

"What? What's going to happen? You know, don't you?" Tom asked.

"Don't worry, we'll live."

"Easy for you to say."

The clouds began to swirl and churn with energy, ready to burst. A drop of rain slapped David's cheek, and he smiled.

"Why are you smiling?" Tom asked.

Whack! A sizable drop landed on Tom's forehead. He wiped it off. David slunk down and wedged himself into the boat floor. He looked up at Tom and smiled. "You might want to hold on to something. Things are going to get bumpy."

"David, what—"

Krakoom! A blue streak of lightning ripped across the sky and exploded with fire, as it pierced a tree on the distant shore. The thunderclap triggered a deluge of rain from the dark sky. The waves, revealed by bright flashes of lightning, rose and fell ever higher, ever wider, threatening to capsize the lot of them into the undulating sea.

Panic quickly took hold of the group. Judas dove to the floor of the boat and clung to the wooden bench. Chaos gripped the minds of those attempting to control the situation.

"We're all going to drown!" someone yelled.

A wave crashed over the boat and knocked most to their knees. What followed was a mass of yelling, screaming and questioning, obscured by the rain and thunder. Tom and David couldn't make out what was being said, but their thoughts were clear: They were all going to die. They'd be capsized and the waves would take their strength and water would fill their lungs. They would sink into the cold abyss, never to be seen or heard from again.

Tom couldn't stand it any longer. It seemed he would have to take action to save their lives again. He hoped this wouldn't become a habit. He climbed to his feet and headed toward the center of the boat. Just then, a second wave careened into the boat. Tom was flung from his feet, and his head collided solidly with the side of the vessel.

In the confusion, only David saw Tom fall. "Tom!" David frantically crawled to his side.

David inspected Tom's head, which was doused with seawater and already covered with blood, pouring from a gash. He was unconscious and probably better for it. This would hurt with a passion when he woke up.

Peter kneeled down next to David and yelled, "Is he alive?"

"Yes," David shouted back.

"David, it is well known that you are wise in the ways of the world. Tell us, what should we do?" Peter asked David, trying to squelch the terrified look on his face.

"Where's Jesus?" David asked, knowing where his line of questioning would lead.

Peter looked to the back of the boat where Jesus was laying. "He still sleeps."

"Well," David said, "Wake him up."

Peter hurried across the boat, doing his best not to be knocked overboard by the tossing sea. He fell to his knees next to Jesus. He took hold of Jesus's arm and shook. "Master! Master! We're all going to drown!" he shouted.

Jesus blinked as he woke from his slumber. He calmly took in the storm, the rain and the lightning. He briefly glanced at the distraught men, all looking to him for salvation. "Help me up," he said to Peter.

Peter pulled Jesus to his feet and then quickly clung to the floor of the boat. Jesus stood alone at the center of the boat. The wind and rain whipped through his hair. David noticed that the power of the storm seemed to invigorate him. Jesus stretched out his hands into the rain and smiled.

David knew what was about to happen and cursed Tom for being unconscious. If he saw this, there would be no more excuses.

Jesus closed his eyes and spoke kindly, as if to a friend. He said, "Stop."

Calm. The clouds pulled back and disappeared like they had been rewound. The wind extinguished to a gentle breeze. The waves were ironed flat. All in an instant. It was as though someone switched on the lights and let the sun come out. No one made a sound as the boat rocked in the placid water.

Tom came to, with a jolt, "Wha—what happened?" he asked, and he held his head in pain.

"Jesus calmed the storm," David explained.

Tom looked up at Jesus, still standing alone in the middle of the boat. "What? C'mon, David."

Jesus turned his head toward Tom, clearly disappointed.

Tom started, "He can't—"

"Where is your faith?" Jesus asked Tom, and then he spoke to the rest of the group, "All of you..."

Jesus stepped over the fearful men and resumed his spot at the back of the boat. He stood, facing the shoreline, silent.

The disciples, minus Tom, had all seen what Jesus did. They began speaking to each other with excited whispers.

"Who is he?" someone asked.

"I don't know!" another replied.

"He calmed the storm! How did he do that?"

"Unbelievable."

"He commands the wind and water, and they obey him!"

Tom's brow furrowed and he looked at David. "Are they serious?" he asked, as he winced with pain.

David nodded and said, "Let's take care of that wound. And no whining; this might hurt."

As David began to clean Tom's wound with seawater, Tom stared across the boat at Judas, who had not moved from his spot. The small man was clutching the bench, hands shaking and jaw trembling. Tom had recognized the name of Judas when they were first introduced so many months ago, but he couldn't remember who he was.

He would have to remember to ask David. Tom feared for Judas on several occasions, as the man seemed to wilt at the slightest hint of danger. Maybe Judas just needed a friend? Someone to look out for him? To inspire him? Tom decided he'd get to know Judas better; maybe they could help each other.

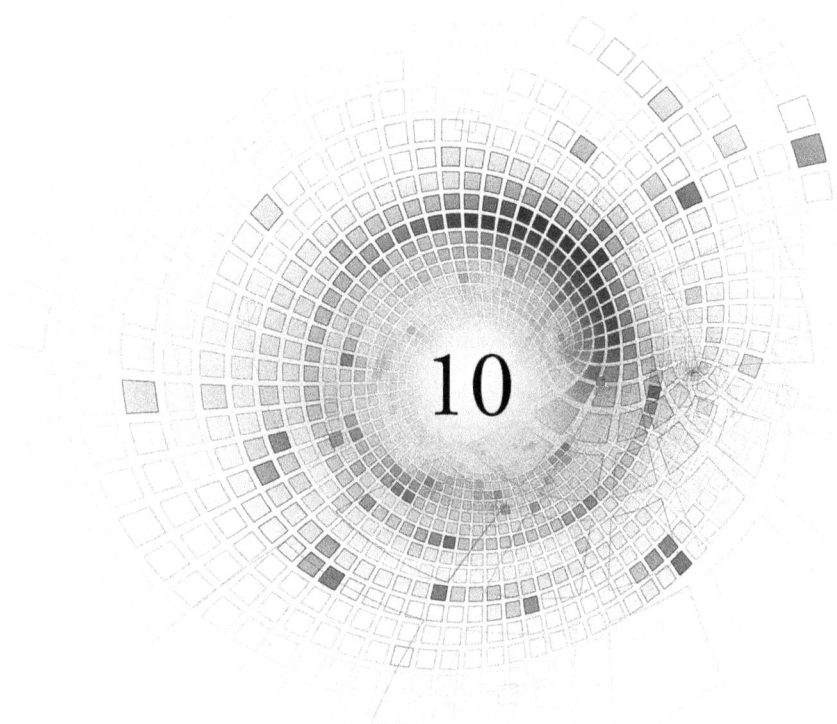

10

PITFALL

29 A.D.

5:32 P.M.

Gergesa, on the Sea of Galilee, Israel

A mile from the extravagant city of Gergesa was a dark valley, hewn into the Earth by years of wind and water. The walls of the two hundred foot chasm were lined with tombs dug into the cliff faces. The air was cool, wet and reeked of stale decay. Some called it The Valley of the Dead. Some simply called it The Valley, but for the past week, no one called it anything at all. No one dared to even think about the valley, as though Samuel, the man now shackled to a cliff face, might hunt them down and devour their children.

Samuel, once a fisherman and friend to many, had been overtaken by an evil force. Some speculated that the Tempter himself possessed Samuel. Those who knew the man had tried to give him time. Perhaps the evil would pass? But after a month, the evil had not passed; in fact, it had grown stronger, deepening its hold on Samuel's body. He was found sleeping in the entrails of ten sheep he had slaughtered, apparently with his bare hands. The Roman Guard was called to action. It took ten heavily armed and expertly trained guards to subdue the man, and two almost lost their lives.

Samuel had been chained to the cliff face in the Valley of the Dead for five days, awaiting his sentence, which all knew would be death. Clothed only in dirty rags, Samuel spoke in strange languages, frothed at the mouth and at times mimic-ked the beasts of the forest. He was truly mad. But for the past five hours, he just sat there, cross-legged with his back to the four Roman soldiers standing guard. The soldiers, fully armored with iron helmets, hard leather chest plates, shoulder pads and boots, all wielded shields, swords and spears. They maintained a healthy distance and a watchful eye at all times.

Greagor, the captain of the group, stroked his favorite sword against a whetstone, sharpening its blade to a razor's edge. With its double-edged iron blade, and its U-shaped, brass hilt, as well as its ornate sheath, it was a spectacular weapon— one that Greagor had used to kill several enemies of Rome. With every swipe of the blade, Greagor kept his eyes glued on Samuel. His lip raised in a sneer, revealing clenched teeth. Not only was this man a Jew, a conquered people with phony free-doms, but he was evil, and Greagor wanted him dead. "We ought to slit his throat now and be done with it," he said.

The other men laughed and agreed, but none took action. They were all too terrified to personally carry out a death sentence. Greagor, pleased that he had made the men laugh, thought it appropriate to further taunt the chained beast. He picked up a sharp stone the size of a fist, and heaved it at Samuel. The rock sailed through the air, sure to strike a painful blow. The soldiers' eyes grew broad with anticipation.

Whack! Stone slapped against flesh.

Greagor stood up. He thought his vision must be playing tricks. But the other men, with petrified visages, saw it, too. Samuel's hand had a firm grip on the stone, inches from his head. He had caught the stone...with his back turned. Greagor sat down and looked at his comrades. All were too timorous to say a word, lest they entice the beast to retaliate.

Samuel looked at the stone through glazed eyes. He smiled and began to rock back and forth, muttering to himself, "Dimito desrafat fier tarsadun," over and over again. Each time he finished the words, he cut a bloody gouge into his arm using the stone. Froth dripped from his mouth and mixed with the blood oozing from his arm. The sight only enticed him further and his rocking grew more fervent. His legs bounced at the kneecaps and his eyelids twitched as though in violent REM sleep.

As Greagor watched with a new respect, he thought he saw something different about Samuel. He was growing more excited...or was it nervous?

⁊

The sea had been calm since the storm magically dissipated, and no one had said much of anything. David had bound Tom's wound as best he could, but it didn't stop Tom's head from swelling. The pain was intense at first, but had dulled slightly when Tom sat still, which wasn't easy to do in a rocking boat.

If only I was alone, Tom thought. He could make a quick jaunt to the future for some Ibuprofen and ice, but it was impossible here in the boat, and it would be even more unlikely as soon as they landed in Gergesa, which was now only one hundred yards away.

From this distance, the city could be seen in its entire luster. Tall, white arches attached several columned buildings to one another. A grand theater bustled with activity to the south, and a temple of Zeus stood tall and proud atop a hill to the north. This was the pinnacle of how Tom had envisioned the Roman Empire, its influence smearing even into the most distant territories. He enjoyed the view despite the drumbeat of pain pounding within his skull.

Matthew, who had been resting on the side of the boat, craned his head up as though he'd been rudely awakened. "Disgusting. Look at all those pigs. Who would tend such beasts so close to the city?" he said to Tom.

Previously, Tom would have thought such a comment to be peculiar, but having learned Jewish culture, Tom knew that pigs were unfit to eat and were looked down upon severely. The fact that such a large herd was roaming on the hill, just outside the city, must have enraged every good Jew for miles. But Tom wasn't inclined to have yet another conversation about the foulness of pigs. He responded with a simple smile and the subject died out.

Within five minutes, they reached the shore. "Someone else can get their feet wet this time!" Matthew yelled. "I've spent my time in the water!"

Peter stood and said, "You got more than your feet wet," as he climbed over the side of the boat, into the water. "Judas, give me a hand."

Judas rather reluctantly got to his feet and threw one leg over the side. As he put his other leg into the water, he lost his balance and fell backward with a yelp, catching his robe on the oar and ripping it lengthwise. Peter thrust his long arm into the water and pulled the flailing Judas to his feet. Judas was panicked and coughed a large amount of water up after taking a breath. Tom wondered if he had ever been submerged in water. The poor man must have sucked in a mouthful.

Judas attempted to collect himself but was clearly distraught. His hands shook as he clutched the side of the boat, knuckles white. Tom felt a deep compassion for the man. "Go ahead to shore, Judas," Tom said, as he patted Judas's hand, "I'll help Peter."

Judas trudged to the shore and sat down with his head between his knees. Tom and Peter dragged the boat full of men to the shore.

Tom then walked to Judas, who looked up with the sad eyes of a child whose new Christmas present had been broken only minutes after being unwrapped. "Look at this," Judas said, as he held up his torn robe. "I look like a beggar."

"Can't you just buy a new one?" Tom asked.

"It's not up to me. The tax collector has the money," Judas whined.

"Tax collector?"

"Matthew. He used to be a tax collector," Judas explained. "Honestly, I think I could do better with the money, but Matthew insisted he had the most experience."

"Why don't you just ask for some?" Tom asked.

"I don't... I couldn't..."

"Then I will."

Judas attempted to stop Tom with an outreached arm, but he was too late. Tom was already approaching Jesus, who was still in the boat.

"Your compassion is growing," Jesus said, as Tom stopped at the boat.

Tom paused. Jesus turned to him. "Helping those in need...aiding Judas. You're learning my ways."

"I haven't changed since the day we met," Tom said, knowing full well it was a lie.

Jesus smiled. "So you say. Ask your question."

Tom felt the urge to argue the point, but could see Jesus already had him against the ropes. "Judas ripped his robe when he fell out of the boat. I was...he was wondering if we could give him some money to buy a new robe."

"Of course," Jesus said.

That was easy, Tom thought, and then he went a step further. "Actually, Judas wanted to know if you could put him in charge of the money. Matthew is great with money and has experience as a tax collector, but Judas...he's just not growing. I think he's up to the challenge of handling our financing." Tom smiled, attempting to hide his sarcasm over his 'not growing' statement. He felt ridiculous saying it, but it seemed Jesus was taking his request seriously.

Jesus mulled over the proposal. He called Matthew over and said, "Matthew, could I have the money purse?"

Matthew handed a leather sack full of coins to Jesus.

"Judas will be handling the money from now on," Jesus said. "It will be good experience for him."

"Are you sure?" Matthew said.

Jesus nodded.

Matthew smiled and rejoined the other disciples, who were mingling with a crowd of people who had rounded the outskirts of the sea in the same time the fourteen had sailed across it. Jesus turned to Tom and said, "If you have not become more compassionate, what are you getting for your good deeds today?"

Tom looked over at Judas, still sitting on the sand with his head down. "A friend," he said.

"Indeed..." Jesus said, as he handed the coin purse to Tom. "Go, tell Judas the good news."

Tom smiled and said, "Thank you."

Jesus watched Tom walk away, then balanced himself, threw his leg over the side of the boat and pressed his foot into the wet sand.

❧

Greagor's muscles twitched as Samuel's head jerked back so fast that it seemed his neck would snap from the force. Samuel's eyes ballooned, as if they would burst, and he immediately stopped shaking. Slowly, mechanically, Samuel cranked his head toward the east, toward Gergesa.

Greagor gripped his sword and slowly drew it, as Samuel stood to his feet. *What in the name of Neptune is this man up to now? Perhaps a lion is prowling the valley?* Greagor wished it to be true. *Let the savages kill each other.*

Samuel's body became rigid, silent, listening. Greagor looked to the east and saw nothing. Believing confrontation was inevitable, he snapped his fingers once, gaining the full attention of his men. He motioned toward Samuel with his head. All four men slowly drew their weapons.

Samuel took a step forward but was instantly stopped, as the chains shackled to his arms and legs grew taut. He looked down at the chains with disgust and growled. Then he slowly moved his right arm back, letting the chain go slack. Then he tugged it forward.

Clink!

The chain snapped like macaroni.

Stepping forward, Greagor moved slowly, shield at the ready with his men close behind him. "Sit back down!" Greagor commanded.

Samuel twisted his body toward Greagor and gritted his teeth together, hissing, "WE WILL NOT!"

Clink!

Samuel shattered the shackle attached to his left arm. Only his feet were still bound. Greagor knew that once Samuel's feet were undone, he and his men would lose their advantage.

"Attack!" Greagor screamed, as he raised his sword toward the blue sky. The four soldiers charged, ready to spill blood.

Samuel turned toward his attackers and smiled.

℃

Tom and Judas strolled through the crowded streets of Gergesa. Judas was all smiles, clothed in a new robe and proudly clutching the money purse. They had been perusing the many shops for almost two hours, and Tom knew it was time to head back. After the ten-minute argument Tom had with David about going into the city alone with Judas, Tom knew that David would send out a search party if they weren't back on time. And Tom also knew that he and David were the only two people in the world wearing watches right now, so David would know exactly what time it was and how late they were.

"We should head back to the beach now. The others are probably wondering where we are," Tom said.

"Just a few moments more. These dates look delicious," Judas replied, as he eyed a basket of dates being sold by a thick shop-keep.

Tom looked at his watch casually, pretending to scratch his wrist. They still had ten minutes. Tom decided to use the time to get to know Judas a little better. "What happened to you in the water today?"

"What do you mean?" Judas asked, looking down at the ground.

"After you fell in. The water was only knee deep, you could have stood up."

"I...I don't know. It happens sometimes. I—I get afraid. I panic. I don't know why. Water, spiders, snakes, even goats...there are so many things. Sometimes it even happens before I know the danger exists."

"Extra Sensory Perception," Tom said without thinking.

"What?" Judas asked

"Nothing...nothing. Hey, try not to worry too much. You're with friends now. Thirteen friends. One of us will always be there to pull you out of the water," Tom said in earnest.

Judas smiled. "Thank you."

"Now let's get going. David's going to be irate if we're late."

"David doesn't like me much, does h—" Judas froze mid-sentence and his eyes darted around like a scared animal.

"What is it?" Tom asked.

"It's happening," Judas said, arms shivering.

Tom saw Judas's hand shaking, his eyes wary and his teeth biting his lip. Judas was panicking. This was what he was talking about, but where was the danger?

"Aiiiieeeee!" A woman screamed in the distance.

Suspicious of the encroaching racket, Tom and Judas looked down the long street filled with people. A wave of screaming grew from the crowd and headed toward them. People ran in every direction, and the crowd parted like the sea for Moses. Tom squinted as a figure ran toward them. *All these people are running from one man?*

Tom turned to speak to Judas, but Judas was gone, ten feet away, hiding with other frightened shoppers. Tom surveyed his surroundings. He was alone in the street. What did these people know? As the man approached, Tom could see that he was hobbling strangely, and he carried a sword. He decided it was best to follow the crowd's lead and joined Judas on the side of the road.

"What's going on?" Tom asked a woman hiding with them.

"It's Samuel! The possessed man!" the woman whispered.

"Possessed? You mean by a demon?"

"Quiet!" the woman whispered. "His guards are surely dead. If it hears you, you will be next." With that, the woman ducked down an alley and ran away.

Tom didn't believe in demons as much as he didn't believe in Jesus, Heaven or Hell. This was all superstitious nonsense. He was tempted to confront the man and prove to these ignorant people that the man was not possessed, but he erred on the side of safety. The man *was* armed, after all.

A hush fell over the frightened crowd as Samuel drew near; Tom could hear the man ranting. Against the tugging urges of Judas to stay down, Tom stepped out from hiding to get a look at Samuel, and then he quickly took a large step back as Samuel passed, nearly tripping over himself and the others behind him.

Samuel was covered in blood from head to toe, frothing at the mouth like a rabid dog. He had open gashes up and down his arms. Shackles and chains still hung from his arms and legs and clanked along the road. Tom focused on the sword and saw that it was Roman. That woman mentioned guards…could this man really have killed Roman guards with his bare hands, while shackled to a wall? From the amount of blood covering Samuel's body, Tom was convinced it was true.

As Samuel passed by, muttering loudly, Tom became aware of what he was saying. "Jesus… Jesus… We will kill him. Yes, yes. Yes we will," Samuel said, oozing hatred.

Tom stood up straight and watched Samuel head down the street…toward the beach…saying… Tom turned to Judas. "Jesus!" Tom shouted.

"Is he gone?" Judas asked, arms still shaking.

"He's going after Jesus!" Tom said, as he headed into the street. "C'mon!"

Tom began running toward the beach and turned back toward Judas, "If we're going to be there for you Judas, you need to be there for us. Let's go!"

Judas shook with confusion. He was paralyzed with fear, but Tom was right. Perhaps they could beat the man to the beach and simply warn Jesus of the impending danger. They would have to move fast, but after a lifetime of running from his fears, Judas knew he was fast. He leapt from his hiding place and tore off down the street after Tom. They were going to save Jesus!

☙

David hadn't had many opportunities to speak with Jesus alone since their adventure began. So he was thankful when Jesus asked him to take a walk, while the disciples handled the crowd that had gathered on the beach. During their walk, Jesus spoke to David of things to come, things already gone by and the weather. Jesus never gave any indication that he knew David was from the future. And it seemed as though Jesus was more comfortable with David than he was with the twelve disciples. They understood each other. David imagined it must be a relief for Jesus to have someone who understood, like two quantum physicists in the middle of the desert...like with David and Tom.

The walk was almost over, and David could see the crowd, now much larger, gathered in front of the disciples. *There must be three thousand people*, he thought.

"Looks like another long day," Jesus said.

"Indeed," David replied, but then he smiled. *Another long day?* In all his life, David never thought that Jesus got worn out, tired of people or stressed by life. But David was beginning to see things differently. Jesus was not only human, he was as human as David, Tom or anyone else, and all this activity, all these people, wore him out.

David scanned the beach and glanced at his watch. Not only did the watch reveal the time, but also Tom's general location. He wasn't far, but still deep in the city. Then again, it looked as though Tom was heading back, and quickly.

Tom was late, but then, so was David. It wasn't that David didn't trust Tom alone in the city. They had both blended into the society and could manage fine on their own. But he didn't want Tom and Judas having an influence on one another. David was relatively sure how things would turn out, but there were so many unknowns about this past that were not recorded in the Bible. He wondered if his and Tom's friendship would survive the years of living the very subject that divided them most strongly. Over the past few months, David had sensed Tom drifting away, becoming obsessed with debunking Jesus. But now, Tom was becoming friends with Judas... What good could come of that?

"Jesus!" Judas yelled from a street running parallel to the beach. "Take cover! A possessed man wielding a sword is coming for you!"

Jesus and David quickly hurried to Judas.

"From where does this man come?" Jesus asked.

Judas was out of breath, but managed to point to a street, which led up a hill.

"Where's Tom?" David asked, suddenly concerned.

"He's coming…I…passed him on the way. He's a slow…runner," Judas said.

A howl from the top of the hill pulled their attention away from Judas. A man was at the crest, wielding a sword high in the air.

David had never seen the man before, but the location and circumstances filled David's memory, "Legion…"

Jesus shot David a look. He had heard. He heard David say the name before it was known. David slunk back and pursed his lips tight, as the disciples arrived with the crowd in tow. He hoped his foreknowledge would be forgotten.

The man with the sword screeched and lunged down the hill toward the beach, toward Jesus. Many in the crowd turned and fled; the rest, including the disciples and

David, simply backed away. "Stand behind me, and do not fear this man," Jesus said, standing his ground.

The crazed man was like a freight train with a sword. He seemed immeasurably dense, like he could crash through a cement wall. And still, Jesus held his ground. The man was only ten feet from Jesus when, "Jesus! Look out!"

Whump!

Tom tackled the crazed man from the side, sending both men to the ground. The crowd collectively gasped. The sword fell from the attacker's hand, but he was not deterred from his goal. He got to his feet and pounded toward Jesus. Tom was on his feet, too, and preparing to make a second attempt.

"Tom, don't!" David shouted, but it was too late.

Tom dove onto Samuel's back and hung on like a baby monkey clinging to its mother. Samuel growled and thrashed about wildly. Tom had wrestled during his high school years, and for a short time he had even considered trying out for the Israeli Olympic team. He knew the headlock he had wrapped around Samuel's throat was unbreakable and should put the man in a deep sleep within a minute. If only Tom could hold on.

Samuel ran backward and slammed into the wall of a fishery. Tom grunted in pain as his backside indented the wall. He gritted his teeth and squeezed tighter still. He was not going to let this man go.

Samuel swung his body from side to side, flailing Tom's legs in the air. It had been a full minute since Tom locked his arms around Samuel, and he had increased the pressure with every resistance Samuel offered up. But the man wasn't slowing down, and Tom's arms were growing sore. He tightened his grip with all his reserves, hoping it would do the man in—finally.

And it seemed to be working. Samuel staggered slowly and then stopped moving altogether. Tom never loosened his grip. But then he felt a hand on his wrist and then a crushing force. He grunted in pain and looked forward. Samuel was slowly, methodically pulling Tom's arm away, like he had all the time in the world and no use for oxygen. Within seconds, Tom's arms were pulled away from Samuel's neck.

Samuel snapped his head toward Tom and took him by the robe. "We will remember you," Samuel said, as his penetrating eyes burned into Tom's memory.

Seconds later, Tom was airborne, as Samuel tossed him like a football. Tom sailed over the crowd and splashed down in the water. Jesus watched him land, and then turned his head back to Samuel the fisherman, staring him straight in the eyes. Samuel froze in his tracks, his fingers only inches from Jesus's neck.

"Come out of him," Jesus said in a calm voice.

Samuel began to twitch from head to toe, as though a thousand needles were pricking him. He fell to his knees and was no longer a powerful beast. He was instantly reduced to a pitiful horde of personalities. "What do you want with us, Jesus, Son of the Most High God? Please! Do not torture us!"

"What is your name?" Jesus asked, as though talking to an insignificant and inferior creature.

"We are Legion. Please do not send us into the abyss! Mercy! Yes, Mercy! Have mercy on us, as you did during the rebellion! MERCY, mercy! There! Send us into them!" Samuel shouted, as he pointed to the heard of pigs foraging on the nearby hillside.

"The swine! Yes! YES! Send us into them! Mercy! MERCY!"

"Go," Jesus said.

Samuel's head arched toward the sky, and his mouth gaped open as the sound of fifty wailing voices escaped his lungs. As soon as the last voice was silenced, Samuel fell and Jesus caught him.

Tom pulled himself to his feet by clinging to the side of the boat. He had heard the screaming voices asking Jesus to have mercy, but he couldn't understand what was happening or how that man had thrown him so far. He was sure his ribs were bruised, and his head pounded harder than ever. It had been years since Tom had run that fast, that far, and then into a fight. He was getting old.

The wall of people blocking Tom's view had fallen silent, so he assumed that whatever happened was over and his assistance wasn't needed. Not that he'd be any help. But what was that? A noise in the distance growing louder...like people screaming...but worse.

The crowd of people standing in front of Tom began to scatter in either direction. *What now?* Tom remained in the water, six feet from the shore, assuming that whatever was going to happen next, he'd be safe there. No one in this time period could manage more than a frantic dogpaddle, anyway.

As the last of the crowd blocking his view moved, Tom saw something he only thought could happen in frightening fairy tales. A herd of fat, wailing pigs barreled down the street and onto the beach. There was no running, no hiding. He was in the herd's path and had nowhere to go. He leapt from the water into the boat they had used to cross the sea, and held on tight.

Tom heard the pigs plow into the water. He heard them screech and then choke and die. He raised his head slightly to see what was happening. *Screak!* One of the pigs jumped into the boat, its mouth full of foam, and then just as quickly, it hopped out of the boat, directly over Tom's head. He screamed and jumped to his feet, then stood like a statue.

Everything was quiet as Tom spun around, scanning the water with his eyes. The entire herd of pigs was floating, dead in the water. He covered his mouth. As the pigs floated out to sea, he saw a clearing through the water to the beach and took it. David met him on the shore.

"What the hell was that?" Tom demanded to know, in English.

"Tom, watch your language!" David whispered.

"What, I can't say 'hell' now, either?"

"You're speaking in English."

Tom fell silent and then collected himself. He continued in Aramaic, "So, what happened?"

"That man you tried to tackle was possessed by a legion of demons. Jesus sent them into the herd of pigs," David explained. "Are you okay?"

"Is that supposed to be funny, ha-ha, or just plain ridiculous?" Tom asked.

"They don't think it's very funny," David said, as he pointed to the crowd standing on the street, away from Jesus, who was still holding Samuel. Tom lowered his eyebrows when he saw the faces of the crowd, and he walked closer to hear what was happening.

Samuel was awake and standing on his own, but still leaning on Jesus for support. A hefty man in the crowd stepped forward and said, "Please, leave us. We... don't want you here."

Many in the crowd began to run away, afraid of Jesus, just as they were afraid of Samuel. Tom knew it was human nature to fear the unknown, and right now, Jesus was the epitome of the unknown. But Samuel did not fear him. "Please, Master, let me come with you," Samuel said.

"It is not for you. Return home and tell how much God has done for you," Jesus replied, as he gently steadied Samuel on his feet.

"Yes, my Lord," Samuel said, and with that he headed away from the beach.

The remaining members of the crowd ran away as Samuel approached, leaving fourteen alone on the beach.

Jesus turned toward the sea and watched as the sun began to set. David and Tom stood next to him. "Maybe tomorrow won't be so long?" David said, with just a hint of a smile.

Jesus nodded and they watched the herd of dead pigs float off into the sunset.

11

BREATHE

1996
6:41 P.M.
Arizona

Tom had been vexed since 1997, when Peggy's Porker Palace removed Honey BBQ baby back ribs from their menu. He had enjoyed the meal twice a week for years, and then one day the ribs were gone. Tom inquired to the reason for the tasty food's disappearance and was told by Peggy herself, "Ain't enough cows with ribs in the world to feed the likes of the beasts eatin' here. Get too many complaints when we run out. Fights break out. Tables get broke. We losin' money 'cause a them ribs. That's the truth."

Tom had seen one of those infamous rib brawls, and he knew Peggy was right. But it was now within Tom's power to enjoy the meal at least one more time. Tom and David picked a night when they knew their past selves wouldn't be dining, and they tore through time and space for a savory meal. They looked forward to modern convenience, which was a welcome change to what they had endured for some time.

They had experienced a dazzling array of events: Jesus fed five thousand men, plus their wives and children. Tom had estimated the true number of people to be closer to eighteen thousand. Plenty of people, time and confusion for Jesus's secret society of helpers (that was Tom's latest theory) to make several trips to neighboring villages, cities and markets and return with enough fish and bread to feed the masses. It was an elaborately staged magic show. One that Tom thought David Copperfield might do better.

In what Tom considered to be one of Jesus's best performances, they witnessed him walk on water. It was truly amazing at first, but Tom found flaws as usual. He noticed Jesus rise and fall with each wave, so he was indeed standing on something, but not the water. A thick fog had rolled in and visibility was poor. At times Jesus's feet could be made out, but generally, the fog blocked Tom's view. He concluded that Jesus had taken advantage of the foggy air to perform a rather stunning visual illusion by standing on a floating plank. Tom was now a firm believer...that Jesus had invented surfing.

Over the months that followed, they saw Jesus heal more men and women from various ailments—all of which Tom believed to be staged, like so many modern TV evangelists. They heard Jesus tell parables, confusing stories that meant something else altogether. David was the only one who seemed to get the hidden meaning on the first telling, but Tom noticed David was changing, too. When he watched Jesus perform miracles, his eyebrows would furrow instead of raise, his eyes would squint instead of widen, and he would attempt to view the event from several angles. Tom saw this behavior, and he knew that David was still a scientist.

He couldn't help himself from dissecting each miracle, observing, measuring and hypothesizing. What Tom couldn't see was the outcome to David's scrutinizing.

Even Tom had become partially distracted from his goals. He became more comfortable in the past and closer friends with Judas, Matthew, Peter and Jesus. The group often acted like college men, wrestling and playing pranks on each other. They once conspired against David and set a trap of Tom's design. A bucket of water was placed on a door, and when David entered the room, the bucket crashed down and soaked him, bringing on a fit of laughter from all present. To Tom and David this was an old prank seen on TV, but to their ancient friends, it was a priceless new gag.

With all that was happening, all they were experiencing, internally and externally, Tom and David lost track of time. Before they knew it, they had been living in ancient Israel for almost two years. Two years... They deserved a break. At night, when everyone was sleeping, they stole off into the darkness, walked two miles from the nearest sign of civilization and made the trip back to the future to enjoy a hot plate of Honey BBQ ribs and a glass of drinkable water.

Tom stretched, making room in his already overstuffed and ballooning belly. He had eaten two portions of ribs—more food than he might eat in three days back in ancient Israel. His stomach had protested at first, but Tom forged on. David hadn't eaten as much, but he did partake in an above average amount of Wild Cherry Pepsi. He had already used the bathroom four times, and Tom imagined David wouldn't be sleeping for another day from the caffeine circulating through his system. But they agreed, while the sweet, sweet taste of modern food wreaked havoc with their now healthy bodies, it was well worth any discomfort.

After being silent while they devoured their meals, Tom finally noticed they were being watched. Every eye was on him and David, curiously inspecting the two hungry men. Tom realized what puzzled the thick bodied and thicker headed Porker Palace patrons; in the excitement to eat good food, he and David had neglected to change into proper attire. They were both still wearing their ancient robes, which were dirty, but still very colorful. They did their best to ignore the probing eyes surrounding them.

"Do you think we should have changed first?" David asked.

"I'm sure they've seen stranger," Tom said, as he downed a glass of water and slapped it on the table as though it were a shot of vodka. "Never thought I'd be so glad to drink a glass of water."

"After returning to the modern world, are you sure you want to go back?" David asked.

"A little late to try changing my mind again, isn't it?" Tom replied.

"Just wondering what you're going to do when all this is over? Jesus will die and rise again, and you'll be a Christian. You're just going to come back to the future like nothing has changed?"

"A: There is no way in hell I'm staying back there a day longer than this takes. B: Jesus won't rise from the grave, and I'm pretty sure he's not going to die either," Tom said.

"So the Bible is one hundred percent fiction?"

"That's my guess. A fictional book based on the life of the original Houdini."

As Tom sat back, happy with his comment, he noticed two rather sizable hicks pointing and laughing at David and him. Tom did his best to ignore the men and continued the conversation. "So is your savior everything you expected him to be?" Tom asked.

David shifted in his seat. "What?"

"Jesus…not everything you expected him to be, is he? Doesn't exactly fit the perfect little cookie-cutter mold the religious world has given him," Tom said.

A sadness filled David's eyes as he stared blankly at the table. Tom didn't expect this response from his normally stubborn colleague. "You're having doubts, aren't you? Now that you've met the guy and he's more human than you want him to be…you're having doubts."

Tom smiled ear to ear and continued, "I mean really, any guy who can be friends with me could never be the savior of the world, right?"

David looked up and said, "Tom, I—"

"Hey, aren't you fellas late fer your Mary Kay party?" shouted one of the two hicks, now standing right next to them.

Tom and David did their best to ignore the man and continue their conversation, "Tom—"

"Didn't you hear him, boy?" a second hick shouted, standing above David.

Tom's patience wore away. All they wanted to do was have a conversation and enjoy a meal for the first time in two years, and these big, fat, annoying hicks couldn't get over the fact that Tom and David were wearing robes. "Listen, sir, I haven't had a single alcoholic beverage tonight, so I'm in no mood. If you could, please take your girthy friend and go get another beer on me. Okay?"

Tom's long stream of lengthy words seemed to confuse the men. They looked at each other and then walked away. David looked at Tom, wide-eyed and attempting not to smile. "I can't believe that worked," David said.

But he spoke too soon. The two lumbering men returned with two more beefcakes in tow. Tom and David were outnumbered and outsized. One of the new men stepped toward Tom and asked, "Did you all call Billy fat?"

"No, I called him girthy," Tom replied.

"That ain't even a word," the man said, as he cracked his knuckles.

Tom couldn't help himself. "They teaching English lessons at the hog farm now?"

The response was instant and massive, "Git 'im!"

Two of the thugs leaned forward, arms stretched out, hands grappling. David was pulled from his bench and tossed onto a table, which he slid across. He careened over the other side, taking two plates of food, a large Coke, four settings of silverware and a small vase of fake flowers with him.

Tom was a little quicker.

He pivoted his bench and thrust his right leg forward, catching one of the assailants in the nose with his heel. The man screamed in pain and fell backward into Billy. The two men toppled back like thick dominos and destroyed a chair beneath them. The man on top of Billy held his nose and whined, "He done broke my nothe!"

"Git off me so as I can kill 'im!" Billy shouted, trapped beneath his heavy-set friend.

"I gat 'im!" the third hick shouted, even though he had yet to get his hands on anybody.

The bulbous man, whose overalls barely fit, surged forward, threatening to crush Tom right there in his bench. Tom used the bench's slippery surface to his advantage and slid beneath the table. The bench cracked as the weight of the overalls-wearing man mashed down on it. If Tom had been still in his seat, he would surely have been compressed beyond the point of breathing.

Tom rushed out from under the table. Two of the men were still squirming around on the floor, trying to get to their feet, but the man with the broken and bloody nose was writhing around so much that the other couldn't roll over onto his belly and push himself up. As for the man on the bench, he wasn't going anywhere fast either. He was wedged firmly between the wall, the bench and the table. Tom imagined it would take the Jaws of Life to cut him free.

The last of the four attackers was at the opposite end of a table, facing David. They were moving back and forth from side to side as the lumbering behemoth attempted to wrap his thick hands around David's throat. The man took the table in his hands and tossed it to the side, as though it was no more than a chunk of Styrofoam. Tom knew he had to act quickly and picked up a plate from his table.

Moving quickly, he rounded the last of several tables blocking his path and slammed the solid plate down on the last hick's head. The plate shattered from the blow, and the man fell to his knees, though he wasn't knocked unconscious. David stood still with wide eyes.

"David," Tom said.

David didn't budge.

"David," Tom said with a smile, knowing David had probably seen his life flash before his eyes. "Let's get out of here before they get moving."

David snapped out of his trance and his eyes met Tom's.

"C'mon," Tom said, and David moved.

Tom turned and headed for the door with David right behind him. They didn't make it two feet before being stopped by a wall of three more rotund, country warriors.

"Where you ladies off to?" one of them said with a smile, as he gnawed on a toothpick.

Tom sighed and without a word, slugged the first man in the stomach.

From the parking lot around Peggy's Porker Palace, the sounds of breaking dishes, glasses and screaming men could be heard echoing from inside the establishment. The front door whooshed open as Tom and David ran out into the parking lot. Both had been trounced fairly well. Tom's nose was bleeding, and David's eye was swollen.

"Quick! Around back!" Tom shouted.

Tom and David sped around the building, out of sight from any locals, and they activated their watches. The two bright flashes of light and two loud bangs, heard and seen by everyone with a window seat at the Porker Palace would later be explained as swamp gas—even though there wasn't a swamp for hundreds of miles around.

Seven angry hicks pounded out of the restaurant and scanned the area for their fleeing prey. It wasn't every day they got to beat down a couple a fairies.

One of the men, struggling to catch his breath said, "Damn! They gone!"

Another followed, "Them drag queens...sure can...run!"

30 A.D.
3:40 P.M.
Outskirts of Bethany, Israel

The twelve disciples, Jesus and David trudged up a steep hill, which led to a lone dwelling, just outside Bethany. They hadn't been walking long, but the steep incline took the muscle out of even the fittest of them. David, Tom and Jesus led the pack.

Jesus looked at Tom and David, attempting not to smile while doing so. They were both bruised and battered from their encounter with the Porker Palace thugs. Tom had been quick with a cover story; that he and David were mugged, beaten and left unconscious in an alley. "The men who robbed and beat you, were they blind?"

"You're not going to get into the 'blind that can see' stuff again, are you?" Tom asked.

Jesus smiled. "No. I mean, were they physically blind?"

"Why?" Tom asked.

"You claim that five large men beat and robbed you," Jesus started.

"Yes..." Tom was unsure as to where this was leading.

"Yet your money purse remains at your hip," Jesus pointed out.

Tom looked down to his hip, where indeed, his money purse still hung. "Huh, I guess I must have fallen on top of it during the fight. Maybe they couldn't see it?"

"Maybe they were blind?" Jesus asked with a smile.

"Not likely," Tom said, wishing Jesus would change the line of questioning. While the truth would never come out, he didn't want to be seen as a liar, not to his friends anyway. Yet Tom couldn't resist the opportunity for a friendly jab, "Why don't you just fix us up with a little God zap?"

David's head snapped toward Tom, his eyes angry. Tom had just crossed the line with that comment. David turned to Jesus, afraid for what the repercussions for such a statement might be. "We're fine. Ignore my ignorant friend. His ego was bruised, along with his face."

But Jesus, seemingly unfazed by the dig, said, "Healing you would only make you forget more quickly the lesson you've learned. Pain and suffering can be wise teachers, and some lessons need to be learned over time."

Tom mentally sifted through an array of witty replies, but never got the chance to utilize one.

"Stop," Jesus said to the group. At the top of the hill was a large home, built of clay bricks, surrounded by fig and olive trees. Jesus stared at the building, absorbing its shape and the surroundings, like he was remembering. At the top of the hill stood a man, whose presence shouted strength and power.

Lazarus had been working outside all day, and the roots of the stump before him lay exposed, yet still clinging to the ground. He gripped a rope tied to the stump and wrapped it around his hands and wrists. With a mighty pull and a scream of exertion, he wrenched the stump and all its roots from the earth.

Tom's eyes widened as he saw the feat of amazing strength from a safe distance. "Who is this guy? Maybe we shouldn't bother him," he said.

"Stop worrying," Jesus said. "It doesn't become you."

Jesus strode toward the man. Tom wondered what death wish had possessed Jesus now.

Mary, Lazarus's sister, ran from the house, long black hair undulating through the air behind her, and shook Lazarus by the shoulder. "What is it?" Lazarus asked, knowing the look in her bright green eyes meant trouble.

Pointing to the road on which the fourteen were walking toward the house, she said, "There, on the road."

From this distance, only the number of men could be made out. Lazarus picked up his shovel and wielded it like a gladiator.

"Get inside," Lazarus said. "Find Martha, and be ready to run."

"What about you?" Mary asked.

"My life is inconsequential. I would willingly give it for my sisters'," Lazarus said. "Now go."

Mary obeyed her big brother's request. She ran back inside as quickly as she had run out. Lazarus took a few broad steps toward the encroaching group and shouted, "Stay where you are, and state your business." His voice boomed.

The fourteen stopped in their tracks. Lazarus had a commanding voice and even more commanding body language. Jesus turned to Tom and smiled, "Perhaps we all need to learn a lesson, eh?"

"What? No. What are you—?"

Tom's brief protest fell on deaf ears. "We're here to eat your food and be served by your sisters!" Jesus shouted.

Tom audibly gasped. Jesus had gone insane. "What are you doing?" Tom asked. "That guy is huge."

Lazarus held up the shovel, ready to strike down the first man to try. "Turn back the way you came, stranger."

"Stranger?" Jesus shouted. "I haven't been gone *that* long."

Through squinted eyes, Lazarus attempted to make out facial features.

Jesus pushed on, "Perhaps I should come up there and beat some sense into you!"

Tom looked at Jesus wide-eyed. He thought all this God business must really have been going to Jesus's head.

Lazarus stood up straight and his head tilted. "Jesus?"

"In the flesh," Jesus replied.

A smile stretched across Lazarus's face. "Mary! Martha! It's Jesus!" Lazarus shouted, as his huge feet carried him toward Jesus.

They met halfway and embraced like true friends. Jesus was lifted off the ground in Lazarus's arms. "It's been too long, my friend."

Tom let out a long sigh of relief. He looked at David. "I thought we were all dead for sure."

"I'm sure that's the same thing he was thinking." David said, as he looked at Lazarus.

Jesus was released from Lazarus's bear hug. He looked at Lazarus's arms and said, "I see you've been working hard."

"Jesus!" Mary shouted, as she just about barreled him over with a hug.

Tom couldn't help but smile at such a happy reunion. He could tell these must have been lifelong friends of Jesus, and Mary...was stunning. Her hair looked soft, but not as soft as her face, and her smile—beautiful, the way it pushed her cheeks into firm apples. Tom was pulled from his wistful distraction when Jesus spoke.

"Where is your sister?" Jesus asked.

"When Martha heard who was here, she got to work on a meal for you and your friends," Mary explained.

"Come," Lazarus said. "Come inside. Our home is your home. Our food is your food."

Lazarus led the thirteen men, who Tom knew were mostly strangers here, toward the house. He had never seen such friendship or generosity. Tom felt instantly at home.

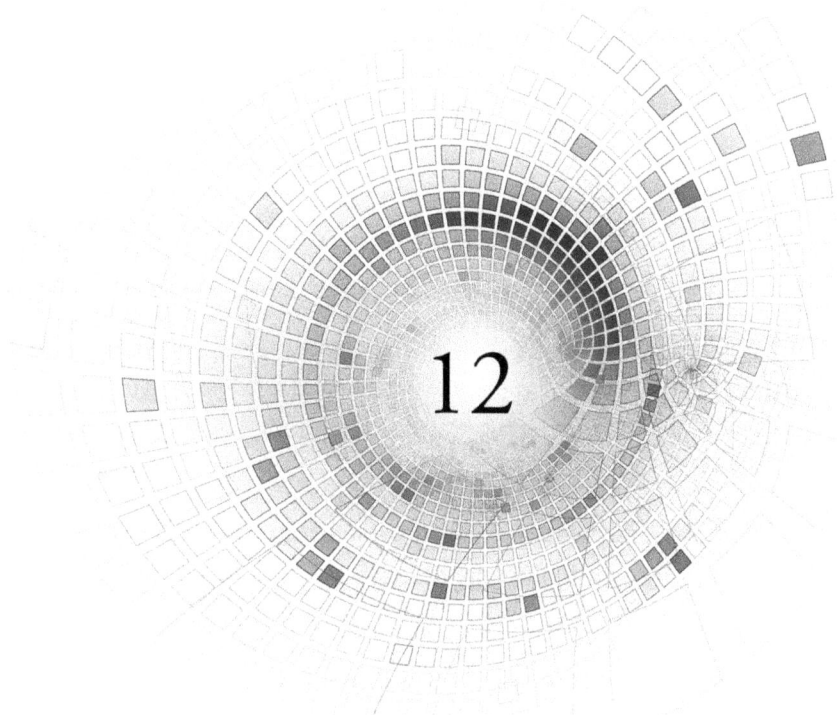

12

EXHALE

2005
2:56 P.M.
Arizona

Thirty seconds after David launched into the past in search of Tom, Captain Roberts, George Dwight and Jake Parrish entered Receiving Area Alpha. Sally watched as Captain Roberts, who looked out of place in his ancient garb and modern crew cut, was allowed free access to any and all classified equipment and material that had been transported to LightTech from the future. Roberts didn't seem to find anything useful in the cluttered room, but Sally was sure he simply couldn't make sense of anything he was seeing. This was the man her superiors were entrusting to save the world.

"Find anything useful?" Sally asked.

"Nothing of interest," he replied.

Nothing of interest? Roberts was a joke, Sally thought. Absolutely every device and sheet of notebook paper within the confines of the room was of interest.

"Of course, finding anything of interest is a moot point," Roberts said. "You and your science team have already combed through this equipment, correct?"

"Of course," Sally replied.

"Then you tell us. Is there anything of interest that might help our cause?" George asked in a tone that suggested she better tell the whole truth, nothing but the truth, so help her God.

Sally picked up one of the remaining time travel watches and handed it to Roberts. As Sally moved her arm toward Roberts, she worked the buttons expertly. Sally was in charge of the science team and held an executive position at LightTech, but had once been a formidable scientist herself. She had studied the watches and had made some discoveries she didn't want known—not yet anyway. She also wanted to protect her two prized scientists. She had been hard on them over the years, and she rarely saw eye to eye with them, but without them, none of this could ever have been possible. And she respected them greatly for that...especially David.

She knew that Roberts would kill them without hesitation. He was the kind of man built for killing, and after the years of training he'd received at LightTech, she imagined he was long overdue to draw blood. She couldn't let that happen, but she also had to make sure the blood spilled wasn't her own.

She pressed the final button on the watch, finalizing the changes she had swiftly made to Roberts's landing zone, placing him ten miles outside his intended target area. The plan was to give him a hike, and hopefully give David a little more time. *Beep, beep.* Sally froze. She didn't expect the watch to make any kind of confirmation noise. Roberts squinted at her, and she could have sworn his hand moved toward his knife. She worked hard not to panic in the following seconds. She knew that even the oddest change in facial expression might draw suspicion. A feeling of dead weight pulled down on her shoulders.

Would her attempts to slow Captain Roberts be found out? She glanced at the watch as casually as she could manage.

Thank God! Sally's tense muscles relaxed. "Top of the hour, gentlemen."

Sally handed the watch to Roberts. It was 3:00 p.m.

Roberts slipped the disguised watch onto his wrist and glanced at the face. "How's this doohickey work?" he asked, causing Sally to roll her eyes.

George and his assistant Jake looked at each other with a tinge of embarrassment. All the years of training and education, and Roberts was still a simple-minded buffoon. Sally saw the exchange and attempted not to smile.

"Push this button once to go back to the prearranged time and place. This has already been programmed," she explained, as she pointed to the appropriate buttons. "Push the same button twice to come back. That's it; even a seven year old could work the watch." Sally was pushing it, and she knew it.

Roberts checked his weapon quickly, making no attempt to hide his angry glare at Sally, as he walked to the center of the room and turned around. "Be back in a minute."

Captain Roberts pushed a button on the watch and waited to be transported back in time. Nothing happened. "It's the other button, the one above that," Sally said, her smirk impossible to hide.

Roberts pushed the correct button, and a blue pulse of light began to flash in front of him. Sally, George and Jake backed quickly out of the room and watched through the glass as Captain Roberts exploded back in time to kill their best and brightest.

Sally turned to George and asked, "So what's our backup plan if Roberts fails?"

"He won't fail," George said with feigned confidence.

"Nonetheless, I'm sure you have a backup plan. What is it?"

George motioned to Jake to explain. Jake stepped forward and said with forced casualness, "We've developed a series of miniature robots that can—"

"Robots? Cut the crap and tell me the truth." Sally didn't feel like being jerked around.

"No joke," Jake said, as he pushed his glasses further onto his nose. "The I-Fly 100 robotic insect series. Each is equipped to deliver a lethal sting that will mimic an allergic reaction. We've tested it on several employees already."

Sally was aghast.

"Not to worry, Sally," George added. "We have an antidote. No one died during the testing."

"The robots are designed to fly, look and act like common pests. They have built in facial recognition software and can operate for seven days using micro fuel cells and solar power."

"How quickly does the poison act?" Sally asked, her stomach knotting.

"Depends on the target," George said with pride. "If healthy, it could take up to two days."

"And you have these all ready to go?" Sally asked.

"Three of them, yes," George said. "You don't have a problem with this, do you?"

Sally was testing her facial control today. "Of course not. I just want to be kept informed from now on."

"Naturally," George said.

"You said you had three. One for David, one for Tom, who is the third for?" Sally asked.

"Captain Roberts, of course. Should he fail to return, his life is subject to termination as well," Jake explained with a smirk that said, 'Well, duh.'

Sally wished she could punch the little brown-nose, but instead said, "You'll let me know when your robots are ready to be sent back?"

"I promise," George said, with a toothy grin.

"Good," Sally said, wishing she had something more stinging to say. She pivoted expertly on her heels and strode away.

Jake looked at George and asked, "Think she's still with us?"

"Sally's a team player, Jake. Always has been," George said.

Jake watched Sally walk away.

George stretched his neck and then said with a smile, "Besides, if she becomes a problem, there's always robot number four."

Jake smiled.

30 AD
8:23 pm
Outskirts of Bethany, Israel

The laughter from Lazarus's home could be heard clear to the walls of Bethany. The past four hours since their arrival had been filled with storytelling, camaraderie and fine dining. The seating was a bit awkward, lounging around a short table from which people would scoop food with unleavened bread. It wasn't Peggy's, but Martha could cook like no other woman in ancient Israel—Tom was sure of that. He was smitten with their hosts. Lazarus was strong as an ox and as funny as a cat in water. Martha was an amazing hostess, never stopping to eat, drink or talk. The woman was a machine. And Mary...sweet Mary. Every time Tom's eyes met with hers, even for the briefest moment, his stomach would turn over. Tom hoped their stay at the home would last longer than most stops.

Half the group, including Tom, Jesus, Matthew, Peter, Judas, Lazarus and Mary sat in one room together, while the rest of the disciples dined in a room across the hall. David had gone outside more than an hour ago and had yet to return. Tom wondered if David had returned to the future again without telling him. Whatever the reason for David's disappearance, Tom wouldn't let it distract him from the incredible time he was having.

Martha buzzed between the rooms and through the corner of her eyes saw Mary laughing flirtatiously with Tom. "Having fun?" she asked Mary with a steely glare.

Jesus looked up at Martha, and his smile faded slightly. Trouble was brewing. "What troubles you, Martha?" he asked, as though clueless.

"Do you not care that my sister has left me to do all the work by myself?" Martha asked.

Jesus smiled pleasantly, "Martha...you're worried about so many things, but only one thing is needed."

Martha put her hands on her hips, waiting to hear what Jesus had to say. "Mary has chosen what is important, and we won't take that from her."

Martha's lips pursed tightly and her eyebrows sank.

"I only mean that my disciples are grown men. Let them tend to their own preparations and join us. We've hardly seen you," Jesus said with a genuine smile.

Martha softened a little. Jesus was getting through. "Stop this foolishness and join us, Martha," Lazarus piped in.

Martha lost any pleasantness and shouted, "I will not!"

But before she could retreat, Lazarus took her by the wrist. "We'll see about that!"

With a strong tug, he pulled her down onto his lap and began tickling her. The room erupted with laughter, while a furious Martha squirmed and screamed in anger, "Let go of me! Lazarus! You stop... HA! Right now! HA HA! Ahhh ha ha ha!"

Lazarus's tickling worked magic, and Martha's anger became undone. Tom watched the entire event unfold as though he were watching a brilliant movie. His own family had been as dysfunctional as they come. He was never close to his parents, and his brother was a moronic bully. The only person he was proud to call family had been snatched from him. Tom caught Mary's eyes, as thoughts of Megan entered his thoughts. He was consumed with guilt. The single reason for him being here, in the home of Lazarus, sharing dinner with friends and staring at a beautiful woman, was because Megan had died so many years ago.

And if she hadn't died? If Megan had survived? What would she look like now? Would they have children? Stuff stockings at Christmas? Celebrate birthdays? Tom's mind flooded with images of Megan, of their non-existent children, of the life he could have had.

The captivating eyes of Mary were too much for him to take. He couldn't betray the memory of Megan, not here, not like this. Tom stood and subtly wiped the wetness from around his eyes. "Where are you going, Tom? Martha was just about to serve us dessert!" Jesus said with a laugh.

Martha ribbed Jesus and said, "You hush!"

"I just need some fresh air, to clear my head," Tom said.

"Maybe you'll find David while you're out there? He's missing the fun!" Matthew shouted with a chuckle.

"I'll send him in if I see him," Tom said, as he left the room.

"Clear his head! As though it were dirty!"

Tom listened to the room laugh at his expense. He often forgot that modern expressions didn't always translate very well. It was something that he couldn't quite master, and it almost always got a laugh. Not that it bothered him, but he knew it bothered David.

Cool, crisp air filled Tom's lungs as he breathed deeply. His thoughts became clear, and the feelings of inner turmoil faded...if only for a moment.

"Thomas?" a sweet voice asked.

Tom turned to the voice, not realizing that his lips had spread into a smile and his eyebrows rose with anticipation. Mary smiled back at him.

"Why did you leave?" Mary asked.

"Just wanted to..." Tom wondered how he could say it right. "...forget some thoughts."

"Of me?"

"No."

"Then maybe...of someone else?"

Tom's heart sank. Mary could see right through him.

She frowned. "If your heart belongs to another, I'll—"

"I'm married," Tom said.

Mary appeared stunned and afraid. "I'm sorry. I did not mean to—"

"No, you... She... I *was* married. My wife died. You—you just remind me of her," Tom said with a smile, as his eyes began to water.

"If the sight of me hurts you, then I will hide myself from your eyes." Mary began to turn away.

"No," Tom said, as he placed his hand gently on Mary's cheek. "Don't."

Mary leaned her face into Tom's hand. He felt the warmth of her skin in his palm and on every ridge of his fingertips. He let his hand linger a moment, as he gazed into her mesmerizing dark brown eyes. "Go back inside," Tom said. "It's getting cold, and I should find David before it gets late. I'll return soon."

After squeezing Tom's hand with her own, Mary turned toward the house. "I'll be waiting."

The door closed behind her, as she entered the house. Tom turned away and felt a surge of guilt churn in his stomach. He had done it again. He took a step and tripped on a root. After recovering, he quickly kicked the root, as if it had caused him to stumble emotionally as well as physically. Tom glared at the root, while a pot full of separate feelings swirled and battled for supremacy in his head. He walked around the house, stomping his feet with every step. *Stupid women! Stupid root! And where the hell is David?!*

❧

Tom circled the home in search of David. If he had gone back to the future again, Tom was going to put his foot down. But before he could formulate the verbal beating he'd give David for skipping out of town, he saw something that made his heart palpitate. A body, lying in the grass! "David? David!"

Tom ran to the body sprawled face up. "David!"

He stood over the body, and looked into David's eye, which for a moment looked glossed over and empty. His fears were instantly suspended when David cracked a smile.

"You should see your face," he said.

"Damnit, David, I thought you were dead!"

David's smile grew wider. He enjoyed the panicked look on Tom's face. It was an expression Tom didn't wear too often, and it showed their friendship was still as strong as it had ever been. "I was just looking at the stars," David explained.

Tom glanced up, but paid no attention to the dazzling array of twinkling stabs of light above. "Everyone's wondering where you are."

"Have you ever seen so many stars?" David asked.

Tom looked up. David was right. The sky was awash with glowing pinpoints—so many that the sky seemed to be glowing. Tom took a seat in the grass next to David, keeping his eyes on the stars the entire time.

"In two thousand years, we'll have television, rocket ships, Cherry Pepsi and satellite radio, but...we won't have this. The world seems so much simpler now. So much smaller. So much more alone in the universe."

Tom looked over at David. He had never heard David speak like this, but he suspected where it was coming from. "You're thinking that maybe you're the one who's been blinded? Maybe I was right from the beginning, and Jesus is a fake?"

David took his attention off the stars and faced Tom. To Tom's surprise, David wasn't angry at all. "Something like that."

"We can go home if you want."

"Why would we go home? You haven't seen him die and rise from the grave yet," David said.

"What? But you just..."

"You think this is the first time in my life I've had doubts?" David let out a chuckle. "I used to believe in Jesus based on what is recorded in the Bible. Fully man, fully God, kind of a hard concept to grasp, so most of us picture him as human in body and God in mind and spirit..."

David sat up and continued, "But now I've met the man, and...he's so human it's frightening. Fully human, fully God... Let me ask you this. Have you ever seen the man sin? Even once?"

Tom sat up, intrigued by the line of questioning. "What do you consider to be sin?"

"Use your instincts."

"Well...he teases people a lot."

"I noticed...and it caused me some doubts, but have you ever felt bad about yourself or someone else as a result?"

"Umm...no. Have you?" Tom asked, truly curious now.

"Not once. I usually end up feeling better about myself and the other people he's teased. He's brought out parts of my personality I haven't seen since I was a child."

"He's a good guy, that's established. But can't you see through that? It's a façade, David. C'mon, seriously. I can find holes in everything we've seen him do so far."

"And you've conveniently missed some of the rather more spectacular events," David quipped.

"Yeah, I planned to be knocked unconscious on the boat. You got me pegged, David," Tom said, growing annoyed. "He's one hundred percent man, that's it. Nothing more. Even you have seen that."

"He's more of a man than I expected, but maybe that's the idea," David said.

"If he's God, why doesn't he just cure everyone in the world with a snap of his fingers. Why doesn't he stop all the injustice in the world, all the crime, war and famine? It's within his power, if he's God. So many people from the beginning of time to our time are suffering. What did they do wrong to deserve it?"

David took a deep breath and let it out slowly as he gazed back at the stars. "Why don't you ask him yourself?"

"That's a great idea. I will."

13

TOMORROW

30 A.D.

9:30 A.M.

Jerusalem, Israel

The streets of lower Jerusalem, slender and flanked by homes squished together like bricks, were abnormally calm on that morning. Typically, the smells of cooking food, ripening fruit and steaming leather filled the air. But today, only the bright roses and dusty road reached the nose. Jerusalem, the capital city of Israel, often buzzed like a beehive, but today—on the Sabbath, the day of rest—all was serene. Tom couldn't decide if it was the kind of peace felt on a warm day at the beach, or an ominous calm before the storm. Either way, he was determined to use the lull in activity to spring what he believed would be the question to undo Jesus's charade.

Much of Tom's previous night was spent in deep thought and careful plotting, inspired by David's insistence that he ask Jesus why bad things happen to good people. There had to be a way to catch Jesus, and Tom was sure he could find it. He hadn't planned on taking all night, but Jesus was a crafty adversary, and these things had to be carefully thought through. But his effort paid off, and he was confident his plan was bulletproof.

That morning Tom insisted they take a walk through the streets of Jerusalem. The sun was rising, the streets were quiet and he would have all the time he needed to find a helper. Of course, he never mentioned his ulterior motive for taking a stroll, but the idea was quickly supported, and they had set out, first thing that morning.

Tom's feet quickly grew heavy and his eyes were sagging a bit, but his plan was masterful, and the thought of executing it successfully gave him the energy to walk the hard streets, though his body protested and cried out for sleep. He strode next to Jesus, in front of David and the other disciples. He was waiting for the perfect moment, the supreme opportunity. He knew that in the city, he wouldn't have to wait long for the occasion to reveal itself.

He wasn't disappointed.

"Some coins for a blind man?" a decrepit man asked. His body was soiled like a dust-covered rag. The man looked toward the sky as he spoke in the direction of the approaching footsteps. "Please, I hear so many of you. One of you surely could share some money, some food…something. Please."

This was it! Tom hustled forward and stood between Jesus and the blind man.

Jesus stopped walking and looked at Tom with an expression of expectation. The rest of the group slowed to a stop behind Jesus. David moved around for a better look at what Tom was doing, face crisscrossed with concern, but he remained silent.

"Something troubles you?" Jesus asked Tom calmly.

"Explain something to me. Why do you allow this?" Tom asked, as he stabbed a finger at the blind man.

"What did he do to deserve this?" Tom said, and then he turned to the blind man and asked, "How long have you been blind?"

The blind man perked up, realizing he was being spoken to. He stood to his feet and stumbled toward the voice that had addressed him. "Since birth, Master."

"Since birth," Tom said. "What sin could he have done at birth to deserve this? Or maybe it was the sins of his parents? I'm not really sure how these sin things work."

Tom waited, sure that his line of questioning would make Jesus stumble. Surely, this was the hardest question addressed to Jesus thus far. Tom's mind raced with anticipation. He would finally outdo Jesus.

Jesus didn't miss a beat.

"Neither this man nor his parents sinned. This happened so that the work of God might be displayed in his life. As long as it is day, we must do the work of Him who sent me. Night is coming, when no man can work. While I am in the world, I am the light of the world," Jesus explained.

Tom stared, dumbfounded for a moment, and then he said, "You lost me. What's all that supposed to mean? Was that another parable?"

Jesus replied by spitting onto the dusty street. He bent down and rubbed the spit into the dirt, creating a small blob of oozing mud.

Tom worried that he had offended Jesus, and that the man was planning to fling the mud at him. Tom took a step back and prepared to duck. Perhaps Jesus was growing impatient with him? Maybe his constant meddling with Jesus's plans had gone on too long, and Jesus was going to expel him? Maybe Jesus would lose his temper and strike him? Tom only wished it were true. That would surely do more to discredit him than this dirty, blind man. He was both relieved and disappointed to see that the intended target for the mud was not himself, but the blind man.

Jesus took the mud and smeared it across the confused blind man's closed eyes. Tom's eyebrows furrowed with confusion and his nose crinkled with disgust. What in the world was Jesus doing?

"What is your name?" Jesus asked the blind man.

"Timothy…" the blind man said. Then the man's eyebrows shot high, and he sucked in a breath of air, as though he had just been astonished. He spoke again. "Are you…are you Jesus?"

"Yes, Timothy," Jesus said. "Now go. Wash in the pool of Siloam."

Timothy smiled and grew excited. "Yes, Master."

Timothy turned and began to hobble down the street. Jesus turned to John, one of the disciples whose kind eyes were hidden by thick eyebrows, and to Peter. He motioned with his head toward Timothy. The two instantly reacted and moved to help the man on his quest to wash in the pool of Siloam.

"That's it?" Tom asked, confused and slightly disturbed by the surreal event. "That's your answer?"

"He'll be back soon enough," Jesus said. "Wait and see for yourself. Or maybe I should rub some mud on your eyes as well?"

"Riiight, the whole, 'those with eyes that cannot see,' stuff again. I'm not blind. I can see fine." Tom said, frustrated. "And I can see right through you."

Jesus chuckled and began walking away. The other disciples followed him and smirked at Tom as they passed. David brought up the rear and joined Tom.

"Is it possible to get a straight answer from that man?" Tom asked, not expecting or desiring an answer.

"If you weren't deaf as well as blind, you might have understood the answer," David replied with a crafty smile.

Tom looked at David. "Funny."

David smiled and laughed, clearly pleased with how things had played out.

Tom stayed quiet. He'd let David have his moment. This wasn't over yet. Not by a long shot.

☙

After Timothy went to the pool of Siloam and washed as Jesus had instructed him, he ran up and down the now crowded streets shouting praises to God. For the first time in his life, he could see the sun, people's faces and dirt. But what was more amazing was that he understood everything he was seeing. He knew a bird was a bird, though he had never seen one in his life. With sight came vision, with vision came understanding—as though he had been able to see since the day he was born.

Timothy's loud praises didn't go unnoticed for long. Like vultures to a kill, a small group of men called Pharisees, the keepers of the law, descended on Timothy. The four men, all dressed in extravagant purple robes, were led by Tarsus, an old man with knobby knuckles and a graying beard. They stepped in front of Timothy. "You say you are the man who earlier today was begging here, at this corner?" Tarsus asked.

"I am the man," Timothy replied.

"How then were your eyes opened?" Tarsus asked.

"The man they call Jesus," Timothy said. "He put mud on my eyes and told me to wash at Siloam. I did as he said, and I can now see!"

"Where is this Jesus?" Tarsus asked, with a tinge of disdain in his voice.

"I—I don't know... I didn't see where he went," Timothy giggled with enthusiasm.

Tarsus gripped Timothy's arm tightly and said, "Come with us."

Timothy had never seen the look upon Tarsus's face before, but he understood its meaning clearly. He gave no objection and followed Tarsus.

Tarsus led Timothy inside a large, ornate building, which glowed brilliant white as sunlight streamed through several windows and reflected off the polished interior.

159

Timothy's eyes had a hard time adjusting to the light and the number of decorations, but he soon took in his surroundings. The roof was open, like an atrium, and sunlight illuminated the space. Encircling him were eight Pharisees, seated around the atrium, all possessing an arrogant scholarly quality. Timothy stood nervously at the center of the room, waiting for something, anything, to happen. Not a word had been said since the initial rapid-fire question-and-answer session that was launched upon Timothy.

"You say...with mud...he returned your sight?" Gamaliel, one of the younger Pharisees, asked the man.

"Yes, and I washed in—"

"The pool of Siloam. We know," Tarsus said abruptly. "The facts of the story have been covered, but there is more to be concerned about."

"Indeed," the prune faced Simeon said. "He performed this act on the Sabbath! He cannot be a man of God."

Silas, a monster of a man, with muscles as large as his ego, nodded his head and added, "No work is allowed on the Sabbath. Any child brought up in the law knows this, and certainly a man of God. He knowingly breaks the law in God's name."

"But...how then can a sinner, which he must of course be, do such...miraculous signs?" Gamaliel asked, and then he turned to Timothy. "What do you have to say of him? It was your eyes that were opened."

"He is a prophet," Timothy said, without missing a beat.

Tarsus reeled back like he had just been slapped. He looked back to the closed doors at the front of the building and yelled, "Let them in!"

The door swung open and an old man and woman entered. They looked horrified to be standing in this room, before these men. They stared at the floor, where they were sure not to make eye contact with the probing eyes surrounding them.

"This is your son?" Tarsus asked the old man, while pointing at Timothy.

The old man glanced up briefly, just enough to see Timothy standing a few feet away.

"Your son, the one that was blind, but now can see?" Tarsus added, as though the information might be useful in identifying Timothy.

"He is our son...and he was born blind, as you have said," the old man responded.

"And what of the man who gave him sight?" Tarsus asked.

"As for who opened his eyes, we will let him speak. He is of age; ask him," the old man said.

Silas turned to Timothy, clearly frustrated, and yelled, "We know this Jesus is a sinner!"

"Whether he is a sinner or not, I do not know," Timothy said, with a modicum of patience. "What I do know is that I was blind, and now I see!"

Simeon jumped in and shouted, "What did he do to you? How did he open your eyes?"

"I already told you!" Timothy shouted. "And you do not listen! Why do you want to hear it again? Do you want to become his disciples, too?"

Every Pharisee in the room gasped.

"You are Jesus's disciple?" Silas asked, aghast.

Simeon interrupted, "We are disciples of Moses. We know God spoke to Moses, but as for this fellow, we don't even know where he comes from."

Timothy had heard enough, and he couldn't stand to listen for another moment. He burst out with emotion, "You're unbelievable! All of you! You don't know where he comes from, yet he opened my eyes! We know that God doesn't listen to sinners. He listens to godly men, who do His will. Have you ever heard of a man born blind being healed? Have you ever? But here I stand before you, healed! If this man were not from God, he could do nothing!"

In all their years as Pharisees, not one of the men in the room had been spoken to in such a way. Silas leaned forward, his eyes twitching. He spoke between clenched teeth. "You were steeped in sin at birth; how dare you lecture us!"

Grabbing Timothy by the back of his robe like an angry lioness to its cub, Tarsus dragged him violently toward the door.

Timothy crashed through the door and onto the street, skinning his knees and tearing his hands on small stones. A number of passersby stopped in their tracks and watched as Tarsus burst from the doorway and yelled, "This man is in sin! Stay clear of his wretched influence!"

Every soul on the street took a step away from Timothy, and for the first time he could see the rejection he had experienced his entire life as a useless blind man. Timothy looked back. The eight Pharisees were moving toward him, fists clenched tightly. He saw his mother weeping into the chest of his father, who mouthed a single word to Timothy, 'RUN.'

Timothy had never run in his life. He wasn't even sure he knew how. But he had to try. If the Pharisees didn't kill him, they'd surely incite the crowd to do it for them. He pulled himself up and stood to his feet. Just as Tarsus raised a fist to knock Timothy back down, Timothy surged forward, running.

Though in dire circumstances, Timothy smiled. Jesus had not only fixed his eyes, but also gave him the legs to run. He looked over his shoulder one last time and saw a growing crowd, led by the angry Pharisees beginning to pursue him. He prayed God would make him fast. He prayed to God to save him again.

❧

As the sun lowered in the sky, Tom, David and Jesus walked the streets of Jerusalem debating as they now frequently did. Everything was fair game. The Jewish Law, morality, what was sin and what wasn't, and the natural world; Tom covered every subject at least three times and each time from a different angle. Whenever his point would be proven wrong or ineffective, he would bend his statements to mean something else entirely, as he worked to find flaws in Jesus's replies. Conversations like these were normally fast, intelligent debates that the other disciples either grew annoyed with quickly or could scarcely follow. The three decided it was best to take such conversations outside.

"I don't understand why you don't answer my questions straightforward, without all the riddles," Tom said.

"Didymus, you are without doubt the smartest of the twelve," Jesus said.

Tom wasn't even flattered by the compliment. He just made a face that said, 'no kidding.'

Jesus continued, "Yet you fail to grasp even the simplest answers. Why do you think that is?"

Tom didn't respond. Jesus was talking in riddles again, and Tom wasn't going to play that game.

Jesus turned to David. "You understand what I teach. Tell me, what is the difference between you and Tom, that he doesn't understand, and yet you do."

David thought for a moment and said, "Well, ahh, I would say... I search my heart for the answers. Tom searches his mind. I have faith. He doesn't."

Jesus nodded in agreement.

"Why not just make David the twelfth disciple?" Tom asked.

"How much more powerful a statement will it be when you come to believe in me?" Jesus replied.

"*If*, not when," Tom said. "So I'm the challenge then? Make a believer out of me, and you can make a believer out of anyone?

"Something like that," Jesus replied.

"Well then, you're God! Make a believer out of me!" Tom said with a sarcastic tongue, whipping the air.

Jesus looked at David with an amused eyebrow raised.

"C'mon, hit me with it!" Tom shouted. "Hit me, oh Lord, and I shall believe in thee—"

Whump!

A man blindsided Tom, and both fell to the ground in a sprawl of arms and legs. David and Jesus nearly burst out laughing, but moved in to see if the men were all right.

Timothy stood up quickly, dusting off his robe and apologizing quickly. "Sorry, masters. Sorry." He was about to continue running when Jesus called out and stopped him. "Timothy, wait."

Tom heard the name, as David helped him up. He looked over and saw Timothy. As their eyes met, Tom realized that they were connecting; Timothy was looking Tom right in the eyes. Timothy was seeing. Tom nearly fell back down, but David held on tight. Tom later thought that his shocked facial expression must have been confusing to Timothy, who had never seen before, but right now, he was distracted by a sudden shift in Timothy's eyes. Timothy was no longer staring at Tom. He was looking just beyond Tom, and his demeanor became that of a scared rabbit.

Tom followed Timothy's eyes and saw a large, angry crowd, led by Tarsus, Simeon and Silas. Tom didn't know who these men were, but they looked important. He looked to David, planning to ask, but kept his question to himself, as he noticed David's body language. David was stepping back, away from the crowd.

Jesus dusted Timothy off with a pleased expression, as though the encroaching mob did not exist. He quipped, "Your eyes are working, and still you walk like a blind man."

"Sorry, Master, I—" Timothy said, as he tried to move away.

But Jesus held him still and asked, "Do you believe in the Son of Man?"

Timothy stopped trying to move. He stood still and looked Jesus in the eyes.

"Who is he? Tell me, and I'll believe," Timothy said, having not yet recognized Jesus.

"You have seen him," Jesus said. "In fact, he speaks with you now."

"Jesus...?" Timothy's face beamed as he recognized the man who had healed his blind eyes. "Lord, I believe!" Timothy said, as he knelt before Jesus and bowed his head.

Tom had little time to hypothesize about what had happened before he was snapped out of his daze by Jesus's loud voice addressing the crowd, who had stopped only a few feet away. "For judgment I have come into this world, so that the blind will see..."

Jesus looked Tom in the eyes and continued, "And those who see will become blind."

"Are we blind, too?" Simeon asked, with as much intimidation as he could muster.

"If you were blind, you would not be guilty of sin; but now that you claim you can see, your guilt remains," Jesus replied, with just the hint of a smile.

The Pharisees got a strange look on their faces. Tom could see that they had been defeated in verbal combat as quickly as he was normally. He knew that for these men to continue the conversation would be futile and would reveal to the crowd that Jesus had beaten them. It seemed the strangers knew this, too. It took ten seconds for one of them to speak.

Simeon squinted. "Are you the one called Jesus?" Simeon asked, changing the subject and dodging a bullet.

"I am."

"We'll be seeing you again," Tarsus said, as he and the other Pharisees turned and pushed their way through the crowd, which dispersed quickly for lack of action.

Jesus nodded in agreement, then turned and walked away. Bewildered, Tom turned to David and said, "I don't think I understand half of what that man says."

David smiled. "I don't think they do either," he said, as he watched the three Pharisees pound away. He turned to Tom and said, "You should hear it in the King James Version."

Tom smirked and looked at the retreating Pharisees, "Who are they?"

"Pharisees."

"They seem to be on the same page as me," Tom said.

David's eyes grew wide. "Stay away from them, Tom. I mean it."

"Why?" Tom asked.

"Think of them as ultra-right wing Republicans," David said.

"*You're* a Republican," Tom pointed out.

"That's not the point," David said. "Left or right doesn't matter. What does matter is that they're the legalistic fringe of the current culture. They're well read, well-spoken and intelligent, but clouded by tradition, and they will defend their beliefs to the point of violence."

"So they're evil?"

David sighed and said, "No. Maybe some. 'Misguided' might be a better word. But others choose a different path. Look, let's just say that nothing good can come from you speaking to *those* Pharisees."

"Afraid they might help me?"

"Aren't you forgetting something?"

"What?"

David looked at Timothy, who was talking with Jesus.

"Timothy can see," David said.

"I was set up," Tom replied without pause, as though it were a foregone conclusion.

"How was Jesus supposed to know what you had planned?"

Tom paused and then said, "You warned him...didn't you? You knew I would try something and came to the same conclusion I did, that if I chose a person for Jesus to heal, someone that wasn't working with Jesus, that he couldn't heal that person. But you warned him, and he had this Timothy pretend to be a blind man along the route he knew we'd take through the city! He knew I'd pick the first beggar we came to!"

"Ugh. Now you're being paranoid." David fumed, as he shook his head and stormed away.

"I'm not paranoid... I'm... I'm..." Tom became distracted by the three figures walking away, their ornate robes dancing in the wind. These Pharisees might be useful. They were the only people who seemed to make sense in this backward culture. Tom decided to find out more about them. Maybe they could reveal the chink in Jesus's armor?

14

BEGINNING

30 A.D.
7:25 A.M.
Jerusalem, Israel

Tom was up and moving at the crack of dawn. He knew it was the only way he could see the Pharisees without being noticed or questioned extensively by David. He worked his way through the streets of Jerusalem, which he was proud to say he had nearly memorized. Finding his way to the upper-city, street-side home of Tarsus was no problem.

Not having been to the upper city too often, he had forgotten how stunning it was. Not at all like the lower city, full of beggars, blind men and the pungent odor of filth. Here, it was clean. The homes were spaced apart nicely, with landscaping and statue decorations. It was like stepping out of the middle ages and into the glory of Rome.

A pang of guilt struck Tom in the stomach as he approached and admired the smooth marble home. He had convinced himself he wasn't betraying his friends. He wasn't plotting against them, just gathering information. David was always one step ahead of him, and it was time to educate himself. He would learn from his own sources what the future was going to bring. Tom knew that by the way David glared at the Pharisees whenever they crossed paths, they must have something to do with a resistance to Jesus's claim to be God. He figured they must know something that David didn't. They must know, and perhaps be able to prove, that Jesus was a fake. Tom was convinced of it.

He knocked on the hand-carved wooden door. No answer. He banged harder and thought he heard some movement inside. *Crash!* Something fell over, and seconds later, the door flung open. "What? What is it?" Tarsus asked, with his eyes half shut. "Every time I send Silva to the market..."

"Sorry, did I wake you?" Tom asked.

"Yes, yes. Now what do you— Wait, I know you... I've seen you with—"

"Jesus, yes, I've been traveling with him."

"Yes. One of his intolerable disciples. Be gone with you, or I'll fetch the Romans!" Tarsus fumed.

"Wait, please. Hear what I have to say," Tom said. "I think we have some opinions in common."

Tarsus eyed Tom, "Meaning?"

"I'm as unconvinced by Jesus's claims as you are," Tom said.

Tarsus scrunched his lips together. "Explain yourself. How would you account for the miracles people say he does?"

"Sleight of hand, deception, some might call it magic," Tom said, as though it were nothing impressive.

Tarsus's upper lip snarled. "Magic! The black arts! You mean to tell me, you, a disciple of this man, believes him to be demon possessed?"

Tom wasn't sure how Tarsus had made the leap from simple magic to demon possession, but reckoned these primitive people had yet to be introduced to the illusionary arts that were more science than magic. But if the modern day equivalent of a magic-using con artist was demon possession, so be it.

"Yes," Tom, said plainly.

Tarsus smiled a toothy grin. "Indeed... Perhaps you would like to speak with some colleagues of mine, as well?"

"I would," Tom said.

"Come in, come in. Let me dress, and I will take you to them," Tarsus said with a full-blown smile.

Tom stepped into the home and closed the door behind him.

☙

Tom managed to sneak back without waking anyone up. He had learned a lot, but not enough. He arranged to meet with the Pharisees again, and they had all agreed to keep their meetings a secret. Tom acted like nothing was different, but he felt different, somehow. He felt like everyone was watching him, like everyone knew. Maybe David was right; he was being paranoid.

Tom was sitting on the hard stone floor of Solomon's Colonnade, which was a row of columns on the east side of the Temple. He had come to the Temple with David, Peter, Matthew, Judas and Jesus, but he had remained distant. He now sat ten feet away, leaning against one of the tall columns, admiring the view, lost in thought. Every time he came to the Temple, he found himself captivated by the beauty of the structure. Truly, his ancestors were master craftsmen. He felt that if there was a God and God actually needed a house, this would be it.

From the colonnade, Tom could see the outer walls and columns of the Court of Gentiles, which he knew was full of merchants selling doves, sheep and cattle for sacrifice. There would be Jewish pilgrims from all over Israel and the Roman Empire, money-changers, scribes and Pharisees. Tom calculated that the entire area took up around thirty-five acres of land. Beyond the Court of the Gentiles, no non-Jew was allowed.

Just beyond the Court of the Gentiles, was the Court of the Women, which was surrounded by beautifully carved columns. On the east side of this court were thirteen trumpet shaped containers, which Tom had learned were for voluntary money offerings. The floors were smooth with two-foot square tiles that led toward a grand, curved, fifteen step staircase. At the top of the staircase was the showstopper of the Court of the Women, the Nicanor Gate, which, when opened, led to the Court of Israel, where only Jewish men were allowed. The gate was a twenty-foot tall, arched doorway with shimmering, solid bronze doors, the glow of which could be seen reflecting on other portions of the temple.

However pleasing to the eye the temple was, there was always an ominous sign of the times, looming high above and attached to the temple. The Antonia, a Roman fortress, which towered above the temple, was constantly patrolled by spear wielding guards whose steel, scale armor and blood-red military cloaks could be seen from a distance. The fortress was plain in appearance but built of thick stone bricks. From its four towers, an enemy army could easily be kept at bay. During recent years, Tom learned it was where Pilate, the local Roman governor was housed. He wondered how people could worship or even believe in God while under such an obvious show of Roman power. Where was their God now?

"Tom, come join us," Jesus said.

Tom stood up, not wanting to act any guiltier than he already had, and he approached his laughing friends, who were sitting on the ground, leaning against the smooth, white columns, engrossed in conversation. "And that works?" Judas asked Matthew.

"Without fail!" Matthew replied. "One look at the girth I lug around and most people believed I was capable of the act!"

"Your pockets must have been heavy with riches," Judas said, wide eyed.

"It's true, they were. But that was the life I lived before," Matthew said, looking slightly ashamed. "Now I'm..." Matthew paused and seemed transfixed by something behind Judas. "...hoping that mob isn't going to be trouble."

"What?" Judas asked, perplexed by the statement.

Matthew stood to his feet quickly and pointed toward the Court of the Gentiles. A crowd was quickly approaching. Peter and Matthew jumped in front of Jesus, forming a formidably tall and wide wall. They had become experts at it over the past years. The mob stopped at the human blockade.

"State your business, and be quick about it. You're interrupting my time in the sun," Matthew said.

A man from the crowd yelled, "We've come for Jesus, the demon-possessed man!"

Matthew and Peter couldn't help but smile. "I'm afraid you've come to the wrong place," Peter said. "No one here is demon possessed."

Another man from the crowd, less convinced than the first said, "You see! I told you demons couldn't heal the eyes of the blind!"

"We know you are his disciples," the first man said. "Let us see him with our own eyes. Let him tell us he is not possessed."

"I tell you the truth," Jesus said, as he walked around Peter and Matthew, into the view of the crowd. "I am not possessed."

An honest looking man stepped from the crowd instantly, but was blocked from moving too far forward by Matthew's thick hand. The honest man stopped and said, "The countryside is torn. How long will you keep us in suspense? Please, if you are the Christ, tell us plainly."

Tom turned to David and whispered, "See, I'm not the only one who can't understand the man."

Cautiously scanning the area for hidden dangers, Tom's gaze fell on David. Tom watched, as David remained silent, studying everything about the situation. Tom observed David's facial expressions change from confusion to enlightenment. He could see in David's eyes that he knew what was happening, what was going to happen. Before he could ask David what he knew, the crowd regained Tom's attention when their words became familiar. They had called Jesus demon possessed.

The words he was hearing, the confusion of these people, were seeds he had planted. Apparently, the secret meeting with the Pharisees had gone well and they had taken his advice. The fact that Jesus was so hard to understand to a large number of people might be the evidence that Jesus was a magician. Upon hearing this from Tom, they translated magician to demon possessed, and while Tom did not believe in demons as much as he did not believe in God, he let them believe what they wanted. As long as they could mobilize people into proving it was true.

Lowering Matthew's arm, Jesus addressed the crowd, "I did tell you, but you did not believe. The miracles I do in my Father's name speak for me, but you do not believe because you are not my sheep."

Jesus began walking around the crowd. He continued, "My sheep listen to my voice; I know them, and they follow me."

A man in the crowd flinched as Jesus took hold of his face, looked him in the eyes and said, "I give them eternal life, and they will never perish; no one can snatch them out of my hand."

Jesus let go of the man and walked back toward Matthew and Peter. "My father, who has given them to me, is greater than all; no one can snatch them out of my Father's hand."

Jesus, now standing next to Matthew, turned and faced the crowd directly and said, "The Father and I...are one."

The crowd exploded. Someone yelled, "He claims to be the Father! He speaks the words of demons!"

The honest man bent down to the ground and picked up a loose stone. "Let's show him what becomes of blasphemers! Stone him!"

The crowd shouted with agreement and searched the ground for stones to hurl. Matthew and Peter pursed their lips and tightened their muscles, bracing for the inevitable. Judas walked backward slowly, past David and Tom, and shuffled away toward the temple. His exit went unnoticed as everyone's attention was on the angry horde. The crowd, now armed with stones, paused, waiting for someone to throw the first stone.

David leaned over to Tom and whispered, "Be ready, this might be a close shave."

Jesus addressed the crowd, showing no fear, "I have shown you many great miracles from the Father. For which of these do you stone me?"

The honest man stepped forward, "Not for your miracles, for your blasphemy! I wasn't sure, but now I know. A mere man is claiming to be God the Father, himself!"

"Is it not written in your law, 'I have said…'?"

Tom whispered to David as Jesus addressed the crowd, "Why do I get the feeling you know what's going to happen?"

"I've read the book, remember?"

"Well then, what's going to happen?"

"I don't know."

"But you just said, 'I've read the book.'"

"All the Bible says about this moment in time is, "He escaped their grasp.""

"That could mean anything."

"Well, be ready for anything."

"Great."

Tom looked back toward Jesus, who was finishing his statement to the crowd, "…that you may know and understand that the Father is in me, and I in the Father."

Jesus turned and walked toward Tom and David, seemingly secure in the fact that he made his point to the crowd that was now analyzing his words.

"That could have gone worse," Tom said to Jesus.

"How fast are you, Tom?" Jesus asked.

"What? Why?" Tom was dumbfounded by the right-field question.

"Run…" Jesus said through his lips, without moving his jaw.

"What?" Tom's brow wrinkled with suspicion.

Jesus leaned in. "My time has yet to come. Run!"

"Stone him!" yelled a man from the crowd.

All at once, the crowd raised the hands full of rocks to the sky, prepared to pelt the blasphemous Jesus. Like an Olympic runner on the starting line, Jesus was off and up to speed in seconds; Tom and David ran right behind him.

With each step forward pushing David faster and faster, he realized he was in the best shape of his life. Before, he couldn't have run ten feet at this speed', without having a heart attack. The feeling of health and vigor spurred him on even faster and he sped past Tom and Jesus.

The crowd quickly made their way around Peter and Matthew, who only received a few bumps and bruises for their efforts. They pursued Jesus, Tom and David toward the temple, toward the crowded and busy Court of the Gentiles.

ca

David, Tom and Jesus bowled through the Court of the Gentiles at full speed. Dove feathers burst into the air as the captive birds flapped their wings in a panic, brought on by the noise of Tom running into a moneychanger's table, spilling coins everywhere and inciting a near riot of looting. The ensuing chaos bought some distance between them and the stone-wielding crowd, but the lead would not last long.

Jesus led the way into the Court of the Women, beneath a sign in Greek, which read: *No foreigner is allowed within the balustrades and embankment about the sanctuary. Whoever is caught will be personally responsible for his ensuing death.*

Tom swallowed hard as he ran beneath and read the sign, which he had never noticed before, as he couldn't previously read Greek. Could he pass as an ancient

Jew? He wasn't sure. He didn't believe in God the Father. He didn't know all the ancient Jewish traditions. He wasn't even from this time. Crap. Tom felt like they were dooming themselves.

The few women that were in the Court of the Women paid little attention to Jesus, David and Tom, as they had slowed to a casual walk before entering the open court. The three made their way across the courtyard and up the curved flight of fifteen stairs that lead to the Nicanor Gate. They paused at the gate.

"This is a dead end," Tom said.

"Through these gates is the house of my Father, who can never die."

"It's just an expression," Tom said.

"And you say I speak in riddles," Jesus replied.

David rolled his eyes, pulled open the large bronze door and shoved the two men inside. They were now in a narrow hall, which was empty at this time of day and which led to the Court of Israel. There was a lower wall on either side, maybe ten feet tall. Tom ran to the wall and attempted to jump to the top. His hands struck the wall a foot below the top. David and Jesus ran to help him up as the voices of an approaching, outraged posse began to echo through the closed doors of the Nicanor Gate.

"We're not going to make it," David said, wondering exactly how Jesus was going to escape the crowd's grasp. Could the Bible be wrong? None of the book's authors were present—maybe they got the secondhand story wrong?

"Give me your hand," came the voice of Judas.

Everyone looked up. Judas was on top of the wall, thrusting his arm down. In all the excitement, they had completely forgotten about him. Tom wasted no time and locked wrists with Judas. He was quickly hoisted to the top of the wall. He and Judas both threw their arms down, and Jesus and David were quickly pulled up and over, just as the Nicanor Gate burst open.

The four watched from above as their pursuers rushed through the hallway and filled the Court of Israel like water streaming out of a spilled bucket. The noise attracted the attention of Levites standing guard in the next courtyard, the Court of the Priests. Four Levites, dressed in pointed hats and robes that contained pockets large enough to hold books of the law, entered the Court of Israel. These men were only slightly physically imposing, but carried all the authority of God, when it came to defending the temple. They could and would kill, should a crime against the temple be committed. And the crowd knew it. To continue in their effort would be suicide. Granted, they could have overpowered the Levites, but doing so would mean certain death under Jewish law. It would also be an unforgivable crime against God Himself.

The mob skidded to a stop in front of the Levites, who didn't have to say a word. Every good Jew knew that the Levites would kill in defense of the Temple, if need be. Roman law forbade murder, even in defense of the temple, but crimes such as these were often overlooked. One by one, the people dropped their stones, fell silent and shuffled back out of the Court of Israel.

Jesus, David, Judas and Tom watched as the crowd dissipated. Now safe, they all relaxed and laughed with nervous tension.

"I fear Jerusalem may be too dangerous for us now," Jesus said.

"Not as long as we have Judas around to pull us out of trouble," Tom said, as he smacked Judas on the back. "Good job."

Judas smiled. He had overcome the piercing fear that had caused him to flee in the first place, and he had saved his friends' lives. He was changing for the better. He could feel it. No longer would fear control his life. *Brave. Reliable. Proud.* These were the words Judas would use to describe himself from now on. He was sure people would see him differently; treat him differently. Things were finally looking brighter for Judas.

15

BUILDING

2005

5:32 A.M.

Arizona

Sally woke up with a start and nearly flung herself onto the rugged industrial floor. Her eyes stung and her mouth was stale, sticky with paste-like saliva. With her nerves shot and her mind distracted by the events of the past days, one hour of sleep was all she could manage. The sleep was welcome, but the fact that she had awakened on her own was very disappointing. She had given orders to be wakened should Tom, David or Roberts return. But she was alone in the room, and no one had come to give her good news, which meant the worst possible news.

Something had gone wrong in the past. It had been hours since Captain Roberts left the present. Had he succeeded, Roberts would have returned to within an hour of his departure. She knew he was either dead or had gone rogue. And she knew what that meant for Tom and David.

Sally stood and stretched. Her back ached. The sturdy loveseat in her office wasn't designed with comfortable snoozing in mind. Her cream-colored office was expansive, meagerly decorated and full of space, but it had become cluttered overnight. Sally spent most of the previous evening riffling through schematics, studying notes and memorizing the functions of the watch, which she now knew to be more intricate than anyone had previously conceived. If only David knew what she knew now. Then again, maybe he did.

Sally dressed quickly, though not in her typical power suit and high heels. She finished the knots on her black running shoes, tightened the belt on her skin-hugging, charcoal pants and straightened her raven hued turtleneck, which showed the curves of her body in a way no one at LightTech had ever seen. She felt silly, dressing like this, like some kind of spy or ninja, black from head to toe, but she knew the main lights would be out for another hour, and she would need to be stealthy if she was going to make it in and out of George's office in one piece.

She tied a black scarf around her mouth, nose and forehead. She looked in the mirror. Her reflection looked like an obsidian sculpture, whose eyes had been colored with a burning brown paint. Ridiculous. She strapped a dark backpack to her shoulders, peeked out her office door and crept out into the dark hallway.

It was a ten-minute trek from Sally's office, on the lower level, to George's office, five floors up. She couldn't use the elevator; there was an armed doorman, even at this time of night. She could have easily walked past him and ordered him to leave his position, but she hoped anonymity would allow her to keep her job, and her life, when this was all over.

She broke a sweat by the fifth floor. She ran every day and she was in perfect shape, but the nervous tension gripping her muscles made every movement a struggle. It was exhausting. She crept to the stairwell door. George's office was just down the hall, but Sally knew this would be the most difficult portion of her covert operation. George, ever the paranoid, had two guards posted outside his office, at all times. But Sally knew George wasn't just being paranoid, he was being cautious. No one puts two armed guards outside a room unless they have something inside to protect. This was why Sally believed the office would contain the robot insects Jake had so proudly described. She would steal the little bugs and make it look like corporate espionage. They had plenty of tough competition that wouldn't be above such a stunt. Hell, even LightTech had engaged in theft and espionage before.

Security was impregnable from the outside in. Getting into the LightTech facility was pretty much impossible. But once inside, security was lax. Though from Sally's perspective, security was downright impervious. She peered down the hallway. *Damn.* The guards were wide-awake and ready for action. She felt sure she could outrun Chuck, the chubbier of the two guards, but the other man, Sean, looked to be in Herculean shape. Probably took his job too seriously. He might be a problem. The only weapon Sally had brought was a five-year-old stun gun she took when she went running, and it could only fire once.

The sound of approaching footsteps from the right caught her attention, and Sally quickly and silently closed the hallway door so that only a sliver of space remained to peer through. She glanced at her watch. *Damn again!* The building would be flooded with employees in a half hour. She ducked back as a body moved past the door, toward George's office and the guards.

Sally watched through the small opening. It was Jake...and he was waving the guards away.

"Chuck, Sean, you guys can take off. Go get a coffee or something. I'll only be a few minutes," he said.

Chuck looked confused. "But Director Dwight ordered us to stay until he—"

"Yes, yes, but who delivered the order?" Jake asked with a raised eyebrow.

"Well, technically, you did, sir."

Sean crossed his buff arms, trying to look like an authority figure and said, "Sir, may I remind you that it's against regulations to—"

"And now I'm telling you to go. Consider it an executive order. Take a walk. Come back in a few minutes. I won't be long."

"But—"

"Now," Jake insisted with a cold gaze.

"Yes, sir," Chuck said. "But just for a few minutes."

Chuck and Sean turned and headed toward the opposite end of the hallway, away from Sally. *Thank you, Jake!* Sally was thrilled by Jake's advantageous appearance, but wasn't thrilled with how he so easily issued orders with executive power. What else could Jake be doing without LightTech knowledge? Jake entered the office, and the door slowly moved toward the closed position. This was Sally's chance! The two guards were nearing the end of the hallway, which turned left, but if she waited, the door might close and lock. She had to risk it.

She opened the door and breezed into the hallway, mixing with the shadows and moving like a cat. The guards didn't hear or sense a thing as they rounded the corner and disappeared into the adjacent hallway.

The door, still ten feet away, was only three inches from closing, and it was moving swiftly. Sally bolted forward and dove to the slick linoleum floor. She hit hard and the air was thrust from her lungs, but she slid quickly. She reached out as the last shard of light from inside the office began to shrink away. The door bounced gently, without a sound and began to reopen. Sally rolled onto her back and caught her breath; she had caught the door with her index finger only a centimeter before it closed.

She returned to her feet and entered the room silently, stun gun armed and ready for a fight. But the office was empty. Jake was nowhere to be seen. The room was pristine and nearly barren. A large desk sat in the center of the room, one chair behind it and two chairs in front. That was it. Sally didn't know where Jake had gone, but she didn't have time to figure it out. She launched into the desk drawers.

Empty. Empty. *Empty.* Where the hell did George keep his secrets? He'd want them within sight of his place behind the desk. He'd want them hidden, but easily accessible. Sally pulled out the plush leather desk chair, which seemed heavier and sturdier than most, and sat down. There was nothing to look at. Just three bare walls and a door.

She was about to give up when she instinctively reached down and pulled a lever, which allowed the black leather office chair to recline. Sally stared at the chrome light fixture on the ceiling. It was very plain, but it was something else about the ceiling that caught her attention. The light in the room was changing. It was getting brighter. Sally leaned forward and snapped her head to the right. The wall had opened up without a noise.

She stood and gawked at the newly discovered chamber. Then she felt a moment of envy: *I don't have a secret room.* But this wasn't any ordinary room—far from it. She stepped into the alcove, and after absorbing its contents, she came to the startling conclusion: *George has a secret lab!* The laboratory was forty feet long and lined with robotic equipment, carefully labeled vials of liquid and even more carefully stored computer components. Jake was at the rear of the room with his back to Sally. He hadn't heard a thing. Sally tiptoed toward him, stun gun in hand.

She walked to within four feet of Jake's back. She didn't want to miss. She felt her face turning purple as she held her breath, frightened to make even the slightest sound. If he moved, she might miss. Even if only one of the electrodes that would launch from the stun gun missed its mark, she would be done. She thumbed the stun gun's trigger and pushed it down. *Click.* Nothing happened. *Click, click, click.* Nothing. *Damn!*

Jake whirled around and gasped. Apparently, not only was Sally's outfit stealthy, but also quite frightening. "Who—who are you?" Jake asked.

Sally didn't say a word, in part, because she didn't want her voice recognized, but she also didn't know what to say. "What do you want?" Jake asked, his voice shaking.

Sally could see his nervous eyes wandering. He was sizing her up. Looking for anything to make sense of this dark figure that had frightened him. He found it in her eyes. The steely gaze. The penetrating eyes. "Sally?"

Sally froze. He had seen through her disguise. She knew Jake didn't think fondly of her. She knew he was stronger than she was. And she knew she had to strike first before Jake came to the full realization of what was happening. Sally was going rogue, and Jake was the only one in her way.

Whack!

Sally acted on instinct, punching Jake in the throat. She had taken a self-defense class five years ago, and she was amazed at how quickly it came back and how well the techniques taught for defense worked just as well for assault.

Jake's legs crumpled below him and he fell to the floor, as his hands clenched his throat. He forcefully sucked air into and out of his lungs as blood rushed to his head. Sally was horrified at what she had done, but she quickly returned her attention to the task at hand. She turned and looked at the countertop where Jake had been working. She saw two cases and opened them both. The first contained four syringes of what she assumed was the antidote to the robot's poison. She opened the second case: empty. Though from the impressions made in the protective foam, this is where they had kept the insect robots, four of them. The fact that they were gone meant that Sally was too late. She would have to alter her plans.

After snagging two syringes, Sally put them in her pocket and stepped over Jake, who was still writhing on the floor. She smiled. She was going to make it. Getting out should be no problem without the guards at the door.

"GUARDS!" Jake's throat had opened up momentarily, and his lungs managed to take in enough air to get out one loud scream.

Sally glared at Jake, and he crawled backward, away from her rage, away from those eyes. His face was two shades of crimson as he struggled to suck in another breath. The door to the office was kicked open as Sean and Chuck burst in, weapons drawn. Sally was caught.

"Freeze!" Sean yelled.

"Move and you're dead!" Chuck shouted, as his sweaty index finger twitched nervously on the trigger of his gun.

Sally's mind raced for a solution. She knew it was only a matter of seconds before she would be killed.

℘

Jesus had led the disciples clear out of the region called Judea, where he believed their lives to be at risk. He made it clear that it was not his time to die, and the entire group, including Tom and David, retreated to the region of Samaria, just north of Judea. Rather than stay in a city, the group had set up shop under the stars and had been camping for a week.

Tom and Judas lay in the grass, far enough away from the campfire to see the bright stars above. The conversation around the fire that night hadn't been as jovial as Tom would have liked. In fact, everything since leaving Judea had seemed more somber, more serious. Tom and Judas had tired of the seriousness and had left the group to talk about the future.

David joined them soon after, waiting just long enough, Tom suspected, so that it wouldn't seem obvious that he was keeping tabs on him and Judas. Tom knew the name Judas held negative connotations in the future, something to do with betrayal, but that was about as believable as Jesus being the Son of God. David sat on the grass next to Tom and looked up at the sky.

"They're beautiful, aren't they? Like sparkling gems floating in the sky," Judas said with a smile.

Tom chuckled. He couldn't help himself.

"What's so funny?" Judas asked. "What do you think they are?"

David cleared his throat and gave Tom a look that said: 'Don't you dare.'

"I think," Tom started, with a semi-sarcastic tone, "I think they are a gift from God, to light our path at night."

"The truest words to exit your mouth yet," Jesus said, as he approached from the campfire. "Are you not cold over here, away from the fire?"

"We're fine," David said.

Judas sat up and perched himself on his elbows. "It was getting too hot by the fire."

"And the conversation was dull," Tom said with a smirk.

Jesus smiled. "I fear it will be the last dull moment for some time to come."

"Are we leaving?" Tom asked.

"Not yet," Jesus answered.

"Jesus!" a voice yelled from the dark.

A single torch light cut through the darkness, as an out of breath man ran toward the group. "I'm looking for the one called Jesus. Have any of you seen him?"

Jesus walked to the man. "I am Jesus."

"Master, I have been sent to you from Bethany, from the home of your friend Lazarus," the man said.

Jesus's face sank. "He has fallen ill?"

The man looked surprised. "Yes, his sisters sent me to you, so that you might come to Bethany and heal him."

"Go then," Jesus said. "Tell them I am coming."

"Yes, Master," the man said. He then returned to the darkness from which he had come.

Tom had heard the whole conversation and walked to Jesus. He saw the look on Jesus's face and realized something wasn't quite right. "We're not going to Bethany, are we?"

"Not yet."

"But you just told him—"

"Mary is a strong woman. Do not worry about her."

"I didn't say—"

"Your eyes say enough."

"We can't just let them wait," Tom said, trying not to appear overly irritated.

"Thomas, his sickness will not end in death. The glory will be to God when His son is glorified through it," Jesus said.

David approached Tom as Jesus returned to the fire. "What a load of crap," Tom said, in hushed English.

David pulled Tom further away from the fire and listening ears.

"Can you believe this?" Tom asked, returning to Aramaic.

"I can believe lots of things."

"You're not worried about Lazarus?"

"No."

Tom scrutinized David's face, looking for answers. Then his jaw dropped open as he came to a realization. "You know what's going to happen. You know everything that's going to happen. But you're not just guessing, you actually know. Don't you?"

"Yes."

"How?" Tom wasn't asking. He was demanding.

"It's all in the Bible."

"Tonight was in the Bible?"

"Yes."

"And whatever it is that happens with Lazarus, you know the outcome?"

"Yes."

"Great. Next you're going to tell me there was a disciple named Tom in the Bible."

"Actually..."

"Not funny."

"And I'm not joking, Thomas," David said.

"Thomas?"

"That's what you're called in the Bible."

Tom's jaw clenched shut for a moment, grinding his teeth. "David, really. This isn't funny."

"Actually, I think you might be the only disciple in the Bible who actually had a nickname."

Tom stared at David, his mind racing with thoughts.

"Do you know how your name translates into Greek?"

Tom didn't reply. He knew David was going to tell him.

David smiled. "Didymus...remarkable coincidence. Now you see why it is so funny that they call you that. Not only did we look like twins, but your name translates to the Greek word for twin, Didymus."

Tom sat down. "I'm in the Bible?"

David nodded happily. "And every Christian child has grown up hearing stories about you."

What David was saying made no sense, but Tom knew he wouldn't lie about something like this. "That doesn't make them true," Tom said.

"But it makes the Bible accurate."

Tom closed his eyes in thought. "What else do you know about me? About what's going to happen?"

"I can't tell you."

"Why not?"

"It might affect the decisions you make."

"You know what happens in the next week?"

"Yes."

"A month from now?"

"Yes."

"How I live? How I die?"

"Tom—"

"You know what happens to Mary?"

David is thrown by the question. "I...no, I don't."

Tom looked away, trying to hide any concerned look on his face that might give his feelings away. But it was too late. David noticed.

"Tom, do you?" David asked suspiciously.

Tom shook his head. "Don't ask me how, but yes."

David couldn't help but smile. He put his hand on his friend's shoulder. "That's great."

"Is it really?" Tom turned around and looked at the stars, trying desperately not to make eye contact with David.

David stood next to Tom and gazed at the glowing night sky. "I promise you. There isn't any other person alive today or tomorrow that Megan would be happier to see you with."

Tom smiled and glanced at David. "What about you?"

"What do you mean?" David asked.

"The woman who inexplicably holds your heart is two thousand years in the future."

David smiled, "A minute won't pass for Sally. I've been gone for years, but to her it will only be a minute."

"It's hard to be away from someone you love for that long. I know."

David nodded. "I miss her smile. Granted, I only saw it a few times in all the years we've known her, but when I did... There was nothing better."

"Well, maybe you'll get to see her smile soon?"

"Not soon enough," David said. "Not soon enough."

❦

S ally grimaced behind her black scarf. This was not going well.

"Raise your hands," Sean demanded, after Chuck had removed her backpack.

Sally did as she was told. She didn't want to incite these guys into pulling a trigger. Jake was still struggling to catch his breath, as Sean ran to Jake and helped him to his feet. Jake struggled to speak.

"What is it, sir?" Sean asked.

Sally knew that if Jake regained the ability to talk he might give the order to shoot. She had to act fast. Sally moved her right hand subtly to her watch and began slowly pushing buttons.

"It's... It's..." Jake was beginning to get out a sentence.

Chuck emptied the backpack's contents while keeping his gun raised at Sally's head. Sally's business suit, heels, nylons and I.D. badge fell out of the bag. She had planned to change into her normal clothes as soon as she made her getaway. She could have easily strolled comfortably back to her office. But that was no longer an option.

Jake pointed toward Sally and said, "That's..."

"Director McField?" Chuck asked. He was holding her I.D. in his hand.

Jake relaxed. They finally understood.

"I think this guy broke into Director McField's office too," the guard said.

Jake's eyes bulged. "NO!" he shouted. "SHE'S... SHE'S..."

Both guards stared at Jake. What was he trying to say? Jake's eyes widened when he saw Sally lower her arms and reach for the gun. "SHOOT HER!" he screamed.

Sally grabbed Chuck's gun and quickly kneed him in the groin. Sally's ears rang with pain as a gunshot ripped through the air. She felt the breeze created by the bullet as it passed her face and shattered several beakers. Sean aimed for a second shot, but Sally had begun moving before the shards of glass from the beakers hit the floor. She ran out the door, through the office and burst into the hallway.

The elevator door directly across the hall opened up with a ding. A stunned guard struggled to draw his weapon as She skidded to a stop and ran down the hallway toward the stairwell. Two shots echoed through the hallway, as Sean leapt from the office and took aim for a third.

As Sally slammed through the stairwell door, a third bullet punctured the metal door behind her, just missing its mark. She scrambled up the stairs, covering two steps at a time. She had a plan. She thought it was stupid, but it was a plan nonetheless. The three guards, two running and Chuck limping, followed quickly, weapons ready to kill.

Jake picked up the office phone and dialed three numbers. "Sir, it's Jake... Better prep...all four. Spencer was right.... Sally's gone crazy... I think she's going back... Yeah... She's got a watch."

Sally's legs burned as she heaved up each flight of stairs. The men behind her were gaining, and if they caught her, would most likely kill her. She couldn't let that happen. She slammed into a thick bulkhead and pushed. The doors were heavy, covered in sand and meant only for emergency use; only a select group of people knew they existed, and from the outside, they were invisible. An alarm sounded as soon as the first ray of daylight entered the stairwell.

Pang! A bullet ricocheted off the stair Sally was standing on. The vibration caused by the bullet sent a tingling sensation up her leg. *That was close.* A few more seconds and she'd be dead. She grunted as she pushed the bulkhead open and ran into the blazing sun. The searing heat of the desert and blinding light of the sun on golden sand was disorientating.

Sally stumbled forward a few feet and covered her squinting eyes. She saw it just in time. She planted her feet firmly in the sand and leaned backward. Her toes protruded over a five hundred foot drop. She was teetering on the edge of oblivion.

"Don't move! Don't move a freakin' inch, lady!" the elevator guard shouted.

"Turn around, nice and slow," Sean said, as he inched toward her, keeping a watchful eye on the cliff.

Sally turned around slowly, but did not move away from the cliff's edge. She had to time this perfectly and make sure she didn't get shot in the process.

"Take off your mask," the guard demanded. "Take it off, now."

Sally punched one last button on the watch as she raised her hand to her scarf and unwrapped it. The guards took a step back when they saw Sally's face. They had been shooting at their boss.

"Sorry for the trouble, boys," Sally said with a smile.

She tossed the scarf at the guards, obscuring their view. By the time the skinny guard plucked the scarf out of the air, she had already jumped.

"Director McField!" Sean shouted, as he reached out for her.

All three men ran to the edge of the cliff and looked over. Sally was plummeting toward the ground. A light began to pulsate. With each flash it grew brighter and brighter, enveloping Sally's body in a blaze of white. The three men jumped back as a sound like an explosion rose from below. They waited only a second before looking back over the cliff. And what they saw, they couldn't believe. Sally was gone. No broken body. No stain of blood. She had vanished. Only a glowing cloud of blue particles remained, carried by the wind.

"Holy... She's...she's gone!"

"This must have something to do with that secret stuff they've been working on."

"Yeah, but where did she go?"

"Not where did she go," Jake said. "But when did she go?"

As Jake finished his sentence, a tingling zap of energy coursed up through the sinews of his back and into his skull. He was suddenly filled with the knowledge of what he had to do next...and it was wonderful.

The guards turned around and saw Jake standing in the bulkhead. He had a gun raised. "Sorry guys, but you've seen too much, and we need to tidy up a bit."

Before any of them could react, Jake fired three shots.

16

RISE

30A.D.
3:12 P.M.
Bethany, Israel

Tom was miffed. Jesus knew Lazarus was sick, maybe even dying. While Tom in no way believed Jesus could heal Lazarus, he knew that they were friends. If Lazarus died, Jesus should be there. They all should be there. But they weren't. Three days had passed before they set out that morning, headed for Bethany. Tom thought that Jesus might have waited the three days with the hopes that Lazarus would be feeling better by the time they arrived, thus negating the need for an actual miraculous healing.

The hike toward Bethany had been quiet and tense. Tom was glad it was almost over. As the hillside home of Lazarus came into view, Tom's heart sank. A crowd of people, maybe a hundred, was gathered around the home. And there was a noise...a wailing.

Is everyone crying?

Jesus stopped in his tracks and looked at the crowd. The disciples followed suit. Tom knew what this meant. He knew Lazarus was dead. And they hadn't been here.

As the fourteen moved forward again and approached the home, Martha burst from the crowd and stormed toward Jesus, consumed by rage. "Where were you?"

She stopped in front of Jesus and punched his chest. *"Where were you?"*

She punched Jesus's chest and arms over and over, lessening the blow each time. "If you had been here earlier, Lazarus would not have died!"

Tom shook his head at hearing Martha say the words, confirming Lazarus's passing. This was madness.

After putting his arms around Martha, Jesus pulled her close. She sobbed into his chest as he ran his fingers through her hair. He held her tight until her muscles relaxed. Then Jesus loosened his grip on her and she wiped her eyes dry.

"But...I know that even now God will give you whatever you ask," Martha said, with the voice of a desperate beggar.

Jesus wiped a stray tear from her cheek and said, "Your brother will rise again."

"Yes, yes, I know, in the resurrection. On the last day," Martha said, defeated.

"Martha...I am the resurrection. I am the life. Whoever believes in me will live, even though he dies; and whoever lives, and believes in me, will never die... Do you believe this, Martha?"

Martha's eyes filled with liquid as she stared Jesus in the eyes. "Yes," she said with a firm voice. "I believe you are the Christ, the very Son of God, who has come into this world."

Martha heard her own words and looked suddenly worried. "Sorry I hit you."

Jesus smiled at Martha and asked, "Now, where is your sister? Where is Mary?"

"Inside. I'll get her." Martha headed for the house.

Appearing weakened by the strong emotions of Martha, Jesus sat at the base of a fig tree, while the disciples dispersed among the mass of mourners. Tom and David stood twenty feet from Jesus, watching the scene as though through a time portal. Tom thought David looked nervous. Did he know what was going to happen? Was he expecting trouble?

Tom attempted to hypothesize about what David might be thinking, but found his own thoughts consumed by concern for Mary. He hadn't seen her yet, and scanned the faces of the people who had gathered at the home.

Like a lighthouse beckoning to a ship in the night, Mary emerged from within the sea of people and headed toward Jesus. Tom felt an incredible urge to run to her, to reach out and comfort her. But she was not coming to him. Why wasn't she coming to him? Perhaps her feelings for him were temporary? Had he misread her interest? He swallowed hard at the thought and continued watching, his feet stuck to the ground like two branches frozen in ice.

He watched as Mary stood above Jesus at the fig tree. He looked up from the ground and met her eyes. It was as if an entire conversation was held using only their eyes. They stared at each other in painful silence, crying. A teardrop fell from Mary's face and struck her shaking hand, as it fell to the earth. She took a deep breath.

"Where were you? You could have saved him," Mary said with a sniffle.

Jesus reached a hand out to Mary, and she fell into his arms.

Jesus wept.

Tom felt a nagging on his tear ducts and gave in, allowing the tears to flow freely down his face. He felt David's gaze and knew he must be realizing how much Mary really meant to him. Tom had never once, not even when he talked about Megan, cried in front of David.

Jesus held Mary by the shoulders and pushed her back, so he could see her face. "Where have you laid him?" he asked.

Mary wiped the tears from her eyes. "It's not far. We'll show you."

Mary and Jesus stood to their feet. "Let me gather the disciples," Jesus said. "Then we will go see about your brother."

Jesus walked into the crowd, leaving Mary alone. As she stood by herself, her face became twisted with agony. She jumped when Tom placed his hand on her shoulder. "Mary," Tom said, with a compassionate voice. "I'm here."

Mary spun around and wrapped her arms around him as tightly as she could. He squeezed her and pressed his face against hers, mixing their tears. He felt as though his heart were being stung by an angry swarm of bees. Lazarus was dead, but Mary was alive. Tom could feel her love for him as they shared the pain of loss that Tom knew all too well.

Watching from the sidelines had become a hobby for David. He wasn't always invited or allowed to take part in everything Jesus and the disciples did, but he was just as happy to watch. And he had never been happier to do so than now. Here they were, two thousand years in the past, mourning the death of a friend, whose sister was falling in love with Tom. David smiled. Tom didn't believe in Jesus, but he sure had a habit of falling in love with women who did.

Tom looked up as Jesus emerged from the crowd with Martha and the eleven other disciples. "We're ready," Jesus said.

Mary smiled at Tom through wet eyes. "Go ahead," Tom said. "I'll catch up with David."

Mary nodded with a faint smile and then ran to Jesus. David rejoined Tom and said, "She's something special, isn't she?"

Tom looked at David, surprisingly serious. "Tell me, David. If Jesus loved Lazarus so much, why didn't he come sooner? Let's say, for the sake of argument, that he did heal the blind guy, and all the other people who claim to be healed.

Why didn't he come here and heal Lazarus? He's caused Mary so much pain by not coming... It seems to me that he's been letting people suffer and die in his name from the very beginning."

"Tom..." It was all David could get out.

"What?" Tom asked. "If God created the universe, he can save a human life. If Jesus is God, he could have saved Lazarus. So he chose not to. If Jesus is God, he could have saved Megan. If Jesus is God... God is a bastard."

Tom couldn't believe David's reaction. David smiled!

"What are you smiling at? I'm being serious," Tom said.

"I can't say why some people die when and how they do. Only God can ever really know that. But some lives can be saved," David said.

"What are you talking about?"

"I think we should follow Jesus."

"Why?"

"Because after eighteen years, you ought to trust me."

David was right. While Tom had lost all trust in Jesus's ability to make the smart choices, David had never failed him. They followed after Jesus and the disciples, along with the rest of the crowd.

As Tom wove his way past the scads of people, he saw a familiar face. Looking at him was the Pharisee named Tarsus, dressed in the common man's clothing, walking with the crowd. Tarsus caught Tom's eye and nodded to him, as men who have a common goal sometimes do.

Tom nodded back.

⁊

Jesus, Mary and Martha stopped in front of Lazarus's tomb, which was simply a cave dug into the grassy hillside. A large, rounded slab of solid stone covered the

195

entrance with an airtight seal. Tom, David and the disciples stopped behind Jesus, the large crowd of mourners behind them.

Jesus walked to the stone and rested his hand on it. Tears rolled down his cheeks. He took a deep breath, looked up at the sky and then turned to David and Tom with a look of determination. "Take away the stone."

Tom looked at David as if to say: 'Is he serious?!' David grinned and headed for the boulder. Tom followed, feeling very silly.

"Wait," Martha protested. "By this time he'll… He's been in there four days… The smell… We can't."

Jesus looked at Martha with kind eyes. "Did I not tell you that if you believed, you would see the glory of God?"

Martha looked at the ground, unsure, but then nodded and backed away, though her look of concern did not diminish. Jesus glanced at David and Tom, signaling them to push. Tom and David braced themselves against the boulder and heaved.

It didn't budge.

Peter, who was standing in front of the crowd with the other disciples, nudged Matthew and said, "Let's help."

Matthew nodded in agreement and grabbed Judas, who was standing next to him. "You, too." Before Judas could object, Matthew had dragged him all the way to the boulder. Tom and David were relieved that help had arrived.

"On three," Tom said.

"What's on three?" Judas asked. Peter and Matthew looked confused as well.

"I'm going to count to three. When I say 'three,' we all push," Tom explained.

"Ohh, why didn't you just say so?" Matthew said.

"One…"

The five men braced themselves against the stone.

"Two…"

Tom dug his feet into the ground.

"Three!"

All five men pushed with all their strength, and the boulder rolled free. A sound like venting gas escaped from the cave as its seal was broken. The crowd covered their noses and backed away. The stone rolled free and became unbalanced. It wobbled and fell onto its side, just missing Judas and exploding a cloud of dirt into the air, which mixed with the smell of death. Tom wondered if this would be the moment of Jesus's undoing that wouldn't be recorded in the Bible.

Walking past Tom, Jesus slowly stepped toward the cave. He grabbed the sides of the cave entrance and leaned in, bowing his head at the same time. "Father, I thank you that you have heard me. I know that you always hear me, but I say this for the benefit..."

Jesus turned and looked Tom right in the eyes, "...of the people standing here, that they might believe you sent me."

Jesus turned his head back toward the gaping hole in the earth. After a moment, he turned his back on the cave and walked a few feet away, facing the crowd. Jesus closed his eyes. "Lazarus!" he yelled. "Come out!"

This is insane, Tom thought.

It went against all reasonable logic, even for the people of this time period. Even still, Tom's eyes were locked on the cave entrance, just as everyone else's were.

A woman in the crowd screamed in terror and ran away. Something inside the cave was moving in the darkness, skulking and shuffling toward the light of day. With each movement, the figure produced a scratching sound, as if a limb or dead body were being dragged over stone. It was like a bad horror movie. What happened next was both fully expected and completely unbelievable. Everyone present, minus Jesus, took a quick step back as a hand wrapped in white burial cloth clasped onto the outside rim of the cave entrance.

All at once, the whole crowd gasped. Several people turned and ran, screaming and horrified. Some fell to their knees, legs too weak to support their weight. Others stood silently, watching, waiting for the horror to continue. Jesus turned toward the cave as a man, wrapped in cloth from head to toe, staggered into the afternoon sun.

"Take off his grave clothes and let him go," Jesus said to no one in particular.

Martha and Mary dashed to their brother and began tearing at the cloth, desperate to see Lazarus living again. Within a minute, they had exposed his head, torso, arms and legs. Lazarus was not only living, but looked to be in perfect health. His skin wasn't pale and wrinkly, as one would think a dead man's skin might look. He was full of life, vibrant with blood coursing through veins, pumped by a strong heart.

Lazarus was alive!

Tom was bewildered. He staggered backward and sat atop the flat stone, which had covered the cave entrance. He watched as Mary, Martha, Jesus and Lazarus were happily reunited. There had to be some explanation. This defied all of the rules of reality, of human existence...except one.

Gripped by a frigid suspicion, Tom suddenly saw through what was happening. There was one rule, one constant of humanity that applied to this situation: deception. He and everyone else here had been conned by perhaps the greatest sleight of hand in history. Tom knew now that David Copperfield had nothing on Jesus. He looked at Lazarus, alive and well and of all things laughing. *He was in on it, that's for sure.* Tom looked at Martha, tears in her eyes, but she could have known. Tom looked at Mary. He had felt her heart break. Her emotions were real. Tom was sure of it.

Jesus had carefully orchestrated this event with his closest friend, Lazarus. They had conspired against everyone they knew and loved to further Jesus's campaign, and they had gone so far as to cause Megan such incredible pain. *Megan? Mary!* Tom realized he was transplanting his feelings of past sorrow about Megan to the present situation. But it still applied. Jesus's crusade had killed one woman he loved and had now injured another.

Mary served Jesus faithfully. Megan went to Africa for him. Mary trusted that Jesus would come and save her brother, and he betrayed that trust. Megan gave her life because she believed in him. *And this is how he repays people who believe?* Deceit. Lies. Manipulation. Tom couldn't allow it to continue. Not anymore.

A set of squinty eyes caught Tom's attention. Tarsus was there, looking at him. He had seen and heard the entire event. Tarsus motioned with his head for Tom to follow, then turned and pushed his way into the crowd.

Tom stood to his feet, resolute. As he took a step to follow Tarsus, David grabbed his arm, "Isn't this amazing?"

Tom looked at David, his complexion full of anger. David looked in the direction Tom was headed and saw Tarsus disappear into the crowd. "Where are you going?" David asked.

"I have something to take care of," Tom said, as he yanked his arm away from David and headed after Tarsus.

David had never felt such hatred from Tom. His eyes were cold and lifeless. *Oh no...* David's mind raced. He remembered the face of the man Tom was following. David had seen him earlier and thought he looked familiar, but couldn't place the face. But he remembered now—Tarsus, one of the Pharisees. Tom was going to see the Pharisees. Or had he seen them already? What was he planning to do? David's heart began to race as he considered all the possibilities.

Careful not to be discovered, he followed after Tom. If Tom planned on betraying Jesus, it would be the first inaccuracy David had seen in the Bible thus far. Could something like this have been omitted? David had witnessed a miracle, a life being brought back to the world, but if the Bible were wrong, if the word of God was inaccurate, it would shake his faith beyond repair. Maybe the events after today would be recorded incorrectly? Maybe there were two betrayers among the disciples? Maybe Jesus wouldn't rise from the dead? David knew the rest of the world was safe from the prospect of a world without Jesus Christ as God, but as for him personally, he wasn't sure anymore. He knew that the choices Tom made in the next few hours could change everything he believed.

⁊

The busy streets of Jerusalem provided David with a series of excellent hiding spots as he chased after Tom and Tarsus, who were now headed for the upper city. David was happy to see that the upper city was busy as well. He moved from building to building, staying in the shadows and acting as inconspicuous as possible. Tom had no idea he was being followed.

David watched as Tom and Tarsus entered an extravagant building, which David recognized as one of the Pharisee meeting places. It was bright white and smooth with columns on either side of the thick, solid oak door. This was truly the Beverly Hills of ancient Israel. David scanned the front of the building and noticed a walkway around the second floor, which he thought must look down upon an open atrium. He knew this would be his only chance to find out what was going on behind that door.

After leaning out from his hiding place behind a well-groomed donkey, David searched the road for prying eyes and found none. The streets this far into the upper city were almost always quiet, save for the occasional heated debate. But right now, the streets were empty, which suited David's plans perfectly. He bolted across the road and hid behind a Roman-made statue of Julius Caesar, meant to remind even the rich who was in charge of their lives. Behind the statue, a tall wall decorated with an elaborate and colorful mosaic of Moses studying the law rose to about four feet below the second floor walkway. David grabbed hold of Caesar's solid forearm, planted a foot on the figure's backside and heaved himself up, praying the statue would hold his weight. Should he tip it over and be caught, it would surely cost him his life. He leaned over with both hands and grabbed the top of the wall, his feet firmly planted on the statue's buttocks.

Just then, the front door of the building swung open and two voices spilled out into the street. Two servants exited and headed toward the lower city, both grumbling about their masters. One of the servants laughed and looked back toward the building. He stopped and grabbed the other man's arm. David had been spotted!

David stared at the men as he hung between the statue and the wall. They looked at him, studied his face, his clothes. David didn't know what to do. His mind raced, and no feasible solution came to mind. He did the only thing he could think to do. To David's surprise, the two servants returned his smile, nodded to him in approval and then they turned and left without a word. David sighed, thanking God that these men had as much contempt for their masters as he did.

With a burst of energy gained by the adrenaline that surged through his body as he was caught in the act, he pushed off the statue and pulled himself up onto the wall. From there it was a quick jump and heave over the walkway's railing. He lay on his belly and slid across the floor to an open window from which he could hear voices. Then he poked his head around the corner and looked into the wide-open room. There were ten Pharisees sitting around Tom, who had the center stage. David recognized several of the Pharisees: Silas, Simeon, Gamaliel and Tarsus. They all had confronted Jesus at one time or another over the past years. And the man Tom was standing in front of...that was Caiaphas, the high priest. David knew this was no ordinary meeting.

Tom felt as uncomfortable with these men as he did at LightTech black tie events, where he was required to shmooze with investors. It was true that he made as much money in a year as most men in a lifetime, but he preferred to live like the average guy. These were the kind of men who loved their money and had no qualms over showing it. But they were a means to an end. Tom was sure they could help discredit Jesus. He remained silent as Tarsus finished up his tale of Lazarus being brought back from the dead.

"He did what?" Caiaphas asked.

"Raised him from the dead!" Tarsus replied insistently.

Caiaphas looked at Tom. "And you witnessed this as well?"

"Yes," Tom said, though he did not believe Jesus had really brought Lazarus from the dead. But that's what Jesus wanted people to believe, so that's what he'd get.

"How?" Caiaphas asked.

"He had the stone removed from the grave by some of his disciples. He simply yelled the man's name and commanded him to come out," Tarsus explained.

Caiaphas leaned back and addressed Tom again. "And you, his...disciple... Why have you come to tell us this?"

"It is true that I am called a disciple of Jesus. But he gave me the title against my will. I do not believe what he teaches. I do not believe he is God or what he does is from God. Truly, I am not his disciple."

Caiaphas was very pleased with Tom's answer. "I see...and would you work to prove such things to be false? Would you work to undo what Jesus has done?"

"That's why I'm here," Tom replied.

"Can you confirm some items for us then?" Caiaphas asked, eager to get on with the questioning.

"Certainly," Tom replied.

"Does Jesus claim to be one and the same as God the Father?"

"Yes."

"Does he claim to heal the sick and lame with power bestowed upon him by the Father, even on the Sabbath?"

"Yes."

"Does he speak openly against us, the teachers of the divine law of Moses?"

"Yes."

"You see! It's as I told you. Jesus does such things, while claiming to be God the Father!" Tarsus said.

David heard every word. He turned away from the window full of rage. He knew if he didn't leave now he would confront the men and perhaps even be killed for his insolence. David had heard enough. Tom was betraying Jesus. He was betraying David. He was making a lie out of the Bible. David knew now that there were two turncoats in the disciple's ranks, and Tom was one of them. He climbed back down to the street and walked away, looking at the ground, full of confusion and questions.

The Pharisees grew more excited. "If we let him go on like this, everyone will believe in him!" Silas shouted. "The Romans won't stand for it!"

"I agree," Simeon said. "They'll destroy the temple and take our nation from us. We must demand that Jesus stop at once."

Tom's eyes bounced from one Pharisee to the next as they eagerly agreed. He stopped on the face of Caiaphas, who cracked a smile, as though he had just had the most wonderful thought. "Do you not realize what an opportunity this presents, for all of us? The death of one man can be the catalyst for something much greater. He will be silenced, permanently, and our nation will become a strong body again as a result," Caiaphas said.

"With us at its head," Tarsus agreed happily.

The room was all nods and smiles. "We must be careful in our actions. Only a conviction of crimes punishable by death will serve our cause. Killing him outright will enrage the masses," Silas said.

Tarsus raised and clenched his fist dramatically, "Then we must turn the masses against him."

Caiaphas turned to Tom again. "Can we count on your help?"

Tom felt sick to his stomach. This isn't what he came here to accomplish. "You...you plan to kill him?"

"Of course," Caiaphas replied.

Tom was terrified. He had handed his friend over to men who would kill him, and yet, if he refused to help now, they might kill him just for knowing. Tom struggled to find words and found only one. "No."

Caiaphas blinked. "What did you say?"

"No…" Tom said nervously. "I came here to prove Jesus was a fake, a simple street magician, not to plot his death."

Caiaphas shook his head quickly as though clearing his mind. "You have given testimony to his crimes yourself. You must understand that he—"

"Hasn't done anything so bad as to deserve a death sentence," Tom interrupted.

The faces of the Pharisees surrounding Tom grew grim, but Tom forged on, strengthened by the weight of his own guilt. "He's broken some of your stupid moral laws. He's said some things that go against what you've been taught, but you're talking about a man who has been my friend, regardless of our differences. I will not help you kill him."

"Blasphemer!" Caiaphas screamed as he stood to his feet, holding a whip in his hand.

Tom eyed the whip. *Where the hell did that come from? Does he keep one handy for moments just like this?* Before Tom could react physically, he was cracked across the face with the tip of the whip. It tore open his cheek.

He held his face in pain and looked back toward the thick closed door. Tarsus stood in his way.

Every Pharisee in the room was on their feet, waiting for the other to make a move. Tom decided it was in his best interest if he acted first. He screamed, and charged Tarsus. The air burst from Tarsus's lungs as Tom heaved his shoulder into the man's stomach and picked him up. Tom continued forward with a stunned Tarsus in his arms and slammed into the front door, breaking it down. The two men careened into the street, Tarsus absorbing most of the impact.

Tom got to his feet quickly and jumped over the immobilized Tarsus, who was arching his back in pain. Caiaphas whipped Tom across the back, opening a bloody gash. Tom fell to his knees as the remaining nine Pharisees encircled him.

This kind of situation wasn't completely foreign to Tom. He'd been in his fair share of brawls over the years, but never were the odds this grim. Ten on one. Tom knew his only recourse was to run, but he was surrounded. He took in each of his adversaries. Several were old for the times, perhaps close to fifty, and Tom imagined that few of them had any experience fighting. Most people in Jerusalem were too afraid of the Pharisees to fight back. But Tom wasn't most people.

Feigning his injuries as more severe than they actually were, he began to beg, "Please, no more. I don't want to die. I'll help you. I'll do whatever you want."

This seemed to give pause to the Pharisees and their ever-tightening circle of bodies stopped. Tom didn't wait another second. While still on the ground, he kicked back quickly and caught Silas in the knee. Even before Silas fell to the ground, Tom was up and charging Gamaliel. He rammed Gamaliel to the ground, but before he could turn around, he was stuck by a flurry of blows coming from every direction. But they were inexperienced and caused little damage. Tom smiled. This was like fighting a bunch of junior high girls. And while Tom was surrounded, Caiaphas wouldn't be able to get in a shot with that awful whip.

Tom caught a fist and parried with a blow of his own. He couldn't see who he was striking, or what happened to them after. All he knew was that after only six swings of his own, the space around him was clear of bodies. He could have sworn he heard one of them yell, "Stay away from him! He's possessed!"

Tom turned toward Caiaphas, who had already raised his whip into the air. A moment of indecision on Tom's part—to run or charge—was all it took for Caiaphas to bring down the whip and cut open Tom's arm. Before he could scream, he was hit from behind with a plank that had broken off the shattered door.

Tom fell forward, but he kept on moving. He crawled as quickly as he could away from the group of men. He felt one last sting of the whip across his thigh as he got to his feet and started running.

The voices of his pursuers faded after ten solid minutes of running. Tom was bleeding and beaten, but he was still in better shape than the Pharisees, who spent most days in lazy debate. Tom slowed as his energy and blood drained from his body.

He had made a mistake. Those men couldn't help him, and right now only one man could. Tom had to find David before it was too late. Tom would make up for betraying his friends. Bible or no bible, history was wrong. Tom was going to save Jesus. Just as soon as David saved Tom.

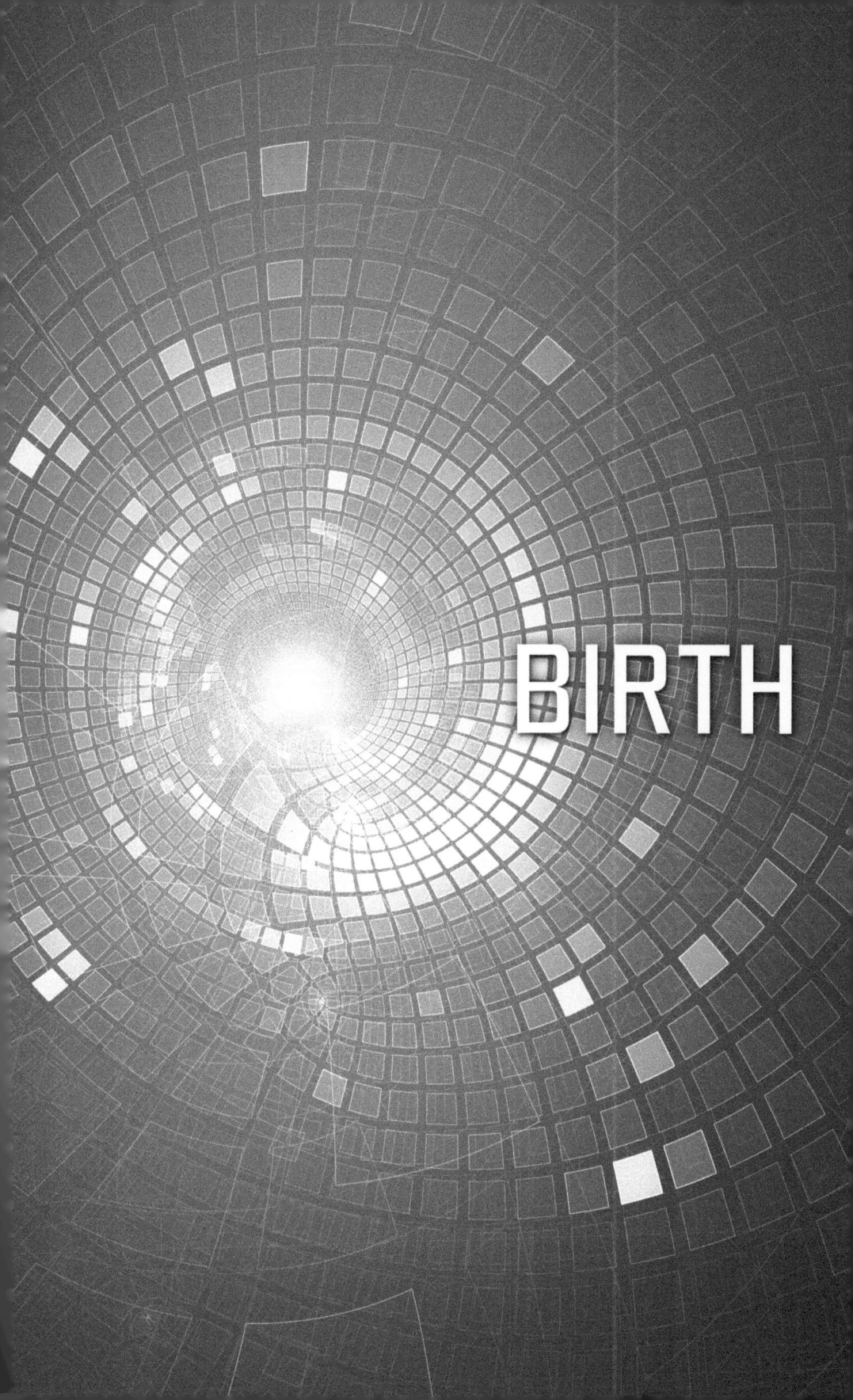

BIRTH

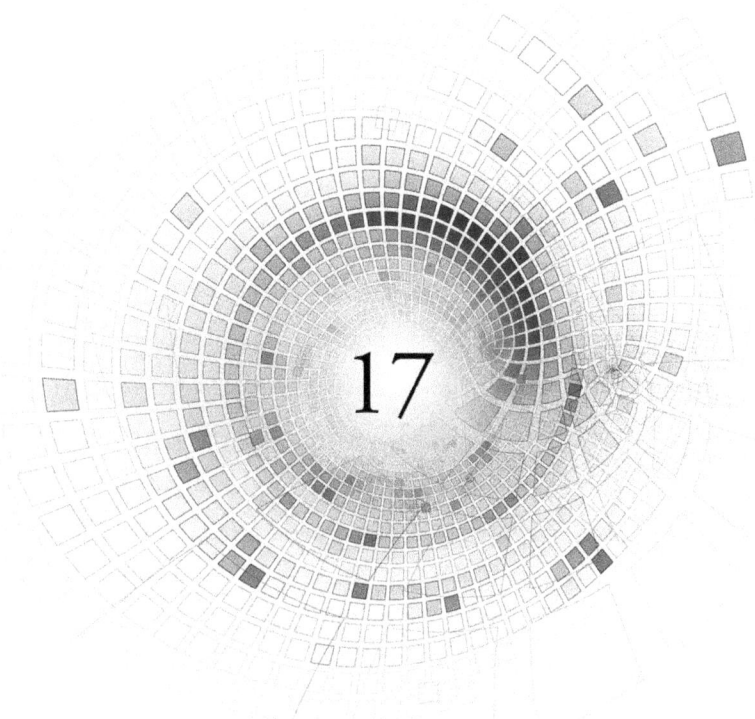

17

ACCEPTANCE

30 A.D.
6:07 P.M.
Bethany, Israel

An old fig tree provided David with a much-needed rest as he leaned against it, gazing out over the green landscape. He had left Jerusalem and retreated to a hillside just north of Bethany, where he and Tom would come to talk and sometimes return to the future for a Cherry Pepsi, rack of ribs or whatever else they missed of their own time. But the scenic view had yet to calm David's nerves. A typhoon of troubling thoughts churned in his mind. Tom had betrayed them. Tom had become the enemy. David wished it weren't true, but he saw Tom with the Pharisees, telling them exactly what they wanted to hear. He had defected, and in doing so he had proven the Bible to be inaccurate.

Damn him.

The urge to pray crept up on David. While David had never been one to consistently pray on a daily basis, it's what he normally did when life got callous, desperate or merciless. But now...now he wasn't sure if it would do any good. But he was stubborn and not ready to give up his faith yet. Only he and Tom had witnessed Tom's betrayal. How could it be recorded in the Bible if no one saw it?

"Lord Jesus," David said aloud, "I know you are here on earth with me now, and I could just as easily talk to you in person, but I also know you can hear my prayers... If Tom is working against you, please make it clear to me what you would have me do? Is this the way things happened? Is this your will? More than that... Please bring Tom back to me. Please turn him away from the men who seek to kill you. Please keep him—"

"David," Tom's voice interrupted.

David jumped. He hadn't heard Tom approach.

"Are you talking to yourself?" Tom asked.

David looked back briefly and saw Tom's silhouette standing in the dark shadow of the tree. "Go away," David demanded.

"I need your help," Tom said.

David was too upset to hear the light rasp in Tom's voice. As David flew to his feet, his head swelled with anger, so much that his eyes burnt. "Would you have me betray Jesus, too?" David yelled, as he grabbed Tom and shoved him against the tree.

"ARGH!" Tom screamed in agony.

David gasped as Tom's face became visible in the fading sunlight. Dry blood was caked around an open gash on his face.

David let go of Tom and took a step back. He could see by Tom's stance, how he was holding his stomach, how he was leaning forward and breathing shallow, that he had been beaten, close to death. "What happened to you?"

"You should see the other guy, or should I say, 'other guys,'" Tom joked with a laugh that made him flinch with pain. "Wasn't exactly a fair fight."

Tom leaned his weight against the tree and slid down to the ground, careful not to catch the open wound on his back on a shard of bark.

David stood above him. "I saw you, Tom. They're going to kill him, and you're helping them."

Tom looked up at David. "No... I'm not helping them."

"Don't lie to me," David said, growing angry despite Tom's wounds. "I saw you with them. I followed you to Jerusalem."

"I'm telling you the truth. I told them I wouldn't help them kill Jesus. I told them I just wanted to prove he was a fraud, that he was my friend and I wouldn't have anything to do with killing him..."

This was news to David. "You did?"

"Next time you spy, try staying for the entire conversation." Tom smiled. "Oh, and I told them that their religious laws were silly."

David put his hand over his mouth.

"That didn't go over too well," Tom said.

"You said that to Pharisees?" David asked.

Tom nodded.

"Be glad they let you live," David said with a nervous laugh.

"I don't think they intended to," Tom said. "David, we have to stop them."

David kneeled down in front of Tom. "We can't stop them."

"Why not?"

"Remember when Jesus called you to be a disciple? And I went back to the future?" David asked.

"Yeah, what about it?"

"I never told you what I discovered."

Tom sat up a little straighter, waiting for the news.

"Tom...the past can't be changed."

211

"Don't be absurd." Tom was near laughing, but held it in for fear of the pain it would cause.

"Did you stop to think about how Thomas the disciple could be in the Bible, before we came back in time? Time can't be altered. Everything we're doing now is already history."

"I'm not following you."

"You've been beaten up, so I'll forgive your mental incompetence."

"Hey," Tom said, as he sat up as though to converse better.

"No one ever goes back in time to kill Hitler. I know this for a fact, because if they had, it would already be history and there would have been no holocaust. The assassination of JFK is never foiled, the World Trade Center still falls, and Jesus will die on the cross. These things can't be changed. The past is already the past, Tom. The changes we make are already recorded in history."

"You're telling me that Jesus is going to be murdered, and there's nothing we can do about it?" Tom said.

"It's already history."

"We'll see about that."

"Warn him if it will ease your mind, but I'm positive he already knows." David stood to his feet and offered Tom his hand. "But right now we need to go see Mary and get you cleaned up."

With a strong yank, David pulled Tom to his feet and helped support his weight. As the pair began the walk toward the home of Mary, Martha and Lazarus, David smiled. Tom hadn't betrayed his friends. The Bible was accurate. David realized he should never have doubted. But his grin swiftly faded as he discerned what that fully meant. The next few weeks would be the best and worst of his and Tom's lives. They would experience the wonder of God and the pure evil of men. He felt secure with how things would turn out for Tom, but he had no idea what his own fate would be. And that's what scared him most.

❧

F ive days passed before Tom felt well enough to leave his bed. His wounds healed well under Mary's tender care. He would have stayed longer, enjoying the attention, but David insisted they rejoin Jesus and the disciples. It would soon be Passover, and Jesus would be entering Jerusalem, the city that loved and hated him.

Tom remembered celebrating Passover with his family when he was a child, and the story of Passover fascinated him. God freed his people when he smote their Egyptian masters by killing every first-born son in the land of Egypt, but sparing the Hebrews, who had marked their homes with the blood of the paschal lamb. The story continued with pillars of fire, Egyptian armies and the parting of the Sea of Reeds. And he could recall his Father complaining about Jews who said Moses parted the Red Sea. "Don't they know their own heritage?" he would shout. "Any good Jew knows it was Yam Suph, the Reed Sea." But what Tom remembered most about the story was how he tormented his older brother, telling him that their house was unmarked as the Passover came and went every year. He would watch at night as every breeze made his nervous brother twitch for fear that God might return for the firstborn again. A month after Tom's tenth birthday, his parents separated, the Passover celebration was forgotten and Tom's interest in Biblical things was replaced by mathematics and girls.

That was a lifetime ago and two thousand years from now. Tom rubbed the memories out of his eyes as he stared down at Jerusalem, glowing in the bright afternoon sun. He couldn't believe what they were doing. Jerusalem was full of people, gathered for the Passover feast, many of whom wanted to kill Jesus. Yet here they were, on a hill overlooking the city, about to enter through the front door. Tom had warned Jesus and found David was right. Jesus knew of the threat to his life. Not only that, he fully expected to be killed.

That conversation ended abruptly, as Tom didn't want to frighten Mary with an angry outburst after she had tended his wounds so gently. And as for Mary, Tom wasn't sure what to do about her. He hadn't felt this way about a woman since Megan...but after Jesus was dead...and didn't rise from the grave... Tom knew he and David would be returning to the future, without Mary. He thought it best to slow things down, so that when he and David disappeared, it wouldn't hurt her too badly. When she had closed her eyes for a kiss goodbye, all she felt was the breeze from Tom's body as he turned and left without a word.

It was one of the hardest things he had ever done in his life, but what they were about to do was even worse. Tom, David and the disciples stood behind Jesus, looking down at Jerusalem. It was a surreal sight. Word of Jesus's coming had reached the city, and hordes of believers had prepared a welcome. Thousands of people stood in front of the city gates waving palm branches and shouting "Hosannah! Hosannah in the highest!" The sound could be heard from Bethany even before they set out that morning.

Tom stood next to Jesus. "You sure about this?"

Jesus nodded.

"Let's get it over with then," Tom said.

Jesus turned to Tom. "Wait," he said, very seriously. "I'm not ready."

Tom sighed with relief. Maybe Jesus didn't have a death wish after all? Was Jesus coming to his senses? Maybe they would leave and Jesus wouldn't be killed and—

Jesus ran behind a tree. Tom glanced at the other disciples, questioning them with his eyes. Most shrugged. They didn't know what was happening either.

Then the answer came in the sound of trickling water. Smiles stretched across the faces of everyone present. "It seems even the Son of God has to relieve himself from time to time," Matthew said with a hearty laugh.

Jesus reappeared from behind the tree, adjusting his robe with a smile. "Okay, now I'm ready."

"Don't forget your handsome steed," Matthew said.

"How could I?" Jesus asked. "Bring him to me."

Peter led a donkey to Jesus, who mounted its back. Tom smiled at how ridiculous this must look. The people at the bottom of the hill were expecting a king, a deliverer from the dark times they had been living, a mighty warrior to slay their enemies and free their nation from the Romans. Instead, they were going to get Jesus, a thick carpenter riding a donkey.

No wonder they killed him, Tom thought.

The group headed for the city. Tom noticed that everyone looked nervous and unsure, except for David and Jesus. Tom wished he knew what they knew. The turning in his stomach was almost unbearable.

Tarsus and Caiaphas stood on the city's outer wall, looking down at the people, who were waving palm branches at Jesus, foul Jesus, riding into their city like a king on an ass. The sheer nerve of the man infuriated them. Tarsus's lip twitched. "If we don't do something soon, the people will not be swayed against him."

Caiaphas squinted in thought as he watched the palm branches sway up and down over Jesus. Caiaphas saw Tom walking with the other disciples and sneered. He had hoped Tom would have died from his wounds. Caiaphas scanned the rest of the disciples' faces, and as he looked at Judas, their eyes met. A thought slammed into Caiaphas's mind as though it was not his own. As though someone had whispered it clearly into his ear.

"If we take him now we will be stoned, but perhaps there is another way," Caiaphas said.

"You have something in mind?" Tarsus asked.

"You see there," Caiaphas said as he pointed Tom out, walking behind Jesus with David and the other disciples.

"Yes, the one who escaped," Tarsus said. "I don't think he'll be of any more use to us."

"Indeed, but if one disciple fails to believe in Jesus so much that he wants to prove the man a fraud, perhaps another will believe Jesus to be so wrong, so evil, that he might want Jesus to die as much as us?"

"If only that were true," Tarsus said.

"Perhaps it already is… Look there," Caiaphas said, as he shook his finger at Judas. "The small one. Judas. I think his name is Judas. Yes, *we know it is.*"

Tarsus looked out and saw Judas, who was now looking at the ground. "Yes, he does seem a bit frail, doesn't he? He should be easy to influence."

"We will take Judas and make him do our bidding," Caiaphas said. Then he squeezed his hands together and said to himself, "Yes. *Yes.* No. Our master's bidding. Yes, our master's bidding. We should go tell him. Yes."

Caiaphas turned away from what he now considered Jesus's last triumph. From here on, he would control the minds and souls of his people. He would use his power to sentence Jesus to death. He would reclaim Israel for the Jews, for the laws of Moses, for the Pharisees…for the Master.

Tarsus and Caiaphas left the wall, eagerly discussing their plans for the future. As they walked, their shadows followed them, as did a third.

෴

Judas strode down a shop-lined street of the lower city. He always took a great amount of pride in his monetary duties, even when it required him to shop for thirteen men. But today's shopping order was easy: bread; Judas had quickly found and bought five loaves. He then had the time to scan the shops for exotic fruit, which he bought and devoured.

No one would be the wiser.

After having his fill of fine fruit, Judas was returning to the upper room in which they were to dine tonight. But something caught his eye. A jewelry stand selling gold and silver items covered in all sorts of sparkling gems.

"Can I help you find something? Some gold perhaps? For a lady or perhaps for yourself?" the stand owner asked.

The extravagant items captivated Judas, his eyes ablaze with interest. The owner saw his chance and seized it. "This would look very nice on you."

"I—I don't know," Judas said, wide eyed.

The owner held up a bracelet. It was gold with two green gems and a red ruby. "This bracelet was part of Solomon's own treasure," the owner declared.

"Really?" Judas's eyebrows rose.

"Try it on. See how it fits you."

Judas raised his arm to the owner, who slipped it on his wrist, mimicking a servant.

"There you are, master," the owner said. "Like King Solomon himself."

"Buy it," a voice said inside Judas's head.

"Yes, buy it. You're a king," another voice said.

Dismissing the voices as his own thoughts, Judas smiled wide as he looked at the bracelet, snug on his wrist. It fit him well, indeed. Judas looked at the owner. "How much?"

Judas had never bought something that wasn't on the order and now that he had, he felt great. True, it was expensive, but he was in charge of the money and no one needed to know. If someone asked, he would tell the others it was a gift. Judas looked at his wrist where the bracelet dangled below the five loaves of bread. King Solomon had nothing on him.

The shopping district of the lower city was nearly behind him as he strode onto an empty street, which was lined with alleys on either side. He was oblivious to the world and almost didn't hear the high-pitched voice call to him. "Hello."

Windows, doors and alleyways spun through his vision as he searched the vicinity for the body belonging to the voice. Where did it come from, and was it talking to him?

"Over here."

Judas pivoted and saw only an empty alley.

"Where are you, child? I cannot see you." Judas said.

"The alley in front of you. Quick, I need your help!"

Judas approached the alley cautiously and peered into the shadows. He thought he saw a small figure on the ground, but it was too dark inside the alley to make out clearly.

"Please, hurry," the voice pleaded. Judas now thought it must belong to a little girl. She sounded scared, maybe hurt. He caught a glimpse of his bracelet, strong, noble and kingly. Helping someone in need felt like the right thing for a man like him to do. He placed his bread on the ground just inside the alley and entered.

Looking at the ground before placing each foot forward, he edged into the alley and stopped just five feet away from a little girl, who was sitting on the ground with her back to him. "Are you lost?" Judas asked.

"I need your help," the girl said.

An old feeling suddenly clawed at Judas. Since he had saved his friends from being stoned at the temple, he hadn't felt afraid. He was a new man, a brave man. He couldn't understand why this was happening again. His fingers grew cold and tingly. He thought of retreat, but he wouldn't leave the little girl to whatever danger might be around. "Tell me, child, what would you have me do?"

"Do you follow the man named Jesus?" the child asked.

Judas's palms grew sweaty and his eyes darted around the alley. What was making him feel this way? His senses pounded on his skull, warning of danger, issuing the call to flee. *But the child!* "Yes, yes I do. Now then, come along. Let's get you out of this alley. Quickly, child."

"Take my hand," the child said.

The girl raised a chubby hand in the air, and Judas took a hold of it. Her grip was loose at first but quickly became like a wine press. The girl whipped her head around toward Judas, revealing a chapped and distorted face, as though her skin was peeling tree bark. "Judas, Judas," the girl said, her voice like an angry old man's. "How trusting of you. Even the prowling lion can look as pure and innocent as a small child. Did not your master teach you that?"

Lungs heaving and heart racing, Judas felt his throat swell with anxiety. What was this? He opened his mouth to scream, but no air escaped. The darkness in the alley began to move, to writhe over the walls and floor like a living shadow. The black mass sealed off the entrance to the alley and he felt more alone than he had ever felt in his life.

He yanked his hand away from the hideous girl and fell backward against the alley's wall. Before he could catch a breath, the girl was standing above him with her rot-smelling face only inches from his. "Do you know who I am, Judas?"

His body trembling, Judas was unable to answer.

"Yes, you do... I can see it in your eyes," the girl said with a smile.

"What do you want with me?" Judas shouted.

"I told you the truth," the girl said, as she stood up straight. "You see. I'm not all bad." The girl smiled wider. "I need your help."

The swirling darkness closed in tighter, reducing the alley to a ten-foot black box, and shrinking. Voices could be heard from the darkness. "You will help us. Yes, help us. Buy the bracelet. It looks so good on you! Like a king! Like a fool! Like a traitor! Yes, yes, yes!"

"Will you help me, Judas?" the girl asked.

The darkness closed in tighter and tighter so that Judas wouldn't have been able to stand. It threatened to crush them both. He felt his life being snuffed. His heart pounded. He wished for death but knew it wouldn't come. He closed his eyes tight, terrified to see what would happen. "*Yes!*" he cried. "I'll help you! Just stop! Please stop!"

A searing heat burned Judas's back, spreading through his shoulders and into his head. Then the pain dissipated. He waited several seconds. He heard nothing, felt nothing. Then he opened his eyes. The girl was gone. He was alone in the alley, as though nothing had happened. Resting his head on his arms, he whimpered and cried like a beaten child.

"*Get up, Judas!*" came a loud voice.

Judas screamed and jumped to his feet. His head twisted from side to side, searching. But no one was there. No girl. No blackness. There was no source for the voice. It was all around him...

No, it was inside him.

"You know where you need to go. Caiaphas is waiting for you. You know what must be done. Judas, I have faith in you," the voice said.

Judas caught his breath for a moment, then ran to the edge of the alley, picked up his bread and ran toward the upper city.

18

BETRAYAL

2005

7:01 A.M.

Arizona

The noise was immense as Sally crashed into the wardrobe department and spilled into a closet of medieval outfits, knocking chain mail, long swords and shields displaying every sort of national emblem, to the floor. She fell to her hands and knees and vomited into a leather boot. David had told Sally about the side effects of time travel, but the twisting feeling in her stomach was much worse than he had described. And she had yet to actually travel through time. She simply used the watch to transport from midair to the wardrobe department, which she supervised. She knew if she was going to save Tom and David, then she better fit in as best as possible. Her current, skin tight, black ninja outfit wasn't going to cut it.

She moved to retch again, but her entire body became rigid, and she held down her bile as the door creaked open. Someone must have heard the noise! Sally ducked behind a rack of British army uniforms and held her breath. She could hear footsteps wandering in the dark, searching for something...for a light switch.

The lights clicked on and set the room ablaze with fluorescent light. "Hello?" came a voice that Sally recognized.

"Director McField, is that you?"

How did Spencer know it was her?

Spencer stopped moving. She could feel his eyes searching for her. "I saw you take the watch, Sally. David told me that if something went wrong that I could trust you. He should have been back by now...and that means something went wrong...but you figured that out already, didn't you? That's why you're going back, too?"

"How the hell do you know all that?" Sally said, as she stood up.

Spencer flashed his teeth with a confident smile, "You hired me, Sally. You know how smart I am."

Sally smirked. Spencer was right. He was smart, but he knew entirely too much. "What do you know about David?"

Spencer adjusted his glasses and made only a halfhearted attempt to hide his proud smile. "I saw him."

"When?" Sally asked.

"Before Tom or David ever went back."

"So did I. Everyone did."

"Correction. The David I saw had come back from the past, dressed in clothing appropriate to the early A.D. period in ancient Israel," Spencer explained. "A closer inspection of the receiving area's inventory reveals that there was, in fact, one item missing, and the second time signature was no glitch in time space, no random effect created by time travel..."

"It was David…" Sally said.

"Precisely. David gave me instructions to follow—which I did perfectly, I might add—and that included locating you, if he and Tom should not return to within an hour of their departure time. I deduced the logical choice of action would be to send someone else back in time, but upon seeing the beefy Captain Roberts slip into the time stream, I knew it was only a matter of time before you took action yourself."

Sally was growing tired of Spencer's lengthy explanations. "All wonderful, Spencer, but get to the point."

Spencer remembered who he was talking to and straightened up. "I'm here to help you, Director McField."

What good could a skinny little scientist do to help Sally now? This wasn't a time for brain storming, hypothesizing or arguing the fate of the universe. She needed action. "Spencer, can you buy me some time?"

"Time is our specialty, Director McField," Spencer said proudly. "Time is our new best friend."

Sally went into detail quickly about Captain Roberts's mission and how he planned to carry it out. She told him about the robot insects with the poison that could kill a man and make it look like an allergic reaction. She told him everything. If David trusted Spencer, she could, too.

"What time do you plan to travel to?" Spencer asked.

"Same time as Roberts, but far enough away so that he doesn't see me."

Sally threw a robe over her ninja outfit and sneakers. She knew the sneakers might be seen, but she also knew she might have to do some running, and not wearing sandals would give her an advantage. She disguised her watch with some twine as best she could and threw a covering over her head and face. She was pale as a ghost and didn't want stick out more than she already would. "Can you keep things busy here for a while? Create a temporal emergency or something? Give me some extra time?"

"Can do," Spencer said with a thumbs-up. "You don't have to worry about a thing here. We've got everything under control."

Sally thought Spencer's speech was strange. He had referred to himself in the plural three times now. But he was probably just nervous and there was no time to have a personal conversation.

"Thanks," Sally said. "You're a good man."

After tapping a series of buttons on her watch, Sally said, "Better stand clear."

Spencer walked to the edge of the room and watched as Sally disappeared into time with a bright flash and a boom. This had been easier than he thought it would be. When the idea to turn the recent events to his advantage had entered his mind, as though from divine inspiration, he wasn't sure it would work. But Sally had played right into his hands, and his recent alliances would make sure he moved up the ladder quickly.

Spencer pulled a cell phone from his back pocket, flipped it open and dialed two numbers. "Director Dwight? Yes, it's Spencer. Director McField just went back... Yes, sir...same time as Captain Roberts... Yes, sir. Thank you, sir. Yes, sir."

Spencer was all smiles as he hung up the phone. Just like that, he had secured David's position as lead scientist of the time travel unit. He was moving up in the world. Spencer giggled to himself and headed out the door for Receiving Area Alpha, eager to begin studying his priceless artifacts from the future.

Spencer was feeling too good to notice the voices of congratulations within his mind were not his own. "Good job! You're so great! But we still have more to do. Yes. Much more work for us to do. Yes! Yes. The future awaits us."

As Spencer left the room, two shadows followed him. After rounding the corner, the second shadow detached and moved down the hallway, toward Director Dwight's meeting room.

❧

Director George Dwight and Jake Parrish sat across from each other on plush leather chairs. The room was small and lit only from above. It was the kind of room perfect for a meeting such as this. Soundproof walls. No windows. No vents. No doors.

"Things haven't gone exactly to plan, sir, but I think we have things under control now," Jake said.

"How's the throat?" George asked.

Jake rubbed his throat. It hurt like hell. "That woman can throw a punch."

"And she's as smart as she is strong, so don't go assuming she's out of the game just yet," George said.

"Yes, sir."

"What's the status on our little friends?"

"Prepped and ready to go. We know where and when Sally and Roberts are, and with the onboard facial recognition software, the other two shouldn't be too much more difficult to track down."

"Has the poison been altered?"

"Of course, sir. The poison acts the same, but its kill time has been accelerated to a half hour. Sally will have little time to find them and administer the antidote. Of course, by then, it will be too late for all of them."

"Excellent. What a regrettable mess this is. It's a PR nightmare, really."

"Spencer and a team are prepping to retrieve the bodies even as we speak. I think a helicopter crash would be a fitting way to dispose of the bodies."

George leaned back with a smile. "You're trying to make director."

Jake smiled. "I believe we have an opening."

"Get this done for me... Consider the position filled."

Jake stood to his feet and headed for an empty wall. "Better have my door etched. This won't take long."

The wall whooshed open in front of Jake. He exited the bare room and turned to the right, his pace quickening with every step. The door closed silently behind him, leaving him alone in the cool hallway. George was a blind fool. Jake was far more than an assistant. He ran this company. He was in charge. As soon as he finished cleaning up George's mess, he would apply himself to usurping his boss and taking this company to places of power never before dreamed of.

"Do you think it's possible?" Jake asked himself aloud.

"We think so." Jake answered.

"So do we!"

"Yes!"

"This is so fun!"

☙

Tom laughed loudly at Matthew's impression of a Pharisee. It was uncanny. Jesus and the twelve had been dining together in a room they had rented for the night. Rarely did they eat a meal so good that wasn't given to them for free. This meal was different, it was bought and paid for, and the men and women who served them were not being charitable. They were being paid. This wasn't just another meal. It was formal, as formal as a meal could be when you're all lying around a table, digging into the same piles of food with shards of ancient Pita bread.

How the meal had begun was even stranger. Jesus had washed all their feet. Tom had grown used to having his feet washed by servants; it was customary here in the past where everyone wore sandals and ate while reclining, placing their dusty feet precariously close to the food. But Tom had never had his feet washed by another disciple, let alone Jesus. He was amazed at how humbling an experience it was.

But the washing of Tom's feet was nothing compared to what Jesus did next. He took some bread and some wine, said something about how it was his blood and flesh and then they all ate it. It took Tom, and he imagined everyone else, some time to shake the feeling that this was Jesus's way of saying goodbye. Tom wished David were here to explain what was happening.

The fact that David wasn't present caused Tom some distress at first because of the recent serious mood. David was waiting outside, eating by himself. Jesus and David had agreed that this meal was for the disciples' benefit alone. But Tom didn't feel up to any big surprises. He could usually judge from David's facial expressions when something good or bad was about to happen, but David wasn't there. Tom did his best to settle in and forget about what might or might not happen. So far, the meal had gone as they usually did. Matthew told jokes.

Everyone laughed.

Tom had been sitting next to the disciple named John, who was likable enough, but who Tom had never gotten to know very well. The two had bonded over dinner as people who eat and joke together sometimes do. There were twelve disciples after all, and all were almost always busy. Groups of friends had formed among the disciples, and getting to know everyone hadn't been the priority over the past few years. But now Tom wondered if he hadn't been missing out on something.

John was smart. Damn smart, and Tom enjoyed hearing his theories on everything from how birds flew to what craters on the moon were. What impressed Tom the most was that John was often close to the mark. If he hadn't become a disciple of Jesus, John might well have been the world's first Da Vinci.

Tom looked up from his food and saw Judas re-enter the room. He had been fidgety and nervous all night. Tom decided to ask him what was wrong in the morning. Right now, he was having too much fun, and Judas was busy ordering food and paying servants.

"Friends, brothers, a moment please," Jesus said, as he stood up.

The room fell silent, and all eyes were on Jesus. "Now that you're all here, there is something I need to tell you...something I need to tell you now, so that when it happens, you will believe what I have taught you. You might not believe what I'm about to say, but be assured, it is the truth... One of you...will betray me."

Everyone stopped breathing. The disciples looked at each other. Was he serious? Who was he talking about?

A rumble of discomfort shot through Tom's stomach. He had almost betrayed Jesus. Did that count? Was Jesus talking about him? Or was it Judas? He knew history believed Judas to be the betrayer of Jesus, but it didn't seem remotely possible. Tom looked for Judas and found him talking to a servant, not even paying attention at the moment. The man had proven to be a good friend, not a killer.

Peter, who was sitting next to John, who was sitting next to Jesus, nudged John with his bony elbow. "Ask him who it is."

John nodded and turned to Jesus, "Who betrays you? Tell us, which one of us will it be?"

There was one last piece of bread on the table. Jesus picked it up. "I will give this bread to the one who betrays me, after I have dipped it in the oil."

Jesus took the bread and dipped it in a small dish of olive oil, garlic and assorted spices. Just then, Judas, who had been all but oblivious to the conversation, as he was talking to a servant about money, leaned down to Jesus's ear and said, "We're out of bread, should I go purchase some more?"

Jesus turned to Judas and replied, "You are kind to offer, but you have not eaten yet. Take this bread to fill your stomach."

Judas took the bread. "Thank you."

"Do what you are about to do quickly," Jesus said. "Time is running out."

"I won't be long," Judas said, and he exited.

Jesus turned back to the disciples, who looked disappointed.

Peter looked at Tom, who looked at John, who looked at Matthew and so on. All were confused and frustrated with anticipation. "Uh, Jesus," Tom said, "What about the bread and betrayal? You were going hand it to the betrayer, but you just gave the bread to Judas...to eat...and he left."

Jesus looked around the table. "It would appear that we are out of bread."

"Judas went to get more bread?" John asked.

Jesus nodded.

"Well can't we use a piece of fruit or chicken leg or something?"

Jesus smiled. "I'm afraid we'll just have to wait on Judas."

No one liked that answer, but what choice did they have? They returned to their previous conversations, which now included speculation as to who would be the betrayer of Jesus.

℘

The rest of the night had gone by quickly and the morning had come even quicker, and still no sign of Judas. Tom wanted to take some of the disciples and search for Judas, but Jesus insisted Judas was fine and the group headed out early for the garden of Gethsemane on the Mount of Olives, just east of Bethany and Jerusalem.

Jesus left the disciples in the garden, which was an olive grove lined with sweet smelling, bright red Crown Anemone. He said he needed to speak to his Father. The disciples carried on conversations like nothing had changed. But Tom could sense a change, as though unseen forces were squeezing his skull. He went for a walk to clear his mind.

After five minutes, Tom stopped and sat on a large rock and took a deep breath. He was constantly amazed at how clear the air was here. In Arizona, there wasn't a lot in the way of air pollution, but on particularly windy days, they'd get blasted by smog from the L.A. basin. Here, the air was always clean.

"Have you noticed where you're sitting?" David asked.

Startled by David's sudden appearance, Tom almost fell off the rock backward, but he quickly recovered. "On a rock."

"What do you see in front of you, down the hill? Picture a thousand people all gazing up at you. Go back a few years."

229

Tom looked around and his mind began recalling the events of the past. He hopped down from the rock and peered at it. "I'll be damned," he said. "This is where it all started."

Tom walked a few feet away and turned toward the rock again. "I was standing here; you were on the rock… Seems like a lifetime ago."

Tom walked to the rock and rubbed it with his hand like it was an old friend. "You might not believe it, but I don't particularly miss the future. I have things here I never had there: a large group of friends, I'm seeing the world, learning. In the future we stopped learning, did you ever realize that? We were just working every day, putting into practice what we already knew. Here we learn something new every day."

"You forgot something," David added.

"Mary. I know. But I have to return to the future. What we've started…the time travel devices… Who else is going to take care of it? Make sure it isn't abused?"

David raised his eyebrows with a humored expression, "I can't think of anyone better than us."

"Right," Tom said. "We have to go back."

After walking a few feet away, David turned and faced Tom. His face was sour.

"What's wrong?" Tom asked, curious as to the change in emotion.

David walked to the rock slowly and leaned against it. "You know how I told you how the past can't be changed, because it's already happened?" David asked.

"You're not having doubts, are you? It's a sound theory," Tom said.

"No, I don't have any doubts. I just wish it were wrong," David explained.

Tom felt a sudden urgency, "Why? What's going to happen?"

"It's already happening."

"What is?"

"Did you see Judas leave last night?" David asked, looking Tom in the eyes.

"Did something happen to him? Is he okay?"

"Did you see what he had in his hand?"

"Just a piece of bread that Jesus—" Tom's muscles tensed. It couldn't be...but the fact was undeniable. "Judas... He gave the bread to Judas! The exchange seemed so casual, it seemed Jesus had forgotten what the bread was meant for...but he didn't, did he?"

"ARGHH!" A man's voice cried out in anguish from the olive grove.

Tom jumped off the rock, ready for action.

David stood up straight. "It's begun."

19

TRIALS

30 A.D.
5:12 P.M.
Mount of Olives, Israel

Tom had never pushed his lungs to the edge of endurance like this before. He was running as fast as he could. And David, the old man, was right behind him. He and David hopped over rocks and wove between trees like rabbits eluding a predator. But rather than running from the predator, they were headed straight for it.

As they rounded a group of trees, the clearing in the olive grove where the other disciples had been came into view. The disciples were in chaos, arguing about what to do, what not to do. No one had a clear course of action.

Dust kicked into the air as Tom came to an abrupt stop. He was completely winded, but he didn't bother sucking in air before speaking. There wasn't time to breathe. "What happened? Tom asked. "Where's Jesus? Who screamed?"

"They took him!" Matthew said. His face then contorted to a disdainful expression. "Judas was the betrayer!"

"I tried to stop them," Peter said, as he held a sword in the air, its metal blade smeared with scarlet blood. "But he took the soldier's ear and put it back on...like I had never cut it off...just put it right back on..."

"Where did they go?" Tom asked in a hurry.

"They're leaving the grove even now. Headed for Jerusalem and a trial by the Romans," Matthew said, hardly believing it himself.

Tom looked at David desperately, "We have to stop them."

"We can't. You know that."

"Even if we fail. History doesn't say we didn't try, right?"

"No."

"Good enough for me."

Being at the top of the hilled olive grove made reaching top speed again that much easier. Tom was thirty feet away within seconds and would soon be out of sight. David followed after him, careening down the hill, arms flailing to maintain balance around the curves.

Matthew looked at Peter, forehead wrinkled. "Stop them? Did they see how many men there were?"

The wind tore through Tom's hair and his muscles burned with life as he rounded a corner on the twisting path of switchbacks, which exited the olive grove. Ten feet in front of him stood a Roman soldier, apparently placed to stop any would-be rescue efforts by desperate disciples. This man alone, while not a huge physical threat to a group of disciples, carried the weight of the Roman Empire. If the soldier was killed, it would be open season on the disciples. The guard saw Tom coming and after pushing his red cape out of the way, drew his sword, thinking a show of force would be enough.

Tom eyed the sword, but knew the outcome of most fights often depended on who struck first, on who was most aggressive. Brute force didn't replace his tactics—brute force was his tactic. Tom ran straight for the soldier.

"Stop where you are!" the soldier yelled, caught off guard by Tom's undaunted charge.

Tom collided with the soldier like a battering ram. The soldier sailed through the air and slammed against a tree. The man slid to the ground and hit his head on a stone. Tom pressed on, satisfied that the soldier wouldn't be running anyone through anytime soon.

David rounded the corner and saw the crumpled guard. Tom was insane! If he didn't stop, he'd get killed. David ran faster, not noticing the shadow watching him from the side of the path, just behind a fallen tree.

Tom dug his feet into the dirt and stopped at the edge of a thirty-foot cliff. He turned around as he heard the crunch of sandals on dirt and saw David rounding the corner at top speed.

David caught a glimpse of the approaching drop off and began slowing his legs, but couldn't stop his forward momentum quickly enough. David reached out and grabbed hold of Tom to stop himself and nearly took both of them over the edge. Tom's muscles groaned as he pushed against the force of David's body.

After coming to a complete stop, David looked down. His feet were dangling over the edge. Tom yanked him back. "That was...that was close," David said with a concerned look.

Tom moved toward the cliff again and peered over the edge. His mouth dropped open. "This is impossible."

A contingent of twenty-five Roman soldiers brandishing swords and spears marched down the trail with Jesus at their center. The group was led by a mob of Pharisees and Judas.

Slumping to his knees, Tom watched helplessly. "Damn it."

"Nothing we did...could have changed what has happened...or what will happen," David said while sucking in air.

"Tell me," Tom said.

"What?"

"Tell me what's going to happen."

"I'm not sure I sho—"

"Tell me, David. Now. I can't change it. At least prepare me for it."

"Not here. That Roman soldier's going to wake up soon, and I don't think either of us could stand any more excitement."

"You're right, let's—"

Pang! A chip of rock between the two men blasted into the air. They locked in on the airborne object and began analyzing the phenomenon.

"What was that?" Tom asked, bewildered.

Tom watched as David searched the area like a frightened meerkat on patrol. What was he looking for? Tom saw David's eyes widen and followed them to the source of intrigue. A glint of light, reflecting off what must have been glass, was all Tom saw before David was moving. "Get down!" David yelled, as he tackled Tom to the ground.

Puch! Dirt exploded from the ground and splayed across Tom's face. "What the hell is going on?"

"It's Roberts! Run!" David shouted.

The two men jumped to their feet and ran back to the path, which led down the side of the cliff. Tom looked back as they descended the steep incline and saw a man dressed in a bright new robe—too new—jumping out of the trees and chasing after them. And in his hand?

A gun.

With a sound suppressor.

Roberts.

The time enforcer.

The killer.

Tom pushed even harder.

It occurred to him that if they continued at this speed, down the path of switchbacks, they would soon run into the entourage of troops transporting Jesus. It was death in either direction. But apparently, David was one step ahead.

David grabbed Tom by the robe and headed off the path. "This way!"

The two men half ran, half slid down the steep grassy slope. If they made it down this portion of the hillside fast enough, they would rejoin the path just before the Roman soldiers. It was going to be close. They might find their lives ended at the tips of Roman spears instead of modern bullets, but there was little choice, and spears had a much shorter range than bullets.

Captain Roberts cursed himself. He had two clear headshots and had missed them both. He could have stopped them dead in their tracks and returned to the future, without having to worry about justifying David and Tom's deaths. One look at the men told Roberts that they had been living in ancient Israel for months, maybe even years. Their clothing was more authentic than his own, and they were speaking Aramaic. Roberts had studied detailed backgrounds on both men. He knew Tom couldn't speak the language, but here he was, speaking it fluently. That meant Tom had been in the past long enough to learn it, which also meant he had broken so many rules of time travel ethics that killing him was well within reason.

After only fifty feet, Roberts gave up the chase. The savage after effects of time travel were still wreaking havoc on his body. That was what had caused him to miss. He should have waited. He should have planned better. He wouldn't make the same mistake twice.

Turning his head to the left, Roberts vomited like he was casually belching. He wiped his mouth and before he could formulate a plan—

"Don't move!" a male voice demanded in Aramaic.

Roberts turned toward the voice. It was the Roman soldier he had watched Tom rough up. Roberts made no attempt to hide his grin. These soldiers were jokes;

237

poorly trained, poorly equipped jokes. Roberts could see it in the man's eyes. He was a coward with a sword, hiding behind the Roman insignia on his armor.

The Roman soldier backed away as Roberts strolled toward him, still smiling wolfishly. Roberts drew his knife and let the sun reflect off it into the soldier's eyes. The soldier blinked and blocked the light with his hand. He regained his sight quickly, but only just quickly enough to see Roberts's fist rapidly approach his face.

The ground sank as the soldier fell on it like a tipped cow. If Roberts hadn't become a soldier, he would have made a champion boxer. After sheathing his bloodless knife, he suppressed his urge to kill. Killing civilians wasn't part of the plan, unless they got between him and his prey. This soldier was lucky. Roberts simply vented a few frustrations. He could have vented them all.

❧

Tom and David ran for ten minutes straight before stopping for air, then quickly made their way to the home of Lazarus, Mary and Martha, where they hoped they could rest and find safety. Their welcome was far more than David expected. They were hugged and kissed on the cheeks, even by the gargantuan Lazarus.

David surmised that Mary must have shared her feelings for Tom with her siblings, because they now treated Tom like family. But the happy reunion was short lived. David and Tom explained what had happened in the garden of Gethsemane: Judas, the soldiers and Pharisees. Lazarus, normally strong and composed, found himself unable to stand at the news.

When Tom and David told the story, they left Captain Roberts's assassination attempt out. There was no way it could be explained so that it made sense.

The night was long for everyone, though Tom and David fell fast asleep after their physically exhausting ordeal. As David lay in bed with his eyes closed, he felt a strange sensation. As a child on the night before the first day of Hanukkah, David would always go to bed early. His theory was that the sooner he fell asleep, the sooner it would be Hanukkah. The night would pass in an instant, and the festivities of the next eight days would begin—only this night David felt the exact opposite. He knew that as soon as he fell asleep, morning would arrive too soon and they would be facing dangers unknown to other men of this time period.

David's theory proved to be correct. As soon as his eyes closed and his body relaxed, it was morning. Everyone was up with the sun, and only ten minutes later, Lazarus was out the door and headed for Jerusalem. Mary and Martha left with Lazarus, encouraged by David to do so. This might be their last chance to see Jesus alive, and he didn't want them around if Roberts showed up.

Tom watched as Mary walked toward Bethany with her siblings. He felt a terrible sadness. He had said a simple goodbye to a disappointed Mary before she left the house. Only now did he realize this moment might be the last time he saw her. He looked at David, who was already nodding to his unsaid question.

The house shrank behind Tom as he tore down the dirt road and grabbed Mary by the shoulders. "Mary, wait."

Lazarus and Martha stopped walking and turned back to see what the delay was. Their impatience was visible, but they didn't say a word.

"A lot is happening," Tom said, as he looked Mary in the eyes. "I don't know what the outcome will be. I don't know what's going to happen to me, where I'll go, what I'll do, but I wanted you to know... I just..."

"I already know," Mary replied.

Then Mary closed her eyes, waiting.

Tom didn't let her down again.

He grasped Mary in his arms and kissed her, lingering for a moment to absorb the soft curves of her lips as they spread into a smile. Tom moved back after their lips had separated and became suddenly serious. "If I must leave...will you come with me?"

"Where will you go?"

"I cannot tell you that. Will you go with me?"

"Yes."

Tom's shoulder fell as he relaxed. This day might turn out all right.

"Time to go, Mary. Time is short." Lazarus said with a strong voice, as he and Martha began walking again.

"I'll see you soon... I promise," Tom said.

Mary nodded, and after a quick kiss on the lips, she ran to catch up with her brother and sister.

The sound of David's feet on the earth announced his approach. David stood next to Tom, watching the three leave. Tom looked at him, his face taut, "Nothing bad happens to her, right?" Tom asked.

"Mary's fate isn't recorded in the Bible," David replied.

"That's not very comforting."

"Well, I'm sure it would have been, had something bad happened to her," David reassured.

"And what about Jesus? When does he die?"

"Tomorrow."

Tom was surprised. "That fast?"

David nodded sadly.

"There's got to be something we can do to get rid of Roberts until—"

Tom became rigid as his mind wrapped itself around their dilemma. It was always Tom's belief that the world was composed of a series of problems. Science was the method humans had invented to find the solutions to these challenges. Being one of the world's most brilliant scientists, Tom believed that there was a solution to every conundrum, and that he could find it—if only given the time. And this problem took no time at all.

"We've been living here for years. We blend in. We're natives. Jews. We belong here, and he doesn't," Tom said.

"What are you thinking?"

"Captain Roberts is about to get a rude cultural awakening. But first we need to get his attention."

Tom began walking higher up the hill.

"Tom, wait. What are you planning to do? He's got a gun and we're unarmed. He's a trained killer and we're—"

"In the best shape we've ever been in."

"What's that got to do with anything?"

"We're going for a little jog. Think TED can keep up with a couple of old men?"

"I think he might be able to pass us," David said nervously.

"Don't worry so much. God's on our side, right?"

David smiled. He knew Tom was being sarcastic, but he also knew Tom was really enjoying this. He had come up with some masterful plan to beat brawn with brains, and he wanted David to see it all unfold in dramatic fashion, rather than just detail the whole plan.

"Fine, but keep in mind: my fate isn't recorded in the Bible either."

"Don't worry, David, I'm sure if you died, they would have mentioned you," Tom replied with a grin.

David smiled and let his muscles loosen a bit. "How are we going to let Roberts know where we are?"

After walking fifty feet toward the Mount of Olives, which was just to the north, Tom cupped his hands and yelled at the top of his lungs, in English, "Hey Roberts! We're over here!"

Tom continued yelling, hoping this wouldn't take too long. He knew all the screaming in English might attract more than just Captain Rob—

"ARGH!" Tom yelled while cupping his arm. He fell to his knee and lifted his hand. It was covered in blood from a tear in his skin. "He's here," Tom said. "Go! Run!"

"But you've been shot!" David protested.

"It's only a scratch, and we don't have time to play nurse. Now move it, old man!"

"Old man? You just try and keep up!"

Tom and David sprinted down the hill toward Bethany.

"Where are we going?" David asked as they ran. "Bethany's too small; we'll never lose him there."

"We're not going to Bethany," Tom replied.

"Where then?"

"Jerusalem."

David's eyes widened. "Jerusalem? That's three miles away!"

❧

D avid looked over his shoulder. Roberts was still there, gaining on them slowly but surely. In front of Tom, David could see the walls of Jerusalem appearing over the hill. They were almost there. If there was more space between them, losing Roberts in the lower city would be no problem, but David knew that wasn't part of Tom's plan.

In fact, Tom had requested that they slow down a few times to let Roberts grow closer. They were in better shape than they expected. The three miles to Jerusalem passed quickly, and they were able to carry on a conversation the entire way. At one point David even forgot they were being chased. Roberts was only fifty yards behind them, the distance an Olympic sprinter can cover in five seconds, the same distance a bullet could cover in under a second.

"We have to slow down again," Tom said.

"Are you crazy? He'll shoot us!"

"Once we get in the city he won't want to make a scene. He'll want to catch us some place private," Tom explained. "And we need him to see where we're going."

"I'm putting my faith in you," David said, as he slowed his pace.

With a jerk of the neck, Tom looked at David. He didn't like the way that sounded, but hadn't the time to make a comment. Roberts had quickly closed to within twenty-five yards. Close enough.

Tom and David entered through the front gates of Jerusalem and merged into the congested streets, which were alive and loud today with the news of Jesus's trial. Tom and David overheard statements of Jesus's guilt, arguments of his fate and threats to his life. They ignored everything and continued toward the upper city, toward the temple.

They reached the upper city quickly. David wracked his mind to try to decipher Tom's plan, but to no avail. They entered the temple with Roberts only fifty feet back, well within shooting range. But the number of people wandering around the outer temple kept his gun hidden.

"Where are we going?" David demanded to know.

"Inside..." Tom replied.

David could see Tom was getting winded. *This had better end soon.*

The pair entered the Court of the Gentiles, which was unusually placid for a Thursday. David surmised that Jesus's trial must have been attracting the people's attention, pausing their worship of God to kill him.

As they neared the entrance to the Court of Women, David noticed a sign above the door that he had never taken notice of before. He read it quickly as they passed beneath: *No foreigner is allowed within the balustrades and embankment of the sanctuary. Whoever is caught will be personally responsible for his ensuing death.*

David smiled.

"Tom, you're a genius," David said, as they passed through the gates into the Court of the Women.

They ran across the Court of the Women, up the curved staircase and to the heavy bronze door at the Nicanor Gate. David and Tom pushed with all their strength to open the gate. Roberts had entered the Court of the Women and was running toward them at full speed.

David and Tom spilled into the Court of Israel. The seven Jewish men who were worshipping in the court shot annoyed glances at Tom and David, who had slammed the heavy bronze door behind them. Out of breath, Tom struggled to speak. "Quickly brothers...fetch the Levites! A foreigner has entered the inner temple...and wants to spill Jewish blood in the house of God!"

The Jewish men reacted at once, running toward the Court of the Priests, shouting for the Levites.

Tom and David were too tired to continue running, and they knew help would soon arrive. They turned toward the bronze door, which had just finished closing behind Roberts. He was out of breath and looked supremely irritated. He walked toward them calmly, like a predator who knows its prey is trapped.

"You don't have to do this, Roberts," David said.

"You know my name. How nice for you," Roberts said, as he continued forward.

Roberts pulled his knife out from under his robe.

"Leave now, and we'll let you live," Tom said with confidence.

Roberts stopped walking. Tom couldn't believe it had worked, but he then realized it wasn't Tom's command that had stalled Roberts's advance. Roberts's eyes were focused just beyond Tom.

The world spun as Tom turned around and came face to face with a massive Levite. The Levite held a grapefruit sized stone in his hand, and his eyes were darting up and down Roberts's body, taking snap shots of every detail: the blond crew cut, the knife's unusual design, the shining object hanging on his wrist and that Roberts was taking the same mental images of the Levite. The two warriors sized each other up, both knowing what the other didn't know was about to get him killed.

Roberts slowly reached into his robe. His fingers touched the butt of his gun. This would be over in seconds. Roberts took his eyes off the Levite for a split second and looked at David's eyes, which were wide, but not staring at him...David was staring...behind him.

Roberts grabbed his gun and spun around. He fired two shots through his robe, which missed their marks. A second Levite, who had crept up behind Roberts, raised his hand. It held a large stone. The Levite brought it down quickly on Roberts's skull.

Falling to one knee, Roberts dropped his weapon. He clutched his knife and lunged at the Levite. Before Roberts could even swing the blade through the air, a second stone struck him between his spine and right shoulder blade. Roberts dropped the knife and fell to the ground again, but refused to scream in pain.

He struggled to his feet again, glaring at the Levites, who had already picked up new stones. The seven Jewish men who had been worshipping stood behind the Levites, their hands armed with stones.

"You will be tried and executed by the Romans for breaking Jewish law," one of the Levites said.

Roberts's eyes twitched as blood from his head poured down his face and into his mouth. He looked at David and said through gritted teeth, "Don't let them take my watch."

Roberts removed the watch from his wrist and threw it at David as hard as he could. The watch landed on the stone floor, five feet from David. Roberts was obeying his orders to the end, protecting time, but his intentions to hurt David at the same time were clear to everyone present.

"No more!" the bigger Levite shouted. "Lay on the ground, now."

Roberts's grimaced in pain and spat at the Levite, who easily dodged the saliva-blood mixture. The spit flew several feet before landing on a tablet one of the men had been studying.

"He has spit on the Word of God!" one of the men shouted.

Roberts stood to run but was barely on his feet when the first of several stones pummeled his body, hurled by the Levites and Jewish men. He staggered forward until a large stone hit his head, creating a sound like a breaking coconut. Roberts's body went lax and flopped onto the stone floor.

"Quickly," one of the Levites said, "remove his body before the Romans see what we have done."

The seven Jewish men rushed forward and picked Roberts up. They carried his body away, supervised by the two Levites. As the group exited into a side passageway, one of the Levites turned to Tom and David and said, "Well done, brothers. Your alert kept the house of God from being defiled by this man. God will reward your service."

With that, the group of men disappeared with Roberts's body, leaving Tom and David alone in the Court of Israel.

David covered his mouth in disgust and sat down. Tom ran to where the fight had taken place and took the knife, watch and silenced handgun. He tucked them inside his own robe and ran back to David. "Let's go," he said. "I don't want to be here to answer questions. Do you?"

"He died to protect time," David said. "If only he'd have given us a chance to explain. He would have known that time is in no danger."

"Stupid people die stupid deaths, David, and I don't want to be next. Let's go."

David got to his feet silently. He had never seen a man killed before. Captain Roberts was an evil man who wanted to kill both him and Tom, yet David couldn't help feel sorry for the man. His stomach turned as the image of Roberts's death replayed in his mind. But what worried David the most was that he knew he would soon see another man die, the ramifications of which would change the world forever.

Tom and David headed through the Nicanor gate and into the Court of the Women. As the gate opened, a sound hit them, like waves of static. They knew the noise couldn't be good, as did everyone else in the temple, all of whom began hurrying toward the exit.

The crowd of concerned worshipers flooded out of the Temple, pulling Tom and David with them. Once outside the Court of the Gentiles, the static became clear. They could hear the chanting of hundreds, maybe thousands of people, repeating the same word, over and over.

"CRUCIFY! CRUCIFY! CRUCIFY!"

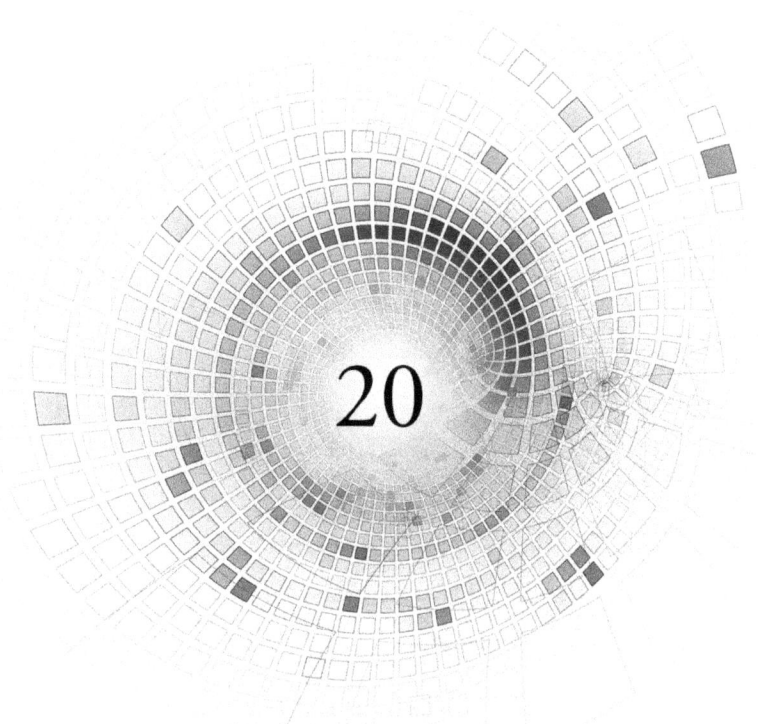

20

VERDICT

30 A.D.

3:23 P.M.

Golgotha ('The Place of the Skull'), Israel

Tom was horrified by the events of the past few hours. Jesus had been taken and beaten. He had been whipped, beaten again and then made to carry a large wooden cross to a hill, while people who only a week ago had welcomed him with cheers and palm branches, now taunted him with insults and stones. Then came the clanging of metal upon metal, as Jesus's wrists were pierced by large nails, binding him to the wood like a plank. After hearing Jesus's screams, Tom had left, knowing that if he heard the tortured sound of his friend again, he might go to the future and return with an assault rifle.

Hours later, Tom and David had struggled against the crowd of onlookers to reach Jesus, to see their friend before he died, but the crowd was too thick and unfriendly to recognizable followers of the man they had nailed to a cross. Tom and David retreated to a hillside opposite Golgotha—which resembled the shape of a human skull—atop which the Romans had crucified three men. Even from his distant viewpoint, Tom could see the stained dirt coating the top of Golgotha. He could see blood dripping from Jesus, his friend, hanging on a cross, twitching and dying for teaching his beliefs.

How could these people think that deserved death?

It was almost too surreal to believe.

Standing beside Tom in equal shock and horror were David, Matthew, Peter, Mary, Martha and Lazarus. They stood silently on the hill, watching, waiting for the inevitable, afraid that any utterance, any disturbance might permanently break their spirits. But when a voice broke through the air, it wasn't one of them; it was Jesus, pushing out his words with his last breath.

"My God, My God," Jesus's voice echoed from Golgotha, "Why have you forsaken me?"

The voice of Jesus was recognizable, but it was coarse, filled with anguish. Then Jesus's body went limp, hanging tight on the nails in his wrists and feet. Tom found his face wet and his throat constricting. Tom fell to his knees and wept quietly, completely unaware of how his friends were reacting.

Mary crumpled into tears and fell toward the ground. Lazarus saw Mary fall through his clouded, moist eyes and caught her just before her head hit the ground. Martha was wailing loudly into Matthew's chest as he held her tightly. Peter stormed off in a rage, cursing the Romans and Pharisees under his breath. And David... Tom looked up at David who was crying, but not like everyone else, who had seen a friend die that they would never see again. David was smiling through his tears.

Confused thoughts raced through Tom's mind in an effort to make sense of David's reaction. Could David really be so confident that Jesus would rise again that he could smile at Jesus's death? Did he really have that much hope? Was he really that naïve?

Tom became aware of his surroundings again and heard Mary crying. As he stood and walked to her, she saw him coming and fell into his arms. He held her as tightly as he could, and she squeezed back. They had both felt the pain of loss before, but now they each had someone to share it with. Tom placed his cheek against hers and held her head in his hand.

"Take me home," she said.

Tom looked toward David, "David."

David had watched Tom with Mary. He had heard her request. "Go."

With nothing else to be said, Tom turned with Mary and they left. Lazarus and Martha followed close behind.

David turned his gaze back to Jesus on the cross. Matthew stood next to him. "You're the most faithful man I've had the pleasure of knowing," Matthew said.

"Not faithful enough," David replied, as he looked at Matthew, who appeared uncommonly small.

"None of us are," Matthew said.

The two stared at Jesus for a few moments, watching as the bloodthirsty crowd dispersed. Matthew shook his head. "I better find Peter before he gets into trouble."

David nodded and placed his hand on Matthew's shoulder. "Until he rises again."

Matthew smiled. "Indeed."

With that, Matthew headed down the hill, leaving David alone.

After a step forward, and then another, David found himself walking toward Jesus at a steady pace. He reached the bottom of the hill, looked up at Golgotha and could no longer see Jesus or the cross. David started up the hill and became aware of how few people were still around. And those that remained were leaving.

The top of Golgotha came quickly as David walked forward, keeping his eyes on his feet. When the dirt beneath his feet turned red, David stopped. He stood still, afraid to look up, afraid to see what he had only witnessed from a distance. But his eyes wandered briefly and found the bottom of a wooden post. He followed the post up and froze on a pair of pierced, bloody feet: Jesus's feet.

David looked up all at once and found Jesus, hanging on the cross, dead. His wrists were nailed to the wood by what looked like railroad spikes, as were his feet, and his side was wet with what remained of his coagulating blood, where a Roman guard had stabbed him after his death. Above Jesus's head, written in Greek, were the words: *Jesus of Nazareth, the King of the Jews.* David's knees shook and gave way. He fell into a kneeling position and found his emotions exploding. He was crying uncontrollably, sobbing loudly. His nose became blocked with mucus. His eyes clouded with thick tears. His head pounded with every quickening heartbeat.

"I'm sorry," he said, like a child pleading to angry parents. "I'm so sorry."

David's memories of Jesus were triggered, and he remembered their first encounter on the Mount of Olives. David had lost control of his emotions on that day as well. And Jesus had stopped his outburst by reaching out, touching David and saying, 'Peace be with you.' But Jesus wouldn't be reaching out for David today. He wouldn't be calming David with kind words. *Well,* David thought, *at least things can't get any worse than this.*

Whack!

David slapped his neck. Something had stung him. He crushed the bug with his hand and brought the remains down in front of him, but he couldn't see through his blurred eyes. A tingle at the back of his neck took his attention away from Jesus hanging above him. What kind of insect had stung him?

David wiped his eyes and blinked several times, making a concerted effort to calm himself and clear his vision. He stared at the insect in his hand. It was still too blurry to make out in detail, but he could see that it was a copperish color from front to back. He could also feel that it was hard and heavier than an insect should be. He blinked three times, and on the third time, his vision cleared.

David looked at the bug and stood immediately to his feet. The insect in his hand was crushed, but he could make out its components...components on an insect? This was a machine! David saw infinitesimal wings made from a clear, ultra-light polymer. He saw miniature gears that gave the robotic wonder life. He saw a hypodermic needle that served as a stinger, and he saw the small, empty vial attached to it.

David felt his neck. It was swelling quickly, and the tingling sensation was spreading down his spine. His eyes widened. LightTech was still trying to kill them, and this time they might succeed.

David ran from Golgotha without looking back. He sprinted down the hill and turned left toward Bethany, toward the home of Lazarus.

Toward Tom.

❧

David's chest felt like it was going to explode, but not from running. He had covered the distance between Golgotha and Lazarus's home in twenty minutes. Now he was only one hundred yards from his destination, but he wasn't sure he would make it that far. His eyes were swollen so badly he couldn't see more than a sliver of light. His thighs stabbed with pain. His calf muscles felt as though they were being twisted into knots. His arms were limp and his organs burned within him. LightTech had picked a powerful poison and it was working fast. David only hoped he could warn Tom in time.

"David!" Lazarus yelled from the home. "David, come quickly! You—"

As blood began to form a rim around his lower lip, David thought Lazarus must have noticed he was moving like the walking dead. But what worried David was that Lazarus sounded panicked before he saw that David wasn't right.

"Tom..." It was all David could say.

After covering the three-mile trek from Golgotha to Bethany, David couldn't go another step. He fell to his knees with all his weight, tearing them open, blood mixing with dirt. Lazarus had starting running toward David an instant after he saw him, which was good, because he arrived just in time to catch David. Lazarus hoisted David over his shoulder and ran for the house like a linebacker.

The conversation between Mary and Martha was muffled and fading as David struggled to listen in. To makes things worse, Mary's voice was quivering too much to tell what she was saying, and the ringing in David's ears was growing louder. David suddenly felt himself lying on his back.

"Lazarus, what's—" Martha said, though David couldn't see her.

"He's sick too."

"What sickness is this? What could do this to a man?"

"I don't know..."

"Mary should say goodbye."

David struggled to make out the voices of Martha and Lazarus, but he understood the meaning of the conversation. He tilted his head to the left and saw Tom lying next to him. Tom looked dead already. What was left functioning in David's brain became a turbine of confusion. This couldn't be happening. David could die, but not Tom. Tom had to—

David heard the front door crash open.

"Who's there?" he heard Lazarus yell.

David's thoughts drifted. He no longer felt his body. He was floating in a black abyss and he saw the face of an angel floating above him, surrounded by a glowing white light... No, not an angel...

It was Sally. He smiled and said, "I've missed you. Sorry I stayed away so long." David laughed. He knew he was dying and that he was talking to a vision produced by his misfiring synapses. But he accepted it. He couldn't imagine a nicer way to pass on than seeing her face again.

"I'm sorry I never told you," David said.

"Told me what, David?"

David grinned ever wider. Now his hallucination was responding.

"That I love you," he said.

"If you hang on and your friend doesn't kill me, you might get the chance."

Now that was odd. What a strange thing for a hallucination to say. David suddenly realized that the voice he heard wasn't inside his head; it was through the ringing in his ears, above it. An incredible sadness swept through what remaining senses David still processed. He realized that Sally wasn't a vision. She was with him now, in the past, and he would never see her again. The ringing in David's ears grew intolerable and waves of color danced in his vision. The last thing David felt before he slipped from the conscious world was a small prick on his limp arm.

With a flash, David felt his arms, legs and head. He could smell, taste and hear. His senses rushed back to him and reality slapped him in the face.

"Whoa, David," Lazarus said.

David opened his eyes to find himself sitting up in bed with Lazarus holding his shoulders. "I'm alive."

"Tom lives as well, though he still sleeps," Lazarus explained.

"How?"

"A friend of yours, I think. From where it is you come from. We cannot understand her language."

David felt a constriction in his throat, but not from the poison he had survived. "Where is she?" he asked.

"Outside."

David made it from the bedroom to the front door in less than five seconds, but his feet became stuck to the ground at the sight of Sally, standing with her back to him, hair blowing in the wind. She was wearing a tight, black outfit, from head to toe. Her gaze was toward Bethany at the bottom of the hill. It was an amazing view that David had often enjoyed, but it paled in comparison to the woman standing in front of him, who had risked her own life to save his. He wanted to watch her, remember her every curve, drink in every hair on her head, but he couldn't wait another second. He ran toward her as quick as he could. "Sally!"

With a burst of excitement and a bright smile, she turned around and saw him running toward her. She covered her smiling mouth and reached out for him. It was a response that was both unexpected and very welcome. David wrapped his arms around her and spun her in the air. For her it had been a day since they last saw each other. For him it had been three years, and he wouldn't waste another second.

David returned her to her feet, gripped her by the waist, pulled her close and kissed her firmly on the lips.

Sally was shocked but surrendered her mouth to David and held him tight. She knew how long he had been gone. She knew how hard the past years must have been for him. His passion for her was tangible, and with his kiss, she felt all the danger, mistrust and deception from the past day disappear.

David released her from his embrace and looked her in the eyes. They smiled at each other. "I'm sorry," David said.

"Don't be."

"But... I don't understand... How long have I been gone in your time?"

"Only a day."

David squinted one eye and scratched his head. "A day? But yesterday you would have killed me for doing that."

"A lot can change in a day."

"And you came back to save us?"

Sally nodded. "I couldn't let my two best scientists die, could I? It doesn't make good business sense."

"No, I suppose it doesn't."

"Have you seen any sign of Roberts yet?"

"Roberts... He didn't last long."

Sally looked surprised, but then she became distracted. "David... When you were...in there...dying. You were speaking English."

David shuffled nervously. "Did I say what I think I said?"

Sally smiled.

"I was delirious. Don't—"

"David... I think..." She stepped closer to him and held his arms. "I know... I love you, too."

David nearly fainted. This woman, who just yesterday was threatening his job, was professing her love for him?

"But...how? It's only been—"

"When you were dying. I thought I was too late. I thought you were going to die. I realized then that if you died, my life would be somehow emptier...meaningless. But even then, I still didn't know...and then you said it, that you loved me, and I knew that second that I loved you, too."

'Stunned' didn't do justice to how David felt. He was simultaneously ecstatic and mortified. He looked into her deep brown eyes; she was telling the truth. "Sally... You don't know how long I—"

Whack! Sally slapped her neck.

"What happened?" David asked.

"Something bit me," Sally said, just slightly annoyed.

David suddenly remembered slapping the bug on his neck. It nearly took his life.

Sally's forehead grew uncharacteristically wrinkled. "David?"

With a wave of concern, David took the hand Sally had used to slap her neck and looked at it. The remains of another robot bug rested in her open palm. "Damn!" he cursed. "How did you cure Tom and me?"

"I injected you with the antidote... David, my neck."

"I know. Do you have any more?"

"I only brought enough for you and Tom."

"What about in the future?"

"It's in George's office. A secret room...but it's got to be guarded like Fort Knox by now."

"Can you think of a time when it's not guarded?"

Sally looked David in the eyes. "It's going to be close."

"I'm used to close."

Sally smiled despite the tingling sensation stretching down her spine. David had become strong, resilient, brave. She adored the man more than ever.

"Come with me," David said, "I have an idea."

❧

George's office was empty and the secret side room was wide open. Jake left in such a hurry that he forgot to close up, which David found very convenient.

David crinkled his nose at the dry, over circulated air. The pale colors of the room were dull to his eyes. The future seemed dead to him now, but the woman next to him was still breathing and he wasn't going to let her go.

David laid Sally on the floor. He didn't want to bring her with him. He thought it would be too dangerous. But her condition worsened so drastically that he couldn't risk not giving the antidote to her the second it was in his possession.

Sally didn't move. Her eyes were swollen shut and her arms and legs had become like Jell-O. Only her chest still moved, slowly rising and falling with each labored breath. David rifled through the small lab and quickly found the antidote. He removed the syringe from its foam protection in the silver briefcase and removed the plastic protective stopper from its tip.

He fell to his knees next to Sally, ignoring the stinging pain from his dried gashes. Then he took hold of her arm and held the needle above her skin. He had never given anyone an injection before. What was that they did on TV? Oh yes. David flicked the syringe twice with his finger and squirted some of the fluid out. *To get the air bubbles out,* he remembered. He placed the needle on Sally's skin and—

"Who the hell are you?"

David looked up. It was Jake, and he was holding a gun.

Jake quickly raised the gun toward David. "David. Of course, David. How nice of you to come back to us."

David froze. Would Jake use the gun? If David didn't inject the antidote soon, Sally would die. If he injected it now, Jake might shoot them both.

Jake walked toward David, taking in his clothing, the amount of dirt on his feet, the length of his beard. "You've been gone for quite a long time, haven't you?"

"What do you want?" David asked, as he noticed a stain of sprayed blood on Jake's clothing. "What have you done?"

Jake looked down at his clothing and smiled. "Security guards can have loud mouths." Pointing at Sally, he added, "They saw her go back. They knew too much. Just like you... So I removed them from the equation."

"We'll get out of your way. We don't want anything to do with you or this company." David said with an honest desperation.

"It's too late for that, David. With those watches, you could change everything. I can't let you do that," Jake said, as he thrust the gun at David's head.

"Take the watches, just let us go."

"I don't think so," Jake said, as he thumbed the gun's hammer.

"Hold it, Jake."

David was relieved to hear Tom's voice.

Jake whipped around and leveled the gun at Tom, who had Captain Roberts's gun trained on Jake's chest.

David saw his chance.

He stabbed the syringe into Sally's arm and pushed the liquid into her as hard and as quickly as he could. Now it was only a matter of time.

"Put down the gun, Jake."

"I'll use this," Jake said, glancing at his gun. "Will you?"

"I'm sure you've seen my report. You know what happened in Zambia. You know I've killed before. What do you think happened to Roberts?" Tom said with a cocky grin.

Jake stood frozen for a moment, his eyes probing Tom's. "No...no...that's not how it happened. You couldn't."

Jake took a step toward Tom. He was a cornered wolverine, ready to attack.

"Slow down, Jake," David urged. "You don't have to do this."

"Shut up, David," Jake said.

David stood to his feet. If bullets started flying around the room, he didn't want Sally being hit. Jake seemed to sense the pressure of David behind him, but he didn't dare take his gun off Tom.

Tom sensed that David was trying to move the action into the office and away from Sally, which was just fine with him. Tom backed up into George's office, giving Jake space to move.

"Keep him coming this way," Tom said to David in Aramaic.

"What are you going to do?" David replied in the same language.

Jake bit his lip and then shouted, "What are you saying? What the hell are you saying?"

"I brought a friend," Tom finished in Aramaic.

Tom's last statement was enough to push Jake right to the edge. His finger squeezed the trigger half way down. He was going to kill them all or die trying.

21

REVELATIONS

2005

7:05 A.M.

Arizona

Tom backed up slowly. He could see that Jake was going to fire, but he didn't want to have to shoot Jake—not if it could be avoided. Tom's back hit the opposite wall of George's office. There was no more room to move, but it might have already been enough.

Just a few more feet, Jake, Tom thought.

Jake's hand shook. His finger began squeezing the trigger. His eyes were locked on Tom, as he pushed forward, aiming the gun for Tom's head.

Tom could see he needed to give Jake time to enter the office. "How about we leave and never come back? We'll call it even, Jake. No one needs to die here."

"We already covered this. If I let you go now, you would change things. For all I know, you might try and kill me in the past, keep all this from happening," Jake said.

"Time can't be changed," Tom explained. "If we had gone back in time to kill you, it would have already happened and you wouldn't exist. You can let us go, and nothing will change."

"Nothing will change because no one is leaving," Jake sneered. "And if time can't be changed, what have you and David been doing all this time, sight-seeing?"

"We can't change the past because we're already part of it. Everything David and I did in the past was recorded in the Bible before we left, because it's already the past," Tom said.

"You don't expect me to believe that you're in the Bible!" Jake was near hysterical laughter.

"It's true," David said.

Jake switched from laughing to ferocity in a split second. "Shut up! Both of you!"

He entered George's bland office through the door to the secret lab, holding his gun straight out toward Tom. He stared at Tom's chest, locked on target, trying to judge which way Tom might jump. He saw Tom look to his left and wink.

What is he winking—ack!

A massive hand reached out and took Jake by the throat. A second hand snatched the wrist of the hand holding the gun. Tom had instructed Lazarus on the dangers of guns and Lazarus already knew how to disarm a man. Lazarus squeezed Jake's hand until he heard a crack. Jake would have screamed if he could breathe, but Lazarus's monster hand held tightly to Jake's throat.

The gun landed on the firm industrial rug. Lazarus took Jake by the shirt, picked him off the floor and heaved him into the air. Jake soared across the office, slid across George's desk and into the black leather chair, which rolled across the floor and crashed into the wall. Jake's body sagged in the chair and then toppled onto the floor.

Tom smiled as wide as the sun; Lazarus was amazing. Tom quickly checked Jake for a pulse. "He's alive," Tom said in Aramaic.

"Good," Lazarus said. "I feared I had killed the man."

Tom entered the lab followed by Lazarus, whose eyes sucked in the strange technologies surrounding him. David greeted them at the door.

"That was close," David said. He looked up at Lazarus. "You all right?"

Lazarus looked stunned by the technology around him. "Yes... I think... What is all this?"

"We'll try to explain later," Tom said, then he turned to Sally and spoke in English. "Right now we have to decide what to do next."

"I'll tell you what we're gonna do," Sally said, as she stood to her feet, supporting her weight on the countertop. "We're gonna make sure no one from LightTech ever goes back in time again."

David smiled. Sally was back.

ᏟᎾ

D avid felt like a child again, sneaking around, trying not to get caught. Only now if he was found, he might get a bullet in his chest instead of tagged, and there was no safety zone. He was sweating, afraid, excited—and he really had to use the bathroom. As a child, whenever David played hide and seek, his nerves would send his bowel system into overdrive and he would have to run inside to relieve himself during the first game. But being in the bathroom for several minutes of the first game also gave him an unfair advantage and a reputation as being a master hide and seek player. Who thinks to check the bathroom during an outdoor game of hide and seek?

"Uh, I realize this might not be the best time, but I've got to use the bathroom," David said with a whisper, as they shuffled down the dimly lit hallway.

"Are you serious?" Sally asked, as she eyed David with one eyebrow arched high on her forehead.

"Yes," David said. He squirmed like a little boy who was about to wet himself. "I won't be long."

Sally led David, Tom and Lazarus down an adjacent hallway to the left. They stopped in front of a blue door. David looked at the door and the white symbol of a woman. He paused at the women's room symbol and opened his mouth to say something that never escaped his lungs.

"David, get in there now," Sally said.

David flung open the door and entered the bathroom.

Tom smiled. Life or death circumstances aside, this was pretty funny.

"We need to augment the watches to transport the entire contents of the receiving area. Do you or David know how to do that?" Sally asked Tom.

"Assuming that's how our future selves transferred the material originally, any watches that haven't been tampered with should still be configured to transfer large amounts of material. It should be a piece of cake." Tom explained.

"I can hear you," David shouted from inside the bathroom.

Sally looked at Tom quizzically.

"He can't go if he thinks people can hear him," Tom explained.

Sally rolled her eyes, spread her lips in a smile and began to walk away. Tom cracked open the bathroom door. "We'll be down the hall," he said with a chuckle. "But hurry up, LightTech is going to be crawling with people soon, and we're going to stick out like Gentiles in the Temple."

"I know, I know," said David from within a stall. "Now shoo!"

Tom and Lazarus caught up with Sally, who was watching Lazarus's confused face taking in mirrors, framed aerial photos and elaborate paintings. "We should send your friend back."

"Lazarus? We might still need his muscle," Tom retorted.

"Look at him. Being brought two thousand years into the future is too much for any man to handle."

Tom looked at Lazarus, who was looking closely at his reflection in a mirror. "Lazarus," Tom said in Aramaic, "Are you all right?"

Lazarus looked at Tom with wide eyes. "This place, this is where you're from?"

"Yes, this was where we worked. Just like Matthew was a tax collector, David and I worked here... But are you all right? Is this too much for you to handle?"

Lazarus shot Tom a glance that said Tom better be joking.

Tom looked at Sally, "He's fine."

"But he's—"

"He's fine, look at his—"

"Hey!" a voice shouted from the other end of the hallway. "Who are you? What are you doing?"

A young guard with bright blue eyes and a blond crew cut, walked swiftly toward them, hand on his holstered gun. There would be no surprise attacks to rescue them this time. They only had one chance.

"Run!" Tom shouted in English, and then repeated it in Aramaic for Lazarus, "Run!"

The three bolted away from the guard, who was already squawking into his radio and drawing his weapon. "This is Daniels. I'm in Delta Sector. In pursuit of three intruders."

Tom knew these hallways would be awash with trigger-happy hired guns in minutes. They had to get out of this sector, and fast. They approached a T-intersection at the end of the hallway. To the right were the elevators, to the left the stairs. "The elevators are guarded, let's take the stairs," Tom said, as they neared the end of the hall.

"No!" Sally shouted, "The elevator's clear."

Tom glanced back at Sally. "How do you know?"

"The elevator guard was one of the three that Jake killed. They were chasing me up the stairs just fifteen minutes ago." With that, Sally turned right and Tom followed.

Pang!

A bullet ripped through and shattered a large framed painting at the end of the hallway, causing Lazarus to dive left. Daniels was running at full speed, gun raised and ready to shoot. Lazarus attempted to cross the hallway to the elevator, where Sally and Tom were waving him on, but a second bullet crashed into the wall, missing him by inches and stopping him in his tracks.

Lazarus ducked and ran back toward the stairwell door. Tom shouted to him, "Lazarus, open that door and follow the stairs down five levels."

"What?" Lazarus shouted.

"Five levels!" shouted Tom, pointing down with his finger as the elevator doors closed.

Lazarus ran to the door and tried to push his way through it, but it held tight. He smashed up against the door and still it didn't budge. Lazarus looked down, saw the doorknob and pulled on it. Still nothing. He could hear Daniels's footsteps approaching quickly as he yelled something unintelligible. Lazarus turned the doorknob by accident as he looked back at the elevator doors, hoping they would open, and he felt the door open slightly. He pulled the door and nearly ripped it off the hinges. Then he ran inside and headed down the stairs with a series of great strides.

Daniels stopped at the crossroads and looked in either direction. He saw the light indicating that the elevator was going down. He looked to the left and saw the door to the stairwell close. He held the radio to his mouth. "Two suspects in elevator 4D, one in the stairwell. I'll take the stairwell. Elevator has stopped on..." The guard looked at the elevator level indicator. "Level 2, over."

"Copy that Daniels, we are en route to Delta Sector, level 2, over and out."

This was the first security breach Daniels had been a part of, and he loved every second of it. When he got the call earlier, it was for only one perp, and he had thought the action would be over by the time he arrived on the scene. But now there were three perps, and he already got to fire his weapon...twice. Daniels secured his radio and raced into the stairwell.

The hallway fell silent until the blue bathroom door creaked open. David peered out. It appeared his penchant for using the bathroom had paid off again. No one ever checks the bathroom—especially a women's room. He had heard the shouting, the gunshots. He knew Lazarus was on his own, and he knew where Sally and Tom would head. He would have to move quickly.

A smile came to his face as he realized he could move more quickly than any other man on the planet.

David tapped the buttons on his watch and then waited for the bright flash and loud noise. But nothing happened. He looked at the watch and carefully pushed the final button again. He waited...nothing. David wasted little time self-debating why his watch had ceased to work. His friends were in trouble and it was time to take action. After deactivating his watch so it wouldn't suddenly transport him if it decided to work again, he ran to the T-intersection at the end of the hallway and took a left into the stairwell.

☙

The supply closet was small, but it made for the perfect hiding place and it was strategically down the hall from the entrance to the control center. Some scientists had shown up for work, but had been promptly sent home by two armed guards who stood watch in front of the control center doors.

Tom and Sally were crouched on the floor amid brooms, buckets and boxes of detergent and deodorizer. The smell was a noxious mix of bleach and dirt, but it beat being shot at.

"So what made you come around?" Tom asked in a hushed voice.

Sally looked at him. "What do you mean?" she whispered.

"I'd almost call you a nice person."

"Funny."

"I thought so."

Sally sat silently for a moment, but then looked at Tom and said, "People change."

"Overnight?"

"My guess is that changing overnight is easier to do than not changing at all over three years."

"What's that supposed to—?"

"You're still arrogant. You still don't know when to keep your mouth shut. And you still have my respect."

Tom's eyes softened, his forehead smoothed and his muscles relaxed.

Sally continued. "Over the years I watched you and David do things I had only dreamed of, and I had to be content to sit on the sidelines and watch. The most I could do to feel useful was to nag. Otherwise, I had no reason to be here."

Tom smiled.

Sally had changed, and he decided he'd better, too, lest he get the old Sally back. He extended his hand. "Friends?"

Sally reached around a hanging mop and took his hand. "Friends. But don't push it."

"Done."

A loud squawking noise from around the corner caught their attention. Shouting voices were blaring from the two guards' radios. They couldn't make out what was being said, but they knew it must be urgent and probably to do with David or Lazarus. The two guards ran past, keys jingling, leaving the control center unguarded.

Tom looked at Sally, whose face had become distorted with concern. "David will be okay. We survived much worse in the past, trust me."

Sally looked at Tom, trying to squelch any worried look. "Let's go."

The pair squeaked open the closet door and glanced down the hallway. The path was clear. Tom knew they must have locked the facility down tight. They didn't want anyone going in or out. He smiled and looked down at his watch. They had an automatic exit no one could block.

Tom and Sally made their way into the control center and found the lights already on and computers twitching with activity. Every computer console in the room was alive, processing equations, searching for information and solving problems.

"What's all this?" Tom asked.

Sally looked perplexed. "I don't know. None of this was on when I left."

Tom kept moving. "All the information in the world won't matter if they don't have that." He was pointing at the equipment in the receiving area, which was lit from the inside.

Tom and Sally quickly took stock of everything in the room. Tom froze on the table that had held the original ten watches. "How many watches do we have in activity right now?"

"Yours, mine, David's... Your friend Lazarus is wearing Captain Roberts's. Only four, why?"

"Damn. We've got two more missing."

"Can we get rid of all this with only the four?"

"Shouldn't be a problem. Though I'd really like to know where the other watches are," Tom said, as he situated the watches in four separate parts of the room. "When and where do we want this stuff to go?"

"Return to sender." Sally said. "I can't think of anyone better equipped to take care of all this than you and David. If it came from your future selves, let's send it back."

Tom worked the buttons on each watch. "Good idea. Our future selves would have lived through all this, so they should be expecting it."

Tom finished prepping the final watch. "Okay, I've got them on a timer. We have thirty seconds."

Tom and Sally quickly exited the receiving area and watched from the safety of the control center. "Fifteen seconds," Tom said.

Tom's eyes squinted. "I just realized something. If all this equipment was sent to us from our future selves, then David and I must make it out of this okay."

Sally raised an eyebrow and smirked with half her mouth. "That's reassuring... for you."

Tom looked at the receiving area. "Five seconds..."

Five seconds of silence passed between them, and on the sixth second, Tom's brow lowered and crushed together. "Nothing's happening."

"Maybe you forgot to push a button?"

"On all four of them? Not likely."

Tom was about to charge back into the receiving area when a voice stopped him in his tracks. "Quite the quandary, isn't it, Dr. Greenbaum?"

Tom looked up. Spencer was sitting on the other side of the room with his feet crossed on top of a desk.

"Spencer?"

"You remember my name? After all those years in the past? I'm flattered."

"How do you know—?"

"It's okay, Tom, Spencer's working with us. He knew about you and David going back in time even before you went."

"How's that possible?"

"I've known for a very long time, Tom," Spencer said with a grin, as he brought his feet down to the floor.

"Why aren't the watches working?" Sally asked Spencer.

Spencer shrugged with a smile, "Because I disabled them. Actually I've managed to disable all attempts at time travel within a square mile thanks to this brilliant mind." Spencer tapped his head. "You really should have given Spencer a promotion. If only we had discovered his mind earlier."

"Spencer, are you feeling all right?" Sally asked.

"Why, whatever do you mean?"

"You're talking about yourself in the plural," Sally replied.

"Were we? Sorry, force of habit."

"How and why did you disable the watches?" Tom asked as he moved toward Spencer, keeping a watchful eye on the little man.

"We're afraid we can't tell you that," Spencer said.

"Why not?"

"Because we said so."

Tom knew something was seriously wrong with Spencer. He had worked closely with Spencer for years. He wasn't talkative. He wasn't sarcastic. He wasn't anything like the man sitting across the room from him.

Spencer sat up straight. With every utterance, his voice was joined by another, and another, until he spoke with the combined voices of fifty separate men, all in unison. "You know what? What? You deserve to know. He does? He does! Tell him! We will! We went to the future. It's really quite a wonderful place. Nice. Nice! War. Famine. Technology. We used this amazing mind to create a device that binds time and space into a solid, unbendable force. Rendering you...stuck. Like glue! Like bugs in honey! Stuck."

Tom's mind began searching for an explanation...began working out the problem... began...remembering.

Spencer stood confidently and held a small device in front of him. "Such magnify-icent power for such a small device. Tiny. Much like that watch of yours, which we find to be a wonderful new toy. So much fun! A wonderful new toy for us!"

269

Tom's mind flashed back two years. The same look in the eyes. The same voice. Tom knew it was impossible, but what other explanation was there? "I know who you are."

"Of course you do. We're Spencer! Friendly, helpful, quiet, Spencer!"

"The body might be different...the cuts on your arms are gone..."

Spencer's eyes widened and he smiled a toothy grin. "Bravo for you. He's so smart. We don't like him. Neither do we," Spencer said, as he put the device down on the console next to him.

Tom's eyes glanced at the device. He knew it was the key to their escape.

"You're welcome to try, disciple," Spencer said in Aramaic, "but you have felt our power twice before." He switched back to English and continued, "You know what we will do to you. Crush you. Break you. Kill you. Yes! Yes..."

Tom looked shocked, he knew who Tom was, is, and used to be. But *twice* before? Tom only remembered the one time, which ended with a herd of pigs committing watery suicide.

Spencer laughed. "It's been two years for you. It's been two thousand for us, but Legion remembers you."

"Impossible."

"You still don't believe that we're real? Fascinating. Astounding. He's so ignorant! We know!"

Sally had stopped moving. She looked mortified. "Tom..."

Tom felt bad about lying to Sally, but what other choice did he have? "Ignore him. He's delusional. Could be a side effect of traveling into the future. Right now, we need to get that device. I'll take care of him; you get that thing and smash it."

Sally nodded and the two began walking toward Spencer, focused on their individual goals. Spencer stood his unflinching ground. "Jesus was a fool to let us go. A fool! He knew we would come back. And we have. Again, and again. He knew we would steal. Lie. Rape. Murder. Our favorite! Just like we did to your wife."

Tom became like a statue, unmoving and solid.

"Remember the golden field? We saw you there. We weren't sure how it was possible then, but we knew who you were. Thomas, the disciple of Jesus. Tom. Didymus. The doubter himself. Here, in the future! Tormenting you was delightful. 'Do you believe ahs dis wuman deed? Ansah me now.' Like the accent? We can throw it on like a light switch! So much fun. We remember that day. So do we!"

Tom's mind raced to compile and hypothesize on what Spencer, on what Legion, was telling him. Legion was in Zambia. Legion recognized him as a disciple of Jesus from thousands of years past, before he had even gone back. Could Legion have known who she was? Who he was? Tom's head ached as he thought that Megan was killed because he went back in time...but he only went back in time because Megan had been killed! Tom's breath escaped him as the vicious circle twisted his thoughts.

"Do you remember the smell of your wife's blood on your body? We do. Delicious! The look on your face was to be cherished. We did that to you, and Jesus let us. He let us. He set us free! Why do you think that is, Tom? Why would Jesus let us go to torment you? To kill your wife? To kill your pitiful Megan?"

Screaming, Tom charged Spencer with the rage of twenty men filling his clenched fists. Searing hot blood was pulsing through his veins, filled with strength-giving adrenaline. He was going to kill Spencer or die trying.

271

22

CONFRONTATIONS

2005

7:35 A.M.

Arizona

David's nose burned from the smell of month-old, gray paint that coated the stairwell walls and railings. With each breath, he became more aware how odd the smells of the future were. In the past, smell made sense. It was animal, dirt, grass, flowers or food. Never anything as toxic smelling as latex paint laid down once a year to keep things looking new.

As David neared the bottom floor, he could hear several men screaming orders in English. The words were repeated over and over as though the recipient of the verbal barrage was not complying. But David knew it was simply because Lazarus could not understand the words being shouted at him. And soon the guards' patience would wear thin.

David reached the stairwell exit and cracked open the door. He peeked out into the hallway, which was white and covered with long red and green painted arrows, pointing to various technical areas. Lazarus was against the wall, surrounded by Daniels and two other guards. All three had their weapons drawn and trained on Lazarus's head.

"Hands behind your head, damnit! Now!" Daniels shouted.

David saw no way for this to end peacefully. But what could he do against three armed guards? He put his hand on his waist and felt something cold and solid. He looked down. Of course. After Jake was knocked unconscious by Lazarus, David had picked up his gun. At the time, he had no intention of using it, but this new situation called for extreme action.

He pulled the gun from under his robe. It was heavy in his hand. He felt dangerous, like James Bond, only he didn't have a license to kill, and he hoped he could completely avoid any violence at all. But he'd do whatever he had to do to make sure Lazarus was returned to the past intact.

David raised the weapon next to his head like they do in the movies and crept silently into the hallway behind the guards. His face reddened as he closed in. His blood was pumping fast, his heart beat like a nervous hamster's.

As he moved across the floor, he heard his footsteps like anvils falling and clanging. He was positive his approach would be discovered and that any moment now, a bullet would pierce his body. He took a slow, deep breath as he came to within a foot of Daniels. He reached out slowly, and then like a striking viper, he had his arm around Daniels's neck and the muzzle of his gun firm against the man's head. "Don't move! Nobody move! Or...or he gets it!"

Well that sounded dumb, David thought. He didn't plan his words as well as his actions, but the outcome was no less effective. Both guards trained their weapons away from Lazarus and onto David.

David pushed his lips close to Daniels's ear. "Drop your weapon. Now, or I'll pull this trigger."

The gun hit the floor and rattled next to David's foot. David turned his attention to the other guards. "You guys don't want to see..." David read the guard's name badge, "...Daniels die, do you?"

One guard remained solid, unflinching. The other began to blink nervously.

Daniels started to shake. "Jim, Clark, c'mon guys... Do what he says."

Jim took a step forward and aimed as best he could at David's head. "Put the gun down, now."

Daniels's face twisted as though he was being stabbed in the back. "Jim! What are you doing?"

"My job," Jim said.

Clark began to lower his weapon. "Jim, man, I don't know. I think we should do what he says. I don't want anyone to get killed."

"Listen to Clark," David said, as he attempted to keep his head hidden behind Daniels's. "We can all walk away from this in one piece."

Clark bent down and placed his weapon on the floor.

"Thank you, Clark," David said.

"You're welcome, sir."

Jim's hand began to shake and his eyes darted back and forth between David and Lazarus. "NO! Pick your weapon up, Clark. Right now!"

David could see Jim's hand shaking, panic overtaking his senses, tunneling his vision. If he didn't shoot someone on purpose, he might do so by accident. David slowly moved his gun away from Daniels's head and aimed it at Jim. He hadn't ever shot a gun before, but he had played Duck Hunt on the original Nintendo system, when it was a novelty so many years ago. David figured it couldn't be too different.

Jim lowered the gun, and then in a split second of indecision, he raised it up again. Determination revived in his eyes, a burst of red exploded through his arm and his ears rang with the sound of an explosion. Jim's gun fell from his limp hand

and clacked on to the floor. He held his hand to his arm and then took it away. It was covered in blood. "You shot me!"

David smiled. He'd shot him. David pushed Daniels toward Clark and Jim, and then he raised his gun at all three of them. "Don't move. Not one of you."

David looked at Lazarus, whose eyes were wide and lips were pursed. "Are you all right?"

Lazarus nodded slowly, rubbing his ears.

"I'm sorry about this, guys, I really am. But I wouldn't do this unless I had to, unless it was important." David pointed his gun at Clark. "Can I have your radio, please?"

Clark took his radio from his belt. "Of course, sir." Clark handed the radio to David warily and then retreated back behind Jim and Daniels, eyes blinking rapidly.

David depressed the button on the radio, "Uh, this is Clark, over."

"Copy that, what's your situation?" came a voice from the radio.

Lazarus took a step back, eyeing the radio incredulously.

"We have apprehended the suspects...uh, we're bringing them in now. Feel free to call off the alarm...over."

"Copy, how many suspects do you have in custody? Over."

"Four, over."

"Copy that. Good work. Over."

"Thanks, we're bringing them in, over and out."

David switched off the radio and dropped it on the ground. He looked at the three guards. "Your radios. Put them on the floor."

Daniels and Jim took their radios from their belts and dropped them on the floor.

David looked around the hallway. *Now what?* His eyes locked on an emergency fire hose attached to the wall. He looked back at the three petrified guards. "Face each other. Get close."

When David had finished tying the fire hose around the men he realized the hose was too loose to hold the men for more than a few seconds. Even Lazarus had failed to get the thick material to tie tightly.

Clark fidgeted nervously for a moment and then found a smidge of bravery. "Sir, you could just leave us here like this, and we won't move."

David smiled. These poor kids were having the worst day of their life. "Sorry Clark, I can't take the chance. There are lives at stake."

David followed the hose back to its glass case where a red valve was labeled: Turn for water. David walked to the valve and twisted it. Water rushed into the hose, blowing it up like a balloon. The three guards were pulled close together by the expanding hose, which resembled an anaconda constricting its prey. When David was satisfied that the men were secured, he turned the valve off, so as not to crush the men to death. "Can you breathe?"

"Yes sir...barely though," Clark said.

"Have a knife?"

"My belt, on the right side, sir."

David pushed his way through the tight fire hose and retrieved Clark's small jackknife. He opened it up and poked a small hole in the hose, which sprayed a mist of water into the air. "There," David said, "You should be able to get free in...twenty minutes or so."

"Thank you, sir," Clark said.

"You're most welcome."

David turned to Lazarus. "Ready?"

Lazarus held up a rag tied in a bundle, full of very heavy items. "Their weapons and talking boxes are in here."

David took the bundle and placed it on the floor next to the bound guards. "Your guns and radios are in this. Try not to shoot anyone today, guys, okay?"

"Yes, sir," Clark said.

David opened the door to the stairwell and looked at Lazarus. "Let's go."

Lazarus and David disappeared into the stairwell and the door closed behind them with a clunk. David led the way swiftly down the stairs. With the heightened security and the watches not working, they were running out of time. They might have to attempt an escape on foot. If that turned out to be true, David knew they would all die.

❦

Tom sailed across the control room and crashed onto a computer console. He had forgotten how strong this Legion, this whatever it was, could make a man. He rolled off the console, onto the hard, cold floor and looked up.

The thick foam dangling from Spencer's mouth was enough to make Sally back away, but what concerned her most was that he was pursuing her. Her face revealed she had never seen something so horrible, so evil. Her normally controlled expression had vanished, replaced by a furrowed brow, crinkled nose and a bit lip brought on by the freshly experienced terror.

After pushing himself onto his hands and knees, Tom heard the clunk of metal hitting cement. He knew what it was. He knew he had it from the beginning, but he wanted to beat the beast into the ground with his bare fists. He wanted to feel the blood of Megan's murderer on his tender knuckles. But he knew he could never win a fistfight with this supernatural creature.

He wrapped his hand around the gun and placed his finger firmly against the trigger. Then, he stood to his feet. "Legion!"

Spencer stopped, his crushing hand only inches from Sally's throat. He looked at Tom, holding the gun, and grinned. "Kill us again, Tom. Yes, kill us! Kill us like you did the Zambian men who murdered your wife."

"I'm planning to," Tom said as he walked forward, gun raised.

Spencer craned his neck like a thinking dog. "Do you remember Samuel, disciple?"

Tom pulled the gun's hammer back with a click.

"When we first met and Jesus sent us into the herd of swine? The pigs. We don't like pigs. Do you remember Samuel after we left his body?"

Tom paused, he remembered Samuel. He remembered thinking he was a different man. He remembered Samuel couldn't recall anything that had happened.

"We took him, Tom. He didn't willingly accept our presence. Nobody ever says 'yes' if we ask them. Never. He didn't willingly do the wonderful things we made him do. He was innocent—by earthly standards anyway."

Tom's eyes widened slightly.

"And you remember the men in Africa. The men you killed. You killed us! We loved it when you did that!"

"Shut up."

"They were innocent of your wife's murder, just like Samuel."

"Shut up!"

"And you killed them! Are you going to kill Spencer, too?"

Mounting pressure filled Tom's skull so that his face felt swollen and red with heat. He hadn't felt the desire to kill a man since Megan had been murdered, and here was the being responsible for her death, and he could kill it again. Or could he? Tom aimed the gun and fired twice. Spencer's body spun and fell to the floor in a heap.

Spencer looked up, smiling, "A futile effort."

"I disagree," Tom said as he looked down at Spencer, who now had a bloody bullet wound in each thigh.

Tom looked back at Sally, whose petrified eyes were locked on Spencer. "Sally... Sally!"

Sally snapped her attention to Tom.

"Get the device," he urged.

Sally nodded quickly and hustled toward the opposite side of the room, where Spencer had placed the device.

"You think this body is affected by pain, while I control it?" the voices of fifty men said.

Tom whipped his attention back to Spencer, who was already on his feet and winding up. "Sally, look—"

Whump! Tom crumpled onto the floor, gasping for air.

Froth flew through the room as Spencer turned to look at Sally and growled. He jumped across the room like a gazelle. Sally stopped and slipped backward onto her hands as Spencer landed between her and the device. She crawled away as he stormed toward her.

"How much does this woman mean to you, disciple?" Spencer said, reaching out for Sally's struggling feet.

Tom pulled himself up, trying to shout, but there was no air in his lungs to create the sound. He couldn't let David experience the same loss he had. He couldn't let David feel that pain. But he couldn't do anything to stop it. Tom fell back to the floor. His ribs were on fire and his legs were temporarily useless.

Spencer took hold of Sally's ankle and pulled her toward him. Her squirming did nothing to loosen his merciless grip.

"Please...please..." Tom said.

Spencer held Sally up in the air by her ankle. He looked at Tom.

"Take me instead. Kill me," Tom pleaded.

"All you Christians are the same. 'Kill me. Take me. Martyr me.' We hate Christians! So do we! We would much rather kill this woman and have you live to be tortured again and again. Ad infinitum! Forever!"

Tom took a deep breath. "I'm not a Christian."

Spencer bit his smiling bottom lip until it bled. "That's right! We nearly forgot! How could all of us forget that? If we kill you now, you'll be ours to torture for all eternity!"

After dropping Sally to the hard floor, Spencer leapt into the air and landed on top of a computer console in front of Tom, crushing the equipment below his feet as though he weighed five hundred pounds. Tom pushed away, but found his back against the cold concrete wall of the control center.

"I have bad news for you... You can't kill me," Tom said, attempting to act as confident as possible.

Spencer hopped off the mangled computer console and onto the floor. "And why is that?"

"The time-travel equipment... I sent it here...from the future. If I died now, how could I send it back in time?"

"Let's see, maybe if David sent it back in time without your help? He is a smart one after all, that David. We hate that name! Stop saying it then!"

Tom had no reply. He hadn't considered that.

"News flash, Didymus, we've been to the future, and you weren't there! He wasn't! We didn't see him. Neither did we!"

"You're lying," Tom said, as he squinted his eyes in an effort to mask his surprise.

"Are we? We suppose we're about to find out."

Spencer reached out for Tom's throat with his right hand, while his left twitched with excitement. Spencer paused an inch from Tom's throat like he heard something or sensed a presence. But his reaction would be too slow.

Whack! Spencer fell to the side and slid across the floor. He shook his head and looked up; above him stood a tower of a man with sledgehammer fists.

Lazarus cracked his knuckles and motioned for Spencer to stand up.

23

RESOLVE

2005
7:45 A.M.
Arizona

om held his chest and grunted as he attempted to stand. As David hurried into the room, he could see Tom was hurt, but he couldn't imagine Spencer capable of inflicting it. Whatever the case, things would come to an end with Lazarus standing between Tom and Spencer, fists clenched tightly, muscles burning with energy.

David hurried to Tom and grabbed his shoulder, causing Tom to flinch away. "Tom, it's me."

"David, thank God."

"What's going on? Why was Spencer attacking you?"

"He's blocked the functionality of the watches with some kind of device he got from the future."

"The future?" David knew his own watch wasn't working, so what Tom told him made sense, but why would Spencer go to all this trouble?

"We need to destroy it."

"Where?" David asked, pushing aside any doubts to Tom's story.

"Sally…"

David stood up straight and scanned the room. He saw Sally lying on the floor, clutching a small device that looked like a pixilated sphere. David looked back at Tom. "Are you all right?"

"Just need to catch my breath," Tom said.

Without glancing to see how Lazarus was fairing with Spencer, David ran across the room. "Sally!"

Sally looked up from the sphere and saw David approaching. "We need to destroy this thing. I've been smashing it on the floor, but haven't made a dent."

"Let me see."

Sally handed the round device to David, who carefully inspected every nook and cranny, looking for an opening, a chink in the armor. He found nothing. "When all else fails…" David said with a hint of a smirk.

David lifted the device above his head and hurled it at the floor. The device hit the floor and rolled to a stop next to a computer console. It wasn't even scratched. David stared at the device with squinty eyes, as though it offended him. He bent down and took the sphere in his hand.

Crash! David jumped back as Lazarus landed on the console in front of him, shattering the expensive computer components beneath his dense body.

David stood up quickly. "Lazarus!"

After rolling off the computer console onto his feet, Lazarus looked at David with a dazed expression. "I'll live."

"What happened?" David asked.

Lazarus rolled his neck and looked at Spencer, who was walking steadily toward them. "He is stronger than any man I have encountered."

David looked at Spencer, gangly and small. "Spencer?"

"It's not Spencer," Sally said. "It's something else."

"What do you mean?" David asked quickly, as Spencer closed in.

"I don't know. He refers to himself as 'we'." Sally's eyes bounced back and forth, searching for a memory. "Tom... Tom called him *Legion*."

David's heart pulsated beneath his ribs like a child squeezing a water balloon. Legion. His palms grew moist. Legion. His eyes stung with sweat. "Legion!"

Spencer stopped and focused his attention on David. "Ahh! The gang's all here! David, so nice of you to join us! We were just telling Tom how nice it was to see him after all this time... It's been so long since Zambia... As we recall, you were there, too... He was there! We saw him, too! We always wondered how you came and went so quickly! But now we know! You were breaking the rules! All of them! Time travel!"

David's knuckles turned white as he squeezed them. "Be quiet, demon!"

"You don't want to hear the rest? I don't think he does. Tell him. You tell him. Let's ask! About how we killed Tom's wife? And what a nice surprise it was to meet you there. We nearly killed you. We wanted to, so badly."

"You killed Tom's wife?"

Spencer giggled as he spoke. "Indeed! It was us! All of us!"

Tom sprinted toward Spencer. "Bastard!"

David reached out his hand. "Tom, no!"

Tom tackled Spencer from the side with amazing speed and force. Both men toppled to the ground. Less than a second passed before Tom shot into the air, kicked off by Spencer. Lazarus reached out his long, strong arms and caught Tom, only inches before his head crashed into the corner of a desk.

David knew this had to end now, before Legion killed anyone. He knew he was the only one that could stop what was happening. He rounded the computer console and headed toward Spencer, who was floating up into a standing position, as though someone were pushing him up from behind.

"David, don't!" Sally yelled.

"He can't hurt me," David replied.

"We'll see about that. Yes, we will. Yes!" Spencer hissed.

Spencer strode toward David, fingernails growing and mouth dripping foam with each step. Spencer raised a hand in the air, ready to slash David's throat with his sharp nails.

David stood his ground, raised an open palm at Spencer and said, "Stop demon, in the name of Jesus Christ."

Spencer gasped like someone had punched him in the gut. "Quiet, human! We are more powerful than even Him. More powerful! We will kill you!"

David's muscles relaxed. He was in control. "I speak in the name and with the authority of Jesus Christ."

"No! No! Stop!" Spencer pleaded as he fell to his knees.

Like a drunken man whose body was caught in an invisible centrifuge, Spencer began spinning himself on the floor, pushing his body with his knees. His eyes were wide and his entire face was convulsing with emotions. His torso began to shake and his teeth chattered loudly. Blood poured from his legs as he dug into them and held on tight. "We will not let go! He is ours! We will kill you!"

"Leave his body, in the name of Jesus Christ!" David shouted. "Leave this room, in the name of Jesus Christ!"

Spencer writhed on the floor and froth spat from his mouth as he spoke. "This is not over! Not over! We will find you again! All of us! We will—"

"Leave this place now!"

The sound of fifty wailing voices shot from Spencer's mouth as he arched his back violently. David shuddered at the sound.

When it was over, Spencer's body flopped onto the floor and lay motionless. David closed his eyes and rubbed them with his hand. It was over. He opened his eyes again and looked at Tom, Sally and Lazarus. All three were staring at him as though he were an alien.

Sally opened her mouth to say something.

"I'll explain later," David said. "Right now we have to figure out how to destroy that device."

Tom took the device from the floor and looked it over. He handed it to Lazarus and asked in Aramaic, "Can you destroy this?"

Lazarus looked at the device. "I will try."

The softball-sized contraption looked the size of a tennis ball in Lazarus's hand. He gripped the sphere tightly, wound up and flung it at the concrete wall, putting every muscle in his body behind it. It whistled through the air like a cannon ball and hit the wall traveling over eighty miles per hour. It shattered into peanut sized shards that rained down across the room.

Seconds after the device was destroyed, the receiving area filled with a brilliant blue flashing light. *Boom!* The room exploded with illumination as its entire contents flashed out of the present and into the future. Only the soft glow of fluttering sparkles remained afterwards.

David smiled, but then noticed Spencer had yet to move. Legion was gone, but Spencer had not returned. David knelt down next to Spencer and placed his hand on Spencer's throat. After a moment, he shook his head, clearly disappointed by the results. David looked up, his eyes wet.

Tom sighed. "He's—?"

David nodded.

"Damnit! Why? Too many people are dying over this. It needs to stop! When will it stop, David?"

David looked at the floor, buying time to find an answer that Tom might accept. He didn't find one. "I don't think you want to hear my answer."

"If you say it has anything to do with Jesus or God's will..."

"It has everything to do with Jesus."

287

"David, Jesus is dead. We saw him die, just like Spencer, and just like Spencer, Jesus is not coming back."

"Maybe we should go back and find out?"

"No, David. I'm done. All we've done is get people killed."

"Tom, you can't just—"

"Can and will, David. I'm going back for Mary, and then I'm—"

Bang! The entrance to the control center exploded open as a slew of guards carrying assault rifles poured into the room like army ants.

"Set your watches," David whispered, as he grabbed Lazarus's wrist and began pushing buttons.

The room filled with a series of metallic clicks as the guards readied their weapons and took aim.

"Time to go..." David whispered through clenched teeth.

All four pushed a single button on their watches.

"No!" Jake shouted as he entered the room and saw four flashes of light expanding and growing brighter behind David and the others.

"Shoot them! Kill them all!" Jake screamed, as desperation caused his voice to crack.

David dove behind a computer console. "Get down!"

Tom, Sally and Lazarus hit the floor next to David and covered their faces as shards of debris burst into the air from computer consoles and desks being ripped apart by scads of hot bullets. David looked at his watch and smiled as it disappeared into a brilliant luminosity. They'd done it.

The series of four loud booms could not be heard over the thunder of the gunfire, but the bright flash of light and glowing cloud of particles revealed to Jake that he was too late.

"Hold your fire! Hold your fire!" Jake yelled after the lights dissipated.

Jake ran down to where Tom, David and the others had been hiding. No one was there.

"Damnit!" Jake shouted, as he pounded his fist into a computer console. He turned his rage toward the guards. "Where did you idiots learn how to shoot?"

Jake turned away from the stone-faced guards before they could intimidate him, as his mind began to sort things out. David, Sally and Tom had escaped him. But at least they were gone. They were out of his way and he could freely proceed as planned. He still had a watch. Jake glanced at Spencer's dead body and saw the watch still attached to his wrist. Two watches. As long as the good doctors and Director McField stayed in the past, Jake could care less. He smiled at his victory.

Jake turned to the guards, who were waiting for orders, but a strange burning sensation in his lower back gave him pause. The millions of pins and needles quickly spread up his spine and into his brain. He could feel something...hear something... someone... Voices, so many voices, rushed into his mind, like an explosion...crowding in...taking over.

Jake snapped his head toward the nearest guard. "Give me your weapon."

The guard looked at Jake quizzically, "But sir, they—"

"Now!"

The guard handed Jake the weapon. "What are you going to do, sir?"

Jake punched a few buttons on his watch and turned to the guard, eyes jet black, mouth foaming, "We're going to kill them! Yes we are! Yes! Yes! Kill them all!"

❧

Tom fell through an endless void. His arms flailed for something to hold on to. His legs kicked for the ground, not knowing when it would come or how hard he would hit. He didn't remember time travel feeling like this before. He didn't remember it at all before.

Everything came to a stop and Tom felt his feet touching solid ground, though there was nothing to stand upon, just darkness. But he wasn't alone. He could feel the breeze created by bodies moving around him, smell their foul breath and hear their slight whispers. Tom spun in every direction. Everywhere he turned looked the same. Up was down and left was right. Nothing made sense.

Then a beacon of light caught his eyes. Like two yellow headlights moving through the darkness on an abandoned street. Then two more, and more, until the vision of headlights disappeared, replaced by hundreds of glowing eyes.

He found himself standing alone in a pillar of light that shone down from an obscured source. He was surrounded by the darkness that had once held him tight. Looking down, he saw a stark floor and in his hands...a sword.

The cloud of angry eyes began to whirl around him, goading him, but he stood still and gripped the sword tightly. As the blackness, full of yellow eyes, swirled in on him, he raised the sword in the air, ready to strike. When the first black shadow reached him and the sword came down, he woke.

Tom's limbs flailed as he fell from the bed. He hit the stone floor hard. "Ugh!" Tom clutched his bandaged ribs. They had been back in ancient Israel for several days now, and while Tom's wounds where healing nicely, his ribs still throbbed from time to time.

"Are you all right?" Mary asked, as she rushed in from the next room and bent down to him.

He rolled over and looked into her deep eyes. He smiled. "I'm fine. Just a nightmare."

"Want to tell me about it?"

"It would scare you."

"It was only a nightmare," Mary said with a smirk.

"I can't remember much of it anyway," he insisted, as she helped him to his feet.

She shrugged indifferently. "I'm glad you're awake. We're eating breakfast soon, and you have a long walk ahead of you." She kissed him on the forehead.

"I'll be out in a minute," he said.

After Mary left, Tom rubbed his eyes with his hands, trying to erase the images of the dream. The blackness, the glowing eyes, they had burrowed into his conscious mind. He shook his head and rubbed his face.

The dream had been as real as any experience throughout the course of his life. Tom reminded himself that scenarios like the one in his nightmare could never happen. They weren't real. Demons did not exist. Legion was some kind of psychosis, some sort of delusion that affected people of the past, brought to the future by their jaunts through time. That was how Spencer had been infected... But that couldn't—

The stress caused by dwelling on supernatural subjects was overwhelming. Tom forced his mind to think of other things. He pictured Mary in the other room preparing food with Martha. He pictured Lazarus working up a sweat outside, pruning the fig trees. He thought of David and Sally, reunited after all this time and finally finding love. This was a happy ending, even if Jesus was dead.

Tom's thoughts drifted to the disciples. Peter and Matthew, laughing, remembering jokes told and drinks shared. He felt like a senior in high school on the last day before summer break. He was going to say goodbye to friends he would never see again. It broke his heart. But there was no reason to stay. Jesus was dead and had been for a week now. There was no message of Jesus being alive, being risen from the dead. Jesus had been a fraud, and Tom loathed him for it.

Tom knew that deep inside he wanted Jesus to rise from the dead, to prove he was God incarnate, to prove that there was some kind of eternal hope, to justify Megan's death, at least to prove she didn't die for a fraud. But she had. Megan's savior was lying in a cave rotting. Just like everyone else eventually does.

The end had come, and David was wrong. Jesus was a fake—of that much Tom was sure. But he was also an incredible man, and Tom missed him sorely. Tom found his eyes growing wet as he remembered Jesus hanging on the cross. The way his body fell limp at the point of death. The way his voice sounded as he cried out to God. It occurred to Tom that he hadn't given the passing of his friend much thought in the week since it happened. Tom's eyes stung, as they grew damp with tears.

"Tom?" David said, as he entered the room. "It's time to—"

David saw his tears and stopped moving.

The embarrassment a man feels when caught crying was the furthest thing from Tom's mind. He left his face wet. "What good came from Jesus's death, David?"

David pulled up a sturdy, wooden chair and sat down.

"And don't tell me that savior of the world crap, either. You know it's BS, too."

"When you first left, when all this began, I had a conversation with Sally. She wanted to know what the danger of you coming back in time to disprove the story of Jesus would be. This was before I knew time could not be changed. What you were attempting, in my mind, could have destroyed everything we know and love about the world."

Tom had wiped the dampness from his face and was staring at David. He was listening.

"Try to imagine a world without Jesus."

"Easy. Megan would still be alive."

"Okay, imagine a world without Christianity."

"Same answer."

"Think beyond yourself, Tom. Think about the global ramifications."

Tom was feeling compliant and let his mind pour over the global ramifications of what David was asking. He thought about several Old World cultures that wouldn't have existed, but they held no emotional tie with him. They would be missed, but really, they didn't matter much. He thought about all the marriages and babies born of Christians and Christian couples—people who met at church, couples whose religious commonalities brought some together and kept others apart. Without Jesus, babies conceived by Christians would never be born and billions of lives would be altered... *Okay, that's bad*, he thought. "I get the picture."

"Do you really?"

"If I had somehow messed up the Jesus story, billions of people might never meet, copulate and have children that formed the future of our world."

"True, but that's just a small part of the larger picture. Frankly I'm surprised, Tom. Maybe all this time breathing fresh air and eating non-genetically engineered and untreated food has dulled your mind?"

"Hey," Tom was offended by the insinuation that he couldn't grasp the whole picture, and he sent the full resources of his cranium to the forefront. Images, colors and sounds, flashed through his mind, putting together a picture of a world without Jesus, like a montage of possible histories and futures played in fast-forward.

David watched Tom's eyes fluttering, revealing Tom's mental processes. David smiled; he knew Tom would figure it out.

Tom looked up. "America."

David nodded.

"I never thought of that... America would never have been born."

"One nation under God."

"Under Jesus..."

"Neither of us were born Americans, but we've made it our home. And I don't think we'd have it any other way. America was founded on a belief system that would not exist without Jesus."

"But not everyone believes in Jesus," Tom added.

"True, but the majority of the founding fathers—not to mention the European civilizations that came before them—did. This is bigger than just America. You would be undoing two thousand years of history."

Tom shrugged. "You're right."

David sat up. "I am?"

"The world as a whole is a better place because of Jesus, God or not. But individuals still suffer because of him. If he were really God, wouldn't he have worked it out so that everyone was helped by his existing, and not just the general populace? What about the people who live and die in his name?"

"He loves them most of all, I imagine."

Tom smiled. "He would, wouldn't he? I miss him."

"Me too," David said.

"Let's get this over with. I just want to say goodbye to Peter and Matthew and go home," Tom said, as he headed for the door. He had proven Jesus to be a fake, but he had also realized that the teachings and life of Jesus had an impact on the world that was greater than any other man in history. Jesus wasn't God, but he had earned Tom's respect.

ↂ

I t took Tom, David and Sally three days to walk the distance between the home of Lazarus and the home where the disciples had been staying since the death of Jesus. Normally the trek might have taken only a day, but between Tom's still healing injuries and Sally's soft feet, the trip lingered on.

They had only a quarter mile left and had entered a grove of red grapes that twisted and stretched its vines toward a white brick home.

Sally looked at the home. "Please tell me that's where we're stopping. My feet are swollen."

"Be glad you're still wearing sneakers," Tom said. "It was an entire year before I got used to these sandals. I don't think my feet will ever become smooth again, even after we get back to our own time."

"Tom, I've been meaning to ask you about that," David said.

"About what?"

"Going home."

"What about it?"

"Are you sure you want to?"

"Of course. What do you mean?"

"Well, there's Mary."

"She's coming with me."

"What about Lazarus, Martha, her family? She has more reasons to stay than you do to go..." David flashed his watch to Tom. "And I can always come to visit."

"I...I just don't belong here... I don't fit in. What good is a quantum physicist in 30 A.D.?"

"Maybe you have more to offer than your science..."

"Like what?"

"Didymus! David!" Matthew's voice boomed through the air, as he barreled toward them.

"Matthew!" Tom shouted with a smile.

Matthew gave Tom a crushing hug, lifting him off the ground. "Where have you been? I have so much to tell you! You're not going to believe it!"

Tom's face was turning red as the air was squeezed out of his injured chest. "Okay! Okay! Just put me down, you big ape."

Matthew put Tom down and noticed him holding his chest. "You're injured? What happened to you? Was it the Romans? Or those wretches in Jerusalem?"

"It's a long story, my friend," Tom said, as he stretched out his chest, realigning his ribs.

"Is it them?" Peter yelled from the doorway of the home.

Matthew cupped his hands around his mouth, "Indeed it is!"

"Have you told them yet?" Peter returned.

"No!"

"Told us what?" Tom asked.

Matthew turned to Tom, looking him straight in the eyes with a large smile. "Jesus...he's back."

David clapped his hands together and started laughing. Sally looked at him, confused. "David, what's going on? What did he just say?" Sally asked in English.

David took Sally by the shoulders. "Before you came, Tom and I were traveling with Jesus. Actually, Tom was one of his disciples." David felt his mind about to go into a tangent of detail that was unnecessary. He blinked hard and focused his thoughts. "Before you came back for us, we saw Jesus die on the cross."

Sally squinted one eye. "Jesus, as in Jesus Christ, Jesus?"

"Yes," David said with a grin. "That Jesus. What Matthew just told Tom is that Jesus is alive again, that he has risen from the grave."

Sally squinted the other eye, "That's not possible."

"I know! That's what makes it so great!" David was giddy with excitement. The moment he believed would come, the scene that every child in Sunday school learns about, was here.

"I'm not laughing, Matthew," Tom said angrily.

"But I'm not joking," Matthew said, as his smile faded.

Tom was losing patience. "Matthew…"

"Come inside. Ask the others!"

Tom stared into Matthew's eyes. He knew Matthew was a jokester, but his sparkling eyes usually gave away any secrets. Tom couldn't see that sparkle, that glimmer of humor, ready to deliver a punch line. Tom could see that Matthew was serious, and that just meant he was crazy.

Tom walked around Matthew and headed to the home. Matthew let him go and turned to David. "David!" Matthew looked David over. "You don't have any injuries, do you?"

"No, just tired from walking."

"Good!" Matthew said, as he picked David up and bear-hugged him.

The air was squeezed from David's lungs as Matthew held him in the air. After David had coughed and laughed sufficiently enough, Matthew put him back on the ground. Matthew's attention then shifted to Sally. He looked at her sneakers, and then back to David. "Who is your friend?"

"I'll introduce you later," David said. "Right now, I don't want to miss what's about to happen."

David headed for the house with Sally. Matthew watched them walk by.

"What's about to happen?" Matthew asked, as he began lumbering after David.

REBIRTH

24

BELIEVE

30 A.D.
4:02 P.M.
Israel

Tom entered the house and found himself surrounded by excited disciples. Peter was the most excited of all.

"Tom, have you seen him?"

"You're not a part of this, too, Peter?"

"Part of what?"

"Matthew's joke about Jesus being alive."

"Joke? Why would Matthew joke about something like this? Why would I? Do you not believe that if Jesus were still in the grave that we would still be mourning him, just as you still are?"

"Peter, people...human beings don't just come back to life."

"That's the grand part," Matthew said, as he entered through the home's front door with David and Sally in tow. "Jesus has proven to us by living again that he is not just flesh and blood."

"Let me guess. He's God, right?"

"Indeed," Matthew said, smiling.

"If Jesus was God why did he allow himself to be killed by men? Couldn't he have stopped it from happening? He didn't have to die to prove he was God. He could have—"

"Healed the blind, cured the sick, the deaf, mutes and lepers?" David was on a roll. "Raised the dead?"

Tom remained silent.

David pressed on. "You've already seen him do these things, but you found ways to discredit him. And now he has died, and you saw him die. With your own eyes, you saw his last breath escape him on the cross."

"Yes, David, he's dead. And I'm not going to believe a dead man is living again."

Peter's shoulders dropped. "We would not lie to you, Tom."

"What will it take for you to believe?" Matthew asked.

Tom rubbed his reddening face, collecting his thoughts. "Unless I see the nail marks in his hands and put my fingers where the nails were, and put my hand into his side, I will not believe!"

Tom felt a hand on his shoulder and heard a familiar voice, "Peace be with you."

Tom's muscles locked. He knew the voice. He knew the phrase; he had heard it delivered to hundreds of people over the past few years. He looked at Peter, who was smiling wide and stepping back. He looked at Matthew, who was holding his hand to his mouth, trying not to laugh out loud.

It couldn't be...

Tom whipped around and gasped. Jesus was standing two feet away. Tom's forehead wrinkled as he felt an array of emotions overtake him.

Jesus reached a hand out toward Tom, who flinched away. "Put your finger here; see my hands. Reach out your hand and put it into my side. Stop doubting and believe."

Tom blinked, trying to clear the rapidly forming tears from his eyes. He stared at the hand held before him. It had a deep, red scar, just below the palm. Tom looked into Jesus's eyes... It was Jesus! Alive! Tom's legs began to shake as the full realization of what was happening struck home. Jesus...was God!

Tom fell to his knees. "My Lord and my God!"

Jesus reached down to Tom and pulled him back to his feet.

Tom was still shaking, "I'm sorry... I'm so sorry."

Jesus smiled slightly. "Because you have seen me, and touched my scars, you have believed..."

Jesus looked at David and continued, "Blessed are those who have not seen, and yet believe."

David grinned, not only because Jesus had paid him the greatest compliment, but because Tom now believed. All this time in the past wasn't for nothing. David felt relieved. He felt justified. He felt better than he ever had before. Tom believed.

David glanced at Sally, whose eyes were wet with tears. "Why are you crying?" he asked. "Can you understand what's happening?"

"I can't understand what's being said, but I think I understand what's happening..." Sally nodded at Jesus. "That man, he's Jesus?"

David nodded.

"And you and Tom saw him die?"

David nodded again.

"And he's alive again...and Tom believes in him now..."

David nodded a third time followed by a laugh.

"But how... It doesn't make sense. It's not possible."

Jesus diverted his attention to Sally. He walked to her, face to face, took both of her shoulders and smiled. "Sally, before there was time, I was; in me all things are possible."

"Come, Didymus, we have much to talk about," Jesus said, as he turned and walked back to Tom.

Jesus practically had to carry Tom out of the home, but they managed to exit through the front door.

Sally watched them leave and then looked at David. Her jaw was slack. "David... He spoke to me in perfect English..."

"I know," David said, as his lips spread into a crafty grin.

✅

Tom took a deep breath, partly because the air was cool and sweet, but also because he was anxious. Here was a man who he had ridiculed for years. A man, who he now believed was God, whom he had plotted against and whom he had schemed to prove fraudulent. Tom leaned back and felt the cool earth in his palms. He looked at Jesus, who sat next to him on the grass-covered hill overlooking the grape grove. "I've done so many things against you in the past years...and I know you know about them..." Tom shook his head, not wanting to continue, but he forged on. "This isn't... This is hard for me. I'm not used to being wrong... I just... Can you forgive me for the things I've done to you?"

Jesus looked at Tom, clearly amused by the trouble Tom was having. "You know, if you'd have really listened to half of what I taught over the past three years, you'd know I already have."

Tom's shoulders relaxed. Not only was Jesus living, he was his old self. "Thanks."

"I believe I have a question of yours to answer," Jesus said.

"You do?"

"I do...and you deserve to know the answer."

Tom waited uncomfortably. What was Jesus referring to?

"She didn't die for nothing."

"What?"

"She didn't die for nothing, Tom. She died for me."

Tom's eyes were wide. "You knew?"

Jesus smiled, "I know everything."

"But..."

"Do you remember Timothy, the blind man whose eyes I covered with mud and instructed to wash in the pool of Siloam?"

Tom nodded.

"Do you remember my answer then? Can you use that mind I gave you to put together the pieces of a puzzle that stretches through time?"

Tom smiled. He enjoyed a challenge, and the fact that it was coming from the mouth of God, made it that much more intriguing. "You said then...that bad things, like the blind man, happen so that your glory might be revealed. So Timothy...he was born blind so that you could heal him, in my presence...so that I would believe and this conversation could take place?"

Jesus nodded. "Now expand that theory to Megan."

"She died so that I would come back in time?"

Jesus grinned.

"So that I would become a disciple... So that this story would be told in the Bible and people like me would relate...and believe?"

Jesus's smile grew.

"And that's why you let Legion live." Tom's mind was wrapping itself around the paradox. "You knew Legion would kill Megan in the future. You knew I'd come back. You knew..."

"Yes."

"Unbelievable..."

"Isn't it though?"

Tom smiled. "What about Legion... He's a demon, right? He's still around in the future. Do you have more plans for him?"

"Legion is a *them*, neither he nor she, but many demons, linked together, lending strength to one another. My plans for Legion are through, though not entirely over."

"What do you mean?"

Boom! A noise like an explosion rang out from the other side of the hill.

Tom looked at Jesus. "That was... It's here?"

Jesus nodded and looked at the bottom of the hill. David and Sally were running toward him. He looked back at Tom, "There is one last thing I require of Legion."

Tom looked worried. *What does that mean?*

David rushed up the hill to Tom and Jesus. Sally was right behind him. "Did you hear that? Someone used a watch," David said.

"I think we know who," Tom said.

"Who?"

Shick Chic. Jake prepped his assault rifle, standing at the top of the hill.

Tom swallowed; he knew Legion had been used to kill in the past. Would he serve a similar purpose here?

"It's Jake," David said, as he took a step back.

Tom took David by the arm and looked him in the eyes. "Not Jake," he urged. "Legion."

Jake jumped ten feet through the air and landed closer to the group. "Yes, we are Legion! Yes! Yes! And we will—Aiieee!"

Legion saw Jesus and recoiled. "The Son of God! Here! No! This can't be! Whose idea was this? Not mine! Mine either! Quiet! Wait! We have an idea...YES! YES!"

Jake raised the assault rifle at Tom.

"No..." David said.

Jake quickly turned the weapon at Jesus and fingered the trigger. "We killed you once, Jesus. We can do it again!"

"No!" Tom yelled, as he pushed Jesus down and took his place.

Bang! A bullet ripped through the air and pierced Tom's chest, dead center. Tom's body went limp, and he fell to the grass.

"Tom!" David fell to his knees next to him.

Sally screamed and ran for cover, which only attracted Jake's attention. *Bang! Bang!* Jake fired two more shots, laughing joyfully with the voices of fifty men. Sally hit the ground hard, lying motionless.

"Stop damnit! Stop!" David screamed. "In the name of Jesus Christ, I command you to stop!"

Jake raised the gun at David. "Quiet, human! We will not!"

David looked desperately at Jesus.

"Do not worry, David. All is well." Jesus looked at Jake. "Stop."

Jake became rigid as though he had been paused, unable to move. Jesus stood to his feet and walked toward Jake.

"No! *No!*" Jake screamed, "Mercy! Have mercy on us, as you once did! Yes! Mercy! It is your way! It is!"

"Quiet, demons!" Jesus yelled.

Jake clamped his mouth shut.

"You have served your purpose on this earth. You have been a plague for long enough, foul creature. You gave up your place in the Heavenly realms, and your time in the world of my children has come to an end."

Jake's eyes were wide with horror.

"Be gone! To the burning abyss for all eternity with you!"

Jake fell to the ground in a fit of convulsions. His body shook violently for ten seconds, and then it abruptly stopped. Jake's eyes popped open and he glanced around.

He saw Jesus. He saw Tom and Sally lying dead, and David staring at him. He looked to his side and saw the assault rifle...and the watch on his wrist. "What did I do?"

Jesus grabbed Jake's wrist and pulled the watch from it. He worked the buttons with his fingers while saying, "It was not you who committed these crimes but the beast to which you gave access to your body, by rejecting my word. Return to your own time and sin no more."

After he pushed the final button on the watch, Jesus placed the watch on Jake's lap and stood back. *Whum, Whum, Whum, Boom!* Before Jake had a chance to register what had happened or where and when he was, he was gone, returned to the future.

As glowing blue particles settled to the ground, Jesus bent down and picked up the loose watch, which was not attached to Jake's body and did not return to the future with him. He placed the watch in David's hand and closed his fingers around the device. "It's over."

"But what about Tom and Sally? They've been shot! They're dead!" David said, as he leaned over Sally's body. "Why did you let this happen?"

"Shot? With what?"

David grew angry. "With bullets!"

"These bullets?" Jesus asked, as he held out a hand.

David looked at Jesus's hand. Next to the scar were three bullets. David turned back to Sally, and she began to stir. A rustle in the grass caught his attention; Tom was already sitting up. He looked back at Jesus. "Thank you."

"It was nothing."

David smiled, "For you, maybe."

Jesus laughed.

"What happened?" Tom asked, as he stood up. "Where's Jake?"

"Gone," David replied, as he helped a stunned Sally to her feet. "Jesus returned him to the future."

"And Legion?" Tom asked.

"Legion will never again torment the people of this world. He has been destroyed," Jesus said.

"We're not dead?" Sally asked. "But, Jake shot us."

David smiled. "He missed."

"But—"

Jesus opened one of Sally's hands and placed his on top. "Open your eyes, child, and believe." Jesus removed his hand, letting the bullets roll into Sally's open palm.

☙

Tom and David sat on the hillside for an hour, speaking about the events of the past weeks, while Jesus talked with Sally. David knew Sally would be getting an earful, but it was probably good for her, having been so shockingly exposed to Christianity, and who could be better suited to aid in the transition than Jesus himself?

But his thoughts didn't linger on Sally and Jesus for long. What he was about to do was one of the hardest things he'd ever done. In a few minutes, David would be returning to the future with Sally...and saying goodbye to Tom. He and Tom had been the best of friends and trustworthy partners for almost eighteen years. Now he had to return to the future without Tom, without his job at LightTech and without any plans for the future.

"So what now?" Tom asked.

"I take Sally back to the future and then... I don't know what I'm going to do. But right now... We say goodbye."

"You say that like you already know I'm staying."

"I do know."

Tom smiled. "You know, your knowledge of the Bible kind of takes the surprise out of things."

David laughed. "Sorry."

"So, what happens to me now? Is that recorded in the Bible?"

"A little, but the rest is recorded in history."

Tom pursed his lips and nodded his head, clearly impressed with himself. "Really. So you know how I die then?"

"Yes," David said as he looked at the grass, avoiding Tom's eyes.

"How?"

"I believe the saying is something like: That's for me to know and you to find out," David said with a smile.

"As long as I outlive you, old man."

David stood to his feet. "Old man... I suppose you're right. We're both old men now, but old men at the beginning of new lives."

Tom stood next to him and looked at Jesus and Sally talking at the bottom of the hill. "For both of us... I'm going to miss you, partner."

"We might see each other again."

"Make sure of it."

David lifted his wrist and shook the watch. "I might just come and pay you a visit every now and again. We still have to create these."

"I'll be expecting you," Tom said, as he extended his hand for David to shake.

David took Tom's hand and pulled him in for a tight hug. Tom cringed in pain as his ribs began to shift. "The ribs, the ribs."

David moved away and laughed. "Sorry, sorry. And you think *I'm* old."

The smile on David's face slowly faded and he said, "We ought to go, or this will take all day."

The two began walking toward Jesus and Sally.

As David grew closer to Sally, he could see her stunned expression. Her eyes were wide and her face was pale. When Tom and David stopped a few feet away, she didn't even look at them.

"Ready to go?" David asked Sally.

"Huh? What?"

Jesus had obviously impressed her with something.

"Did we miss something?" Tom asked.

"I was just telling Sally about the future, the past, things to come that have already happened." Jesus explained.

Tom chuckled. "You know, for the first time, I think I actually made sense of what you said."

"Won't be the last time," Jesus replied, and then he looked at David. "You're leaving?"

"You know I am," David replied.

Jesus nodded. "We'll speak again soon."

David tilted his head. "We will?"

"Ask Sally. I told her all about it," Jesus said, before he hugged David tightly.

David took a few steps back after Jesus released him. He wanted to do this quickly. He wasn't one to linger at goodbyes; it just made the pain worse. "Better stand back," he said, as he and Sally set their watches.

Tom and Jesus walked fifteen feet away and turned to watch David and Sally leave. David and Sally pushed the final buttons on their watches, and a bright light began to flash all around them.

Whum, Whum, Whum, Boom!

With a flash of light, David and Sally disappeared from the past.

Tom looked at Jesus and said, "You know, if you had pulled something like that, you might have been more convincing."

Jesus smiled. "You haven't seen anything yet." Jesus put his hand on Tom's shoulder and the two headed back toward the house, where Matthew and Peter were waiting in the doorway.

"You mean to tell me walking on water wasn't enough? Feeding five thousand men wasn't convincing? And calming that storm wasn't eye-opening?" Jesus said.

Tom smiled. "I guess... I was just blind."

Jesus turned away from the house and looked out toward the horizon. Three figures approached on the path—Lazarus, Martha and Mary. They were rushing forward, toward Jesus and Tom.

Tom turned and saw only Mary, her sleek black hair bouncing with every rushed footstep. Tom turned quickly to Jesus. "Tell me she lives a good life."

"How could she not, Didymus? She will be with you."

"My life so far hasn't exactly been ideal."

"All in the past," Jesus said. "The future is yours to write."

Good enough, Tom thought. He sprang forward, arms extended. Clutching Mary around the waist, he spun her around. It was the loving embrace he'd longed for since that day in Zambia, the day that had started everything.

He understood why Megan gave her life. He also knew that Mary would do the same, and he loved her all the more for it. But what stood out in his mind, more acutely than anything else, is that like Megan and Mary, he would willingly give his own life if called to do so.

He had a feeling that day might come...but not today.

25

A.D.

Somewhere

Sometime

As David strode up a grassy hill, he stared at the ominous sky, swirling with black clouds and energy. The flapping of his robe grew louder as he neared the peak. In one hand, he held Sally's hand. She was blindfolded and following David carefully up the steep incline. In his other hand was a large umbrella and a 16oz. Wild Cherry Pepsi.

"Where are we, David? It smells like it's going to rain. I better not get wet. I don't want to get wet."

"Patience, my dear. You're going to enjoy this...even if you do get wet."

"Great," she said.

David stopped at the top of the hill and looked at the view, which stretched for miles. "Incredible..."

"What? David, can I take this off now?"

David untied the blindfold and pulled it away from Sally's eyes. She blinked a few times and then gasped. "What is it?"

"Better get under if you don't want to get wet," David said, as he sat down on the grass and opened the umbrella.

Sally sat next to him and huddled under the umbrella. "Now tell me what this is."

"Ever heard of Noah's Ark?" he asked.

"As in the flood?"

David nodded.

"Is this?"

David nodded again. "It took me fifteen trips through time to figure out when the flood began, but I'm pretty sure it's any minute now."

Sally looked at the view again. Below them was a lush valley and at the center of the depression was an unbelievably large wooden boat, just sitting there on the ground, supported by hundreds of wooden planks on either side. On the side of the boat was a large open door and a long board, which served as a ramp. An old man and three younger men pulled the ramp into the boat and closed the hatch.

After twisting the cap off his Wild Cherry Pepsi, David took a sip and looked up at the sky, tilting the umbrella away from their heads. A drop of water hit David square in the forehead, and he laughed. Sally pulled the umbrella back over them, and the pitter-patter of raindrops began tapping out a song on the fabric.

"Here it comes," David said.

The rain picked up quickly, and each drop grew in size. Soon it sounded like TV static at high volume. Sally and David could hardly hear each other laughing. David reached into his robe and pulled out four flat, orange, pieces of plastic.

"What are those?" Sally shouted.

David put one of the objects to his lips and blew as hard as he could. The object expanded as he continued to blow. He pushed a clear plastic nozzle in and held the fully inflated object up. It was round with a hole in the middle. "Floaties...you know: water wings." David said. "Just in case."

Sally smiled and took one of the floaties from David's hands. They blew them up and put them on together. David looked at Sally as she watched the water swiftly flooding the valley. She was so beautiful sitting there in her bright orange floaties. David knew he had to take the chance. Maybe this was God's plan for the two of them, all along? Maybe God had more in store for them both? Sally had yet to tell David about her conversation with Jesus. He knew their adventures were just beginning. Today would be no different. He reached under his robe.

Sally caught the glimmer of what looked like just another raindrop, but upon closer inspection revealed an engagement ring. He held it in front of her eyes. His face was an expressive mix of elation and terror.

"Will you?" David shouted over the rain.

There was a pause as Sally stared at the ring in David's hands.

"I bought it from an Egyptian merchant in 500 B.C. I don't have a receipt but if you don't like it, I'm sure I can—"

"David, shut up," Sally shouted with a wide grin.

He stopped talking and looked into her eyes.

Her next words were indiscernible, but he could read the expression on her face and the shapes her soft lips were making.

The answer was 'yes.'

David jumped to his feet and tossed the umbrella into the air, where it got swept up by the wind. He pulled her to her feet and kissed her as water poured over their bodies. Sally leaned into David's ear and said, "You have a date in mind?"

He smiled. "Whenever you want. Time is on our side."

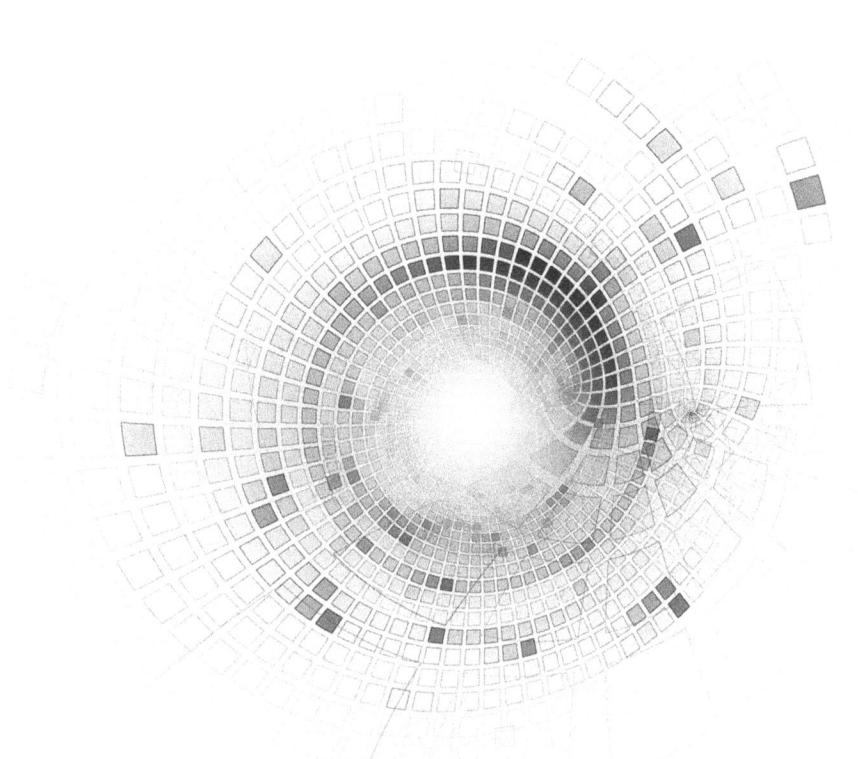

THE FATE OF THOMAS

Thomas is believed to have carried the word of Jesus to Parthia or Persia. He died in the name of Jesus, slain with a lance. He is believed to have been buried in Edessa, in Mesopotamia, where confirmed reports about relics supposed to be his, exist from the Fourth Century...but the story of the events between his time with Jesus and his martyrdom has yet to be told.

Acknowledgments

Back when I first wrote *The Didymus Contingency*, I had a long list of friends and family in my acknowledgements. It was the first time I'd written one, and I was determined to thank everyone who had supported me over the years. But now, ten years down the line, I'm not going to thank individual people. And it's not because I'm a jerk now; it's because there are more people to thank than I could possibly include in these pages. With every passing year since I first self-published this novel, the number of people supporting it, and me, has grown beyond the level I ever thought possible. Even though my writing is more polished now, I frequently hear that *The Didymus Contingency* is people's favorite novel. I've heard from Buddhists, Mormons, Atheists, Wiccans, Agnostics and Christians alike, all saying that this story about Jesus is their favorite, and during our current state of constant outrage, that's an amazing thing. So I would like to acknowledge all the people who have read *The Didymus Contingency* and enjoyed it, despite their own, possibly conflicting, beliefs.

About the Author

Jeremy Robinson is the international bestselling author of fifty novels and novellas including *MirrorWorld*, *Uprising*, *Island 731*, *SecondWorld*, the Jack Sigler thriller series, and *Project Nemesis*, the highest selling, original (non-licensed) kaiju novel of all time. He's known for mixing elements of science, history and mythology, which has earned him the #1 spot in Science Fiction and Action-Adventure, and secured him as the top creature feature author.

Robinson is also known as the bestselling horror writer, Jeremy Bishop, author of *The Sentinel* and the controversial novel, *Torment*. In 2015, he launched yet another pseudonym, Jeremiah Knight, for two post-apocalyptic Science Fiction series of novels. Robinson's works have been translated into thirteen languages.

His series of Jack Sigler / Chess Team thrillers, starting with *Pulse*, is in development as a film series, helmed by Jabbar Raisani, who earned an Emmy Award for his design work on HBO's *Game of Thrones*. Robinson's original kaiju character, Nemesis, is also being adapted into a comic book through publisher American Gothic Press in association with *Famous Monsters of Filmland*, with artwork and covers by renowned Godzilla artists Matt Frank and Bob Eggleton.

Born in Beverly, MA, Robinson now lives in New Hampshire with his wife and three children.

Visit Jeremy Robinson online at www.bewareofmonsters.com.

319

Lightning Source UK Ltd.
Milton Keynes UK
UKHW011840131021
392145UK00004B/1039

9 781941 539484